making it real

making it real

The Canonization of English-Canadian Literature

robert lecker

Published in 1995 by
House of Anansi Press Limited
1800 Steeles Avenue West
Concord, Ontario
L4K 2P3
Tel. (416) 445-3333
Fax (416) 445-5967

Canadian Cataloguing in Publication Data

Lecker, Robert, 1951–
Making it real : the canonization of English-
Canadian literature

Includes index.
ISBN 0-88784-566-5

1. Canon (Literature). 2. Canadian literature
(English) – History and criticism. I. Title.

PS8071.4.L43 1995   c810.9   C95-930322-7
PR9184.3.L43 1995

Cover design: General Theory
Printed and bound in Canada.

House of Anansi Press gratefully acknowledges the support of the Canada Council, the Ontario Ministry of Culture, Tourism, and Recreation, Ontario Arts Council, and Ontario Publishing Centre in the development of writing and publishing in Canada.

For Emily

CONTENTS

PREFACE

THIS BOOK WAS COMPLETED in the months leading up to the second Quebec referendum on the future of the province and Canada. In such a political climate, no one who writes about Canadian literature can pretend that they are engaged in an apolitical activity. No one can pretend that it is possible to speak about Canadian literature without interrogating the country. Yet, in most Canadian criticism published these days, one seldom encounters this type of interrogation. Either we assume that the relation between the country and its literature is now so well established that there is little need to speak of it, or we assume that the relation is so questionable that it is scarcely worthy of address.

The result of both perspectives is that contemporary English-Canadian criticism now finds itself unable or unwilling to comment on the country at precisely the time that such commentary might have contributed to the national debate about Canada's future. Today, it is risky to be a literary critic who believes that the study of Canadian literature affects this future. I have to take this risk. This doesn't mean that I want to return to the days of using criticism to celebrate Canada for Canada's sake. Those days of feel-good criticism are long over. But I do want to encourage critics of Canadian literature to recognize the national bias that informs their work, and to ask whether this bias has extraliterary connections that need to be explored. Such an exploration is particularly important when it comes to teaching Canadian literature to Canadian students. When that happens, we are inevitably teaching them about their country; for this reason, we need to have a clear sense — or a clearer sense — of the relationship between pedagogy, criticism, and citizenship. In most recent studies of Canadian literature, this relationship is downgraded or ignored.

Canon studies are inevitably connected with cultural formations. One of my aims in this book is to understand how the country has been conceived through the study of its literature, what values govern this study, and how these values affect the ability of readers and academics to intervene in a constructive national critique. Another aim is to understand how I have been constructed by a Canadian canon that, in some ways, I helped to invent.

Ever since I have been writing about Canadian canons, people have encouraged me to say more about my experiences as a publisher and editor, to comment on my own involvement in Canadian canon-making. This encouragement has always surprised me, since it never occurred to me to ask other editors or publishers to examine their own contribution to the field, and it never struck me that they could be objective or unself-interested, even if they did agree to such a self-examination. This is the stuff of memoirs, not of criticism. So I have generally tried to avoid the confessional. Nevertheless, in a book devoted to Canadian canons, I can't pretend that I am innocent of contributing to canonical formations, and indeed I have profited from these formations. This may mean that whatever questions I pose about Canadian canons are inevitably coloured by my own business and editorial interests. But at least I can say that my potential lack of objectivity is countered by considerable experience that allows me to speak both as a professor and as a publisher/editor who has worked in what I call the industry of Canadian literature for twenty years.

The eight chapters in this book bring together many of the essays I have published since 1990 on canon formation in English-Canadian literature. An abridged version of chapter 1 appeared in *Critical Inquiry* 16 (1990): 17–32. An earlier version of chapter 2 was published in *Mosaic* 26.3 (1993): 1–19. Chapter 3 was first published in *Essays on Canadian Writing* 51–52 (1993–94): 32–82. Chapter 4 appeared in *Open Letter* 9.1 (1994): 25–80. Chapter 5 was published in the *American Review of Canadian Studies* 24 (1994): 197–216. Chapter 6 appeared in *Canada Ieri e Oggi 3*, a publication of the Italian Association for Canadian Studies (Fasano: Schena editore, 1992). Chapter 7 appeared in *PMLA* 108 (1993): 283–93. Chapter 8 was published in *Studies in Canadian Literature* 18.2 (1993): 1–26. I am grateful to the editors of these journals for allowing me to reprint this material. All of these works have been revised or expanded for inclusion in this volume.

I owe many thanks. My biggest debt is to the Social Sciences and Humanities Research Council of Canada, for a research grant in aid of this project. Without that assistance this book would never have come to fruition. I am also grateful to the Ontario Arts Council, for helping to support my writing, and, finally, to McGill University, for funding much of my travel to some of the conferences where the ideas in this book were first presented and tested.

Several people helped to clarify my ideas and to identify weaknesses. Above all, I wish to thank Mary Williams, for her patience, her constant encouragement, and her eagle eye. I benefited from the editorial and critical interventions of Neil Besner, Gary Boire, Russell Brown, Nathalie Cooke, Michael Darling, Frank Davey, Jack David, Margery Fee, Carole Gerson, W.J. Keith, Philip Kokotailo, Shirley Neuman, Michael Ross, Denis Salter, Bruce Whiteman, and Lorraine York. Special thanks are due to Jennifer Caylor, Rachelle Kanefsky, Peter Lipert, Angela Marinos, Shawn Phelan, and Cynthia Sugars, each of whom assisted me in my research and in solving technical and copy-editing problems. Rosemary Shipton's detailed commentary, and her copy-editing, were also of enormous help. I am deeply grateful to Martha Sharpe for her support and expertise at every stage of the production of this book, to Paul Davies for his superb typesetting, and to Don McLeod for preparing the index.

A final note of thanks must go to Charlotte Stewart-Murphy and Carl Spadoni, for their assistance in my visits to the Archives and Research Collections Division at McMaster University, and to Sarah McClelland, Jack McClelland, and Malcolm Ross, for giving me permission to quote from archival material relating to the New Canadian Library Series.

making it real

Making It Real

THE FIRST AND EARLIEST ESSAY in this book was written about six years ago and published in *Critical Inquiry* in 1990. Frankly, my original intention in writing "The Canonization of Canadian Literature" was to stir up some dust. I had been looking at English-Canadian literature and its critical landscape for almost twenty years, and it seemed that the criticism was getting tired. Too much had been accomplished. Too fast. In three decades we had witnessed the creation of a full-blown industry — a powerful, government-supported network comprised of academics and publishers involved in the teaching, study, and promotion of Canadian literature and literary criticism. This industry contributed to the formation of the institution of English-Canadian literature, a university-based culture devoted to the study of the nation's literature, a culture defined by rules, customs, and ways of speaking that made the members of the institution (and the literature it studied) seem separate, special, and powerfully self-sustaining.

In my role as co-editor of the critical journal *Essays on Canadian Writing* (founded in 1974), and later as co-publisher of ECW PRESS (established in 1977), I played a part in the growth of this industry and therefore I bear some responsibility for its successes and failures. In many ways, my reflections on what I have called the institution of Canadian literature comment implicitly on my own activities as a publisher, editor, and professor involved in the rapidly expanding field of Canadian literary studies during the 1970s and 1980s.

These activities have not always encouraged me to see the industry from the serene perspective of one who was happily capitalizing on its advancement. By the late 1980s I was beginning to feel that the institution and its members were suffering from complacency. Hierarchies had been established. There were no heated debates and there was little in the way of contestation. Orthodoxy was up. Passion was down. The operative metaphor was closure. I was struck by how many critical projects — including several initiated by ECW PRESS — were devoted to wrapping things up, as if the whole young enterprise of studying Canadian literature was already close to ending. Yet in many ways, despite all the books and grants and essays and reviews and theses and interviews and conferences, we still knew very little about the values informing the institution's judgements; and we knew even less about how those values had achieved and maintained their currency. If the study of Canadian literature was wrapping up, I wanted to know how it had happened.

There were some fundamental questions to ask. Why had there been so little commentary on the nature of the Canadian literary institution itself?[1] How did this institution display its past? Why did Canadian critics within the institution tend to write about some authors or texts and not others? What forces of inclusion and exclusion accounted for the choices made in our critical studies and literary histories? How were the selections appearing in anthologies of Canadian literature the product of these forces? How were students affected by this kind of canonical activity? What was it that made Canadian literature worthy of being defined as somehow different? What was the relationship between Canadian literature and citizenship? Why did no one seem to be asking these questions?

In my initial attempt to address some of these issues, I argued that the formation of the English-Canadian literary institution was driven by the desire to see literature as a force that verified one's sense of community and place. In this view, literature becomes a medium that refers us to the connection between writing, culture, and nation. Implicit in this view is the assumption that valuable writing underwrites a national-referential aesthetic. This assumption inspires most Canadian criticism written up to the 1980s; in fact, ever since the nineteenth century, canonical activity in Canada has been driven by different applications of the national-referential ideal, and by the assumption that a country without a national literature is not a country at all. As T.D. MacLulich observes in an essay that provides an excellent discussion of the relation between nations and their literary institutions, "nationalism has always been part of the cultural air that Canadian writers and critics have breathed. This desire to identify a distinctively Canadian literature has its origins in the widely prevalent assumption that every self-respecting nation ought to have its own linguistic and cultural identity" ("Thematic Criticism" 19). MacLulich goes on to show that Canadian literary nationalism has its roots in European romantic nationalism, and that Canadian critics from Thomas D'Arcy McGee to Frank Davey have all been inspired by this essentially romantic-nationalist belief that literature can be defined in national units. For each of these critics, but of course in very different ways, the pursuit of such definition is crucial to formulating a version of cultural distinctiveness.

As it developed, the Canadian literary institution promoted self-recognition and national recognition in order to confirm its own canonical status. No wonder. Those who are responsible for creating canons are simultaneously involved in solidifying their position as canon-makers. By canonizing texts, they canonize themselves and their institutional milieu. The irony is that as the insular and self-containing power of the institution developed, there was less and less need for the institution to question itself or to determine how it was connected to civic life, even though it was through the belief in such connection that the institution initially evolved. In its present form, canonical activity in Canada encourages critics to live inside their institutional walls, secure within a specialized, private, professional guild. It does not encourage them to be critical or to talk about Canada in critical ways. It does not encourage them to be public.

As I point out in chapter 3 — "Privacy, Publicity, and the Discourse of Canadian Criticism" — there is no strict private/public binary, no strict division between institutional and noninstitutional worlds. There are critics who deliberately address public and private audiences. The lines often get blurred. Most Canadian critics don't feel wholly comfortable with privacy because they are haunted by the idea that criticism is responsible to the public, to the nation. The formation of a Canadian literature industry during the 1960s and early 1970s complicated this sense of responsibility because it demanded new ways of talking about literature. It said: come inside, speak inside. But the traditional ways of discussing literature, which were dominated by narratives of nation, still pulled, still had considerable force. It is precisely because Canadian critics were always marked by their split allegiance to privacy and publicity that their discourse is so tortured in its wrestling with the problem of social obligation.

The introduction of European critical theory compounded the confusion experienced by Canadian critics who — during the 1960s and 1970s — perceived themselves as participants in an emerging industry that was founded on a nationalist aesthetic at precisely the time when such an aesthetic was being undermined by post-structural thought. Unlike their counterparts in other countries, Canadian critics initially experienced theory as contamination and infection, precisely because they retained such a strong sense of public responsibility. Theory was inside, and Canadian criticism was going inside, but it was going with reluctance and guilt. For critics who were making this move, some pressing questions remained: How could they embrace theory while remaining responsible to their ideas about the connection between literature and culture? How could they be public in their literary interests *and* professional in their critical habits? As they moved into the realm of privatized discourse, Canadian critics found themselves torn between worlds. They were forced to speak two ways at once, to address two audiences, to double talk.

The public side of Canadian criticism endorsed a correspondence between author, literary text, and social context. In doing so, it affirmed that those who spoke about this relation were anchored — citizens inhabiting the very state they had the professional ability to describe. Robert Kroetsch is right: in any number of ways, people involved in writing about Canadian writing keep trying to construct their country, to write it into existence, to make it real (even though they know that their very utterance makes it positively unreal).[2] But Canadian literary critics didn't always recognize that they were creating the country in this way, or, if they did, they didn't always see their action as something valuable outside the industry itself.

Eventually, the devaluation of Canadian critical discourse as a public mode of address undermined the public value of the industry. It could no longer intervene in questions about Canada because it had invested heavily in strategies designed to circumvent those questions. Most recent studies of Canadian literature assume that the relation between literature and nation is tainted — a subject to be avoided — even though it is precisely this relation that inspired the formation of the institution and allowed it to (briefly) thrive. The history of institutional Canadian criticism no longer strikes me as a purely nationalist project; now I see it as a conflicted narrative, driven by the double desire to reject and accept its Canadianness. The problem today is how to write literary criticism that is postnational *and* national, how to *imagine* that Canada is really real.

Because one facet of the initial critical desire to invent Canada was a displaced expression of nationalism, arguments about the need to make the country *un*real (or to value nonrepresentational texts) were seen as antinational, disloyal, and institutionally subversive. While several Canadian critics did seek to question cultural norms — to construct different versions of national desire — they were marginalized precisely because they did not conform to the dominant view. Often, they had to engage in tactical manoeuvres in order to explore their different constructions of the nation and its literature in ways that were palatable to the entrenched, nationalist-realist school. For the most part, however, the Canadian canon reflected the interpretive needs of its canonizers, who legitimated texts in their own image — texts that were national, rooted, realistic, democratic, conservative, topical, moral, safe. As I say in "The Canonization of Canadian Literature," the institution *is* the canon; its members *are* the texts. This could be read as a gloss on Raymond Williams's assertion that "the true condition of hegemony is effective *self-identification* with the hegemonic forms" (118).

The situation has shifted a bit since I wrote "The Canonization of Canadian Literature," which appears here in its full original form (the version published in *Critical Inquiry* was substantially abridged). The nationalist-referential assumptions that guided Canadian criticism into the late 1980s seem to have been undercut by contemporary theory, but many of those assumptions are still there. Canonical and institutional power are still tied to nationalist concerns. Although we may theorize Canadian literature in new terms that fly by us on an annual basis, the central question of value in Canadian literary history and criticism remains largely unexplored.[3] I think this is because we have failed to make this history and criticism interesting or to show how it is full of narrative force. The museum is still closed. The curators are inside. Canadian critical discourse is still dying for life.

Of course we have lots of well-researched and informative accounts of Canadian literary history, and much solid criticism. But many of these stories are unbearably polite; they lack tension, passion, candour. When was the last time you remember hearing a Canadian critic speak with passion about a strongly held critical view? Yes, we have A.J.M. Smith arguing with John Sutherland about the value of native and cosmopolitan literary traditions, Robin Mathews arguing with just about everyone about how critics have sold out to American capitalism, Lorraine Weir taking issue with Linda Hutcheon because she has "normalized" the concept of postmodernism, and Tracy Ware attacking my views for being theoretically naive, but contestations — especially those in which the contesters *exchange* views — are rare. Everybody seems quite comfortable, and would prefer not to be too involved.

It is in response to the anaesthetizing politeness of so much Canadian criticism that "The Canonization of Canadian Literature" calls for a dramatization of Canadian literary history and its narrators, one that would do more to vivify the critics who have influenced Canadian literary values, one that would show how those critics were conflicted narrators whose writing, like the literature it was devoted to, struggled with the self-defining problem of how to make it real. After all, literary historians (like all historians) are staging our history. They are story-tellers. As Eric Hobsbawn says, history "is not what has actually been preserved in popular memory, but what has been selected, written, pictured, popularized and institutionalized by those whose function it is to do so." For this reason, Hobsbawn concludes, "all historians, whatever else their objectives, are engaged in this process inasmuch as they contribute, consciously or not, to the creation, dismantling and restructuring of images of the past which belong not only to the world of specialist investigation but to the public sphere of man as a political being" (13). Dominick LaCapra makes a similar point when he argues that "all forms of historiography might benefit from modes of critical reading premised on the conviction that documents are texts that supplement or rework 'reality' and not mere sources that divulge facts about 'reality' " (11).

I have tried to provide some examples of this kind of critical reading in the two essays on Northrop Frye and Frank Davey — both critics who have had an enormous impact on Canadian literary studies, and both of whom are seldom treated as narrators in their own right. Similar essays could be devoted to a host of Canadian critics who have coloured our perception of who we are and how we should read.

I don't see the problem of dramatizing Canadian literary history as any different from the problem of dramatizing anything else you want people to be interested in. You've got to have tension, disagreement, energy, a story line; sometimes people will get angry. Pick up most Canadian criticism and you will see how tame it is, how worried we are about engaging in debate. How can we expect the literature to come alive for our readers if it soon becomes clear to them that it is not alive for us? Or if they see that it is not an issue of passion, even if we all know we are talking about *Canadian* passion, which is never really passion at its best?

Students. They are one of our last links to the public. (I can say "our" quite confidently because I know how small my audience is. It is comprised mainly of academics teaching Canadian literature and their students, a testimony to how restricted and isolated the study of Cana-dian literature has become.) What is our responsibility to these students? The critiques of "The Canonization of Canadian Literature" written by Davey and Ware made me realize, perhaps for the first time, that in most contemporary discussions of Canadian literature (includ-ing my own) the public is left outside, while professionals develop the orthodoxy of specialization in the confines of an increasingly privatized club.

As I argue in chapter 3, the idea that there might be a public audience for Canadian criticism now seems absurd to most specialists in the field. Within the institution, debate about issues deemed of communal interest seldom occurs. There is no discussion about the relationship between literature and community. We don't seem to believe that the public audience has any literary competence, or that it belongs at our academic affairs. We talk privately. We hoard what we own. We have bought into what Edward Said calls "the cult of expertise and professionalism" so thoroughly that a "doctrine of noninterference" has set in ("Opponents" 2). This doctrine lies behind the view that "the general public is best left ignorant," while "insiders" are "endowed with the special privilege of knowing how things really work and, more important, of being close to power" (2). For Said, this doctrine has turned the act of reading into "an act of public depossession" (5). This "epistemology of separation and difference" (21) appears prominently in the contemporary study of Canadian literature. But it is not new; it has been evolving as a force aligned with professionalism for the last thirty years.

It's not difficult to see why this epistemology took root. If one objects to any formulation of the nation as an entity that can be described — that is *worth* describing — then one has to fall back on a pluralist vision of the country that sees it as a conglomeration of competing forces and centres of power. This is the view endorsed by much contemporary Canadian theory. But if one promotes this view, there is no reason to describe the conglomeration as *Canadian*, and no need to speak to the Canadian public (or students) about it. Only if there *is* something identifiably Canadian is it worth asking what that identification is all about. Contemporary Canadian literary criticism refuses to speak from where it lives. Yet it still lives — here. This is not just any place. It is a specific place. Which makes me wonder (again): Is it possible to speak about Canada and the postnational at the same time? Or to imagine that Canada is a dreamed place that is absolutely real? These are some of the questions we need to ask, particularly when we express scepticism about there ever being a collective so innocently called "we." Still, I think Richard Ohmann is right when he says: "There is just no sense in pondering the function of literature without relating it to the actual society that uses it" (39).

The argument that there is no monolithic Canada is self-evident. Once this is accepted, there is no choice but to imagine the "actual society" in an entirely new way. Since the mimetic assumption that it's out there (and can be framed) no longer holds, we have to think of different methods of explaining the country to ourselves and to the public. It is not enough to say it's *not* out there, because in so many ways the idea of Canada remains a powerful force. We have to explain that whatever idea we have of the country is constructed, and that everyone can participate in this construction. Everyone can make it real, which means that the country can become a collective fiction that is constantly renewed. After all, Canada is nothing less than a dramatic narrative about community. The strongest expressions of this community will be those that recreate the country by imagining it anew.

How does one begin this process of imagining the nation? Or of ensuring that the imagining process survives? Or of teaching students to enter into the process? You can't do this without providing a point of departure, a vision of the nation that you propose in order to destabilize it. In the absence of such a vision, we are truly lost, for then there are no points of reference, nothing to hold on to, nothing to make us believe we have anything in common, nothing to make it seem real.

The chapter entitled (interrogatively) "A Country without a Canon?" explores the problem of such idealism, the difficulty of talking about Canada in the full knowledge that while Canada cannot be described as any kind of totality, it still affects us as a totality on a day-to-day basis. The essay also touches on an issue that will be central to my discussion in "Privacy, Publicity, and the Discourse of Canadian Criticism" — the extent to which professionals are responsible for engaging in discourse about their imagined country within a public arena. In "A Country without a Canon?" I ask whether teachers and critics of Canadian literature have any moral responsibility to recognize the force of the community that empowers them or that provides them with the subject about which they get paid to speak. I do this by trying to imagine what it would be like to live in a country without a canon, or to teach a national literature that some people say is too young to be codified, too new to be enshrined.

While a country without a canon may be free, plural, ahistorical, and self-conscious of the material conditions that account for its contingent status, it may also be a country without moral conviction, without the means of recognizing difference, without standards against which ethical and political choices can be judged. This is why I argue that some recognition of canonical authority is ultimately crucial to the promotion of change and difference. If there is nothing entrenched, then there is nothing worth fighting against. As Louis Montrose observes, the interrogation of cultural canons provides an important means of determining how "versions of the real, of history, are experienced, deployed, repudiated, and by such means they may also be appropriated, contested, transformed" ("New Historicisms" 415).

Strong canonical formations are capable of inciting strong anti-canonical reactions. Canons enable us to be critical. They construct difference. They are necessarily political and therefore fundamental to the way we represent ourselves. If this is the case, then one must ask whether any form of subversion can be effective in its ends if it does not know and cannot articulate the nature of the canonical model it hopes to subvert. A recognition of an all-embracing plurality or otherness — which runs counter to the valorization of central (institutional, canonical) authority — does not correct imbalances in power; it neutralizes power by promoting the cliché that everyone is the same in his or her difference. To avoid such neutralization — to effect real social and political change — we must recognize and value precisely those forces we wish to undermine or explode. A key problem in the contemporary study of Canadian literature is our tendency to label and dismiss the idea of canonicity as the ground of difference. Another problem is that we have not theorized a model that allows the central and the marginal to be seen as mutually dependent and constantly in play.

The promotion of such interdependence is crucial in a publicly political sense, for students (who import the vision of Canada they are taught into the public sphere) cannot be asked to contribute to a country they believe is so fragmented as to be ultimately unknowable and therefore unchangeable. For this reason, it is essential first to recognize and value the national-referential model, in order to devalue it and show that the vision it proposes (one nation: its textual reflection) is fundamentally deceptive.

By introducing students to the hegemonic model and then encouraging them to challenge it, we will also be encouraging them to be critical in a way that can affect their daily lives, as Canadians, or as people thinking about Canada and its multiple ways of being whole. This is why I argue that even if there is no Canadian canon, we can still assert that there are valuable benefits to be derived from canonical pursuits, and that these benefits are particularly relevant to people who confront the absence of canonical authority. Weak canons, or non-canons, can do little to promote contestation or social change. In the absence of canonical authority, no authentic questioning, and no new forms of inquiry, can occur. Political change — an exemplary form of critical activity — is dependent on the creation of canonical ideals that must necessarily be undercut.

One need not have an agreed-upon canon in order to follow these critical-idealist pursuits. In fact, if there is no Canadian canon, the prospect of imagining one seems all the more inviting at this time, simply because as a canonically unformed culture we still have the opportunity to imagine our community anew. What I am suggesting is that our belief in a canon and our imaginative construction of it are far more important than its actual presence, even if such presence could be identified. In other words, the imagined community holds much more potential than any actual community ever could.

Although it would be nice to believe that teachers of Canadian literature could use their skills to enable students to become more critical of their country, pedagogy and criticism in recent years have encouraged students to focus on texts at the expense of questions of nation and on theoretical speculation to the exclusion of real political involvement in the events of national political life (although it is certainly true that some theory — especially feminist theory — does teach students to interrogate cultural norms, even though these may not be specifically Canadian norms). Today we seldom see examples of Canadian literary criticism that actually suggest a relation between the literature and the country.[4] In fact, the very suggestion is often treated as a sign of bad taste, mainly because it is rooted in the disgraced mimetic assumption that literature reflects life or in assumptions about the relation between literature and culture that are rooted in Arnoldian humanism. A number of Canadian critics writing today are working to find new ways of exploring this relation between nation and narration (Bennett, Blodgett, Davey, Findlay, Gerson, Hutcheon, and Slemon come to mind), but the overriding sense is that the fictions of Canadian literature and the fictions of Canadian culture have been divorced.

The pursuit of specialization and special interests has prompted academics to turn inward, toward professional values and discursive models that are increasingly uncivic. "Opponents are therefore not people in disagreement with the constituency but people to be kept out, nonexperts and nonspecialists, for the most part" (Said, "Opponents" 19). The message conveyed by this professional solipsism is that Canadian literature can no longer be spoken of in terms that are comprehensible outside the academy, or, more alarming, that literary critics within the academy no longer feel that it is necessary to pursue such terms. Of course, the impulse to be understood outside the academy would originate in the belief that there was information that the public and professionals could discuss. In this case, the information would be about the construction of Canada, its literature, the narratives we share.

Because the public (or popular) understanding of the function of literature remains grounded in representational values, there are few ways in which the populace can become interested in theories of textuality that challenge or ignore representational assumptions. The result is that the public's view of Canadian literature is very different from the professional's view, both in terms of what constitutes Canadian literature and in how it can be understood. Ask a few well-read, literate people who follow Canadian writing how they enjoyed such classics as *As for Me and My House, Roughing It in the Bush,* or *The Studhorse Man.* You will probably be told that they haven't heard of them. The industrialization of Canadian literature has created a whole world of Canadian literary classics that readers outside the academy (and many within it) know nothing about. It doesn't matter whether the specialization attached to theory has in fact alienated the public, for as Montrose says:

> One can object that the attack on postmodern theory for retreating from public discourse into a superspecialized and rarefied vocabulary is a profound misrecognition, but the very pervasiveness of this misrecognition is evidence of the enormous gulf that still separates postmodern theoretical discourse from general public understanding. It is easy enough to argue in principle that postmodern theory is a struggle to constitute a new discourse of cultural generality that will transcend academic specialisms. But it is difficult in practice for that theory to make itself publicly intelligible and available. ("New Historicisms" 432–33)

What are the implications of this separation of professional and public consciousness? There is nothing inherently wrong with specialization; every national literature has a group of works known mainly to specialists in the field. But there is certainly a gap indicated by the fact that books considered to be classics inside the profession remain virtually unknown outside it. The gap indicates the extent to which the profession has become self-supporting; apparently it does not need to address any kind of public beyond the institution in order to survive. This is a dangerous and possibly suicidal assumption. As the study of Canadian literature moves further and further indoors, it will become less and less socially relevant, so private in its venture that no one will be able to see it. Finally, in all practical terms, it will disappear from public view. This trend will only be reversed if Canadian criticism finds new ways of recovering its public function.

In "Privacy, Publicity, and the Discourse of Canadian Criticism" I explore this schism between the professional and the public spheres. My contention is that the Canadian literature industry at present is marked by its refusal to address concepts of nation, mainly because the mimetic-nationalist values that informed earlier Canadian criticism have been undercut by contemporary theory. The result is that students are seldom taught to see a connection between the Canadian literature they read and the Canadian space they inhabit, or, if they do, they are taught that the connection is so problematic and subjective that the ideas of collective action and community begin to seem worthless. In other words, the teaching of literature can provide no means of effecting collective political change in the "real" world because the nature of this world — in Canadian terms — has been radically called into question. The term "Canadian" in the study of Canadian literature seldom forms part of discussions about the texts under study.

This is a fundamentally alienating message. It is the message many students take with them when they leave the university, and it is the same message that leads them to believe, as members of the public outside the institution, that there are few points of contact between the public and the professional worlds. This perceived separation is reinforced by the professionals' use of increasingly sophisticated and shifting theoretical language. Such language conveys to the public that it has no means of communicating with the academy, which speaks another tongue. Conversely, many professionals who teach Canadian literature find themselves unwilling, or unequipped, to participate in public discussion about the country whose literature they teach. Frank Davey argues that we live in "a state invisible to its own citizens, indistinguishable from its fellows, maintained by invisible political forces, and significant mainly through its position within the grid of world-class postcard cities" (*Post-National* 266). Maybe the country is invisible, gone. Maybe Davey is right. But if he is, why bother thinking about Canadian literature at all? The challenge is to show that Davey is wrong. I suspect he would welcome such a challenge, mainly because he has devoted his academic career to studying a literature that is distinct by virtue of its Canadianness.

There is little reason for students to invest in an invisible country. How can they be critical of it or contribute to its growth if they cannot see it or imagine it? If students find it difficult to be critical of their milieu it may be because, in many of their courses, so little attention has been devoted to examining the ways in which a specifically Canadian milieu does exist. Even to raise the issue of what a "specifically Canadian milieu" might be seems dated, something one might have talked about in the late 1960s, but not today (when we need to talk about it more than ever). Yet academics continue to call themselves "specialists" in Canadian literature and to align themselves with organizations devoted to putatively nationalist causes such as the Association for Canadian and Quebec Literatures or the Association of Canadian College and University Teachers of English. It is hypocritical to assume that one can be professionally identified with things "Canadian" while at the same time repudiating or ignoring the connection — however artificial it may be — between the country and its literature. This artificiality needs to be exploited, not set aside.

I find it paradoxical that contemporary literary criticism seems to have deprived Canadian literary critics of the ability or the desire to be critical of Canada, to use the tools they have developed in the interests of democratic change. By introducing the idea that all experience is constructed through language, post-structural theory undermined the assumption that the critic could effectively comment on the relation between literature and whatever is imagined to be a real Canadian ethos. The reconceptualization of the country — a political act — cannot be effective when it is contained solely within the private sphere. The critic needs to step outside. The first stage in this process involves a recognition of social reality — a reality that most contemporary pedagogy teaches students to ignore, or to theorize as a linguistic construction that is fundamentally removed from their lives.

Texts do have a relation to the social world. The privatization of Canadian literature has devalued this relation and has therefore undermined our ability to be critical of that world. This means, of course, that many of the myths associated with the idea of a community that can be described as Canadian must also die: the myth that there ever was a coherent canon of Canadian literature; that Canadian literature transparently depicts some kind of cultural reality; that the study of literature might unite diverse people in their desire to understand more about their country. The death of these myths has a price. The removal of critical discourse from the public sphere has discouraged the expression of collectivity. Worse, it has made the idea of collectivity seem redundant. Yet without some form of collective experience there is no shared history, no narrative to imagine together, no story to change.

Although "Privacy, Publicity, and the Discourse of Canadian Criticism" traces the privatization of the discourse of Canadian criticism, it also suggests that there are some signs that the ground may be shifting. Several critics are now calling for more accessible critical language and for more direct involvement in the public sphere. Postcolonial theory is drawing attention to various forms of cultural domination and is encouraging critical activity that reinterprets historical and cultural values.[5] Whether these calls for a shift in the discourse will encourage a more widespread movement remains to be seen.

If Canadian literary critics have distanced themselves from the public, they have frequently distanced themselves from history, too. Of course, we do have detailed studies of Canadian literary history, and there are many people who have devoted enormous efforts to interpreting and recording the literary-historical facts. But what I often miss in these histories is a sense of what it was like to be reading Canadian literature in another time. The research involved in preparing chapter 4, the essay on anthologizing Canadian fiction, certainly increased my curiosity, for the more I examined the ways in which the reputations of Canadian authors were explained by our literary histories, the more I became aware of just how sanitized and canonized — how removed from history — these histories are. Perhaps this is because so many of these histories still endorse an emphasis on text at the expense of context. By the same token, the history of communal experience has been subordinated to author-centred studies. Questions of audience, society, and readership are seldom addressed.

There are dozens of Canadian writers who had huge popular appeal in their time. Their audiences were enthusiastic about literary styles and genres very different from those we tend to value today. What did it mean to be part of a community of readers that existed prior to the industrialization of Canadian literature? How did it feel to be one of those readers? Why did so many Canadian writers — once considered exemplary — drop from view? How can we explain the rise of certain reputations? The fall of others? How much did historic fame or shame have to do with political allegiance, writers' feuds, the giving or denying of prizes, certification, grants? I touch on some of these questions in "Anthologizing English-Canadian Fiction," but my primary aim is to collect data and raise some questions that literary histories tend to ignore.

We often think of canonical texts as the products of some kind of informed critical consensus, or we speak of how they have stood the test of time, or of the ways in which they somehow embody a tradition. Yet anyone who starts digging into national literary canons will inevitably be struck by how haphazard their construction can be.

One of the strongest forces behind the canonization of Canadian literature is McClelland and Stewart's New Canadian Library series. The New Canadian Library was originally conceived by Malcolm Ross in the early 1950s. By the end of that decade it had become the major vehicle through which Canadian literature reached the high-school and college market in paperback form.

Many of the works selected by Ross for inclusion in the series came to be seen as essential Canadian reading within the schools. As the demand for cultural self-recognition increased during the 1960s and 1970s, more and more courses devoted to Canadian literature were introduced. Many of these courses relied upon the growing list of books selected by Ross; and many teachers relied upon the critical introductions that accompanied each NCL volume to provide them with critical access to these Canadian texts. (A number of the New Canadian Library titles were unknown to teachers and critics — a scary thought.)

Despite the fact that many of the people who were reading the books had never heard of various titles in the series, McClelland and Stewart began to refer to the works it included as Canadian classics. It wasn't long before they began to promote the New Canadian Library as a collection that contained *the* Canadian classics. In its 1992 catalogue the publisher described the entire series as a "true library," one that was "synonymous with literary excellence." In one sense, McClelland and Stewart was absolutely correct in making this grandiose claim, for many people had come to believe that the series would eventually encompass most of the "great" Canadian works; for this reason, each new title released in the series achieved instant special status, simply by virtue of its inclusion.

Because the New Canadian Library had such an impact on canonical activity in Canada, the values accounting for the selection of works to be included in the series are certainly worthy of examination. Yet, to the best of my knowledge, no one has undertaken such an examination, perhaps because the series is considered too sacred, or too entrenched. It just *is*. There are, of course, endless reviews of NCL titles, and many of these comment on the worthiness of the series as a whole, but I haven't seen anyone try to explain why Ross selected certain books and not others (except for David Staines, the current general editor of the series, whose sustained praise for Ross in his introduction to *The Impossible Sum of Our Traditions* is so hyperbolic and genuflective that it really can't be seen as reliable or disinterested). In other words, the topic of the canonical choices informing the New Canadian Library selections has seldom been broached, despite the fact that the series has contributed so much to the formation of canonical value in Canada.

When I decided to undertake such an examination, I paid a visit to the McClelland and Stewart archives at McMaster University to consult the papers relating to the New Canadian Library; I also visited the University of Toronto to read the Malcolm Ross papers housed there. The first thing I discovered in both these locations was just how few people had consulted what appeared to be the only sources of information about the formation of the series. I wonder why. Second, I learned that the business of selecting titles for inclusion in the series was often quite haphazard. The selection process was guided by Ross, but it also responded to financial considerations and the intervention of influential writers, friends, professors, and critics. Equally significant was the publisher's desire to capitalize on certain segments of the school market, even if Ross didn't always endorse this desire.

None of this in itself is very surprising: every publisher must respond to market conditions, the cost of obtaining permissions, the need to create an image that can be used in effective advertising, and so on. As a publisher myself, I know this. However, I was surprised to discover how little attention was paid to literary issues or questions of critical assessment. On some occasions it seems that Jack McClelland or members of his staff selected books for inclusion in the series without Ross's knowledge. On other occasions it appears that books unknown to the publisher (and sometimes to Ross) were suggested for inclusion. What kind of classics were these?

The essay on the New Canadian Library, chapter 5, suggests that much of what we recognize as canonical fiction in Canada is the product of forces that were as much economic as they were aesthetic. Perhaps they were more economic than aesthetic. Perhaps quality is not such an important factor when it comes to determining which books will form a national canon.

This conclusion, which could probably be applied to most reprint publishing ventures, seems to alarm some people who want to believe that literary values are independent of financial considerations, and that the selection of great works — in this case, so-called great Canadian works — cannot be primarily market driven. When I delivered a preliminary version of my essay on the New Canadian Library at an academic conference, a number of people objected, not to my findings, but to the fact that I would be so vulgar as to make them public. (One conference participant said: "You don't have to air our dirty laundry in public.") This reaction served to confirm my impression that the New Canadian Library had achieved high canonical status: whatever values it embodied, they were too canonical to be challenged. Canons are always most potent when they remain distant, untouchable, boxed.

This should probably make us want to unbox them. At the very least, it should encourage us to look more closely at the ways in which the perception of canonical value affects our response to so-called classic texts. In chapter 6, "The Rhetoric of Back-Cover Copy," I look at how the canonization of a much-vaunted novel — Sinclair Ross's *As for Me and My House*— has completely altered the ways critics speak about the book. The shift in critical rhetoric attached to Ross's novel demonstrates that the more classic a work becomes, the more its function is apprehended as critical, rather than aesthetic. The classic text becomes a vehicle through which we read a critical message; at its most extreme, the claim for the critical value of the novel supplants the claim for its value as literature. In his afterword to the most recent NCL edition of

As for Me and My House, Robert Kroetsch encourages us to read the novel as a means of accessing something else — "contemporary art" — and as a guidebook that will teach us something about the nature of fiction and its construction. At the same time, we are encouraged to read it as a prairie novel that will tell us about "our culture and psyche" and "the larger story of the Canadian imagination." In this paradigmatic expression of doubled value, Ross's text is packaged in a way that both evades and embraces the narrative of nation. The novel comes to be read, ironically and canonically, as a reflection of the tension between the local and the universal — a displaced version of the tension between private and public critical value that characterizes postindustrial Canadian criticism.

In its recent catalogues, McClelland and Stewart has begun to refer to the entire New Canadian Library series as a group of texts that are "indispensable to an understanding and appreciation of the country itself" (*English and Communications 1992*); in other words, they have become educational tools that convey multiple canonical instructions, all in a single package. The rhetoric of canonicity begins to outstrip itself as it claims greater and greater distinction for the already-classic text. The new NCL afterwords are by "distinguished writers, critics, and scholars." Their covers "feature specially chosen masterpieces of Canadian art" (aren't masterpieces *already* chosen?). Ultimately, the rhetoric of canonicity masks the enormous differences between these canonical works that are being described as the already-classic.

Like the people who produce copy for the catalogues and back covers of New Canadian Library editions, the writers, critics, and scholars who provide the afterwords to recent NCL texts often blur the distinction between the functions of criticism and fiction. The generic distinctions that once marked off criticism as "secondary" and the novel or poem as "primary" have collapsed under the weight of contemporary theory, which is reluctant to privilege one form of narrative over another, or to establish a hierarchy of narrative modes. My commentary on *As for Me and My House* explores one version of this collapse.

The idea of reading criticism as narrative may be a result of canonical exhaustion, but it can also be liberating. Eli Mandel once suggested that Margaret Atwood's *Survival* could be read as a ghost story. There are many other Canadian critics whose work can be profitably read as fiction. When criticism is treated as narrative, all kinds of interesting transformations can take place. We begin to see that writers of criticism, like writers of poetry or fiction, are influenced and frequently driven by the literary forms and tensions they have studied or appreciated in the work of others. We begin to see that critics are often embarked on a voyage, and that each new analysis represents a stopping point in a continuing and frequently archetypal personal journey.

There is nothing new in this observation — Hayden White has been making it for years — which makes it all the more remarkable that so few works of Canadian criticism have been treated as narratives with their own tensions, formal preoccupations, discursive strategies, and metaphoric structures. The same comment applies to works of Canadian literary history: we seldom read these works as narratives created by individuals who are fulfilling specific agendas, articulating certain needs, and writing themselves into history as they write their historical accounts. The last two essays in this book represent initial attempts to stage this kind of reading. I look at two specific documents that have had a profound impact on the study of Canadian literature: Northrop Frye's conclusion to the first edition of the *Literary History of Canada* (1965) and Frank Davey's essay entitled "Surviving the Paraphrase," which was originally presented as a conference paper in 1974, then published by Davey in 1976 and again as the lead essay in his book by the same title in 1983. Although both works originally appeared many years ago, they continue to affect the ways in which Canadian criticism is perceived today. It is clear that both Frye and Davey saw these documents as pivotal narratives in their own critical *oeuvres*.

Frye's conclusion depicts in narrative form his evolving sense of how critics necessarily become involved in their critical creations; further, it reveals the degree to which this involvement provides a measure of the critic's own imaginative development. Frye reads Canadian literary history as a romance that implicates him in its structures. Because his conclusion glosses the fall-and-redemption myth that inspires much of his work, it illustrates his conception of literary-history-making as a simultaneous act of self-making. Viewed from the perspective of Frye's own transforming voyage through it, the conclusion appears in a new light as a romance about the creation of the idea of Canada, a metaphoric conception that is transhistorical, autonomous, and distinctly literary.

Davey's "Surviving the Paraphrase" is, in many ways, devoted to countering the effects of Frye's conclusion. Davey rejects the notion of an idealized "peaceable kingdom" (Frye 848), just as he rejects the totalizing claim that Canadian literary history can be read as a monolithic narrative. In Davey's view, such a denial of plurality, difference, and conflict serves to neutralize the literature in question; it creates the illusion that there is harmony where there is really discord and fragmentation. Worse, Davey argues, Frye's perspective encourages critics to focus on cultural questions at the expense of literary language and form; by doing so, it bypasses the technical qualities that make the works of individual writers distinct.

Although the two documents at first seem antithetical in their aims and interests, an exploration of their narrative strategies suggests that they share more than one might have thought. Both describe a quest undertaken by a narrator in search of redemption. Both present an alienated speaker who seeks integration into the social order. Both narrators attempt to construct a social order that will house them. Both envision this social order as primarily imaginative, linked as it is to the transformative power of the written word. By the end of his story, the narrator of "Surviving the Paraphrase" discovers, ironically, that he has been driven by a desire that is similar to Frye's — the desire to imagine Canada, again and again and again, through a variety of critical acts. This is not the expression of a critic who truly believes his country is "invisible to its own citizens" (*Post-National* 266).

Every time literary critics address Canadian literature, they also imagine the country. Every time we try to unimagine Canada, we make it that much more visible, that much more real. But how often do we read critical versions of this construction? How often do we step back and talk about where we think we are living, or about how Canadian literature is part of the world in which we live?

In "A Country without a Canon?" I ask whether we have any moral responsibility to recognize the force of the community that empowers us or that provides us with the subject about which we speak. My feelings on the matter have guided me in writing this book. As teachers and critics of Canadian literature — as professionals who are trained to think about the country — we need to talk more about the community we inhabit. We may be subjected by that community. It may seem fragmented and even foreign. We know that any totalizing idea of the country is false. But we cannot transmit this knowledge effectively unless we can define what we are describing in more convincing terms than by simply calling the country monolithic, or by describing its multiple forces as purely institutional. In the end, I don't think we can identify ourselves without the simple recognition that there is a world, a nation, a community (a canon?) that positions our act of identification and leads us to reach conclusions about how we live, or teach, or read.

Part One

Canon and Context

1

The Canonization of Canadian Literature: An Inquiry into Value

IT IS STARTLING TO REALIZE that Canadian literature was canonized in fewer than twenty years. Here is how it happened:

At the end of World War II, Canadian literature was not taught as an independent subject in Canadian schools. There was no institutional canon. In 1957 McClelland and Stewart introduced its mass-market paperback reprint series entitled the New Canadian Library. It allowed teachers to discuss the work of many Canadian authors who had never been the subject of formal academic study. The New Canadian Library was truly "new": prior to its conception, there was no "library" in use. There were no Canadian classics. Northrop Frye recalls that, at that time, the notion of finding a classic Canadian writer remained but "a gleam in a paternal critic's eye" (Conclusion [1976] 319).

Frye's comment must be placed in context: he was remembering the efforts that produced the first *Literary History of Canada* in 1965. Its publication "gave a definitive imprimatur of respectability to the academic study of Canadian writing" (MacLulich, "What Was" 19). It made a Canadian canon seem possible; to many, it made the canon seem real. According to its general editor, Carl F. Klinck, the *Literary History* project "began in 1957" and "required six years and the work of many hands." It was "accomplished by the Editors and twenty-nine other scholars" who wrote with "the support provided by the Humanities Research Council of Canada and the Canada Council," two government funding agencies that made "twenty-two separate short-term grants in aid of research." "Not one application was refused" (Klinck, 3: vii). The publisher also received "a substantial grant-in-aid" for its efforts to promote the "national recognition of our literature" (Klinck,

3: xii). As they congratulated one another, government, academia, and the publishing industry joined hands to create a national canon. The institution called Canadian literature was born.

Since 1965, what is commonly referred to as the "explosion" in Canadian literature has produced all the by-products of canonization run rampant. In short, "an entire new gallery, one labelled 'Canadian Literature,' has been added to the literary museum presided over by our English departments" (MacLulich, "What Was" 20). So strong is the desire for canonization in Canada that this gallery has been erected (with great elaboration and cost) at a time when, as John Guillory says, "the canon has become the site of a structural fatigue, where pressures conceived to be extrinsic to the practice of criticism seem to have shaken literary pedagogy in fundamental ways" ("Canonical and Non-Canonical" 483).

The museum that houses the new gallery called Canadian literature is run by academic literary critics who remain studiously impervious to "the unveiling of the canon as an institutional construction" — an "unveiling" that, in other countries, has created what Guillory describes as "a legitimation crisis with far-ranging consequences" ("Canonical and Non-Canonical" 483). While their American counterparts are arguing that "all prior literary histories are [now] rendered partial, inadequate, and obsolete" (Kolodny 291), and while the editor of the *Columbia Literary History of the United States* "candidly admits, 'we are not so sure we know what American literature is or what history is and whether we have the authority to explain either'" (quoted in Kolodny 294), Canadian critics and literary historians have turned a blind eye to these delegitimizing activities. Following a path charted by some of the earliest commentators on Canadian writing, they continue to enshrine the literary models they have invented in the hope that such activity will provide the canonizers with what they have always wanted: an image of themselves and of their values.

These values are easy to identify: a preoccupation with history and historical placement; an interest in topicality, mimesis, verisimilitude, and documentary presentation; a bias in favour of the native over the cosmopolitan; a pressure toward formalism; a concern with traditional over innovative forms; a pursuit of the created before the uncreated, the named before the unnamed; an expression of national self-consciousness; a valorization of the cautious, democratic, moral imagination before the liberal, inventive one; a hegemonic identification with texts that are ordered, orderable, safe — texts that work through what Lorraine Weir calls "'shareability'" and the "strategy of containment" ("Discourse" 27). Although the student of Canadian literature can find many examples of works whose qualities run counter to those I have just listed, the fact remains that the canon is the conservative product of the conservative institution that brought it to life. The power of the canon and the power of its members are inseparable: the institution *is* the canon; its members *are* the texts.

In Canada, this identification of the institution with its texts is best illustrated by the proceedings of a conference on the Canadian novel held at the University of Calgary in 1978. The most important result of this conference was the publication of a list of the 100 "most important" Canadian novels, prepared "as a guide to those interested in the masterworks of our literary tradition" (Steele 158). This "guide" was the result of a ballot "distributed to Canadian 'teachers and critics,' who were invited to choose 1) the most 'important' one hundred works of fiction (List A); 2) the most important ten novels (List B); and 3) the most important ten works of various genres (List C)" (Steele 150). The ballot was prepared by Malcolm Ross, with the assistance of McClelland and Stewart, publisher of the New Canadian Library; Jack McClelland was highly visible at the conference. Most of the "important" works of fiction, it turned out, were published by his company. This aroused some suspicion, but it did nothing to stop the canonizers from pursuing their incessant desire: to identify Canadian classics at any cost. Their "coming-of-age party" had been a grand success, for there was a sense in which the conference "dealt with the total literary institution" (MacLulich, "What Was" 18, 19). The "Golden Age for Canadian Literature" had arrived (Stouck, *Major Canadian Authors* 280).

By 1982 McClelland and Stewart had established the Canadian Classics Committee, the mandate of which was described in a press release dated 31 May. It was "formed to define and prepare a list of Canadian literary works that merits the designation 'classic.'" The committee, which comprised "a group of distinguished scholars and educators from across Canada," tautologically defined a "classic" as "a book indispensable for the appreciation of Canadian literature" and announced that it would soon issue "its first list of approved literary classics." Once the list had been issued, the committee noted, it would "authorize publishers of approved editions of each work so nominated to carry the official imprimatur of the committee." The committee declared that it was "independent" and "self-governing." Then it thanked the publisher for his financial backing and support.

Today, Canadian literature is taught at virtually every high school, college, and university in the nation. "Certified" Canadian classics abound. Doctoral dissertations are written annually on dozens of Canadian literary topics. Tenure-track university appointments are regularly offered in the field. Massive government support through numerous funding agencies, along with the institutional support of academics, accounts for the proliferation of canon objects associated with the Canadian literature industry: reference guides, critical studies, specialized journals, bibliographies, articles, anthologies, films, research grants, awards, medals, and even teacher-oriented "crash courses" in what has become its own thriving discipline. A card game entitled Canadian Writers ("Suitable for ages 7 and up") is now available.

* * *

Something profound happened to the study of Canadian literature after the *Literary History* appeared in 1965. Given the canonical exercises that marked the Calgary conference, one would think there was widespread support for the values implicit in the canonized works. Certainly the volume of criticism directed at interpreting these works suggests widespread support. Yet it is remarkable that all this interpretation directed at the canonical texts has produced no sustained discussion of one of the most crucial, problematic, and theoretically important questions that gives the Canadian canon its power — the question of how the literary values it embodies achieved and maintain their currency. Such a discussion would naturally involve a parallel exploration of the forces accounting for the production of the authorized version of Canadian literary history we have been taught to read. It would also acknowledge what Louis Montrose calls "the historicity of texts" and "the textuality of history"; this textuality creates multiple histories "that necessarily but always incompletely construct the 'History' to which they offer access" ("Renaissance" 8). In Canada, these histories remain ignored or uncreated; by extension, the examination of literary value has also been evaded. While we do hear calls for evaluative criticism, we seldom find criticism that investigates the values we have enshrined.[1] We do not know why we read the books we read or why we say they are good. We do not know why the Canadian canon includes certain texts and excludes others. No one can account for the taste informing the list of the 100 "most important" novels chosen at the Calgary conference. No one can say why certain Canadian authors are major, or minor, or seldom mentioned at all.

Why has there been this lack of attention? Because the canon was created so rapidly, and because it was, like all canons, an institutional construct, the efforts of its creators were directed toward verifying the structure they had invented. To verify this structure was to verify the institution itself. As Hayden White observes, literary histories and the canons they enshrine have "specifiable ideological implications" (69); they are "verbal fictions, the contents of which are as much invented as found" (82). The Canadian canon — and its so-called history and tradition — has been invented so quickly that it tends to mask something else that has been constructed — what Harold Bloom calls the "historicized dungeon of facticity" (2) that places us "so far inside a tradition, or inside a way of representing, or inside even a particular author, that only enormous effort can make us aware of how reluctant we are to know our incarceration" (1).

By ignoring the values informing literary history, and by pretending that there is a *history* rather than histories, Canadian critics have shown little awareness of their incarceration in facticity. Our canon remains unique by virtue of its rapid rise to power at precisely the time when other canons and literary institutions are being named, explained, torn apart. Canadian critics continue to accept what Montrose calls the "unproblematized distinctions between 'literature' and 'history,' between 'text' and 'context' " ("Renaissance" 6). Although a "poetics of culture" (the term is Stephen Greenblatt's) is entirely relevant to the study of Canadian literary histories, Canadian critics show little interest in exploring "the range of aesthetic possibilities within a given representational mode" or in examining how that mode is tied to "the complex network of institutions, practices, and beliefs that constitute the culture as a whole" (Greenblatt, "Introduction" 6). Because they ignore this network and because they pretend that history is stable and knowable, literary historians in Canada have sanitized their subject to death. It has become an accessible, bound-up object, divorced from chaos, power, change. Text and context are sundered; language and history are at odds.

If other national literary canons have begun to decompose in the face of current ideology and theory, it is because the "fantasies of ortho-doxy" enshrined in these institutions have also begun to decay while the forces accounting for exclusion and "difference" have replaced orthodoxy and become a "central critical category" (Guillory, "Ideol-ogy" 195). In Annette Kolodny's words, the delegitimation crisis "asserts as its central critical category not commonality but *difference*" (293). Such an assertion obviously undermines the canonical values associated with commonality: the orthodox belief in a great tradition; the notion that a national literature expresses shared cultural values; the idea that any literary or cultural undertaking can be explained in terms of inclusion. Only when we begin to focus on the forces of exclusion, difference, and "defamiliarization" can we finally "stand before the vast array of texts — canonical and non-canonical alike —

and view them as more or less complex assemblages of rhetorical and stylistic devices whose meanings and value have been variously constituted over time by changing audiences" (Kolodny 303).

An awareness of delegitimation and defamiliarization "empowers us to understand that the critic's nagging obsession to locate any and every text within a graded, evaluative hierarchy, irrespective of history, is no more (and no less) than one facet of an ongoing process by which competing interest groups vie for cultural hegemony, in part by defining what shall be invested with merit" (Kolodny 303). The same awareness empowers us to reformulate our notion of literary value in terms proposed by Jane Tompkins, terms that ask us to determine "how and why specific texts 'have power in the world' (or do not attain power, as the case may be) at any given moment" (quoted in Kolodny 304). These current theories about literary value, or about what Barbara Herrnstein Smith describes as "a more general rethinking of the concept of value" (10), now appear "to bracket the majority of theoretical problems over which criticism has not unfruitfully labored, among them the problem of literary language" (Guillory, "Canonical and Non-Canonical" 503). As Montrose observes, they encourage us to "resituate canonical literary texts among the multiple forms of writing . . . while, at the same time, recognizing that this project of historical resituation is necessarily the textual construction of critics who are themselves historical subjects" ("Renaissance" 6).

* * *

Why has the delegitimation crisis had so little impact on Canadian literary theory or on the writing of Canadian literary history? Why have the values informing the Canadian canon remained virtually unquestioned from any perspective? These questions can be addressed through the realization that Canadian criticism is marked by a general reluctance to acknowledge that the canon comprises what Guillory calls "the hieroglyph of a social relation" between the canonizer and "the school." The school defines and promotes the canon in order to define and promote itself. Therefore, the canon "must be confronted as the cultural capital of educational institutions" ("Canonical and Non-Canonical" 495). It is the currency used by the institution the canonizers inhabit. For them to destabilize the canon would be to devalue their currency. It would depreciate the value of their house and make them poorer. To avoid such depreciation, canonizers need only maintain the canon that sustains their reflection. The unwillingness to explore the canon paradoxically attests to its power. It testifies to what

Herrnstein Smith calls "the correlation of validity with silence" (8). This correlation is a predominant feature of the Canadian critical landscape. Some history would be helpful here.

I have already suggested that in Canada the canonical departure point is marked by the publication of the first *Literary History of Canada* in 1965. In his conclusion to this history, Frye set the nonevaluative tone that would characterize most future discussions of Canadian literature. Frye argued that to study Canadian literature properly, one must outgrow the view "that evaluation is the end of criticism," for had evaluation been "a guiding principle" in the creation of the *History*, criticism of Canadian literature would have become "only a huge debunking project," leaving it "a poor naked alouette plucked of every feather of decency and dignity." Frye claimed that his nonevaluative stance was consciously anticanonical, for the "evaluative view" that he rejects "is based on the conception of criticism as concerned mainly to define and canonize the genuine classics of literature" (821). Frye believed that there *were* "genuine classics," but that they had not appeared in Canada. Not yet. Twenty years later, as we have seen, Canadian classics had appeared in droves.

The rapid appearance of the Canadian canon and its classics was a direct result of the values that were everywhere present in Frye's conclusion, and everywhere denied. Silence *was* golden. Frye's evaluative denial was paradoxical and prophetic: it was unnecessary to call for evaluation because the act of evaluation was over; the *Literary History* — and all the values it incarcerated in its dungeon of facticity — was complete. Power had been established through all that was denied. Frye's refusal to evaluate lends credence to Herrnstein Smith's view that "one of the major effects of prohibiting or inhibiting explicit evaluation is to forestall the exhibition and obviate the possible acknowledgment of divergent systems of value and thus to ratify, by default, established evaluative authority" (7).

How is this "evaluative authority" embodied in Frye's original conclusion to the *Literary History*? In one respect, the document can be read in the context of Frye's other theoretical works, since it argues that "literature is conscious mythology" (836) and that "the forms of literature are autonomous: they exist within literature itself, and cannot be derived from any experience outside literature" (835). But in the conclusion this argument soon breaks down. Without saying so, Frye suggests that there is a Canadian literary form that is extraliterary in origin, a form that is the product of "the obvious and unquenchable desire of the Canadian cultural public to identify itself through its literature" (823). Such a value is chiefly concerned with cultural self-recognition. Literature becomes a means through which Canadians can know themselves and verify their national consciousness. The value of Canadian literature is that it reflects the value of the nation. Excellence becomes a matter of the writer's ability to express this value.

Few today would question the assertion that Frye is a cultural nationalist. I am more interested in exploring the literary values implicit in his nationalist stance. Frye's conclusion makes it clear that there is a formal value attached to the nationalist one — the value of representational realism. Again and again he emphasizes that what differentiates Canadian literature — what makes it unique and therefore valuable — is that the Canadian writer allows us to "remain aware of his social and historical setting." Because so much Canadian literature is "as innocent of literary intention as a mating loon," its value lies not in "the autonomous world of literature" but in its ability to transmit "cultural history" and to provide "an indispensable aid to knowledge of Canada" which "records what the Canadian imagination has reacted to." Therefore it is most significantly studied "as a part of Canadian life" (822).

All of the terms employed by Frye suggest that what is valuable to him in Canadian literature are those works that establish a relation between national consciousness, literary history, and a kind of idealized mimesis. The same relation provides the currency used by the institution erected after Frye's conclusion was published — the institution that sanctified the Canadian canon as we know it today. Because the institution is fundamentally narcissistic, it wants clear, mirrorlike images of itself and what it sees: the stuff out of which representational realism — and most canonized Canadian literature — is made. Realism confirms the school's position in space and time. It says: you are fixed, concrete, authoritative. You exist. Your unwarped image means truth. It is this search for placement, solidity, and identity — embodied in various critical statements and culminating in Frye's conclusion — which allows Eli Mandel to observe that "as soon as we add the word *Canadian* to criticism, we move the object of our concern into a particular space and time, a geographical and historical context, where what might normally remain simply an element of the background — the sociology of literature — becomes the foreground" (*Contexts* 3).

During the 1970s the so-called thematic critics (most notably Margaret Atwood, D.G. Jones, and John Moss) developed Frye's ideas by valorizing the literary expression of nationalism so central to the evolution of the canon. Their nationalist bias, and its debt to Frye, is widely recognized. But this recognition has obscured the mimetic value attached to the search for "cultural history" that was articulated in Frye's conclusion. The Canadian works of criticism that were canonized after the conclusion are the products of this value. As Frank Davey has observed, "Thematic critics in Canada have been interested in what Canadian literary works 'say,' especially what they 'say' about Canada and Canadians" ("Surviving" 6). Davey's argument — that this value is objectionable because such critics "have largely overlooked what literary works 'mean' " — is revealing. It demonstrates a unified and unitary view of what makes Canadian writing valuable — a view that supports those works that are *not* concerned with what concerns Davey: "matters of form, language, style, structure, and consciousness as these arise from the work as a unique construct" (1). Davey objects to the principle of inclusion implicit in these canon-making critical works, one that embraces texts that present Canadian readers and critics with an image of themselves.

The rhetoric of the thematic critics reveals that what they value most is not the abstract concept around which their books appear to cohere — call it "survival" (Atwood 32), "national identity" (Jones 4–5), or "the 'garrison mentality' " (Moss, *Patterns* 15) — it is the mimetic potential of the works they study. Because Canadian criticism and Canadian literary history are inevitably fictions — narratives about their own strategies of knowing and naming the world — we can say that the mimetic forms they assume and the values they support *reflect* the mimetic forms they canonize and call valuable. As Hayden White observes, "Although historians and writers of fiction may be interested in different kinds of events, both the forms of their respective discourses and their aims in writing are often the same" (121).

The created fictions of the thematic critics are mimetic narratives; they attempt to secure a fundamental relation between people and their world and to record the evidence of this relation. For Jones, "English-Canadian literature tends to be haunted by the sterility of a materially abundant but overly mechanical order imposed upon life" (9). The artist may attempt to exorcise this materialistic, mechanical ordering, but in the end, as at the end of Jones's study, the artist remains grounded in reality: ultimately, he or she must try to "celebrate the actual" and to find the "authentic reality" of "our own identity" (183). For Atwood, "a piece of art . . . can also be . . . a mirror. The reader looks at the mirror and sees not the writer but himself; and behind his own image in the foreground, a reflection of the world he lives in" (15). At the end of her study, Atwood reaches the same conclusion as Jones. She argues that only "when literature names situations we can recognize" will "writer and reader connect in an area we call real life: it's our situation that's being talked about" (241). Moss is also interested in works that offer "visions of reality from fixed perspectives" (*Sex and Violence* 5). Because he is pulled toward "discussions about the mimetic aspects of the work — about, that is, the relationship of the work to the world" (Brown 159), Moss maintains that "the time and place to which we most need access are here and now. The Canadian novel can give us these at least, the dimensions of our experience of ourselves" (*Sex and Violence* 5).

Just as the works of criticism canonized after Frye's conclusion were the product of mimetic values, so the creative works interpreted by these critics gained value according to their ability to record time and place. This value, as in the criticism, was a displaced form of nationalism. Nine of "the first ten novels" selected at the Calgary conference were clearly works that operated according to the mimetic conventions of representational realism.[2] These conventions had dominated Canadian fiction for decades. As George Woodcock notes, "it was characteristic of Canadian fiction when it began to emerge as something special and distinguishable that its practitioners tended to be formally unadventurous and even conservative and to concentrate to a degree long abandoned by novelists in culturally more settled countries on the content of their books — on what they had to say rather than on how they said it" (83). The implication is that what makes early Canadian writers "special and distinguishable" is precisely their conservatism, their dedication to content over form.

The Calgary conference served to illustrate the canonical value of mimesis that writers and critics had come to share. And while some did (and still do) take issue with the list distributed at the conference, that list remains the single most prominent and thorough indication of what the Canadian canon has become (the entire list is reprinted in Steele, *Taking Stock*). The conference also confirmed the intimate relation between the canon and the "evaluative authority" of what had become the institution called Canadian literature. The power of this institution, as of all canonical institutions, lay in its ability "to impose fictions upon the world and . . . to enforce the acceptance of fictions that are known to be fictions" (Greenblatt, *Renaissance* 141). The Calgary conference emphasized this institutional control over multiple forms of fiction by ranking novels as well as works of poetry and criticism. The first work chosen in the "open" category was the *Literary History of Canada*. This selection dramatizes the intimate connection between the critics and the paradigmatic canonical oracle. MacLulich accurately observes that "there is a sense in which the Calgary conference . . . dealt with the total literary institution" in Canada ("What Was" 19), an institution that clearly reflected the power and influence of its inhabitants: academic critics throughout the country, the "specialists" in Canadian literature who promoted the canon and rose to power on its muscular back. These specialists were a breed apart from the early Canadian academics who agreed with F.R. Scott when he argued, in 1955, that "to establish a continuing literary tradition in Canada significant works of Canadians must be kept in print" (Whalley 9). Now that the canon was established, and now that the texts supporting the institution called Canadian literature were deeply enshrined and unassailable, it became permissible, even fashionable, for Canadian critics to recognize and question the canon. (Their questions merely acknowledged and reinforced the canon's currency and authority; it was *worth* questioning now, more than ever.)

One of the speakers at the Calgary conference — Robert Kroetsch — confessed his "reluctance" and "need" to "locate/discriminate the canon of Canadian fiction" ("Contemporary Standards" 9). Kroetsch's comments are revealing because they are the product of his special status: as an academic who became a canonized Canadian novelist, he represents the bridge between creative and critical value so central to the Canadian "school." Kroetsch's desire to locate and discriminate the canon can be seen as a desire to locate and discriminate himself within the canon that allows him to speak with its authority as an author, critic, and (self-proclaimed) shaman/sham. But because this desire for inclusion within a great Canadian tradition outweighs Kroetsch's desire for exclusion, he remains baffled by the very canon that has created and crowned him. "I still haven't grasped," he says, "why we make room on the crowded shelf of fiction for one book, and not for another. How and why do we insert a particular text into the row of existing texts, or into what might be called the supertext?" (11). This is an important question, but Kroetsch never really answers it. He soon becomes diverted by his own need to define a canon and to list the "important novels that I haven't yet read" (16). (How does he know these works are "important" if he hasn't read them? The answer reveals that Kroetsch's recognition of the canon born from silence is committed and complete.)

Kroetsch does point to one feature of the Canadian canon that I have identified as a value: the idea that the Canadian novel is "a kind of weather report," "a matter of here and now" that "demands of us an exact measuring and an exact response" (13). He calls attention to the canonized writers' "attention to history" and to those novelists who, "book by book, would seem agents of the world, not its creators" (15). Kroetsch is correct when he identifies the chief characteristic of the

Canadian novelist: as a mimetic agent, he or she makes us "feel at home," "names us into safety," and provides "a victory of humanism — when some of us are sceptical about the humanistic tradition" (17). The value implicit in this statement is that what is good is what is recordable, verifiable, coherent, and concrete. Canada is "a country in which literature is expected to be conservative," Kroetsch says (14). For Canadian readers, the novel serves to validate our communal position in time and space. In this way, it serves the same function and the same end as the work of the thematic critics — that of valorizing mimetic, as opposed to expressive, literary-historical forms.

Another participant in the Calgary conference — Barry Cameron — argued against what he saw as the prevailing notion "that the writer is implicitly a spokesman or agent of a society and that literature's main function is to present visions of society." This notion is attached to criticism that "looks at language not for itself, but primarily as a referential or representational tool that points to something beyond or outside language" ("Response" 28). Yet Cameron's desire to reverse this perspective — to focus on language before world, on form before content — is actually a means to an end that has everything to do with cultural representation, with the relation between the work and its world. In a 1977 essay written with Michael Dixon, Cameron argues that "privileged criteria or 'special pleading' on the grounds of national origin are invalid" and that "Canadian literature deserves treatment as part of the autonomous world of literature" (138). They maintain that an understanding of formal values is "the key to an understanding of what Canadian means as a literary term" (141). The lingering emphasis on Canadianness is revealing: ultimately, for Cameron and Dixon, as for Frye, the "autonomous world of literature" is secondary to that which is emphatically Canadian. And even as they eschew the "sociological bias" of the thematic critics who pretend "that literature consists only of content" (141), Cameron and Dixon encourage their readers to determine "whether there is anything indigenous about our literature" (142).

If it can be said that the Calgary conference marks a canonical high point in the institutional creation of Canadian literature, then it can also be said that the values associated with this canonical orgy had never been more pointedly expressed. As Laurie Ricou noted in his response to one of the conference papers, "we are in some danger in this country, as our attempt to find the ten best Canadian novels might also suggest, in assuming that there is one right way for criticism, of declaring an orthodoxy from which no variation is allowed" (Panel comment 98). Ricou was correct: a mimetic orthodoxy had developed that valued what Eli Mandel called "the difficult work of naming one's place and time" ("Regional" 114).

* * *

My observations on the canonization of Canadian literature between 1965 and 1978 are meant to suggest that the value of the classics that were created during this period was a function of their ability to represent nationalist currency through a displaced formal equivalent: mimesis. I mean further to suggest that mimetic discourse is the appropriate instrument of power in an institution that seeks to verify its solidity and authority over time. Of course, these suggestions truncate the received version of Canadian literary history. We know there are some works that are valued precisely because they are experimental; and we know it would be possible to write a history of experimental Canadian poetry or prose. Such a history might challenge the canon, but by doing so it would only attest to the authority of the model from which it deviates — a conservative, historically oriented model aligned with nationalism and mimesis.

The historical equation between nationalism and mimesis appears in most of the comments made on Canadian literature since it became the subject of criticism in the early 1800s. Carl Ballstadt shows that early Canadian critics "regarded literature in which the fancy was given free reign as being inappropriate to a new country," and that they endorsed literature that "would take inventory of a new country, to begin the process of naming and familiarizing." When Ballstadt notes that these early critics "felt that factual and informative literature would best suit the needs of a people seeking to establish themselves" (xvii), the nationalist impulse behind their critical values begins to emerge. This same impulse appears in the works of a variety of nineteenth- and twentieth-century critics who argue that the best way to validate the nation is to encourage a national literature that "emphasizes practicality and modesty in intention, a serious, factual, and scientific stocktaking to pave the way for fiction and poetry in which fancy would not be the sole component but which would flourish on a solid foundation of accurate and particular accounts of experience" (xxi–xxii).

Although the relation between nationalism and mimesis seems self-evident, the connection in terms of literary value is seldom made. While it is true that Canadian critics have historically argued in favour of a literature that would identify the nation, and while it is equally true that "nationalism has always been part of the cultural air that Canadian writers and critics have breathed" (MacLulich, "Thematic Criticism"

19), few will admit that this desire to reflect upon the country led to the valorization of the type of literature best suited to this kind of reflection: realistic fiction. In the only study that addresses this question, MacLulich argues that in Canadian fiction, the "documentary" value inspiring Canadian novelists is derived from the "social realism that is the hallmark of the nineteenth-century novel" (*Between* 12), a realism that prompts our best-known writers to "build their fiction around characters and situations that are recognizably drawn from their own society" (*Between* 11). If such a value informs the Canadian tradition in fiction — and the works canonized at the Calgary conference suggest that this has indeed been the case — it is puzzling to consider why the value of realism as a nationalist tool has not been more widely recognized. My sense is that this value is so deeply entrenched that it has become unnecessary to mention it.

The impact of this realist-nationalist equation upon the selection and formation of the Canadian canon is profound, precisely because it continued to be held as a value throughout the twentieth century. Yet its continuing presence is obscured, not only because its value is *assumed*, but also because when the value is expressed it acquires a variety of forms. We may refer to it as thematic criticism, or the sociology of literature, or the documentary mode, but the informing value remains the same: asserting the existence of the nation by supporting literature that records its existence. When critics such as Davey or Cameron and Dixon argue that Canadian criticism must transcend its fundamental conservatism — which they see as a function of its preoccupation with culture, history, and sociology — they simply identify the continuing presence of the realist-nationalist impulse that dominates Canadian literary history.

If literary history is "a fiction written by those who wish to retain a record of their own values" (Allen and Anderson 3), and if I am correct in asserting that in Canada these values are fundamentally mimetic, then it should be possible to see the history of Canadian criticism as a mimetic construct. I have already mentioned some points of departure for this kind of history: the early emphasis on realism and nationalism in nineteenth-century Canadian criticism, the debate between native and cosmopolitan values that emerged after the two world wars, Northrop Frye's implicitly nationalist-realistic stance in his conclusion, and the mimetic forces underlying the work of the thematic critics and informing both the presentations and the selections made at the Calgary conference in 1978. But what happened to Canadian literary value *after* Calgary? One way of answering this question is to look at some of the critical documents on Canadian literature and literary history published since the 1978 conference. Has the canon really been redefined? Has critical value shifted? I don't think so.

If the nature of critical value in Canada *has* changed, the shift only serves to expand upon and solidify the nationalist/mimetic overlap that has characterized the study of Canadian literature since the 1800s. The title of Robin Mathews's *Canadian Literature: Surrender or Revolution* (1978) indicates the critical drift toward a form of nationalist criticism that is simply a heightened and more militant expression of what is a historically established value. When Mathews writes that "Canadian poetry has always used the native, the documentary, the intelligent, the civil, the typical, the concrete, the present in human relations," he reaffirms the same equation between the value of literary nationalism and mimesis that was affirmed by Canadian critics throughout the nineteenth and twentieth centuries. This value seeks "the typical, the concrete, the present" before what Mathews, quoting Charles Olson, calls " 'the *primitive-abstract*' " (160), by which he means those forms of writing that are not grounded in a socially verifiable, realist aesthetic. "Writing poetry for the Canadian people means writing in contact with ordinary Canadian life, without pretentiousness" (161). It means that "the Canadian poet ought to write the Canadian language. . . . discover Canadian roots, know Canadian literature, Canadian history" (162).

It is astonishing to realize that a similar, infinitely conservative view informs D.J. Dooley's *Moral Vision in the Canadian Novel* (1979). This study is not a bizarre effort at parody; it sincerely advances the view — amidst contemporary notions of the death of authorial and textual privilege — that if the novelist "wins our respect, it must be because his characters have the stuff of life about them and because he has created a convincing social and moral context for them." After all, Dooley argues, "the world must be shown as a place in which the choices made do perceptibly affect reality. If the novelist cannot convince us of this, then he has failed completely" (ix). The value implicit in these criteria favours more than the so-called moral context that can be conveyed through representational realism; it disfavours the same works that MacLulich and Mathews see as threatening — works that are abstract, nonlinear, discontinuous, metafictional, and cosmopolitan in their formal and aesthetic assumptions. It is not surprising to discover that Dooley — who believes that "style, for all its brilliance, cannot do the work successfully" (ix) — dedicates his study to another proponent of the social-realist school: Carl F. Klinck, the first general editor of the *Literary History of Canada* and Dooley's "first Professor of English."

Dooley's tribute suggests that critical studies of Canadian literature are often part of the same value system informing the *Literary History* —

values that affirm Northrop Frye's belief that, in Canada, the "literary imagination" is "a force and function of life" which "tells us things about this environment that nothing else will tell us" (822). Is Frye's view any different from Kroetsch's view of the Canadian novel as weather report? Both critics advance the notion that the purpose of critical evaluation is, in John Moss's words, to "illuminate society" and to "illustrate real life from a Canadian perspective" ("Bushed" 161).

The critical value that equates quality with verisimilitude is not confined strictly to the assessment of Canadian novels and poetry. Short stories are also evaluated from a mimetic perspective. The selections in Wayne Grady's *The Penguin Book of Canadian Short Stories* (1980), which range from nineteenth-century sketches to relatively contemporary tales, are informed by the editor's belief that the "most characteristic feature" of the Canadian short story is "a realism so intimate and natural that what it describes is often mistaken for real life" (v). Even if we ignore the literary naïvety that allows Grady to confuse realism with reality, it remains clear that, for him, as for most other mainstream anthologists involved in creating the tradition, the criterion for inclusion necessitates the selection of authors who fulfil a "social responsibility" and "bring the unarticulated soul of an entire community into sudden and radiant being" by interpreting for us the "complexities of human life" (vi). Such a criterion merely sustains the prevailing orthodoxy, one that positions author or critic as a "mediator between the literature and society" and allows the mediator to proclaim "Canadian reality as real" (Moss, "Bushed" 162, 171).

Grady suggests that what distinguishes Canadian short fiction is its participation in a realist tradition. In Canada, as elsewhere, the concept of tradition is usually invoked as the vehicle of value in time; that is, it provides a temporal validation — a fictionalized explanation — of why certain literary works tend to appear during certain highly and subjectively defined historical segments. Because tradition can never be any more than the narrated desires and dreams of its creators, we know that the assertion of a tradition is always a sign of the asserter's need to create a world. In Canada, the need is to create a world that is as convincing as possible — a realistic world. The more tradition is asserted (the more the realistic fiction unfolds), the more obvious becomes the asserter's desire to formulate a linear, coherent, framed, and named world at any cost.

If one seeks to align this notion of history with the values of a critical school, one need not look far to find the values of F.R. Leavis. Although it might seem ludicrous to assert that Leavis still provides the central values by which a Canadian author is judged, this seems to be the case.

The appeal to Leavis is not difficult to explain when one considers the nationalist-mimetic pursuit that informs the canonization process in Canada. Tradition tells us that the nation has solidity, that its history is ongoing and real. Tradition also tells us that literary taste is best created and maintained by an elite; in Canada today, as in Leavis's time, this elite is comprised of those who run the institution — chiefly the academics who name the classics and create the literary histories to accommodate them. In the tradition created by this elite, realism, nationalism, and literary history are conjoined; they become interchangeable terms that are rooted in a single but all-encompassing value promoted by the institution.

Most members of the Canadian literary institution eventually pay direct or indirect homage to Leavis. Dooley mentions him on the opening page of his study. In *A Due Sense of Differences* (1980), Wilfred Cude argues that for him, as for Leavis, evaluation must be the end of criticism, for "the most important thing a critical book can do is to distinguish the finest works of a given literary tradition" (xii). Cude's attempt to distinguish several Canadian classics soon becomes confusing. On one hand, he argues that a classic "is of necessity a unique work" that finally "stands alone" (xii). Although this "solitude" and "creative uniqueness" would seem to undermine the notion of history (if a work stands alone, it needs no cultural or historical context to support it), Cude relies upon Samuel Johnson's belief that a work must "please many and please long" (17) to determine whether the novels he examines are truly classics ("the consensus that coheres about a classic is not subject to error" [18]). But because Canadian literary time is foreshortened, and because the so-called Canadian tradition is a recent construct that does not yet include several of the works treated by Cude, he relies on what he calls "the scientific technique of predictivity" to determine which works are worthy of evaluation (13). "Once the first approving arguments appear in the train of a classic's publication, for those with eyes to see and ears to hear, the consensus may assume convincing proportions at any time" (21).

This logic may seem irrational and absurd, but in Canada the consensus informing the canon has assumed such convincing proportions that dozens of classics have been chosen by those who seem to support Cude's assertion that "we need not entangle ourselves in controversy about the intellectual mechanisms underlying the value-judgments that lead to the consensus" (16). In these words, Cude pays tribute to another critical tradition in which he partakes — the "correlation of validity with silence" (Smith 8) that lies at the heart of Frye's conclusion to the *Literary History* in 1965. This is why Cude is able to say that "Frye is perfectly within his rights to deplore the excesses of the critical rating game" (16), even as he rates and ranks the works he calls classic in his study. The confusion is not difficult to explain. Like several other critics who call for evaluation in criticism, Cude assumes that to evaluate is to explore value, when in fact the very act of evaluation serves to bypass any exploration of value because the enacted values are so entrenched that they have long been forgotten by critic and audience alike. Evaluative criticism, in being value-loaded, paradoxically escapes the weighty burden of the currency that allows it to appear respectable, powerful, discriminating, rich.

The evaluative approach is endorsed by a number of Canadian critics. Moss writes that "the responsible Canadian critic must learn to correlate, discriminate, evaluate" and to approach works "in relation to other works in the Canadian tradition" ("Bushed" 176). W.J. Keith, a former member of McClelland and Stewart's Canadian Classics Committee, writes that in his undergraduate experience at Cambridge "evaluation was assumed as a natural outcome of reading and thinking" ("Quest" 156). In Keith's words, Leavis "remains for me the greatest English literary critic of this century." It is Leavis's principles of evaluation that allow Keith to argue that anyone who consults the list of 100 novels selected for the Calgary conference "would obtain an excellent grasp of the mainstream of Canadian fiction" ("Quest" 159).

This "mainstream" is synonymous with the canon and tradition. But, as we have seen, the "mainstream" was largely the creation of academics in control of the literary institution. In a candid digression, Keith notes that if academics refused to determine which works were classics, problems would ensue, for "who would decide the question of what is a permanent part of our literature and what isn't: the publishers? the booksellers (including those who control the chain book stores)? the popular reviewers? the writers of literary gossip-columns in our newspapers? The prospect is disturbing" ("Quest" 163). It is "disturbing" because the idea that anyone but academics could pronounce on the value of literary works amounts to an invitation to anarchy. The "general reader" knows nothing. At all costs, control must remain within the established school and the traditions it has created in order to validate itself and perpetuate its judgements. John Metcalf puts it this way: "Theories about Canadian literature tend to reflect the larger social attitudes and nearly all the visions of our literature are nationalistic, chauvinistic, smug, and amazingly *white*" (*What Is a Canadian Literature?* 13).

The impact of the Calgary conference did not wane. The proceedings were published in 1982. Finally, the list of "the most 'important' one hundred works of fiction" was available for anyone to consult (Steele 150). It was composed, virtually in its entirety, of realistic, linear, conventional novels that were the central, defining texts of the new Canadian tradition — one that valued works which affirmed the country and its people, one that had already answered the question posed by Atwood in *Survival* (who posed it after Frye): "Where is here?" (17). The answer is provided by the creators of the Canadian canon: "here" is all the texts that tell us we are here. It is in all the texts we sanction for study. To ignore these texts is to be not-here; it is to disappear.

In his attempt to counter the threat of such a disappearance, David Stouck adopts what is by now a familiar line: the notion that there is a Canadian tradition, that it is fundamentally realistic, and that Canada's canonized authors all attach themselves to this tradition. In *Major Canadian Authors: A Critical Introduction* (1984), which we are told is "the first book to focus exclusively on major authors and their works" (ix), Stouck is able to refer to several authors who have produced "at least one major piece regarded as an indisputable classic in the canon of Canadian fiction" (x). Stouck's claim is significant, if only because it suggests that the status of the works canonized during the 1970s is no longer subject to discussion. How else can one explain the fact that the *first* book on the topic of major authors is able to deal with writers who are *already* the major authors of classic works in the canon and to pronounce their status to be "indisputable"?

What makes these works important to Stouck? The conservatism of his selections suggests that, for him, as for his canonizing predecessors, the value of the work was largely representational. Here are the opening words of his concluding chapter:

> The reader may be surprised that this study of Canadian literature concludes with an essentially old-fashioned writer. [Alice] Munro's themes are the ego-centered, familiar ones of initiation and romantic love, her techniques those of pre-World War II realists such as Eudora Welty, James Agee, Frank O'Connor. Where, it might be asked, are the more experimental writers, the avant-garde? (273)

Where indeed! Stouck recognizes that these "experimental writers" have received "little critical or popular recognition." Yet he makes no effort to rectify the situation. The exclusion of these writers is, for him, apparently part of God's plan. Stouck's explanation for his neglect of these writers supports the arguments I have advanced: "The reason for this is partly nationalistic, because experimental writers have found their models and sources of inspiration outside the country" (27). With these words Stouck identifies the crucial principle of exclusion that governs the creation of the Canadian canon: works that are inspired by non-Canadian models are not "major" and are not worthy of study. They are excluded because they are somehow treasonous in their alignment with things foreign. And they are excluded because, in being "experimental," they are antirealist, anticonservative, anti-Canadian.

The same principle of exclusion applies to Stouck's assessment of Canadian poetry. Experimental — by which Stouck means contemporary — poetry is dismissed within a page, because the *major* writers, even "in the early 1980s," were "still engaged in giving a realistic account of growing up and living in Canada" and in "creating a literary map of the country" (277). But Canadians need not worry about the fact that "interest in the works of writers whose inspiration comes from outside the country will lag behind." In the end, "the best of their work will eventually come to have its place in the tradition of Canadian literature, just as the writings of women, blacks, and other minority groups have found a significant place" (277). After all, the "tradition" can accommodate some aberrants — even women and blacks. Through such an accommodation, the canonizers can demonstrate their liberalism by admitting a few token savages — such an unruly bunch! — into the mimetic museum. Why not? They liven up the permanent display. They give it a little colour.

A more ambitious view of Canadian literary history is offered by Keith in his *Canadian Literature in English* (1985). Keith's wide-ranging study is not only inspired by his belief in a Canadian tradition that synthesizes the dual influences of British and American literature, but also by his sense that the critic must, above all, evaluate the works in question. As I have argued, however, the act of evaluation and the investigation of value are two entirely different forms of inquiry. If we want to arrive at the values that account for Keith's evaluations — something we are entitled to know — we must infer them by examining the principles of exclusion and inclusion informing his work. Like his predecessors, Keith is interested in invoking and supporting a tradition of Canadian literature — one that constitutes a "main stream" of "authors who may be considered 'major' because they have dominated the country's literary language, shaped its consciousness, and so fostered the native tradition" (x). For Keith, status is explicitly a function of power, of domination.[3] Writers who do not "dominate" are excluded from the "main stream." This does not explain how the writers who *are* included manage to "dominate" language or shape the country's consciousness. One gets the sense that the articulated standard of evaluation is at odds with the unarticulated values that account for Keith's judgements and selections. Tracy Ware observes that "the cardinal stylistic virtues, for Keith, are clarity, poise, polish, and restraint," and therefore "Keith is inevitably uncomfortable with those writers who emphasize the inadequacy or exorbitance of language" ("Notes" 571).

This kind of discomfort leads Keith to reaffirm the fiction of a Canadian literary tradition that is fundamentally conservative, moral, and realistic. Neither radical politics nor radical aesthetics have a place in such a tradition. This explains why "there is little point in writing much about Milton Acorn here," since Acorn is "an avowed Marxist-Leninist" who does not fit the pre-established frame. As Keith says: "This is a book about the continuities of cultural tradition and Acorn's main concern is to challenge the established tradition whenever and wherever he encounters it" (104). Therefore, he has no place in a book entitled *Canadian Literature in English*. The same principle of exclusion accounts for the fact that some of Canada's most innovative, experimental, and prolific writers — including bill bissett, bpNichol, Matt Cohen, Leon Rooke, Audrey Thomas, and Ray Fraser, to name a few — receive no comment, or are dismissed within a sentence because, as in the case of Rooke and Thomas, "they have failed to display a coherent, unifying vision" (172). This "vision" is nothing but the projected fantasy of one member of an established school that wants to see itself as coherent, unified, and enduring. The writer or critic who does not share these values and the notion of a "unifying vision" has failed. That's all there is to it. Conformity is what counts.

In one sense, MacLulich shares Keith's notion of the Canadian tradition as a unique combination of British and American influences. But here the similarity stops. Keith confidently asserts that "the Canadian literary tradition is now sufficiently established that it can be discussed in relation to the literatures of Britain and the United States without embarrassment" and that it "impressively forms itself as the embodiment of a scattered and elusive people's communal vision" (*Canadian Literature in English* 9). MacLulich is more doubtful about the survival of this vision because, in his view, "writers and critics today are being forced to declare their allegiance either to the traditional notion of fiction as mimesis or to the new notion of fiction as pure verbal invention" (*Between* 17). This "interest in the innovative, the experimental, and the post-modern" is dangerous, MacLulich argues, because "the infatuation with new writers and their works often means that the pioneers of the Canadian tradition in fiction are in danger of being pushed aside" (*Between* 18).

It is not surprising to discover that for MacLulich, as for Keith, Dooley, and Stouck, these pioneers wrote in the mode of "social realism"

(*Between* 12) and created "documentary" works with "characters and situations" that are "recognizably drawn from their own society" (*Between* 11). What is surprising is to learn of the threat to this realist tradition posed by the so-called radical innovators. As I have tried to suggest in my brief survey of the criticism on Canadian literary history published before and since the Calgary conference (up to 1988), there is no threat to the established order in creative or critical terms. We continue to value and to teach the canonized works, and these works embody precisely the values that MacLulich sees as threatened.

If the conservative, mimetic values associated with the canonization of Canadian literature are truly being challenged today, one would expect some evidence of this challenge to appear in the critical journals devoted to the study of Canadian literature. But as recently as 1986, in one of the most prominent of these journals, *Canadian Literature*, it is still possible to discover an epistolary "dialogue" between an editor of the canonized journal and an uncanonized critic. The critic complains that the "ideological commitments" of the journal are subject to question because it supports arguments that are "grounded in Aristotelian rhetorical conventions" and because it refuses to "deconstruct the assumptions of a culture" or to participate in "that massive process of rethinking the languaging world." Instead, the journal — and others like it — "are effectively suppressing the very response which they should foster" (Weir, "Dialogue" 4).

To judge from these words, the canon — and the critical values aligned with it — are in little danger of collapsing. The dissident can be admitted to the superstructure and can even be treated with deference and respect. In this case, the editor thanks the dissident for the "challenge" (Ricou, "Dialogue" 6). By doing do, he announces that absolutely nothing has changed. The journal has asserted its liberal viewpoint; that is more than enough.

The widespread currency of the values informing the Canadian canon makes it virtually certain that so-called experimental works of criticism — those that are involved in the process of "rethinking the languaging world" — will never be accepted by the school. Or, in order to gain some kind of transient acceptance, the rethinking process will be recast in terms that are acceptable to the school. In Canada, the very act of such recasting serves to expose the fundamentally conservative values held by those who seem most prepared to challenge canonical values.

* * *

My conclusion: most Canadian critics find it impossible and even treasonous to deal with the Canadian canon in terms other than those embodied in the canon itself. We may hear calls for criticism that will uninvent, demythologize, or decentre text and world; and we may find occasional celebrations of noncanonized writing. But the canonized criticism, like the enshrined poetry and fiction, remains conservative, moral, documentary, sociological, and realist in approach. As Barbara Godard notes, "Canadian critics have resisted a politics that is blind to the experience of the human subject" ("Structuralism/Post-Structuralism" 34). For this reason, "generalized analyses of critical theory of the type produced in the United States and England by Jonathan Culler and Terry Eagleton have not been part of the Canadian scene. Critics have been less interested in the grammars or deep structures of narrative than they have in readings of texts" (33). Nothing has changed.

Given the entrenchment of the canon and of critical methodology and consensus, it is natural to wonder what purpose is served by an essay that argues, as this one does, that no progress can be made toward a new view of Canadian literature and its canon until we begin to question and theorize the values informing the works we study and the language we bring to bear on our study. In ignoring such questioning we have ignored the single factor that makes us different: history. Before we subject Canadian works to poststructural, or Marxist, or *any* kind of critical or theoretical approach, we have to stop, stand back, and ask how and why these works got where they are. What historical conditions gave them their power? What new conditions might rob them of that power? To answer these complex questions it is essential that Canadian critics make their first goal the rehistoricization of Canadian literature — not in terms of the vague notion of value embedded in the rhetoric and propaganda of our inherited school, but in terms of a new and rewritten conception of history as a narrative that is not received but created, not dictated but free, false, in flux.

I began this chapter in an attempt to demonstrate how rapidly and fully the Canadian canon was established during the same years that other national literary canons were being torn apart. Then I tried to show that the value supporting the Canadian canon expresses a conservative, yet profound desire for unity, community, coherence, authority, place, and, yes, grace. Should these desires be abandoned? Should the Canadian canon be deconstructed in the face of current theory? Perhaps. But before the process of replacement begins — before the *necessary* canon is invented anew — it might help to situate ourselves in a historical drama that has always been denied. Our literary history remains to be invented in multiple forms. The material is there. We have writers and critics who are kings, psychopomps, devils, saints. We have stages full of weird characters who are dying to speak. We have obsessions, power struggles, treachery, demons to hate and love. There are voices everywhere. But we've shut them out. We inhabit a silent museum. We protect the permanent display. Our position is secure and unexciting.

But we can change things. Whoever reads Canadian literary history can write it anew. To re-view and renew Canadian literary history in this way would be to liberate ourselves from the worn-out methodologies and antimethodologies we believe we should believe in or believe we should import. It would be to discover what the governing narratives are behind the fictions that surround us, the ones we have so quickly crowned and those that remain hidden, waiting to be found.

2

A Country without a Canon?
Canadian Literature and
the Aesthetics of Idealism

IN A RECENT REVIEW of Charles Altieri's *Canons and Consequences*, Bernard Harrison poses some important questions about the relation between canons and culture. He asks:

> Can a culture survive without a system of values rich enough to preserve it from eventual disintegration through mere alteration of manners and ways of thinking? ... And can such systems of values exist without canons: without bodies of works, in literature, history or philosophy, generally regarded as "important": works to be brandished, sniped at, accused, devalued or revalued, which by manifesting the values of the tribe in each succeeding generation permit the renewal of a living sense of both the scope and the limitations of those values?

While such questions have been central to discussions of canonicity outside Canada, the study of canons and canonicity in English-Canadian literature has been less productive than one might have hoped, mainly because the relation between culture and value (the central canonical matrix) remains largely unexplored. Although the 1980s produced some scattered commentary, and even a few direct challenges to what was perceived as canonical authority (see MacLaren, Powe, and Stuewe), the first book on the topic did not appear until *Canadian Canons*, the collection of essays I edited in 1991. There is still no sustained consideration of how a (shifting) Canadian canon — if such an animal exists — can be seen as historically contingent, politically self-serving, ideologically generated, and culture-ridden. As in most discussions about Canadian literature, there is no sense of debate, by which I mean a focused and disruptive exchange of ideas on a topic considered worthy of dispute. Even the most pointed challenges to what has been called the Canadian canon have been met with indifference rather than hostility. (I think here, in particular, of works by John Metcalf and Lorraine Weir.)

This indifference contrasts sharply with the conditions prevailing in France, the United States, and Great Britain, where for years critics have been engaged in what John Guillory calls "a legitimation crisis with far-ranging consequences" in which "pressures conceived to be extrinsic to the practice of criticism seem to have shaken literary pedagogy in fundamental ways" ("Canonical and Non-Canonical" 483). Writing in 1990, Paul Lauter asserts that "today, canon study is perhaps as popular a subject for academic disquisitions as post-structuralist 'theory'" (144). It is precisely because the range of "canon study" outside Canada is so popular and extensive that it cannot be summarized with ease. In his review of the influential collection of essays entitled *Canons* (which appeared in 1983), Louis Renza noted that

> Recent critical trends clearly suggest that . . . canonical self-certainty is on the wane. Almost daily, it seems, critical articles and scholarly works appear informing us that we have wrongly overlooked the value of this or that writer's work because the inherited, pedagogically assumed canon has simply seen fit to relegate them to the status of "minor literature" — or has even forced them to disappear from canonical consideration altogether. (258)

For Renza, revisionist arguments about the canon, which constitute "a declaration of intellectual guerilla war against canonical thinking or cultural imperialism" (268), are encountered "almost daily." For Canadians, even today, it is "almost never."

The very desire to bring this debate to Canada is seen by some theorists as an expression of a "colonial cringe" (Godard, "Canadian?" 12) that is rooted in "an idealization of critical practice in other countries, particularly that of the United States" (Davey, "Critical Response" 674). What seems overlooked, however, is that the debate about the canon outside Canada — and especially in the United States — is grounded in non-American, poststructural attempts to "theorize power, action, agency, and resistance" (Bové 61). As Guillory observes, "the problem of canon-formation is one aspect of a much larger history of the ways in which societies have organized and regulated practices of reading and writing" ("Canon" 239). To argue that a Canadian

interest in canonicity is colonial, or that it is irrelevant to Canadians, is
to ignore the ways in which the canon debate contributes to crucial
interrogations (of politics, of ideology, of gender, of subjectivity) that
know no national bounds. Davis and Mirabella go so far as to say that

> The study of the canon has been one of the most important issues to
> come out of recent examinations of the institution of literary studies.
> The political implications of the very existence of a literary canon and
> what that canon means in terms of gender, race, class, nationality, and
> ideology are enormous. It is no coincidence that the current public
> debates over the quality of education and the success or failure of
> Western civilization hinge on the issues stirred up by revising the canon.
> (125)

Despite these claims, the debates raging in other countries simply don't
appear in Canada. Why is this the case?

The answer to this question seems to depend on whether one believes
that Canadian canons (or *a* canon of fiction or poetry) exist, whereas
in other countries the liberal critique of the canon has flourished
because national canons are *assumed* to exist. Those who do claim the
existence of a Canadian canon can be quite assertive in their claim. To
Paul Hjartarson, for example, there is no doubt about the existence of
a Canadian canon:

> The question is *not* whether a canon exists and, if not, whether we should
> formulate one. The canon *does* exist; we *have* already formulated it. We
> formulate it every day. The canonical texts are those that figure promi-
> nently in our own discourse — they are the texts we teach, we write about,
> we cite. The classical texts, in short, are those *we* value. (67)

In this construction, the "we" who value the "classical texts" are
emphatically university teachers; the canon has absolutely nothing to
say to a community beyond the institution's walls. Other critics who
perceive a Canadian literary canon see it as a displaced expression of
nationalist ideology: "Canadian literature, perceived internally as a
mosaic, remains generally monolithic in its assertion of Canadian
difference from the canonical British or the more recently threatening
neo-colonialism of American culture"; it retains a "nationalist stance"
and has "not generated corresponding theories of literary hybridity
to replace the nationalist approach" (Ashcroft, Griffiths, and Tiffin
36). Leon Surette asserts that the valorization of nationalist thought
is synonymous with the valorization of Canadian literary history

("Creating"). Dermot McCarthy reaches a similar conclusion when he writes that

> The gathering of the scattered texts into a "permanent form," the selection and organization of a literary canon, and the ideological program of nation-building and identity-definition, all cohere isomorphically from the beginning in Canadian literary history. (33)

Although the notion of referential and mimetic discourse has been undermined by a recognition of the materiality and contingency of language, the assumption on the part of many critics is that if there is a Canadian canon, its formation and development is referential: the canon is seen as a vehicle through which the value of the nation as a cultural force is represented and conveyed. This perspective grounds my earlier discussion in "The Canonization of Canadian Literature," where I argued that there was a Canadian canon, that it valued mimetic forms of discourse, that it viewed literature as a displaced trope of nationalism, and that it was the conservative byproduct of the conservative institution that supported its enshrinement. I also suggested that the Canadian canon was so solidified that, as a topic, it was beyond controversy, a factor which accounted for the characteristic lack of debate in discussions about Canadian literature and literary history.

The objection to this conception of a Canadian canon is best summed up by Frank Davey in his commissioned response to my essay. For Davey, the Canadian canon I had constructed was academic, humanist, unitary, realist, conservative, nationalist, and narrow in its denial of those forces that have refused the neo-conservative aesthetic that governed my canonical universe. For this reason, Davey felt that my concept of the canon restricted discursive choices, offered no sense of contestation, and erected a one-sided canonical monolith that denied plurality and difference. Davey concluded that " 'Canadian criticism' is nowhere near as monolithic as [I depict] it, that class, gender, ethnicity, region, national politics, business practice, and discursive and institutional inheritance play much larger roles in these struggles than [my] use of 'institutional' implies" ("Critical Response" 680–81).

One critic who appears to support these objections is Tracy Ware, who endorses Davey's assertion that there is no monolithic Canadian canon. If there is a Canadian canon it is elastic, shifting, and impossible to define as a particular group of texts:

> The Canadian canon has always been fluid: the available anthologies are so inclusive that no course can exhaust their possibilities, and different

instructors and institutions use and even construct very different anthologies. Thus Canada has all of the uncertainty but none of the dogmatic resistance necessary for a "delegitimation crisis." Canonical interrogations "have not deconstructed the monolith in any way similar to the way it has been deconstructed in other countries" — read "in the United States" — because there is no monolith here. ("A Little Self-Consciousness" 487)

In this chapter I would like to examine the implications of the position advanced by Davey and Ware. To do this, I will begin by turning their shared assertion into a hypothetical statement: there is no recognized Canadian canon; there never was a central Canadian canon; there may never be one. I am not so much interested in proving or disproving this claim as I am in exploring some of the moral, ethical, and cultural questions raised by such a position. What does it mean to be a country without a canon? How does the absence of a canon affect our sense of agency and difference? How does such an absence colour our notions of community, time, and place? Is there any way in which such an absence marks a loss, or gain?

*   *   *

The first thing one observes when confronted with the view that there is no Canadian canon is the apparent evidence to the contrary. If there is no canon, what are people such as W.H. New and W.J. Keith writing their literary histories of Canada about? Or what is the *Literary History of Canada* about? Why do so many of the same figures get included in or excluded from these histories? Why do so many anthologies of Canadian poetry include Archibald Lampman's "Heat"? Why do so many anthologies of Canadian fiction include Morley Callaghan's work? Why is there an eight-volume series (covering thirty-six authors) entitled *The Annotated Bibliography of Canada's Major Authors*? And what about Margaret Atwood, Robertson Davies, Margaret Laurence, or Mordecai Richler? Surely they are canonical figures in Canada.

In order to support the assertion that these are *not* canonical figures, or that there are *no* canonized works, one has to fall back on the distinction between canonical and curricular value. This distinction is examined by Virgil Nemoianu, who observes that "curricular works are those that are chosen to be taught in class, to be included in anthologies, those that are read by and fed to large numbers of individuals in a linguistic and social community at a given time." Curricular authors "are chosen for utilitarian reasons, to satisfy some needs — political, ethical, practical — and to create bridges of compatibility between an essentially recalcitrant phenomenon and the needs or preferences of structured societies with their ideological expressions" (219). Curricular formation is a product of "the prevailing prejudices and sensibilities, writing style and aesthetic tastes" of "a given age" (219–20). "Curricula are, in a sense, negotiated accounts between the definitional and hegemonic features of a given historical time and place and the broader and inchoate canonical domain proper" (220).

In contrasting canon and curriculum, Nemoianu argues that canons embody communal ideals: "They incorporate values, questionings, intentionalities, plots, and constants of human nature"; they are shaped by "communitarian orientations." From his idealist perspective, Nemoinanu observes that canons are shaped by a number of parameters: "majority preference" — those works "chosen by most readers in a historical cross-section"; "multiplicity of attached meanings"; ability to invoke transcendence of the contingent through "interaction and compatibility with different value fields and kinds of discourses"; "aesthetic durability"; and last, but of central importance to my discussion, canons are the "outcome of democratic pressures" — they mediate between the "highbrow and the lowbrow" (221) and are chosen by popular demand over time; in this sense, their texture is heterogeneous and nonelitist. Nemoianu even goes so far as to assert that "it is exactly when and if canonical authors come to be maintained by curricular elites and become their exclusive possession, that they are in danger of losing their canonical status" (220–22).

This model of the distinction between canon and curriculum is both conventional and controversial — conventional because it makes assumptions about consensus, transcendence, and durability that have been undermined by recent historicist thought; controversial because it asserts that canonical works are informed by communal, democratic values. At first glance, these assertions seem outrageous and offensive: What community does Nemoianu speak for? What majority? Whose version of transcendence? Whose values? Because Nemoianu never really addresses these questions, his examination stops short of providing a convincing defence of canonical ideals.

A much more engaging defence of these ideals is offered by Charles Altieri, who is, in my view, the theorist who has made the most effective challenge to the critical historicist stance. Altieri is concerned with investigating models of human agency as they are formulated by canonical ideals. His positivist model proposes that canons provide us with concepts of authority that allow us to resist local and current abuses of power. In Altieri's view, canons promote the recognition of moral categories and therefore have an ethical dimension. Further, he argues that canons begin to make historical language possible by generating a "cultural grammar for interpreting experience" ("An Idea" 47). For Altieri, there are some powerful advantages conferred by the maintenance of canonical ideals: the ability to articulate fictions of history and community, and to position those fictions in relation to other fictions that are powerful because they are different. Canon, culture, community; they are all entwined.

In Canada we have a shifting but identifiable curriculum that is often misread as a canon (chapter 1, "The Canonization of Canadian Literature," is an example of this type of misreading). By this I mean that we study works whose temporal impact is brief, whose cultural grammar is local before it is national, whose idealizations are not those we can identify with the values held by a community at large. A good way of demonstrating this assertion is to consider the popular appeal of some Canadian works that have been institutionalized and are often thought to be canonical, say, Sinclair Ross's *As for Me and My House.* While the novel may appear on course curricula throughout the country, and while much has been said about its ostensible excellence, it is not a canonical work. The average, well-read person out of the academy has never heard of it. In fact, many well-read people within the academy have never heard of it. This so-called Canadian classic was published in 1941 in New York, but not in Canada. Its first Canadian publication was delayed sixteen years, until it was released by McClelland and Stewart as part of the New Canadian Library series in 1957. Even today it remains a purely curricular work. It has no claim to public interest. It does not mediate between popular and academic demand. It transmits no cultural grammar.

What about such writers as Atwood, Davies, Laurence, or Richler? Surely they have achieved canonical status — they are all popular writers who have a large following and are also taught in the schools. True, but popularity within a given historical time, and curricular adoption within that time, are not indicative of canonical status. A decade ago Hugh MacLennan was still considered to be a major writer worthy of study; I doubt that this is still the case. Even Davies's and Richler's early works are now fading from popular and academic view.

Such rapid transitions in curricular taste suggest that there really are very few Canadian texts that have stood long enough to gain canonical authority, and fewer still that have seemed important for more than a generation. There is no stable canon that we can look to as a point of reference, even if our most profound desire is to question and undermine that reference point.

Of course I realize that I have uttered a number of blasphemies: that a country as young and regionally diverse as Canada might be expected to produce even one truly canonical text (a version of the search for the great Canadian novel); that anything as plural and contingent as culture or history could be caught in a text, or represented, or be agreed upon as being in any way true; that even if culture could be caught or represented, it would constitute a valid point against which other measurements about social and institutional values could be made. As critics, we have learned to value cultural-historical relativism over canonical stability, to challenge the text's socio-literary situated-ness rather than endorse it, to show how the authority behind even the most canonical of texts is undermined by its own internal conflicts, to see the dominant canon as the repository of bourgeois patriarchal values that retain power through the exclusion of all divergent ideologies. In this respect, most theorists seem to support Barbara Herrnstein Smith's arguments "against the transcendental or universal valorizing of our canonical texts" (Scholes 148). For Herrnstein Smith, "what supports canonical texts is not so much their own merits or relevance to our purposes as the way they have already been inscribed into an intertextual network of reference. That is, they are culturally important because they have been culturally important" (Scholes 148).

If any of these revisionist, historicist tendencies had been applied to Canadian texts rigorously enough to make me believe that there were texts — perhaps urtexts — that *had* canonical authority, I would be much more optimistic about the state of Canadian literature. But the absence of such tendencies returns me to the assertion I am exploring: that we have no canon at all.

If there is no canon, are we better off? Certainly the current assumption, outside Canada at least, is that a deconstruction of the canon will have beneficial effects. It will empower minority groups that have been excluded from the white male bourgeois power base; it will privilege heterogeneity over homogeneity, difference over uniformity, margin over centre, performativity over pedagogy, the postmodern over the modern. Such anticanonical theorizing will lay to rest the myth that canons transmit traditions or transcendent historical ideals, will in fact lay to rest the myth of history itself, both as a temporal category and as the repository of transcendent values.

Is such a condition desirable? Linda Hutcheon expands on this question when she asks:

Must tradition's legacy be kept or is that particular formulation of the issue of history going to lead to an immobilizing nostalgia rather than a critical reformulating and revisiting of tradition? Must we seek social cohesion when that is, in fact, what has been masking social difference in the name of a dominant power group? (*Poetics* 209)

To address these issues, I return to Altieri. If we give any credence to his views, we have to grant that, in the absence of a canon, a number of social constructs attached to canonical ideals will also vanish: consensus, community, social responsibility, and ultimately ethical challenge. Those who say good riddance to such worn out idealizations need to confront the downside of repudiating the canon. While the country without a canon may be free, plural, ahistorical, and self-conscious of the material conditions that account for its contingent status, it may also be a country without moral conviction, without the means of recognizing difference, without standards against which ethical choices can be judged. If you eliminate the canon, you eliminate it at a price. The challenge is to decide whether we want to pay this price.

For teachers, the canonical dilemma poses additional problems. What are we saying to our students about values, ideals, and community if we attack the canon? What are we saying if we say there is no canon? What are we saying if we support it? Perhaps most important, what are we saying if we say nothing at all? Do we have any moral responsibility to recognize the force of the community that empowers us or that provides us with the subject about which we speak? I think we do. We may be subjected by that community, may be interpellated by it, may define ourselves as all that it is not, but we cannot be convincing in our dissent if we are incapable of describing what we are dissenting from in more convincing terms than labelling it monolithic or institutional. An objection to my argument here would be that I treat culture and community narrowly, as specifically literary. This is true. But the questions raised by the canon debate in literary terms can easily be applied to current theorizing about cultural studies that goes beyond the purely literary. (Recent essays by Bonnie Braendlin and E. Ann Kaplan demonstrate this connection.)

These questions and observations put me in a deliberately double bind when it comes to thinking about a Canadian canon. I know that intellectually I have to accept the validity of Frank Davey's position: canons shift; they are fluid constructs; there is no monolith; there is no community, no grammar of consensus; there are only a host of separate centres, each vying for power and control. Or maybe there are no centres at all. Yet emotionally I also reject this stance: I want to find a Canadian community; I believe there are Canadian ideals; I do not want to consider the canon only as an instrument of power, and I do feel, with

Altieri, that it can function as an agency of shared values. The problem with this belief is that it is to my advantage to say there is a Canadian canon, just as it is to my advantage to say that there isn't one. Both positions empower me. After all, the most canonical statement you can make is that there is no canon. By extension, isn't my desire for community (or my recognition of the community's absence) just another way of fortifying the master's house? And speaking of that house, am I not fundamentally powerless to change it? As Audre Lorde puts it in the title of an important essay on the construction and deconstruction of feminist value, "The Master's Tools Will Never Dismantle the Master's House."

The assumption behind Lorde's essay is, of course, that it is valuable to dismantle the master's house. Note that the strength of her argument owes much to the strength of the house she is attacking. Because the canonical ideal has been highly valued, it also comes into sharp focus as a force to be devalued. Ironically, however, the strength of this devaluation is dependent upon the strength of the model it subverts; in other words, strong canonical formations are capable of inciting strong reactions to them. Canons construct difference. They are *necessarily* political and therefore fundamental to the way we represent ourselves.

I am aware that this observation suggests a circularity that could be seen as reinforcing a master/slave relationship: the canon subjects the dissident by making her/his self-definition dependent upon the authority she/he is trying to subvert. I am also aware that, even in the face of this circularity, real and important changes have taken place in reaction to perceived canonical norms. To put it another way, strong canons provoke strong responses, and those responses are capable of promoting real change.

Although "canon study ought to be able to lead us out of a narrowly construed set of professional concerns and back into the broader social and political world" (Lauter, "Canon Theory" 143), the liberal critique has undermined this canonical potential. The case for liberal pluralism — which paradoxically asserts the value of democratic representation at the expense of canonical elitism — does not always work in favour of disempowered individuals or groups. Nor does the contemporary historicist rejection of the essential, the ideal, the true, and the universal always work in favour of the marginal or the plural, or in favour of concrete change. To recognize contingency and relativism from an anti-essentialist (and anticanonical) stance, or to express disbelief in the belief that human ideals can be imagined and achieved, is to turn society into a semiotic field that means little to those who have been excluded from institutional power. As Elizabeth Fox-Genovese observes:

> From the perspective of those previously excluded from the cultural elite, the death of the subject or the death of the author seems somewhat premature. Surely it is no coincidence that the Western white male elite proclaimed the death of the subject at precisely the moment at which it might have had to share that status with the women and peoples of other races and classes who were beginning to challenge its supremacy. (134)

Craig Tapping similarly explains that the failure to maintain canonical ideals is in many ways a failure of theory, because

> despite theory's refutation of such absolute and logocentric categories as these — "truth" or "meaning," "purpose" or "justification" — the new literatures . . . are generated from cultures for whom such terms as "authority" and "truth" are empirically urgent in their demands. Land claims, racial survival, cultural revival: all these demand an under-standing of and response to the very concepts and structures which post-structuralist academicians refute in language games, few of which recognize the political struggles of real peoples outside such discursive frontiers. (quoted in Slemon 5–6)

Without canons, there is no alterity. From this observation it follows that weak canons, or noncanons, can do very little to promote contest-ation or social change. With this in mind, I return to an earlier observation about the Canadian canon: because it does not exist, there is no debate about it. A less extreme formulation of this hypothesis would say that the lack of debate in Canadian criticism is directly related to the absence of canonical conviction. Lacking a Canadian canon, we have been unable to articulate difference. Alterity has been submerged. Ideology has been bypassed, blanketed, blanked out. We know no difference. We know no canon. We know no country. We are not.

From this perspective, the absence of a Canadian canon, or even the assertion that there are many canons, begins to seem like an unhealthy sign. It means that we have not identified literary ideals that are worth defending, and that, consequently, we have developed no literary ideals that are worthy of being attacked. Such a condition produces stagnation and complacency. To guard against such complacency, it is crucial to affirm the value of canonical ideals, in the full knowledge that such ideals are questionable, that idealization itself is only a relative con-struct, and that the very notion of idealizable values is no longer tenable in the face of critical historicist assaults on the concepts of permanence and continuity. This sounds like an impossible compromise that can only produce bad faith. For how is one to reconcile the need for canonical ideals with the recognition that such ideals are usually understood as exploitative and socially repressive?

To address this question as it pertains to the study of Canadian literature, I want to turn to Altieri again. It is obviously unreasonable to expect a country as young as Canada to have developed a viable literary canon. But how long do you get to remain young? If Canadians are old enough to contemplate the breakup of the country through the departure of Quebec, they are also old enough to begin to value the canonical experience and to appreciate the benefits it offers to students, teachers, and the community at large. What are these benefits? If we were dealing with an established canon, we might ask how that canon reflected certain common ends, how it functioned as a communal agency, how it mediated challenges to this representation, or how it served what Altieri calls "curatorial and normative functions" ("Canons" 2). The curatorial function of canons is "to preserve rich, complex contrastive frameworks, which create . . . a cultural grammar for interpreting experience"; the normative function recognizes that "canons involve values — both in what they preserve and in the principles of preserving" ("An Idea" 47). If I respect the assertion that there is no Canadian canon, it follows that we cannot speak about what values the canon actually embodies. Instead, we have to engage in a broader level of inquiry concerning the functions and benefits of canonical ideals.

Altieri identifies "at least three competing cultural functions" of the traditional canon: first, "it institutionalizes idealization as a force shaping our sense of what communities we wish to identify with and what selves to pursue"; second, "it challenges individuals and new movements in the arts to meet certain criteria of self-representation if they choose identities within certain communities"; third, "it is capable of focusing those discussions about the ends of politics that are very difficult to develop if one's major interest lies in demystifying prevailing beliefs and resisting all cultural positivities" ("Canons" 3).

Altieri fully understands that these claims for ideal canonical functions seem to resist contemporary demands for canonical expansion that would satisfy new political constituencies; they also seem to evade the new historicists' suspicion of using norms from the past as models, the Foucauldian recognition that canons institutionalize hegemonic power, and the understanding of subjectivity fostered by such thinkers as Althusser and Lacan. Yet an idealized model of the canon offers a paradoxical alternative against which current ideologies can be measured. The existence of this alternative does not guarantee any ultimate respect for difference or subjectivity, nor does it offer to deliver "truth," but it does ensure that claims for difference are positioned in relation to a historical backdrop that is more abstract and therefore less politicized than the current debate. Such abstract positioning, of course, is anathema to historicists, who argue that all historical moments are relative and contingent. Their argument, however, does little to come to terms with people's apparent desire to make connections between their experience of the past and the present. Nor does critical historicism provide us with a means of measuring the relevance of our actions, or the ethical force of whatever values we hold. As Altieri puts it, "despite our very different contemporary commitments we can share those ideals of interpretation that secure readings of the past sufficiently determinate in historical terms to distance the text from those political interests, and thus to make it available for a wide variety of significant challenges and applications in the present" ("Canons" 9). Such readings of the past are also crucial to the fiction of our future. As Lauter observes, "what is at stake, after all . . . is what a society sees as important from its past to the construction of its future, who decides that, and on what basis" ("Canon Theory" 143).

While an appreciation of canonical value can enhance our understanding of current theoretical and social issues, it can also enable us to articulate, and preserve, the needs and values of community even if what is preserved is nothing more than a fiction of value, a "biased and limited version of cultural history" (Altieri, "Canons" 12). In this context, Robert Kroetsch's statement that "the fiction makes us real" (*Creation* 63) takes on canonical significance: we recognize *ourselves*, our *plural* selves, through the fiction we write, and, by extension, we recognize our community by preserving certain fictions. In the paper he delivered at the Calgary Conference on the Canadian Novel, Kroetsch recognized that part of him "insists that, essentially, one of the ways in which we build a culture is by selecting and elaborating a few texts" ("Contemporary Standards" 12). As the agency of such selection and elaboration, "the canon can offer a grammar promising . . . a set of models and provocations and communal identifications enabling us to explore new aspects of identity and give rich and contoured explanations for our choices" (Altieri, "Canons" 27). The positivist case can be put even more bluntly: "The very idea of fostering better or richer selves requires our sustaining idealizable frameworks" ("Canons" 29).

A fully vested canonical community recognizes that the canon makes certain demands, that it conveys established hegemonic priorities, and that these priorities are tied to a previous order that is open to challenge. Yet the important point is this: the challenge is framed in response to the demands and values articulated in the canon. It follows that in the absence of such canonical authority, no authentic questioning, and no new forms of antifoundational inquiry, can occur. It is *against* the canon and in the *light* of the canon that we learn to read and then to interpret. At the very moment we declare our mistrust of canons as agents of hegemony, exploitation, and questionable historical idealism, we have to recognize the canonical ideals we valorize through this mistrust. What this means, of course, is that if we want to deconstruct canons, we must first invent them and acknowledge their power. Dissent is always a function of defining power and faith. The most provocative Canadian critics, and the most thought-provoking, are precisely those critics who have powerfully imagined the canonical ideals they seek to question and undermine: Frank Davey pits fragmentation, power groups, and region against his imagined central Canada as monolithic force; Barbara Godard articulates theories of language and marginality that contest referential, empiricist discourse; Linda Hutcheon constructs the ex-centric against the centre, the postmodern against the modern; Robert Kroetsch talks about uninventing the invented, unnaming the already named.

What becomes apparent is that canons serve to facilitate debate, encourage change, and force those addressing literary and social issues to take responsibility for their positions, no matter how subversive or self-serving. It follows that a country without a canon can have no authentic dissenters, because there is no authentic focus for dissent. At this point, one might logically wonder how the dissenters I have named (in this case, Davey, Godard, Hutcheon, and Kroetsch) could have succeeded as dissenters if there is no canon. The answer is that either there is a canon (and the assertion that there is no canon is insupportable) or, in the absence of one, each of these critics has fictionalized a private canon against which they can develop their antithetical views. But if the canonical model is private, how are we to explain the widespread interest in these critics' views?

I can conclude only that other people share their idealizations, however fictionalized they may be. Does this mean that there really is a Canadian canon? Not necessarily. Yet I hope I have raised enough doubts about the absence of a canon to propose a modification of my original stance: there may be no canon, but there might be an *imagined* canon — an imagined community? — that we share. In this model, the sharing of idealizations confirms a shared ideal. The canon gains strength as the instrument of idealization precisely because it does *not* exist, any more than the country behind the canon can be said to exist. *Everything* is imagined — the country, the canon, its ideals. In imagining this imagined community, I hope that my debt to Benedict Anderson's exploration of the narrative relationship between humans and their national communities is clear. I am particularly interested in the ways in which various theorists — most notably Timothy Brennan — have appropriated Anderson's model in terms that make it relevant here. Brennan follows Anderson (as well as Ernest Gellner, Eric Hobsbawn, and Terence Ranger) in asserting that nations do not correspond to realities that can be scientifically, politically, or materially defined. Nations are abstractions, "imaginary constructs that depend for their existence on an apparatus of cultural fictions in which imaginative literature plays a decisive role" (Brennan 49). For Anderson, this role is nothing less than the contemporary means by which a people are invented. I would extend this observation to include the canon: it is one of the imaginary constructs through which nations articulate their dreams and values.

I can project several reservations about the arguments I have advanced in favour of imagining a canon. The most potent would be the suspicion that the advocacy of an ideal subordinates the recognition of plurality and difference; the distinctions between gender, race, and class; the postmodern and postcolonial focus on particularity and place; or the ways in which notions of high and low culture are now seen as contingent and constructed. To empower these crucial distinctions is to endorse what Frank Davey calls "theories of 'interest' or 'conflict' " (*Reading* 3) in which "there can be no absolute value . . . only ideological positions that are relative to the interests of those who hold them, positions that operate as value only within those parts of society in which they receive at least unconscious assent" (7). This sounds like a defence of identity politics because it implies that identity is positioned in relation to economic and historical contexts and that identity shifts as these contexts shift.

Such theories of interest may recognize difference with a vengeance, but it seems to me that the end-product of such recognition is anarchy, or at least a kind of radicalized, self-consciously ideological narcissism that thrives on itself, rather than on any shared notion of community, be it real or imagined. As Hazard Adams observes, "with only power criteria available . . . what remains seems to be only the struggle *for* power and either the cyclical reemergence of sheer ego or totally dominant external oppression" (760). This neo-conservative defence of difference offers no standard against which its own assertions can be judged, no "internal correctives" that can address the narrow belief that people truly want to be involved in a "contingent war of competing powers" (Altieri, "Canons" 11). Besides, such a war produces its own narrative of power, its own agenda to reconstitute critical authority through the very mechanism that interrogates it. As Bernard Harrison explains, Altieri's critique of historicist accounts of the canon

> raises the issue of what values the historicist reader supposes his own readings and canonical unmaskings to serve. One answer is simply liberation for its own sake: the supposed value attaching to the state of being undeceived. But that path merely leads to subjectivism and to the endless schism characteristic of sectarian political conflict. (25)

Even if we succumb to the narcissism that to me seems implicit in the politics of identity, we must still recognize that we are positioned and empowered in relation to standards, however false they may be; that we do not stand alone but in relation to time and space; that we cannot identify ourselves without the simple recognition that there is a world, a nation, a community (a canon?) that positions our act of identification and leads us to reach conclusions about how we live, or teach, or read. Joel Weinsheimer states the idealist case in bold terms:

> The universe of the classic comprehends everything shared and common, everything that is intelligible without the need for explanation, everything that is assumed as apparent and indisputable, everything upon which further thought can be based. The classics not only ground a sense of community but are the locus of common sense. (140)

Postcolonial theorists have stressed an equally powerful connection between community, narrative, and identity. One thinks again of Anderson's "imagined communities," and of his assertion that the value of the nation is "the most universally legitimate value in the political life of our time" (12).

Like nation and narration, community and canon are conjoined. The canon enables us to think about our historicity in relation to a model. The same may be said about race and gender. We consider these interests in relation to a model, and we argue for the importance of this consideration because of that model. Here I can return to my earlier assertion: without this model (without a canon) there can be no authentic dissent. Besides, what is the point of dissent if it is not to achieve a positive outcome for oneself and for others? And if we grant this assertion, we have to ask what constructive outcomes are possible within a metaphysic that preaches only the reality of partisan self-interest. On what basis will those who only seek power or recognize difference communicate? As Altieri puts it:

> The more we insist upon differences, the more we must find ways of locating what those different groups share which will allow them to work together or at least not destroy one another. But how then do we insert that potential for sharing into the model of agency within which difference must play so powerful an explanatory force? ("Canons" 15)

To this question I can add others. Should there be no ideals against which we measure personal and social choices? Should we disempower institutions that have developed mechanisms for testing or fostering those choices? If we want to be better, to learn more, or to speak with others, we are compelled to support a network of "idealizable frameworks" ("Canons" 29).

So what are the alternatives to dissenting views about canons, or, in this case, to the dissenting assertion that there is no Canadian canon? Dissent is only valuable if it shows us how to improve or reconceive not only what empowers or disempowers us as individuals, but also what empowers or disempowers the community that denies or grants our difference. It would be ethical to show how this community intrudes upon any construction of self, and it would be ethical to illustrate the ways in which this community has the positive effect of encouraging dissent. Hazard Adams points to this ethical dimension of canonical activity as a form of "right action." He says: "the form of this right action ought to be that of providing creative opposition which does not negate prevailing power and what *it* negates but civilizes it through a Heraclitean oppositional supplementation and change" (753).

I am not suggesting that canons should remain closed or that they are monolithic constructions that never change, but I am asking us to observe the ways in which canons are the products of forces that are popular *and* learned, marginal *and* central, radical *and* conservative. Altieri observes that "there is so much contradiction within the canon that it serves more as a grammar than as a code of values, more as example of possible intensities and modes of self-representation than as a vehicle imposing any particular model of behaviour" ("Canons" 29). Altieri's conception of this canonical contradiction is identified by other theorists, such as Ross Chambers, as a canonical dialectic that makes possible "discussion and challenge." Chambers describes the canon as "a site of ideological split" that is fundamental to change (18). Joel Weinsheimer speaks of canonical benefits in similar terms. For him, "the question of the classic and of history itself is how to think unity and plurality, sameness and difference, without denying either" (135). If we do not have a canon, we cannot say what it does not represent. We cannot say how it neglects to describe the ways in which it is not Canadian. We need to construct a Canadian canon that is deliberately flawed and failed.

At this point it is reasonable to wonder how any of this speculation about the value of a canon can be related to the study of Canadian literature if there is no Canadian canon. How can any of this theorizing about canonical ideals be applied if there is nothing that it can be applied *to*?

Even if there is no Canadian canon (a hypothesis this chapter is beginning to make me doubt), we can still assert that there are valuable benefits to be derived from canonical pursuits, and that these benefits are particularly relevant to people who confront the absence of canonical authority. One need not have a canon in order to follow these pursuits. In fact, if there is no Canadian canon, the prospect of imagining one seems all the more inviting at this time, simply because as a canonically unformed culture we still have the opportunity to imagine our community anew. What I am suggesting is that our belief in a canon and our imaginative construction of it are far more important than its actual presence, even if such presence could be identified. In other words, the imagined community holds much more potential than any actual community could.

If it is true that the chief feature exhibited by canons is the ways in which they articulate a cultural grammar, then we might stop and ask how such a grammar could ever be identified in a country that is so culturally fragmented, so regionally diverse, so subject to the influence of conflicting groups and powers. Canon theory might provide a microcosmic response to this challenge.

The response would go something like this: although contemporary literary critics and theorists in Canada have popularized ideologies of division, margin, and gender (in much the same way that politicians have promoted ideologies of regional disparity, minority rights, or those of race and sex), they have been able to do this precisely because they are in fundamental agreement about the need to create and articulate a Canadian ideal that would encompass division while at the same time reflecting a sense of national community and purpose. This is, of course, a skewed, Canadian form of expressing E.D. Hirsch's much-debated contention that "a certain extent of shared, canonical knowledge is inherently necessary to a literate democracy" (quoted in Ohmann 49). In less controversial terms, a similar connection is made by Lauter, who writes that "the question of the canon becomes a conflict of values, and therefore, translated into public policy, of politics" ("Canon Theory" 129).

When Frank Davey talks about "the linguistic struggle of groups or regions for power and authority within the country" (7), he frames his discussion in relation to the revealing title of his book — *Reading Canadian Reading* — a self-reflexive phrase that positions Davey's dissent firmly within a cosmology of Canadian reading, which is a product of the very community that empowers Davey to write about how the empowering community is centralizing and therefore dangerous. Earlier, in his provocative essay entitled "Surviving the Paraphrase" (an essay that objects to the "messianic attempt to define a national identity or psychosis" [3]), Davey reaches the paradoxical conclusion that "one by-product" of the nonthematic study of Canadian literature he recommends "would be an implicit statement about Canadians, Canada, and its evolution" (8).

It is ironic that Davey articulates the "messianic" centralist urge that defines so much current (and not-so-current) theory in Canada. In *Reading Canadian Reading* he recounts his impressions of the Future Indicative conference on theory held in 1986, and notes that even the most advanced theorists in the country (those who "had come out of the wilderness of thematic criticism") often offered, as he says Barbara Godard did, "a vision of relatively continuous history and advancement" (2). In the words of Robert Kroetsch, another conference participant, such theory provides a double-sided "righting of the culture" (2). Davey himself points to "the polyphonous (and harmonist) view of Canadian literature and culture suggested by many of the other papers" (2–3). It is interesting to consider the ways in which each of these observations about the conference are made in a spirit of dissent that is related to an ideal. In this case, contestation and complicity are entwined. Those who have come out of the wilderness of thematic criticism are obviously on some sort of Canadian pilgrimage. The peaceable kingdom at the end of the road is there. Those who envision history and advancement must have a dream of Canadian progress. And those who think that theory can right and write culture must imagine that there is a culture to be righted and written.

* * *

In Canada one cannot speak about our failure to achieve canonical awareness, simply because it is too soon to have achieved it. One can, however, speak about the benefits such awareness might confer, and one can attempt to identify the features associated with this ideal. This means creating models of our community and interrogating those models. The absence of a true Canadian canon reflects our inability to identify what it is that makes us Canadian. Yet I believe that we have achieved much more in the way of cultural self-recognition than we are prepared to acknowledge, and that even the most ardent defenders of critical historicism share in an act of cultural recognition every time they write about or teach Canadian literature. Every time we engage in an act of cultural recognition we do more than simply affirm a hegemonic past; we simultaneously participate in the contemporary act of creating — imagining — a community. And communities, as Benedict Anderson reminds us, "are to be distinguished, not by their falsity/genuineness, but by the style in which they are imagined" (6).

The future of Canadian literature — of Canada — can go two ways. If we do nothing to imagine our community — what we share despite our theoretical leanings — then we will continue to operate in separate camps, each camp caught in its own solipsistic web, with its members murmuring about power struggles. The end product of such positioning is not independence and freedom, but fragmentation and finally anarchy. But if we take a step toward imagining community, we will have advanced some basis of communicating within a shared social and cultural narrative. Such a narrative would not deny difference, nor would it deny challenge or change. On the contrary, those involved in it would recognize the crucial interdependence of idealization and dissent. Once again, Altieri's thoughts are relevant. He says: "Canons themselves may form the very society they lead us to dream of and, as we dream, to see ourselves in our limits and our possibilities" ("An Idea" 55). Those dreams might redeem us. After all, if we inhabit a country without a canon we are free, in the most radical sense, to write the fictions of our fate.

3

Privacy, Publicity, and the Discourse of Canadian Criticism

Instead of defining themselves as historical agents of change whose constant renovation of cultural and professional discourses extends beyond the rule-oriented circulation of knowledge, intellectuals see themselves as executing a kind of work unattached to anything except their own writing. In other words, intellectuals may identify with the general human interest, but in fact their identity derives from their work routine as people who stand somewhat outside the ordinary commerce of society.

— Jim Merod, *The Political Responsibility of the Critic* (40)

HOW HAS THE DISCOURSE of English-Canadian literary criticism changed over the past forty years? Have Canadian literary critics worked as "historical agents of change," as Jim Merod would have all critics work, or have they stood "outside the ordinary commerce of society," inhabiting a private realm that has an increasingly diminished public function?

My immediate answer to these questions is that Canadian criticism has become a private affair, removed from public access, divorced from its communal frames.[1] This happened partly because the (late) introduction of European theory to English curricula encouraged the use of critical approaches that were foreign to the Canadian reading public. But it also happened because, after the 1950s, the study of Canadian literature became a new industry that required new levels of specialization in order to sustain itself and grow.

Evidence of this industry was everywhere. Beyond the establishment of numerous courses in Canadian literature at the high-school and university levels (rising to 9.2 percent of the total course offerings in Canadian universities by 1992),[2] there was a proliferation of material designed to assist teachers and literary critics involved in the burgeoning field of Canadian literary study: reference guides, critical studies, journals, bibliographies, articles, anthologies, films, grants, awards, and medals.

Although the industrialization of Canadian literature was supposed to make the subject more accessible — more public — the emphasis on specialization encouraged teachers and critics to value theoretical approaches that the literate, educated reader did not understand. As these approaches became more sophisticated (and less comprehensible), the discourse of Canadian criticism was gradually removed from the public sphere. Criticism became a private function attended by a growing professional elite. The elite grew in power, solidified the club. Inside, the language became more and more theoretical. The discussion of Canadian literature got politicized. Internal factions developed. The idea of addressing an interested community of readers — so prominent in preindustrial Canadian criticism — broke down.

Now, at the end of the century and a few decades after the industry emerged, the idea that there might be a public audience for Canadian criticism would seem absurd to most specialists in the field. Even within the institution, debate about issues deemed to be of communal interest seldom occurs. We have come to inhabit a professional world in which critical discourse is perceived as spectacle rather than exchange, in which information is delivered, rather than discussed. There is little sense of generosity among participants. Our discourse is increasingly feudal, private, and territorial. We have gone inside. We are hoarding what we own.

I call this going inside privatization, not only because it connotes business, which is what the industrialization of Canadian literature involved, but also because it suggests an intimate, cloistered realm populated by people who have developed the intimate discourse of being alone. Because it is not open to the public, this discourse is fundamentally undemocratic. With few exceptions, it is not concerned with Canadian values, or Canadian issues, or even Canadian literature. Yet it calls itself Canadian literary criticism. On behalf of what authority, what constituency, does it speak?

In contrast, I call the nonprofessional realm the public sphere, drawing partly on Jürgen Habermas's view that "publicity" appears whenever people who are affected by discursive norms participate in the creation of those norms and in determining their validity (see *Structural Transformation*). For Habermas, the public sphere designates a theater in modern societies in which participation is enacted through the medium of talk. It is the space in which individuals debate about their common affairs, and hence an institutionalized arena of discursive interaction. This arena is conceptually different from the state; it is a site for the production and circulation of discourses that can in principle be critical of the state. (Nancy Fraser 110–11)

I think of publicity as the act of engaging in this type of discourse. In other words, the public discourse I imagine is *critical* in a positive sense because it makes us aware of a social order and therefore shows us what we can change. The public critical discourse I imagine is accessible, interesting, and problematic to people who read within and outside the academy. For those involved in the teaching of Canadian literature, public critical discourse is inevitably involved with a conception of the country.

In one sense, no theoretical definitions of privacy or publicity are really necessary (the impulse to provide such definition is a big part of the problem): if you live within the institution — if you teach Canadian literature — you know how narrow your audience is. You speak to a few, and you speak in a way that will be acceptable to your peers. You do not address "the public." Your discourse is tailored to the few. It is private.

Of course, there is no strict private/public binary. There is no strict division between institutional and noninstitutional worlds. There are critics who deliberately address public and private audiences. The lines often get blurred. In fact, most Canadian critics don't feel wholly comfortable in privacy because they are haunted by the idea that criticism is responsible to the public — to the nation. The industrialization of Canadian literature complicated this sense of responsibility because it demanded new modes of private address. It said: "Come inside, speak inside." But the traditional discursive order, dominated by narratives of nation, still pulled, still had considerable force. It said: "Stay outside, talk outside." To be outside or inside. Public or private. Park bench or boudoir.

In this chapter I will argue that the industrialization of Canadian literature made such discursive choices traumatic. It confronted critics with profoundly new rhetorical dilemmas. The movement toward privatization allowed the discourse to lose its monologic, nationalist, and hegemonic focus. But the movement away from nationalism was also divisive, both for the social order and for the individual involved in that order. Critics were hailed by their new institution. They were called to serve it. How have they served?

Not many people have addressed this question. Although we do have studies of the evolution of Canadian criticism before and after its industrialization,[3] and other treatments of the process of institutionalization itself,[4] I cannot find a narrative that describes how the discourse of industrialization reconfigured its audience. How has the construction of this audience shifted in the industrial years? What changes in critical language have accompanied this shift? What are the political implications of these discursive transformations? To what extent is postindustrial critical discourse in Canada conflicted by its professional status?

The politics of professionalism has always affected the study of Canadian writing, but the character of this activity remained a backdrop until Canadian literature was industrialized during the 1960s and 1970s.[5] This industrialization involved the creation of discursive strategies that would accommodate the strains placed on professor-critics who were unaccustomed to addressing their new audience — the students, teachers, publishers, and government agencies whose job it was to solidify the institutional and pedagogical bases that had been established in an incredibly short period — roughly between 1958 and 1965.[6]

As they moved into the realm of privatized discourse, Canadian critics found themselves torn between discursive realms. They were forced to speak two ways at once. To address two audiences. To double talk. Postindustrial critical discourse became divided by its desire to inhabit two spheres. To write a history of postindustrial critical discourse would be to write a history of this double desire. And desire is always contradicted.

In what follows I describe some of the ways in which this conflicted desire is represented in Canadian critical discourse. I focus on how postindustrial Canadian criticism addresses its audience, imagines its constituency. I also consider some of the political implications of these postindustrial forms of address, a topic central to many of the discussions about professionalism that have involved a number of prominent critics writing over the past decade.[7] The professional debate is not just about "the role of theory and the vocation of the humanistic intellectual" (West 22), or about the ideology of reading, pedagogy, institutional behaviour, interpretive communities, discursive choices, history, or nation; because it concerns all of these areas, the debate is about political agency and ends.[8]

I

The preindustrial concept of publicity in Canadian critical discourse was never innocent; it was always hegemonic in its unstated assumptions about the critic's role as the agent of patriarchal, representational, nationalist, and canonical forces (see Gerson). The discourse was always strategic, always political, always conflicted. The history of Canadian criticism is full of examples of dissent, of splinter movements, of protest groups. But there was no debate about Canadian literature on an institutional level, simply because institutionalization was a late-1950s phenomenon.

Most pre-1950s criticism was an amateurish public cheerleading discourse aligned with patriotism. It was driven by a monologic interest in myths of nationalism, communal value, and the importance of nation-building through literary building. As Heather Murray says:

> Early critical work was eclectic, and most often intended for public consumption. This 'amateurism' of study remained a feature until, perhaps, the end of the Second World War; kept in place in large measure by the restriction to undergraduate teaching and the lack of an infrastructure — grants, journals, libraries, professional associations — that make sustained activity possible. ("Resistance" 56)

The publicity of this early critical work was clearly aligned with its non-professional status. It was this kind of publicity that allowed nineteenth-century anthologist-critics such as Edward Hartley Dewart to assert that "a national literature is an essential element in the formation of national character" and to wonder "whether the whole range of history presents the spectacle of a people firmly united politically, without the subtle but powerful cement of patriotic literature" (ix). (Dewart's statement typifies the larger pattern of European and North American nation-building that characterized the nineteenth century.)

The industrialization of Canadian literary study was originally designed to extend and to capitalize upon the kind of sentiment expressed by Dewart, one that valorized the transparent equation between critical discourse and nationalist political action. As Donna Bennett observes, "most of the criticism of the fifties was in effect a catalogue of national literary traits and often took the form of a manifesto" ("Criticism" 157).

The shift toward privatized discourse proceeded slowly during the 1950s, not only because the institutional structures facilitating privatization were not yet in place but also because the rhetoric of publicity that informed most Canadian criticism up to that time remained entrenched. This rhetoric was about much more than making the Canadian writer or Canadian literature accessible to the public. It was also about the political value associated with such publicity. Through their increasingly civic presence and accessibility, Canadian writers and critics served the political function of providing public relations for the nation; in this sense, they were government agents.

Although they remained unpaid by the state until the Canada Council was founded in 1957, writers served the state and contributed to a shifting sense of value in the type of literature produced and how it was taught. Increasing emphasis was placed on realist literature because it validated the assumption that the writer could portray a distinctly Canadian world.[9] Even in critical commentary on Canadian poetry, the importance of establishing a mimetic link between writing and nation was assumed. In his *Poetry in Canada: The First Three Steps* (1958), R.E. Rashley observed that poetry after World War II had its origin "in the actual experience of people in Canada, and its value is in the fact that it does deal with the significance of life in Canada" (xiv). Implicit in this statement is the assumption that writers, readers, and critics share a community, that such sharing enables the community to envision its future. If you can imagine a future, you can act.

This was the underlying concept of publicity informing the first university-aligned conference on Canadian literature, which was held at Queen's University in 1955. The purpose of the conference was "to examine the problems of writing in Canada" (Whalley vii). Although the conference was originally intended for poets, the organizers decided that "it would be advisable to convene a more inclusive group" so that "any charges of preciosity or special pleading . . . would in this way be automatically disarmed." This group included "not writers only, but publishers, editors, librarians, and booksellers." The procedures followed at the conference were also designed to ensure public access: from the published proceedings we learn that "formal papers would be read to delegates and the public in the evenings to delineate areas for discussion; issues raised in the papers would be examined by small discussion groups . . . the chairman of each group reporting to a plenary session of delegates" (viii). There was a sense, at least in the rhetoric, that there was work to be done and that the conference participants would do this work together.

In his preface to the proceedings, George Whalley makes it clear that this public stance promoted a healthy debate and exchange of views on a wide variety of issues:

> Unfortunately the *ipsissima verba* of the group discussions are beyond record — the conflicts of perfervid devotion and chilly good sense; the blunt assertiveness and allusive urbanity; the obtuse bulldozing attacks parried by the weapons of prim but inflexible good manners; the shameless misrepresentation of other people's motives and the deft counter-attacks

on behalf of cool reason and cold fact; the passages of swift verbal
duelling and of blind pummelling; the lamentations over the decaying
body of Western Civilization and the rallying cries that were meant to
reconcile ineradicable differences; the explosive rage and muttering
frustration of the defeated, the smug condescension of the victors; and
over all this, the mercurial impassivity of the chairmen rendered intoler-
able by their disarming public confessions of savage partiality. (x)

For Whalley (who is being parodic, satiric, and ironic here) these
"delights" nevertheless contributed to an exciting conference characterized by discursive exchange. Such forms of exchange — disruptive,
unruly, impassioned — are crucial to the function of publicity because
public debate performs a *critical* activity that is simultaneously *political.*
The absence of such debate is one sign of the breakdown of the public
sphere. Today, we seldom experience spirited debate of the kind
exchanged at the Queen's conference. At our academic gatherings we
do not address the issue of the public; in fact, we are suspicious of such
universalizing terms as "the public." We seem to assume that our
critical efforts are disconnected from social change. The politics of
agency has become the theorization of agency, and we believe that
theory is action. Yet there is no world for us to act upon, largely
because we have undermined the assumption that there is a relation
between critical activity and a "real" world to be criticized, especially
via texts.

Compare the mood and aims of any contemporary conference on
Canadian literature to those apparent at the Queen's conference.[10]
There, the valorization of publicity seemed to be all-encompassing, if
somewhat blinded by its idealism. Whalley's observations concerning
the public nature of the conference were echoed by F.R. Scott, who
introduced the published proceedings with a metaphor undoubtedly
derived from his support for the CCF. Scott notes that "scholars . . .
business men, professional men, and trade unionists gather in their
national associations," and "from the interchange among these small
groups comes much of the sense of community which exists in Canada
despite all the barriers erected by race, religion, language, and geogra-
phy." For Scott, the central question was "Have Canadian writers such
a sense of community?" (1). The conferees addressed this question by
imagining their involvement in a "literary assembly line," with the
writer as producer whose work was "passed along the line to the
publisher, magazine editor, or CBC programme director" and then on
to the public "on the printed page or through broadcast." The assembly line extended further, of course, to embrace other aspects of

dissemination: "libraries, bookstores, critics, and book reviewers" (2).

The metaphor of the literary assembly line is the metaphor of community. As Scott put it: "All these workers on the assembly line participate in a common undertaking, however much their interest and outlook may vary; when they are all citizens of one country they have further points in common" (2). Reading Scott's comments today, one is struck by the importance he places upon asserting commonalty: "The Conference as a whole was able to develop something approaching a collective body of thought. The afternoons were entirely free for the forming and renewing of those friendships out of which a sense of community is built" (3).

The desire to locate a public and to affirm community expressed at the Queen's conference was unique in its vocal recognition of the problems faced by Canadian writers, but the discursive model it embraced — that of a group of individuals meeting and debating with the public interest in mind — was not really new. The same model formed the basis for most commentary on Canadian literature up to that time, for the desire for community expressed at the conference was a contemporary version of the dominant belief that the dissemination of a national literature was essential to the recognition of community on a national scale. In other words, the publicity of the nation's literature both formed and publicized the nation.

If the Queen's conference was a high point in the discourse of publicity, it was also a turning-point in the discourse of Canadian criticism, for in their desire to promote Canadian writing — to increase its publicity — the conference participants took the first step toward privatizing the communal discourse they pursued. Many of the conferees observed that "criticism of Canadian literature scarcely exists at all; that few universities and schools give Canadian literature courses, and if they do are hard pressed to find copies of the books the students should read" (Scott 4).

The conference organizers were driven by their desire to capitalize Canadian literature by maximizing the writer's publicity. Ironically, it was the *means* of achieving this publicity that introduced the discourse of the private sphere. Scott made a crucial distinction between this conference and others: for him, the Queen's conference

> was not so much a *writer's* conference as a conference on writing and its dissemination. For this reason relatively little time was spent on the art of writing itself; most of the discussion centred around the problems of publication, of reaching an audience, of the acceptance of the role of the writer in contemporary Canada. (3)

He asked what "steps should be taken to make the public more aware of the good writing that was available"? (3).

There were seven specific recommendations: 1) increase the prominence of Canadian literature in public-school curricula and textbooks; 2) increase the number of Canadian works treated in English courses at the university level; 3) encourage the government to fund library purchases of Canadian literature; 4) preserve the literary tradition by republishing out-of-print works in new, inexpensive editions (via government support); 5) increase the level of state funding to writers; 6) introduce a cash component into the Governor General's Awards; and 7) encourage the government to purchase more Canadian books for distribution abroad.

The implementation of these recommendations over the next few years moved Canadian literature into its industrial phase. Malcolm Ross's New Canadian Library series (and other series that followed its lead) provided the texts on which the industry would be based. Ross wanted to appeal to a broad cross-section of Canadian readers; his intentions were noble, and even his publisher was prepared to take a financial risk in the interests of patriotism (if not always in good writing).

Ross imagined that one way of reaching the public was through the university curriculum. But as the series gained acceptance in the schools, Canadian literature became an increasingly curricular affair — a fact reinforced by the publisher's decision to encourage academics to write critical introductions to each volume. The appearance of these introductions changed the status of these literary works and of literary study. Now they were seen as texts that required professional interpretation. By reinforcing the idea that the books in this series were serious enough to be explained to the reader (who was not sophisticated enough to understand them without help), the New Canadian Library paradoxically undercut the public's ability to feel comfortable with its literature. These were mass-market texts which — especially in the 1960s when paperback publishing was relatively new — signalled their popular and accessible status. At the same time, their new, professional status signalled that they were texts that had to be explained — by professionals — in critical introductions and in courses at school.

The specialized discourse of these introductions increased over the years. Gradually, the New Canadian Library series started to cater to university teachers and students of Canadian literature. As Canadian criticism became more and more valuable as a commodity, academics began to read fiction as criticism, to describe novels as pedagogical tools. They began to study "the constructs, values, and fantasies" of other critics (see chapter 6). Canadian critical language became a subject in its own right. Now it was treated as a topic worthy of analysis. This marked a profound shift in the valorization of publicity. The message to the "general" reader was clear: you need special knowledge to understand the literature we are talking about; the more specialized your knowledge, the more powerful you are; the institution can grant this power, but first you must come inside.[11]

When George Woodcock wrote his editorial to the first issue of *Canadian Literature* in 1959, he recognized the growing publicity of the country's literature and addressed his own fledgling magazine as "a potential guest of the literary public of our country," a magazine that would serve "writers, scholars, librarians and — by no means least — the curious reader" (3). In its attempt to address such a broad readership and in its acknowledged debt to "the literary public," *Canadian Literature* was obviously concerned with a high level of publicity. However, threats to this publicity could already be identified. Woodcock emphasized that while some might argue that such a magazine should appeal to a "little clan," *Canadian Literature* would refuse this claim, because it sought "to establish no clan, little or large. It will not adopt a narrowly academic approach, nor will it try to restrict its pages to any school of criticism or any class of writers" (4). This was a very public stance. But the very fact that Woodcock's editorial is charged with repudiating these threats to publicity demonstrates their growing power. Woodcock wanted the study of Canadian literature to be open to everyone — academics and nonacademics — but the discourse he employs suggests that such all-embracing publicity had already come to an end.

II

The idea that publicity was threatened would have seemed very odd to anyone involved in the study of Canadian literature in the early 1960s. After all, Canadian literature appeared to have become much more public. There was the New Canadian Library series. There were courses on Canadian literature cropping up around the country. Federal and provincial agencies were funding Canadian writers, researchers, and publishers. The so-called explosion of Canadian literature had begun. Now the literary nationalists' dream of promoting the country by disseminating its literature could be fulfilled. Now critics would be funded and paid to speak on the nation's behalf. Public money was being invested; public accountability was involved.

The introduction of state funding supported the belief that Canadian criticism and Canadian experience were intertwined. This belief was not new; only the support was. As Carole Gerson notes, "the need for a literature which speaks to Canadians about Canadian experience in a Canadian environment was as current a topic in the 1860s as the 1960s" (*Purer Taste* 36). Yet the literary institution produced by this industrialized publicity began to develop a discourse that was definitely unpublic. Now that Canadian literature was in the schools, new pedagogical strategies — and the specialized discourse attached to these strategies — were required. As the study of Canadian literature proliferated it necessarily became more specialized. At the same time, the introduction of European critical theory into North American English curricula bolstered this move toward specialized discourse. Although the effects of this shift did not appear in published Canadian criticism until the early 1970s, theory was in the air.

In the initial phases of this specialization, critical discourse demonstrated a predictable overlap of private and public interests, both of which were in search of new definition. Evidence of this overlap is suggested by the fact that so many of the critics writing from within the institution were also poets whose creative milieu was outside the university. These poet-critics tried to bridge the gap between outside and inside; they struggled with the challenges faced by the writer developing a new sense of public and private space.

Although the poetry and criticism written at this time by such figures as Louis Dudek, D.G. Jones, Eli Mandel, James Reaney, and Warren Tallman were very different in form, each contributed to the growing sense that a radical shift had occurred in the public perception of the writer and the writer's role. One way of identifying the nature of this shift is to compare the attitudes toward publicity voiced at the Queen's conference in 1955 with those expressed at a similar conference that took place in Quebec in 1963. The Foster Poetry Conference, held in West Bolton, brought together such figures as Leonard Cohen, Louis Dudek, John Glassco, Ralph Gustafson, D.G. Jones, Irving Layton, Eli Mandel, F.R. Scott, A.J.M. Smith, George Whalley, and Milton Wilson — to name but a few of the participants who would contribute significantly to the institutionalization of Canadian literature over the decade.

This conference shared with its predecessor at Queen's a tremendous sense of excitement and energy. In his preface to the published proceedings, John Glassco likened the "essence of the gathering" to "a convulsion, an electrical discharge, and an orgasm" (7). Again, like the Queen's conference, this one was characterized by heated debate:

> There was a constant sense of clash and conflict, not only between the
> forces of tradition and revolution, between the elders still presumably

> stumbling around in post-war academic darkness and the clear-sighted
> children of a putative post-nuclear dawn, but between sharply differing
> conceptions of the role of the poet in society and even of the nature of
> poetry itself. (6–7)

With these words, Glassco identifies a crucial feature of the Foster conference that distinguishes it from the earlier meeting at Queen's: the writers had become self-conscious about their social role as Canadian poets and about the ways in which this role was perceived within the academy. Milton Wilson led a seminar entitled "The Reviewer of Poetry," in which it was pointed out that "poets are themselves among the most active reviewers." But for whom did they review? Or, as Wilson phrased it, "who is the audience? . . . which of his possible readers should the reviewer imagine he is writing for?" (52). In responding to Wilson's questions, Dudek (who was, like Wilson, a university professor) wondered "whether the reviewer shouldn't be enough of a critic to do some charting of the trends and influences in Canadian poetry and to try to place the book in its aesthetic and intellectual context" (55). Significantly, Irving Layton, who wanted nothing to do with the professoriate, "objected to what he took to be a subordination of the poet to historical movements or to the books he'd read" (55). Yet most of the participants seemed to agree with the (unattributed) observation of one of the conference participants that "the Canadian poet's sense of existing in a literary community (despite the size of the country) was surprisingly strong (even a bit cosy)." The same participant "wondered whether it wasn't one of the reviewer's functions to provide a link in this sense of community." As a means of establishing this link, Eli Mandel suggested that "it might be worth-while to try, say, an archetypal approach" (Wilson 56).

I have dwelt on these elements of the Foster conference because they point to an emerging distinction between privacy and publicity. The claims to publicity were still strong: there was an atmosphere of debate and exchange; the image of a literary community spanning the country was invoked; the poet was seen as a vital link holding this community (the nation) together. But now the claims to privacy were getting stronger: the poet was compelled to be self-conscious; poetry was subject to academic involvement; many poets were now poet-critics and professors; the notion of the audience had come under scrutiny; there was a call to identify and clarify influential intellectual traditions; new critical terminology ("an archetypal approach") had been introduced, and it was terminology that not every conference participant necessarily understood.

This gesture toward academic and theoretical specialization was the most obvious sign of the trend (in Canada, as elsewhere) toward privatization — a trend that would produce later conferences filled with language that was extremely specialized and entirely removed from the discourse of the "cosy" community that had once debated in nonprofessional, and often antiprofessional, terms. Beyond the conference, the concept of community was also being redefined. Compare, for example, George Woodcock's concern with publicity in his opening editorial to *Canadian Literature* in 1959 with Frank Davey's introduction to *Open Letter* in 1965. Unlike Woodcock, Davey made privacy his purpose: he wanted *Open Letter* to reflect the views of its editors, who inhabited "an ostensibly private world of baffling values, problems, place-names, and personages." Yet the word "ostensibly" suggests that, at this point, Davey remained uncertain about the possibility of asserting privacy over publicity, uncertain about the "baffling values" he would confront in going private.

While it seems clear that this privatization of Canadian critical discourse was largely a function of the introduction of Canadian literature into the university curriculum during the 1960s, it would be inaccurate to claim that it was solely the process of institutionalization that prompted a conflicted withdrawal from publicity. There were other factors accounting for the shift. During the 1950s Northrop Frye had developed the view that literature, national identity, and cultural development were intertwined — a traditional concept in Canadian criticism, but one that gained new power as a result of Frye's archetypal, mythopoeic theories. These theories had a profound effect on Canadian poets and critics at precisely the time when the future of national identity was being threatened by fears of American cultural takeover, by new communicative theories (especially McLuhan's) that seemed to presage the extinction of the nation state, and by a general sense that mass culture and populism would submerge the distinct culture many Canadians felt made them unique. The cultural nationalism that developed in response to these perceived threats was a broad and very public defence mechanism. But when it was applied to the study of Canadian literature, this mechanism became a potent instrument of privatization: in order to be worthy of being defended, Canadian literature had to be defined as something different.

Anyone who has studied Canadian literature is familiar with the various means by which this difference was defined. The most obvious attempt to identify literary difference emerged with Frye's theories of the "garrison mentality," which he advanced in his conclusion to the first edition of the *Literary History of Canada* (1965). If this new concept of a garrison mentality did not signify a profound shift toward the valorization of privacy, nothing did. For the thematic critics who followed Frye in the 1970s, the notion of a garrison mentality justified the development of theories that focused on survival and isolation as central metaphors of Canadian experience.

All of the critiques levelled at the thematic critics, and, by extension, at Frye's conclusion, miss a crucial point: whether or not these theories were reductive, whether or not they were applicable, they were still *theories* of Canadian literature developed in an institutional setting. In other words, the major effect of Frye's conclusion — such an ostensibly public document — was to bring the study of Canadian literature further indoors. As it turned out, the garrison mentality Frye theorized was not so much in the literature as in the institution proper, which was explaining itself to itself more and more, to the outside world less and less. The garrison mentality was privacy writ large.

The rise of privacy at the expense of publicity meant that new, specialized terminology and theoretical concepts were increasingly applied to the study of Canadian literature. Because such terminology was applied, the study became more elitist, self-conscious, and protectionist. The sense of exchange and debate that characterized preinstitutional publicity was replaced by pedagogy that privileged oratorical over conversational modes of address. What was once a literature available to the community had become the property of scholars who began to write for each other, rather than for the public. As a result, the professional Canadian critic's ability and desire to intervene in public discourse about Canada were reduced.

III

By the 1970s Canadian literature was entrenched in the high-school and university curricula. The number of critical works being published on Canadian literature had increased dramatically. Many graduate students were earning doctorates in Canadian literature. They were needed by the expanding profession. The teaching of Canadian literature was seen as politically expedient, for by introducing students to their national literature, teachers were also introducing them to their country. Pedagogy was politically responsible and justifiable; it promoted a vision of public life, and promoted those involved in furthering this vision. However, this vision was very different from the one imagined by Whalley at the Queen's conference because it was a pedagogical construction of public appeal. The publicity endorsed within the institution was manufactured publicity; it was a state-supported public-relations campaign. This campaign was inevitably compromised and conflicted, because the shift toward pedagogical involvement in publicity meant that publicity had to be treated in pedagogical terms that could be positioned within the discourse of English studies in general. Suddenly the new specialist in Canadian literature was forced to speak about Canada and things Canadian in a way that would be acceptable to his or her peers.

This discursive requirement produced a fundamental reconception of publicity. Whereas the preindustrial discourse of Canadian criticism imagined a broad public readership, postindustrial critical discourse constructed a much more limited audience — one comprised of specialists and students who would judge each other. Such forms of judgement introduced a hierarchy of discourse. New scholars in Canadian literature sought out new discursive modes in order to gain the acceptance of other scholars. The relevance of these modes was self-evident on the level of pedagogy: students learned to speak about Canadian literature in a certain way and were rewarded for speaking this way.

Most of the specialists trained in the study of Canadian literature had been taught by senior academics who accepted the assumption that literature was referential and that literary language was transparent. From this perspective, the mimetic claim that a nation could be represented in its literature did not seem at all far-fetched. It testified to the belief that there was a pre-existing national reality, and that the critic's task was to confirm this reality. Homi Bhabha explains that in this mimetic view, "the 'image' must be measured against the 'essential' or 'original' in order to establish its degree of *representativeness*, the correctness of the image. The text is not seen as *productive* of meaning but essentially reflective or expressive" ("Representation" 100). As Barry Cameron remarks, most critics writing during the 1970s wanted to establish this kind of representativeness. They "were concerned with establishing a general grammar of Canadian literature *as a whole*, and with discovering in Canadian literary texts certain kinds of patterns. These 'patterns' were, further, deemed to characterize the nation or reveal the national character" ("Theory" 111).

Writing in 1990, Cameron finds it necessary to use quotation marks to qualify his description of this form of criticism as "poetics," an indication of how outmoded he considers this modified nationalist discourse to be. Also outmoded, from his perspective, are many of the assumptions about publicity that informed critical discourse in the 1970s, particularly as it was employed by the thematic critics, who are charged with grounding their criticism in a false empiricism and in making "presuppositions about 'Canada.' " Cameron's critique is an excellent example of privatized value in action. He says the thematic critics assume the presence of "an entire culture with an assumed unity. . . . Literary history in these terms turns into Canadian Studies; through an analysis of 'Canadian' symbols, images, and myths, litera- ture is able to function potentially as a means of national identification and a force for national unity" (111–12). Their works "all attempt to raise a national consciousness in order to render intelligible and justify our living together" (113).

Cameron speaks in measured tones, but the subtext of his discussion is clear: from a contemporary vantage point — from the vantage point of European theory — the idea of criticism that attempts to "justify our living together" or that emanates from "collective concern with coun- try" is passé (113). This is the kind of statement that can be made in 1990, when publicity — and the value of "collective concern" — is almost dead. Cameron seems to welcome the decline of publicity. I find this tragic. It may be welcoming disaster.

Unlike Cameron, earlier critics didn't find it so easy to repudiate publicity. They devoted a lot of energy to reconciling two forms of discourse: one, public, compelled them to address national concerns that went beyond the classroom or the tenure committee; the other, private, compelled them to address pedagogical and professional con- cerns that turned their language inward. Of all the critics who have addressed Canadian literature, few have faced greater discursive challenges than the thematic critics, precisely because they were forced, through their writing, to negotiate the tension between the public and the private spheres. In this sense, their work deserves to be recon- sidered, not so much in terms of its effectiveness as textual criticism, but in terms of how this process of negotiation, which is unique to the early phases of industrialization, created a critical narrative that was literally beside itself in its desire to accommodate private and public value.

Frye's conclusion to the first edition of the *Literary History of Canada* is the first narrative to grapple with this negotiated discourse. It projects an idealized, peaceable kingdom of Canada that can be reached by reading literature as an autonomous grammar of redemption. This kingdom is the promised land of publicity; it is the perfect realm that literature allows us to reach together. Frye's pastoral version of publicity contrasts sharply with his vision of the garrison mentality (a trope of privacy) that he found in so much Canadian writing. His conclusion was criticized for generalizing about English-Canadian literature (his idealization of Canadian literature was too public) and for theorizing a mentality of isolation that was at odds with the obvious publicity of so much Canadian poetry and prose (his reading of Canadian writing was too private).

The temptation to embrace the private realm (to write from within the garrison) and to search for the peaceable kingdom (to escape the garrison) was a theoretical expression of the tension Frye experienced between his desire to work within the university (to go private) and to work outside the university (to minister within the public sphere). If it is true that "no essay in Canadian literary criticism has been more influential than Northrop Frye's 'Conclusion'" (Daymond and Monkman 460), it is because the document struggles poetically with the central, but largely unrecognized, critical issue of its time: the extent to which the Canadian critic was responsible for addressing a community.

Of course, there are many who will argue that there is no single community to serve, that the very idea of a monolithic, homogeneous "public" that can be "addressed" is a distortion of history and a denial of the material conditions that contribute to the actual heterogeneity of public life — a heterogeneity that Canadian critical discourse has largely denied. But whether there is or is not a coherent public out there is immaterial. If you believe it's out there, if you write to it, then it's there. If, as Cameron says, "the writing of literary history systematically forms the objects of which it speaks," and if history "is an object constructed by understanding" ("Theory" 108), then it is up to literary history to construct or deconstruct its communal arena.

Influenced as they were by Frye's theories, it seems inevitable that the thematic critics would have experienced some of the tensions between privacy and publicity that gave the conclusion its narrative power (see chapter 7). In *Butterfly on Rock*, D.G. Jones recognizes his debt to Frye and positions himself — typically for this period — as a critic who must bridge the gap between privacy and publicity, between what he calls the garrison and the wilderness. In Jones's model, we are estranged from the land and must reclaim it in order to recover a "greater sense of vitality and community" (136).

On one level, Jones's belief that "we are the land's" (3), that "we must now move into our own cultural house," that we must deal with "a common cultural predicament" (3, 4) is, as he recognizes, an assertion of nationalism that goes back to the nineteenth century. But Jones turns this "question of national identity" into a metaphor. For him, "national identity is not to be equated with simple national pride, political independence, or some inevitably chauvinistic self-assertion" (4–5). The meaning of national identity is redefined as "an imaginative stance towards the world," which is essential if one is to "take a stand, act with definitive convictions, have an identity" (5).

There is a political agenda behind Jones's attempts "to define more clearly some of the features that recur in the mind, the mirror of our imaginative life" (3). Writing in the years immediately following the publication of Frye's conclusion, he senses that the garrison mentality has taken hold, that it may have taken hold of him, that he has become a poet writing from inside. Or he is both outside and in. The "sense of exile" (5) that he finds in Canadian poetry and prose is his own exile from the wilderness of public space. The feeling "of being estranged from the land and divided within oneself" (5) is the feeling he projects onto the literature, a reflection of his own division between the public and private spheres.

Jones's attempt to resolve this division involves "the need to make a transition from a garrison culture to one in which the Canadian will feel at home in his world" (7). In these words Jones expresses a longing for the link between privacy and publicity that he sees vanishing, even as he writes. He wants desperately to be integrated, to be part of the world out there, to be part of the collective identity he wants poetry and criticism to form. But the very insistence of his need to bridge the gap between an alienating privacy and a politically engaged publicity suggests that the gap can no longer be bridged.

Jones is the first to connect the endorsement of publicity with the achievement of political power. And he is the first to argue that, by extension, privacy is powerless as an instrument of real political change. The tragedy Jones recognizes in the shift toward privacy is the tragedy of being unable to act.

Like Jones, John Moss and Margaret Atwood struggle with versions of the tension between public and private discourse. They are on the cusp. There is no need to dwell on their similar theses, which adopt Frye's garrison-mentality theme. I am more interested in how they address their audiences — how they construe their public arena. Atwood's *Survival* thesis is the expression of a poet who feels victimized by privacy. Writing in the early 1970s, Atwood, an ex-academic, sees the academic walls closing in on Canadian literature. She wants to break the trend toward privacy. She wants a public.

Jones tried to write a critical book that would awaken Canadian readers to their collective identity. But his discourse had already become so private that only academics could interpret his message. *Butterfly on Rock* had little popular appeal. Atwood tried to write a critical book that would allow readers to overcome privacy; it would argue that they could be "creative non-victims." They could be in the world. They could change their circumstances. They could be political. *Survival* was addressed to a pretty broad public. It was enormously popular because people outside the academy understood what Atwood had to say, and because she provided an accessible model. I am not particularly interested in whether Atwood was right or wrong, or in what her personal biases as a critic proved to be. I am more concerned with the academic reception of *Survival* because it demonstrates the extent to which publicity had been downgraded in just a few years. Critics complained that the work was superficial, that it ignored central Canadian works, that it was too negative in its outlook, that its thematic bias was reductive. In short, Atwood was condemned because she simplified and popularized her selections, and was partisan in making them.

One of the most potent attacks was launched by Frank Davey, who complained that *Survival* was "of limited use to educators" because it was so partial in its selections (*From There* 34). If the book was of such "limited use," why did it outsell all other critical books on Canadian literature combined? The point is that it was not useful to Davey, who was no longer concerned, as a critic, with reaching students, high-school teachers, or the so-called general reader. Privacy had supplanted publicity.

By the end of the 1970s, the idea that the discourse of Canadian criticism could serve a nonspecialist audience had been gradually repudiated. It would no longer be possible to argue, as Moss did in *Patterns of Isolation*, that a study of Canada's literature could reveal "much about the processes of our emergence into national being" or about "the indigenous character of the Canadian community" (7). As Cameron notes, "such collectivity and such versions of 'the' national character came under increasing scrutiny" ("Theory" 113). Even the idea of addressing university students now seemed to be a secondary concern. Canadian critics began to write for each other. All of a sudden the community seemed smaller, more concentrated. By going private, Canadian critics removed themselves from the possibility of affecting public action.

Not all critics divorced themselves from political concerns. A notable exception is Dennis Lee, whose "Cadence, Country, Silence: Writing in Colonial Space" (1973) engaged the increasingly passé question of what it means to speak as a Canadian from a culturally indigenous space. Lee recognizes that if we inhabit a "problematic public space" (if that space is "radically in question for us"), then "that makes our barest speaking a problem to itself" (37). But then again, Lee wasn't a professional; he could still address the public sphere.[12] Meanwhile, other critics were trying to distance themselves from that sphere as they engaged in research that was "becoming theoretical rather than practical, turning upon its own presuppositions, upon the structure of the model itself" (Godard, "Structuralism/Post-Structuralism" 27). The inward turning described by Godard is an expression of the impulse to privatize through theory.

One of the critics most committed to this form of privatization is Davey, whose "Surviving the Paraphrase" (originally presented as a conference paper in 1974) and *From There to Here* (also 1974) were largely responsible for repudiating the notions of publicity attached to nationalist — and particularly thematic — Canadian criticism. Davey's quarrel with thematics is well known, but the ways in which it is attached to his developing elitism as an agent of privatization is seldom noted. In his early criticism, he tries hard to portray himself as a democratic liberal who would replace the thematicist's monolithic view of Canada with a vision of a postmodern nation that was a "decentralized and retribalized culture" (*From There* 23). Such a culture would stand in contrast to the "elitist, formalistic, anti-democratic, and anti-terrestrial movement" of modernism (*From There* 19).

This seems like an eminently public vision of a new Canada, and it suggests that the critic who endorses such a vision is a kind of liberator who will be nonelitist, antiformal, democratic, worldly. But as it turns out, Davey is quite formal in his assumptions and quite exclusive in imagining the community he wants to address. For example, he chooses the writers for inclusion in *From There to Here* on the basis of their "pre-eminence as artists" (according to what pre-established standard?), and their "influence" (Davey thus endorses pre-existing authority), and according to "their presence on contemporary high school and college curricula" (even though he scorns criticism designed for high-school and college students). In a retrospective examination of the impulses that led him to write *From There to Here*, Davey complains that "criticism normally addresses itself to the student or general reader rather than to the writer or literary critic," and that "criticism is not a dialogue among equals but a monologue by the initiated to the naive" (*Reading Canadian Reading* 37). "I wanted," he emphasizes, "to address critics and writers rather than students, to develop a visibly polemic vision of Canadian writing rather than imply a stable critical consensus" (*Reading* 40).

From Davey's privatized perspective, students are devalued, unworthy of critical address. He feels the same about "the popular press," which is motivated by "superficial nationalism" (*From There* 15). These are the statements of someone who is clearly interested in hierarchies, in power. The problem facing Davey is how to achieve power, in a peda-gogical milieu, when you don't want to address students and you downgrade the popular press. The answer, of course, is to seek out increased power "among equals." (Davey has recently agreed to serve as the president of the Association of Canadian College and University Teachers of English.)

I do not believe that Davey is entirely self-serving. He does seem committed to effecting political change. His recent books on Kim Campbell and Karla Homolka — notwithstanding their specialized discourse — effectively reposition him in the public domain. He is now writing for the popular press he once abhorred.[13] But in his earlier work he chose to embrace privacy, and so also chose to endorse discursive strategies that made it historically difficult for him to operate in public space. Many bridges have been burned. Yet some remain. Despite the persona he has developed as a postnational and antipublic critic, Davey obviously believes in something Canadian and he often encourages us to find out what that something is. Even in "Surviving the Paraphrase" Davey argues that "one by-product" of the non-thematic study of Canadian literature "would be an implicit statement about Canadians, Canada, and its evolution" (10). This sounds a lot like what the thematicists said, as does Davey's assertion that "Canadian literature is a highly useful frame of reference for approaching particular literary problems" (11).

One is prompted, when reading such statements, to conclude that Davey is a conflicted critic — the most interesting kind. The discourse he employs indicates that, at least initially, Davey was confused about the responsibilities involved in going private (see chapter 8). In this sense, the theoretical narrative he has created strongly resembles those equally conflicted narratives written by Frye, Jones, Atwood, and Moss. By valorizing privacy over publicity, Davey could assume the role of antihero, centralized and empowered by his very alienation from centralized power. As others pursued their own forms of antiheroism, privacy began to define itself as the dominant view.

The hegemony of privatization was implicitly and explicitly a hegemony of theory. In their turn toward new concepts of language, Canadian critics were of course not alone. Many came to embrace literary theory after their American and European counterparts; but embrace it they did. The gradual alignment of theory with academic professionalism in Canada might suggest that the privatization of critical discourse here was not really unique; it was happening everywhere. True. But theorists in other countries were not writing against such a powerful alignment of theoretical expression with nationalism as they were in Canada; they were not professionals in an industry that had grown up in a decade; they were not accountable to a public that envisioned the critic as someone whose job it was to provide a narrative of nation; they did not look outside without feeling uneasy about being inside.[14] The introduction of European theory was traumatic because it suggested that nation didn't really matter (language mattered) at a time when Canadian critics felt compelled to believe that nation really did matter. In other words, theory was perceived as anti-Canadian, as threatening because it was American or international, because it didn't encourage us to talk about ourselves. The challenges faced by postindustrial Canadian critics were compounded by the need they felt to use theory to speak about something that theory didn't often speak about: countries.

It is precisely because Canadian critics have always been marked by their split allegiance to privacy and publicity that their discourse is so tortured in its wrestling with the problem of social obligation. Unlike their counterparts in other countries, postindustrial Canadian critics experienced theory as contamination and infection. The disease was inside, Canadian criticism was going inside, but it was going with shame and guilt. How could these critics face the public? How could they be Canadians *and* professional critics? They had to speak in two voices. One voice spoke in tropes and theories about the benefits of going private. Privacy meant the text, not culture; language, not logos; writing, not theme; reader, not community. The public voice — the other voice — got fainter and fainter as privacy drowned it out. Every postindustrial Canadian critic is bedevilled by these voices; the most challenging of these critics are those who battle to be univocal, but who find that, as Canadians, they can't. They are condemned to be multivocal and polyphonic, to be public as well as private, to inhabit both stage and boudoir.

A good example of this double habitation appears in Barry Cameron and Michael Dixon's "Mandatory Subversive Manifesto" (1977). According to the authors, it had been in the works since 1973. It is usually read as a critique of the "Canadian" in "Canadian criticism" and of those schools of Canadian criticism (read "thematic criticism") that did not treat the literature "as part of the autonomous world of literature" (read "Frye"). Cameron and Dixon argue that "privileged criteria or 'special pleading' on the grounds of national origin are invalid" (138).

While the effect of this document was "to reinforce the thrust of Davey's essay" because it rejected "the popular sociology of Frye and others" and because it "stressed the importance of *formal* comparative contexts" (Cameron, "Theory" 117), the manifesto, as a discursive critical act, is also like Davey's because it subverts publicity and simultaneously upholds it. The authors may want to reject Frye's "popular sociology," but they still believe in the autonomous world of literature described by Frye. For Cameron and Dixon, the chief problem is that "Canadian criticism generally fails in its primary task, to mediate between writer and reader" (137) — a failure of publicity if I ever saw one. Cameron and Dixon reject arguments grounded in national origin, but still suggest that "the aim" of "the ideal of education in any society" is "to preserve continuity and community by transmitting from one generation to the next essential 'lore of the culture' " (143). It is the failure "to agree upon what is essential" that has "fragmented" the "house of learning" and made it impossible for students ("the young") to know the "essential lore" that can only, presumably, be taught by responsible teachers and critics (the old?). Such essential(ist) teaching is valuable, the authors maintain, because it provides students with "insights," through literature, "which not only validate their immediate experience as Canadians but also situate that experience within the tradition of their common birthright" (143). By encouraging students "to explore the complex relationships between art and experience" it may be possible for teaching and criticism to contribute to the formation of "an informed citizenry" (143).

This certainly doesn't sound like a revolutionary manifesto. In fact, the rhetoric of publicity it employs begins to sound more and more like an apology for the privacy it endorses. The authors are clearly struggling to define the value of "Canadian" in criticism and are trying to position themselves both for and against notions of "tradition," "birthright," "informed citizenry," "continuity," "community," and "essential lore." While they struggle with their vision of public and private responsibility, Cameron and Dixon also provide a warning: the drive toward privacy results in "compartmentalization and isolation" (143); " 'Canadian literature,' as an academic subject, is a recent creature of this Balkanizing spirit" (143).

Because they are reluctant to part with some of the totalizing claims offered by the thematic critics, I do not see Cameron and Dixon or Davey as offering a clear alternative. What they provide is the conflicted alternative of privacy/publicity so characteristic of Canadian critical discourse in its early postindustrial phase.

A prime example of this discourse emerged at the infamous Calgary Conference on the Canadian Novel, held in 1978. In many ways, the conference exhibited extreme features of privatization, even though it was billed as a public affair. The topics of discussion were all academic. Many papers demonstrated the participants' profound uneasiness with the very idea of a national canon — the same idea that would have struck earlier critics as an ideal. "Canadian literature experts" determined the "selection criteria and specific titles to be considered as the most significant of Canadian novels." The aim was "to recapitulate and discuss the 'state-of-the-art' or the direction of literary scholarship to date" (Steele 157).

The public was invited, but not to speak. This silencing of the public demonstrated the extent to which the institution of Canadian literature had erected its walls. In his conference paper, Laurie Ricou addressed this issue when he expressed concern that "we are in some danger in this country . . . in assuming that there is one right way for criticism, of declaring an orthodoxy from which no variation is allowed" (Panel comment 98).

Very few of the participants seemed to notice the extent to which this orthodoxy had become entrenched. Robert Kroetsch did. In the middle of a meditation on canonicity, Kroetsch commented on his own two-sided sense of responsibility, on "the tension between idiosyncrasy and the communal good, between individual pleasure and communal concern," which "is always there" ("Contemporary Standards" 12). (It is not surprising that Kroetsch felt split; like most Canadian writer-critics, he is reluctant to cut his link with the nonacademic world.) But most of the papers delivered (including Kroetsch's) were in some way devoted to theorizing the discourse of Canadian criticism and to repudiating the claims of the thematic critics who had done so much to negotiate the treacherous waters between the private and public spheres.

The value of the thematic critics as mediators went unnoticed at the end of the 1970s, mainly because no one needed to negotiate. Negotiate what? The institution seemed secure. Language-based theories and the advent of deconstruction made fragmentation and antimimetic values seem safe (because the institution was secure) and desirable (because the institution needed to reproduce itself). The backlash against the canon-making activities at Calgary was the expression of a community that felt protected enough to challenge the very texts on which its existence was based.

At this time, only two critics tried (unsuccessfully) to challenge the industry and its self-consciousness. Russell Brown published "Critic, Culture, Text: Beyond Thematics" (1978) — a provocative reading of current criticism which was radical in suggesting that the thematic critics were culturally and antithetically valuable. Brown's essay has consistently been misread as an attack on thematic criticism — a sign of the industry's growing desire to silence unorthodox forms of dissent. John Fraser wrote "The Production of Canadian Literature" (1978), an insightful essay that has been almost totally overlooked, perhaps because it offers a Marxist analysis that puts the achievements of industrialization in doubt. Fraser examines how the construction of an audience in the mid-1960s and early 1970s was a function of the multinational and state desire "to boost Canadian literary production for spurious national ends" (153). This ambition failed because Canadian writers had not been effectively sold to the public and because publicity itself had not been effectively sold by literary critics — its professional agents. As a result, "Canadian writers started in the 1970s to stress the themes of privacy and disillusion"; they turned to "spectacle" rather than engagement, performance rather than debate (155). According to Fraser, the problem was that "literature was held to be, in any event, an enclosed, specialized subject" (161). The literary industry had withdrawn from the public. And, as Fraser recognizes, "it is the industry alone that makes possible a relation with the public" (156).

IV

By 1981, John Moss went on record to repudiate thematic criticism because "the conditions of our cultural history that engendered such criticism passed. . . . Its purpose, to redeem the literature from the imperialistic darkness and assert its social worth as the voice and vision of national sovereignty, had been served" ("Bushed" 165). Apparently there was no longer any reason to save us from the "imperialistic darkness"; thematic criticism had done the job. Moss's viewpoint was a classic expression of the relevance of Canadian criticism to cultural sovereignty; it was profoundly *un*-new. Quite novel, however, was Moss's recognition that the job had been done too well. The institution was now so secure that it had actually alienated the public. "The fault," according to Moss,

> lies with the critics of Canadian literature who in cleaving from the mainstream, in devising arbitrary criteria of evaluation, in subverting worth to rhetorical utility, have generated an orthodoxy that bewilders outsiders. Instead of proselytizing for the literature among the literate, as it intends to do, such criticism limits access to it. ("Bushed" 164)

I don't fully understand what form of criticism Moss recommends as an alternative to this orthodoxy, and I'm not sure what "mainstream" he means, but his statements are still interesting because they are among the first to identify the public/private dichotomy openly as an inside-outside phenomenon and as the source of a communicative failure. And, as Moss recognizes, "once an orthodoxy has set in, it is difficult to dispel" (165).

The repudiation of thematic "orthodoxy," which continued through most of the 1980s, occasioned some particularly trenchant attacks. In *Clearing the Ground* (1984), for example, Paul Stuewe argues that thematic criticism is "simplistic," denies "overall literary excellence," and has produced "acclaimed 'masterpieces'" which are in fact "tainted fruit" (5). For Stuewe, the "critical establishment" was "hooked on an understandably addictive but nonetheless debilitating theory" (101). In *A Climate Charged* (also 1984), B.W. Powe similarly objects to the "narrow nationalism of the thematic critics" (83), who have entrenched a way of speaking about Canadian literature that denies the true exchange of views, honest criticism, and debate.

If the thematic critics were attacked for being too narrow, simplistic, and reductive, they were also taken to task for being too specialized. Their criticism, some felt, was far too esoteric for the common reader to understand. Powe argues that the most damaging effect of the industrialization of Canadian literature is that "the University becomes the final audience for the work of art. . . . The artist as teacher becomes an academic-critic, and the critic reverently reads other academic-critics, and begins to study criticism itself as if *it* were the primary object of attention" (68). In such a scholastic atmosphere, Powe asserts, art "becomes an object of contemplation and structural mechanics, a battleground for Theory and private games. Without a public, literature echoes in a void" (69). In other words, "the problem is with polarization and specialization, with the widening gap between the University's universe and the public one" (70). (It is interesting to note that neither Powe nor Stuewe are academic critics; apparently they conceive of themselves as writing to an audience outside the academy. But their work has only been discussed within the academy. This says much about the extent to which the audience for literary criticism has become a strictly professional one. For Powe and Stuewe, there is no public left.)

No one paid much attention to the alarms sounded by Moss, Powe, and Stuewe; no one offered a way back to publicity; and only a few critics maintained it was worth seeking connections between the private and the public spheres. In "The Function of Canadian Criticism at the Present Time" (1984), W.J. Keith, who had earlier rejected thematic criticism (see Keith's "Thematic Approach"), argued that "we still have a mission: to have our literature recognized as an essential reflection of our national life" (14). T.D. MacLulich observed that "if literature is removed from its social context, then hybrid literary-political categories such as Canadian literature become meaningless." He warned that "if we discard thematic criticism entirely, we may wake up one morning to discover that we need to reinvent it in order to justify staying in business" ("Thematic Criticism" 33).

Stuewe offered a contradictory view. He predicted that if thematic criticism is permitted to advance it will produce

> a series of ever more depressing reading experiences culminating in an aversion to Canadian books as a whole. If left unchecked, this state of affairs can only lead to a complete breakdown in communication among writers, critics and readers, and produce a severely fragmented literary culture. (5–6)

Stuewe assumes that there is such a thing as an *un*fragmented literary culture; he wants the dream of homogeneous cultural unity, and he believes that criticism can deliver it.

Today, of course, our understanding of the material conditions affecting cultural formations, our belief in the constructedness of literary communities, our valorization of postmodern self-questioning and fragmentation, and our immersion in a pluralist society all make it difficult for us to accept this dream. One can no longer invoke metaphors of community and family to describe Canadian commonalty. A Canadian family — perhaps the family itself — is too public for the discourse of privacy. This may explain why the editor of the proceedings of a 1987 conference called Family Fictions in Canadian Literature found it necessary to mention that the organizers' colleagues "wondered about our wisdom, and we ourselves felt obliged to include W.J. Keith's open letter, 'To Hell with the Family!' in the companion volume to this book" (Hinchcliffe 5).

What is striking about these examples of Canadian critical discourse is their concern with declining publicity. Here it is important to reflect again on how the notion of publicity had been transformed. Prior to the industrialization of Canadian literature, publicity was connected with generally accepted ideas about the common good and social intercourse. Canadian literature was seen as a means of achieving these ends. Readers, writers, and critics shared a common language, and this common language allowed them to participate in public debate, even if publicity was characterized by tension, class consciousness, and polemics. The industrialization of Canadian literature compelled critics to find new ways of speaking in the institution that would promote them through the ranks. But because the public role of the Canadian critic was so entrenched, the demands posed by privatized discourse also compelled critics to speak in new ways that expressed the tension between public and private value. This is why thematic criticism was criticized both for being too nationalist (it was very close to the pre-industrialized public sphere) and for being too specialized (it was the first curricular discourse to represent the private sphere).

One reading of the development of critical discourse during the 1980s is that it became increasingly private, decentred, and theoretically based, to the exclusion of the public. In other words, the predictions uttered by such critics as Powe, Stuewe, Moss, Keith, and MacLulich did come to pass. During the late 1980s nationalism became a dirty word in critical discourse. The introduction of theory excluded the public. Political factions within the industry were staking out their territory, waving ideological flags, and certainly making no concessions to others who did not share their points of view, even though most of the politics focused on the need to respect difference, to deconstruct hierarchies, and to construct a more plural and all-inclusive model of discursive activity.

So this private discourse, which now had merely token public claims, came to be heard by a more and more fragmented community that was divorced from public life. Publicity itself had been internalized, hijacked by the private realm. No wonder the private realm is, within itself, conflicted, contradicted, and paradoxically public. It is not a matter of saying that the private realm rejects publicity, common language, community, nation, democratic exchange. The private realm co-opts these forces and, by doing so, destabilizes itself. The private realm is wedded to the publicity it abhors. It needs publicity as alter ego; it demands that publicity be represented in order to say that its representation is false. Privacy thrives on publicity brought inside. Privacy affirms publicity in order to attack it. Privacy desires publicity. And the object of desire is always the product of repressed lust.

From this perspective it becomes possible to understand that post-industrial Canadian critical discourse effects a privacy that is false. It is false because every repudiation of publicity accepts publicity as a force still potent enough to be rejected. If we look back through the development of postindustrial discourse, we see that those who speak for Canadian literature always speak two ways: the thematic critics address a communal "we," when their audience is really a more restricted academic milieu; Frank Davey wants to write books for his colleagues, but he also allows his paraphrastic guidebook to appear in a series happily entitled Our Nature–Our Voices; Cameron and Dixon want no " 'special pleading' on the grounds of national origin" (138), but wish "to preserve continuity and community" (143); Stuewe and Powe want Canadian academic criticism to respond to higher standards, but they want the same criticism to be accessible to the common reader; and so on. In case after case, the discourse of Canadian criticism is a doubled discourse, haunted by public and private needs.

If I am correct in asserting that there is no exclusively private discourse in Canadian criticism, then I must also assert that there is no evidence to suggest that theory has taken over. Since I align the specialized language of theory with the private realm, evidence of such a takeover would be provided by critical discourse that rejected or ignored publicity or its tropes. Very few examples of such discourse can be found, precisely because Canadian critics have never been able to escape their debt to publicity; after all, the debt is only a generation old. But as the discourse becomes more theoretical (as it celebrates its privacy), its inescapable recognition of publicity becomes covert or antagonistic; publicity is the demon that must be subdued, a haunting force to be exorcized, or addressed in a whisper.

A striking expression of the alignment between privacy and literary theory occurred at the Future Indicative Conference on Literary Theory and Canadian Literature, held at the University of Ottawa in 1986. Compare F.R. Scott's comments on the public aims of the writers gathered at Queen's University in 1955 and John Moss's account of the type of people present, or imagined to be present, at the Ottawa conference:

> As Bakhtin leaps from the sidelines to centre stage, as Derrida clambers out of the orchestra pit and into the prompter's box, and Lacan swings from the flies, as Foucault, Lévi-Strauss, Saussure, Barthes, and a throng of others rhubarb their way through the text, one recognizes just how connected all the disparate elements of this critical extravaganza really are. (2)

This "extravaganza" seems to have baffled and tired Moss, who sees the critics around him as circus performers, hawkers, and con artists. "After an exhaustive day of discourse on critical theory," Moss confesses, "it was exhilarating, the following morning, to return to literature itself" (2) — a comment that reveals Moss's own dis-ease with the private discourse of theory and shows him struggling to convert it into something public, which he equates with Literature. He went on to edit the conference proceedings for publication. Moss warns the reader that "what you encounter may at times seem esoteric" or "baffling," because it is "the arcane pleasure of a few genuine and brilliant eccentrics" (3), but he is determined to offer a particular solution to this problem: if you look closely enough, eventually you will be able to see that this arcane and esoteric pleasure is really a very communal thing. After all, "these critics, in common, think in public." Really? For Moss, they are "mavericks" who invite us to share "the marvellous reward of comprehension sometimes at the very limits of under-standing" (3). Good public fare.

In one way or another, all of Moss's comments focus on the closeted nature of this critical discourse: "If *Future Indicative* accomplishes noth-ing else, it has brought enough of the best of these people together and into the open" (3). But how public was this coming out? In his con-versation with Robert Kroetsch that opened the conference, George Bowering complained that "there is no audience, but there is the text; one is always alone except for the text" (Bowering 6). Bowering succinctly described the private world he had entered when he observed that "the continuousness of the attacks on unity is the only continuous-ness that I can think of" (6), meaning, of course, that Bowering could not think back any further than, say, 1974. The privatization of his memory had left him with the ability to recall only twelve short years.

Although Bowering was probably speaking about *textual* unity, his statement applies equally to a conception of the country: from the privatized perspective of the Future Indicative Conference, the so-called unity of the nation was under continuous attack. So was the unity of the canon. This attack puzzled some members of the audience at the conference. One said: "We're at the point in our literature where we ought to be struggling to form a canon, and yet we're rifling the canon" (Bowering 19). Another expressed the nostalgic pedagogical desire to "get through to that higher concept of the tradition of the writing community" (24).

But even the status of this "community" had been downgraded at the conference in favour of the self-conscious presence of the presenters themselves. Kroetsch identified what he saw as "a failure, a failure of the social contract in our literary community. The audience has failed in its obligation to read seriously, to take the act of thinking seriously" (Bowering 10). Kroetsch thus endorses the increasingly elitist private view that the reading public ("audience," "community") is uncommit-ted, unserious, ill-read. I don't think he is complaining about people who value popular culture over literature; I think he is referring to an audience that *does* value literature, and, in his estimation, this audience is still not serious enough. His comments suggest that he is an author in search of a serious audience. Like most writer-critics in Canada (I think of people like Bowering, Davey, Scobie, or Van Herk), his dis-course has been co-opted by privacy to the extent that he can no longer be understood by nonspecialists. The poet's nonacademic audience is gone. As Davey says in *Post-National Arguments*, Canadian poetry is "read mainly by university-educated readers" (7), as is Canadian literary criticism, if it is read at all. (Yet, even today, the public will still buy the preindustrial criticism of writer-critics such as Hugh MacLennan or Robertson Davies, who can make important points in language that any educated and intelligent person can understand.)

Ironically, Kroetsch's comments at the Future Indicative Conference suggest that it is the Canadian literary institution that has failed to school students properly in the art of "serious" reading. They also suggest that one cannot read for fun (too unserious), or to learn more about the world (too mimetic), or to be involved in the lives of fictional characters (too participatory/communal). Reading "seriously" means reading theoretically, an activity with which the majority of educated university students have trouble. Most students and general readers persist in reading representationally; they want to find in literature a reflection of their world. This is not reading seriously. Reading seriously means correcting the mimetic assumptions that guide most students. It means saying to them: there is really no coherent world out there for fiction to grasp; there is no community worth idealizing; there is really nothing for you to hold on to, but you should continue to study literature and to read Canadian writing because it is Canadian. We never find out why, because the question can no longer be asked. Too essential.

So what models are available to the student or the general reader who engages in such study? Because, as Barbara Godard noted in her conference paper, "research is becoming theoretical rather than practical, turning upon its own presuppositions, upon the structure of the model itself" ("Structuralism/Post-Structuralism" 27), there is no sense that the model can provide a means of identifying the public elements of community that we share.

In the paper he presented at the conference, Barry Cameron revealed the extent to which the study of Canadian literature had become the articulation of a close-knit club: "Most of us are marginalized in our departments because of our interest in theory, and we were all feeling pretty good about this opportunity to speak openly, lovingly, about theory, satiating ourselves without embarrassment in the marvellous jargon of the new criticism" ("Lacan" 150). Yuck. Those who have not mastered this "marvellous jargon" must seek a different kind of satiation. But what are we to make of a critic who revises his previously published work by deliberately *introducing* such jargon, as is the case with Cameron (see Darling)? Clearly the author who revises in this way has also revised his notion of audience, or wishes to address an imaginary audience that he hopes to sate.

If this imaginary audience is also postmodern, as it was often conceived to be by the conferees, then it can be said that, of all the presenters, only Heather Murray (in a very perceptive paper that remembered history) was prepared to criticize "the somewhat utopian assumption that broken is better, that the fragmented text is somehow more subversive than its coherent counterpart" ("Reading" 81). Murray's radical conclusion is that "analysis of the discursive organization of culture and cultural study" is needed, and it requires "collective and interactive endeavour" (81). For her, Dennis Lee's emphasis on the interaction of "civil space" and voice is still crucial to this collective enterprise. And the collective enterprise is still crucial to the realization of political action, one aspect of which would be what Murray imagines as a Foucauldian "literature of resistance" (81).

Such resistance is clearly evident within the private realm, which has become internally politicized. Yet the question remains: How effective are these politics in the public sphere? If we say there is no need for specialists in Canadian literature to interact with the public, the question is moot; we live only in the club. But if we say there is a public politics of Canadian literature, we have to figure how to get back outside. In the end, the subversion of publicity is a subversion of political power. It is, of course, deeply paradoxical that the discourse of Canadian criticism — traditionally rooted in the publicity attached to preserving a communal ideal — should, in such a short time, destroy that ideal. The paradox extends further when we realize that the repudiation of publicity is destructive of privacy itself, for how long can the members of an institution survive when their discursive circle keeps narrowing, becoming more and more private, and cut off from the very nation under whose rubric those practitioners of privacy speak?

By the end of the 1980s, the political value of being inside or outside started to appear in criticism as a subject worthy of consideration in its own right. In part this was a predictable response to Marxist and postcolonial theories of discourse and institutional analysis that had finally made their way to Canada, but it was also a much more direct response to the incredible self-consciousness that had developed within the industry of Canadian literature. We had reached a closeted point of intimacy. We knew ourselves inside out.

Frank Davey's *Reading Canadian Reading* (1988) is the best example of how this late-1980s self-consciousness gets aligned with a political agenda that is still very much the expression of the private sphere. Davey's book opens with a reflection on the Future Indicative Conference. Davey invokes the same image of clubbiness identified by Cameron. He speaks of the conference participants "as a group seemingly unaware that they were a decided minority in Canadian literary studies, a minority whom most publishers of literary commentary in Canada, whether newspapers, review journals, or university presses, are content to overlook or placate by token inclusion" (3). (Strange, how such marginalized professors still seem to have lots of power, get invited to lecture in foreign countries, get big research grants, and publish all over the place.) The group has a postconference lunch. (Davey wants us to know that they *eat* together, that he enjoys their "company and wit" [3].) They talk about Canadian theoretical texts. They talk about the "narrow field of recurrent reference" in the conference papers (2), especially Davey's "Surviving the Paraphrase." Still, Davey is not happy — the papers weren't political enough; to him this means they were not "theoretically self-aware" (17).

Nonspecialists or students have no place at this kind of self-congratulatory table, at least not in Davey's view. After all, too much criticism has been influenced by its "dependency on the needs of secondary and post-secondary education: most critical books have been intended, at least by their publishers, as readings for college and secondary-school students and teachers. The chief assumption of these books is that criticism is an act of mediation" (13–14). But what kind of totalitarian criticism would nonmediation produce? And to whom would it speak? Not to the public. For Davey, the public is oppressive, as is the government, which both serves and constitutes publicity. As Davey says, "educational literary criticism in Canada" (read "publicly aware criticism") "took place within the larger context of the expansion of Canadian literature and Canadian art as a deliberate ideologically-grounded public policy of the Canadian federal government" (15). It follows, then, that to escape such ideological indoctrination, one must repudiate public policy. But this argument cannot hold, for, as Davey recognizes, we never escape our ideological grounding, be it national or institutional. The challenge, then, is not to transcend or deconstruct the monolith — which is impossible as long as we operate under the assumption that there are Canadian literatures or a Canadian nation — but to find a mode of political activity that is publicly viable.

Although Davey understands, perhaps better than any other Canadian critic, the market forces that account for inclusion and exclusion, and although he clearly wants to effect a political shift, he is reluctant to admit that institutional, postindustrial critical discourse in Canada has been divorced from the public because the public does not understand it and therefore will not buy it. Why should the public invest in the "theories of 'interest' or 'conflict' " that mobilize literary critics (3) when those critics have failed to explain to the public how those theories are relevant to people beyond the institution's walls? Just think of the contrast between Davey's stance and the position adopted by Clara Thomas, one of the first professors of Canadian literature. She went out and spoke about Canadian literature to high-school students and teachers, women's clubs, and golden-agers. She wasn't wary of being too popular in her approach. She insisted on reaching the public. Very few people do this any more.

Davey complains that popular newspapers in Canada are theoretically naïve, that they don't recognize the repressed political stakes involved in their enterprise, that too much time has been invested in making Canadian literature accessible to high-school students, and, further, that to encourage such accessibility is somehow to be critically irresponsible, as if the critic's last task were to educate nonspecialists and students. This form of education creates dangerous "illusions of harmony" that conceal repressed political stakes (17).

In making these charges, Davey neglects to consider the elitist assumptions behind his charges that some people — including literary critics, journalists, high-school teachers, and even professors — may wish to reach a larger audience by appealing to wider, sometimes even populist, needs. Yet for Davey, the assumption is that

> criticism normally addresses itself to the student or general reader rather than to the writer or literary critic . . . [This] invites into the ideological configuration the Canadian education system's bourgeois assumption that literary study should be pleasant, healthy, stimulating, but not distressing. (37–38)

To counter this bourgeois assumption, Davey recommends that we see criticism as "a dialogue among equals," so long as the equals are "the writer or literary critic" (37), a recommendation that reinscribes precisely the bourgeois ideology it seeks to counter.

In *Reading Canadian Reading* — a self-reflexive, ironic title that points inward and outward at once — we reach the point of private discourse at which public needs are seen as secondary, and, often, as the object of contempt. However, as Davey's title makes visibly clear, the Canadian part of his reading — sandwiched as it is between his interpretive acts — is still central, substantive, the filling between the bread. It is disingenuous for Davey to pretend that the Canadian part of the title is not absolutely central to the critical project at hand. The politics of "Reading Reading" might be happy to stay self-absorbed, to remain inside. But any author who is reading *Canadian* reading wants his criticism to be intimately connected to the country whose coherence he repeatedly denies.

V

Most recent Canadian criticism seems to have reached a point of exhaustion — or exhaustion has become a central critical metaphor. When I set out to write "The Canonization of Canadian Literature," my original title was "The Death of Canadian Literature." Of course the literature itself is not dead; excellent writing is published in Canada all the time. My mistake was to confuse the literature with its criticism, a sign of the degree to which I had been engulfed by the privatization I helped to promote.

My quarrel was actually with the discourse I had come to inhabit, and it was this discourse that struck me as dead. Closure was everywhere. *Essays on Canadian Writing* and ECW PRESS contributed to this closure. Bibliographies had been completed, literary histories produced, guidebooks published, curricula defined, major and minor figures delineated. The study of Canadian literature seemed to be wrapped up. The profession seemed so tired. When public critics such as John Metcalf tried to spice things up by challenging academic versions of Canadian literary history — as he did in *What Is a Canadian Literature?* (1988) — no one paid the slightest attention to his many convincing arguments. He was bypassed by the club. But even inside, there were no good fights, no debates (by which I mean an exchange of differing ideas as opposed to an attack on someone's ideas), no burning issues that seemed to capture the group's attention.[15]

What was this group? My nostalgic recollection is that when I began to study Canadian literature in the mid-1970s, there was a profound sense of excitement in the air. A new field lay before us. I believed there was an *us*, that we had common concerns, that we were in the process of discovering a literature together. We could make it whatever we wanted. And because we were a small group, we had the opportunity to exchange views in ways that were denied, say, to our American counterparts. Besides, they were dealing with a relatively secured canon. We were the ones with choices to make; the possibilities gave us power.

We took this power and entrenched it. Hierarchies appeared. The subject became more and more academic. Some energy got lost. We pushed things further. To me, a canon appeared. The very idea that there could be a Canadian canon marked a solidification. If we all agreed, what would we wish to speak of, anyway? I experienced this canon as loss. Paradoxically, this canon, which seemed to be the product of consensus, left me feeling alone. The sense of community was gone. There was no longer a viable *we*.

Maybe I was just getting older. But I wanted to write against this stagnation, wanted to find something we could argue about. My essay did inspire some controversy, but the comments it provoked served to heighten the sense of isolation I was trying to battle. My critics seemed to agree that I was so entrenched in the institution — so privatized, in my terms — that any form of canonical critique was ultimately blinkered and self-serving. If the same comment could be made about most of those who spoke from a postindustrialized Canadian critical perspective, it meant that we had all become isolated and powerless. Was agency gone? And if it was, how could I reclaim it?

The question led me to test the idealist assumption that canons facilitate the creation of grammars of dissent. In "A Country without a Canon?" I argued that "without canons, there is no alterity. From this observation it follows that weak canons, or noncanons, can do very little to promote contestation or social change" (9). Here I struggle with my own need to resolve the contradiction between canonical value (a privatized affair) and social value (a very public affair). But the very idea of social value, in this context, is a sham. After all, my audience comprises a few people — specialists with an academic interest in what is being written about Canadian literature. As a publisher I have been able to interact in the public sphere, but as a critic I am still embracing privacy. There is work to be done.

One critic who is working to bridge the gap between privacy and publicity is the *new* Frank Davey, whose recent books demonstrate a profound interest in repoliticizing the discussion of Canadian literature and culture. In *Post-National Arguments: The Politics of the Anglophone-Canadian Novel since 1967* (1993), Davey presents a "post-centennial study" (6) that questions Canada as "a monolithic and idealized construct" (13). He argues that in Canada, "readers, critics, and often writers have been diverted from awareness of the political dimensions of literature" by "two ideologies": "the aesthetic/humanist and the national" (15). Davey wants to counter these ideologies by providing a political reading that considers "the social and conflictual processes that produce culture" (17).

It is precisely because they have denied these conflictual processes that English-Canadian literary works (and criticism) have been prevented "from participating as fully as they might in national argument" (18). Davey thus seeks to introduce a new thematics — a contemporary version of an earlier publicity that saw contestation as an effective means of foregrounding national and literary concerns. I can't engage with all of Davey's observations, and I still find him addressing an academic milieu. But whether we agree with all of Davey's interpretations — or with his public stance — is secondary to the current importance of his strategic attempt to read Canada and its narratives as a contradicted drama that is active and ongoing. In *Reading "Kim" Right* (1993) he is even more concerned with the politics of reading on a national scale. Here he is able to employ his abilities as a textual critic to deconstruct Kim Campbell as sign — a strong example of how criticism can enter the public sphere. While it is true that not everyone will understand that Kim Campbell is really Anne of Green Gables, it is clear that Davey is trying to broaden his audience by seeking more public — and political — frames of reference. He is now writing columns on politics for the *Globe and Mail.*

* * *

Although Davey's recent interest in the politics of Canadian criticism may signal a shift in theoretical concerns, very few professionals have followed his lead. Feminist critical intervention has produced a number of important studies, but these tend to explore text-based issues at the expense of public involvement. Postcolonial theory is drawing attention to various forms of cultural domination and is encouraging counterdiscursive activity that reinterprets historical and cultural value. As Stephen Slemon points out, this activity is concerned with the problematization of "a mimetic or referential purchase to textuality" that is related to "principles of cultural identity and survival" (5). (Notice that Atwood's term is back.) These principles are crucial to our future. Yet, to date, the focus of postcolonial theory in Canada remains postcolonial *theory*; I have seen no attempts to politicize the discussion outside textuality, with the exception of Dionne Brand's "Who Can Speak for Whom?" (1993) and Gary Boire's "Transparencies," an essay on sexual abuse. It remains difficult to valorize the importance of "real" political or social issues, especially Canadian issues, in the current regime. Postindustrial critical culture in this country is still private and aloof.

Many questions about publicity and politics remain unanswered. Does the Canadian literary critic have any responsibility to work for public political ends? Is it too late to reinscribe publicity as a discourse marked by debate, exchange, and interest in communal purpose and common good? Can we bridge the gap between new theories of language and highly traditional ideas about our social value as critics concerned with specifically Canadian literature? Do we have a responsibility, still, to configure and address something called "the country"? How can we explain our professional scepticism about the nature of this responsibility to nonprofessionals? To what extent does our future as professionals depend on our ability to provide such explanations?

By introducing the idea that all experience is constructed through language, post-thematic theory undermined the assumption that the critic can effectively comment on the relation between literature and whatever is imagined to be a real Canadian ethos. This is why Philip Marchand, in his review of *Post-National Arguments*, concludes that Davey has "undercut any effective political agenda . . . by insisting on 'the textuality of all experience.' " In other words, Davey relies on language to skirt "the real"; and, as Marchand puts it, "if reality is simply competing and overlapping discourses," it becomes impossible to address "the fiction we call 'Canada' " or to decide whether it is "worth preserving" (D3).

Marchand's observation is eminently contemporary. It grants the constructedness of the nation through language, but insists that this fiction must still be addressed and evaluated. This evaluation of the imagined nation is political because it is critical. But in this context, political agency is also a means of testing other modes of address, other narratives that are intentionally constructing the nation. The conflicting models produced by such testing form the country as collage — the end-product of every discursive representation of Canada as an imagined nation. The collage is strategically communal. Or, if it isn't, at least it provides a means of creating a discursive publicity that respects nonprofessional modes of address.

Somehow, we have to invent a new publicity. The motivating force behind such an invention may be cynical: if specialists in Canadian literature do not find a means of embracing publicity — if they do not explicitly address the national fictions behind their profession — there is no guarantee that this political constituency within the profession will be renewed. On this level, it is a matter of survival, of jobs.

On another level, it is a matter of preserving the country itself. There are compelling and less cynically self-interested reasons for inventing a new publicity. To talk and write about Canadian literature — beyond exclusively esoteric theoretical discourse — is to insist on its continuing value, however resituated this value might be. Canada is worth talking about. The more we talk, the more we form the subject of our speech. But the formulation and reformulation of the country — political acts — cannot be effective when they are contained solely within the private sphere. The critic needs to perform outside, too. In Edward Said's terms, the critic must stage his or her relation to the world by developing a critical consciousness that stands "between culture and system." "To stand between culture and system . . . is therefore to stand *close to* . . . a concrete reality about which political, moral, and social judgements have to be made and, if not only made, then exposed and demystified" (*The World* 26).

The first step in this process involves a recognition of social reality — a reality that most contemporary pedagogy teaches students to ignore. As a result, Jim Merod observes:

> The social and political context of interpretive activity, a complex area deserving scrutiny, thereby remains separate from the texts and methods of reading that constitute criticism proper. This division perpetually reasserts itself as if critical writing and critical teaching were caught between an authorized "inside," a body of professional interpretive practices, and an unauthorized "outside" that is the world of institutions, of human uses. (2)

For Merod,

> the work of criticism is unavoidably interrelated with a social and political context that cannot be siphoned off as so much bilge and that the work of making criticism a viable activity for students requires the teacher to show how that relationship works. It requires us to show that texts are strategies, that they carry values that exert a force in the social world. (11)

The privatization of Canadian literature has devalued this social world and has therefore undermined the relationship between the criticism we write and the politics that operate outside the university. Today we know — we are taught — that there is no monolithic group of texts that embody national experience and that there is no unproblematized vision of Canadian life. This means, of course, that many of the myths associated with the idea of national experience must also die: the myth that there ever was a coherent canon of Canadian literature; that Canadian literature transparently depicts some kind of social reality; that the study of literature might unite diverse people in their desire to understand more about their country; that Canadian literature is "the bond of national unity" (Dewart ix).

The death of these myths has a price. The removal of critical discourse from the public has discouraged the expression of collectivity. And because all political change is ultimately public, the privatization of

Canadian critical discourse has restricted its ability to encourage real change. This is a dangerous situation, for, as Heather Murray reminds us:

> The current critique of English — for its eurocentrism, its under-representation, its privileging of the "literary" over other linguistic forms — is a critique generated in large part from outside the academy, and it comes to rest on English as a synecdoche for the humanities and even higher education more generally. This is not a new phenomenon: witness the undereducation debates of the '50s and '60s, the Canadian content debates of the '60s and '70s, and the more recent discussions of "cultural literacy." Why us? Why does the debate not focus on history, for example, or fine arts, or sociology? The fact that it *is* us shows that in the public perception, the work we do is viewed as already (and at the least, potentially) distinctive and important. We do things the other disciplines don't. Disciplinary survival may well lie in taking up this challenge — in making that "real" our curricular ideal. ("Delivering the Curriculum" 18)

Without a vision of the real, it becomes difficult for critics to ground their work in the actual cultural space they inhabit. The deliberate critical activity of identifying that space would provide the basis for intellectual solidarity and politically engaged exchange that recognized the relation between pedagogy, knowledge, and public power. As critics, we can modify Canadian society, so long as we address it as something that can be represented — by us. This will of course be impossible if we believe that criticism should move "away from its orientation towards empirical referents, away from hermeneutic or interpretive impulses exclusively, towards a self-reflexive concern about methodology and theory" (Cameron, "Theory" 121).

In different ways, a number of Canadian critics have begun to demand a more direct involvement with the empirical details of public life. Arun Mukherjee complains, by way of quoting Said, that the "mission of the humanities" is "to represent *noninterference* in the affairs of the everyday world" (quoted in Mukherjee 23). For Mukherjee, such noninterference is symptomatic of the "ahistorical realm" in which contemporary teachers of literature "ply their trade" (23). Gary Boire argues that if Canadian criticism is to fulfil a truly "substantive social function" (the phrase is Terry Eagleton's), if it is to survive, "it must begin a truly critical remembering of history, a demystified reappraisal of its own purpose in reading, and writing about, our past writing" ("Canadian" 14).

There are other ways of deliberately intervening in "the affairs of the everyday world." In the session entitled "Explaining Ourselves to the Public" at the 1993 ACCUTE conference in Ottawa, Shirley Neuman argued that academics must begin to address the public and to consider what they can explain to the public. She noted that most of the titles of papers in the ACCUTE program could not be explained to such an audience. She emphasized that the study of English is a profoundly ethical discipline that bears on large social issues. And she provided some useful strategies through which academic professionals could engage in these issues in the public sphere. These strategies include doing community-service work on theatre and library boards; coordinating public reading groups; reviewing in local newspapers; giving lectures in local libraries; becoming more involved with alumni; engaging more directly with popular culture; helping people to learn to read and write; and speaking understandably and unpretentiously. Of course, Neuman recognizes that in the current academic reward structure, which places a premium on published research, such public activities may not lead to promotion and tenure. This is something to change, politically.

In a recent article entitled "Writing the Canadian Flag," which appears in *Alphabet City*, a magazine devoted to politics and popular culture, Len Findlay calls for direct political involvement — in Canadian terms. He argues that

> Professors can make a difference by going beyond canons but also by teaching them in poststructuralist ways; by acting through their various institutional assemblies and associations as effective cohorts of a professional class which too often mistakes timidity for prudence, civility for truth, but which still "represents" one of the best hopes we have for "real" social change; and by participating in far greater numbers in the discussion and definition of public policy. (46)

Findlay's explicit conclusion is implicit in Davey's work:

> Rather than lamenting the persistence of the nation state or attempting to preserve it by rolling the dice or pushing the panic button, we have to make do with it as a problematic but serviceable entity which counters the tendency to see society as simply a random concatenation of social atoms or possessive individuals abandoned to the tender mercies of multi-national corporations. (47)

How do we make this "serviceable entity" work? The question puts a special pressure on critics of Canadian literature whose work is, by definition, aligned with some conception of the nation. As a group of public professionals, we are compelled to stand on guard. The most basic political act is to articulate the conception that informs our work and to share it with students, colleagues, and the public. A fundamental premise behind such activity is that the country is worth imagining. Our job is to find out how and why.

This is one means of preserving the entity we inhabit. But we can do more than preserve. By clarifying the role of Canadian criticism we may find ways of allowing ourselves to *be* critical, not only of Canadian literature but of Canada itself. We can practise criticism that speaks both within and without. This kind of criticism would redress the privatization that has rendered the politics of Canadian criticism all but useless as a public force. It would allow Canadian critics to extend their intellectual agency. It might broaden our understanding of the social effects we can achieve. It would probably make people angry. It might even make things fun.

Part Two

Canon-Making

4

Anthologizing English-Canadian Fiction:
Some Canonical Trends

THERE ARE DIFFERENT KINDS of national literary canons. There is the canon we carry in our heads at any given time — the collection of works we think of as major or central at certain historical moments. Even though we realize that this canon is ephemeral, we often treat it as if it were more permanent than it really is. By idealizing the canon in this way we promote idealization itself. In other words, the imagined canon comforts us, makes us feel grounded, lends solidity to what we know is actually in flux.

The imagined canon feels communal because different people often seem to agree about major and minor classifications, about which writers or works are more important than others. This apparent agreement creates the illusion of consensus and shared value. The imagined canon leads us to believe that we have something in common; it fosters the illusion that there is something valuable we share. We sense that if we destroy this imagined canon we will be alone, confronting our solitudes and our difference. To fictionalize our sense of community, we fictionalize canons.

Most acts of literary evaluation in Canada take place against the backdrop of imagined canons, even if those canons are seen as negative forces that embody exclusionary ideologies. An imagined canon can always be attacked for what it is — a dream, a temporary web of value, a fantasy divorced from history, a narrative hanging tenuously in space and time. From this perspective, any canon will appear to be contingent, variable, the product of real material and institutional forces that are beyond individual or imaginative control. All canons are imagined. All canons are real. The imagined canon may be really real.

Over the past few years I have been thinking about the difference between real and imagined Canadian canons. Sometimes I have assumed that there is a durable canon of Canadian fiction, without having statistical evidence to back up my assumption. This denial of proof — of factual data — demonstrates the extent to which an imagined Canadian canon has centred me, granted the illusion of community, made me feel there was a canon out there that was long-standing, shared.

I wanted to test the dimensions of this imagined canon by engaging in an exercise that built on some form of statistical analysis. Because some of my earlier arguments about canonicity in Canada were based on the belief that there was a recognizable canon of Canadian fiction, I decided to focus my analysis on short fiction published in historical anthologies of English-Canadian literature, mainly because I wanted to see how the canon of fiction was represented in collections of literature that claimed to speak on behalf of the country as a whole.[1] I also focused on short fiction because the database, although large, was manageable in terms of my resources. For the most part, my analysis is devoted to short stories, with the understanding that many anthologists present excerpts from longer works as short stories.

Glen M. Johnson points out that "although 'the compiling of anthologies' gets mentioned as an important factor in canonizing, studies of the actual compilations have been rare" (112). My approach to the compilations I examine is descriptive and analytic; it is primarily a reading and interpretation of the information presented in the table comprising appendix A (see page 142).

Aims and Methods

My specific aims were quite simple: to determine which authors had been most popular among anthologists since the first anthology of Canadian literature including prose was published by Watson and Pierce in 1922; to chart the rise and fall of certain reputations and to see which authors had experienced a resurgence in popularity; to raise questions about the principles of selection accounting for observable trends; to explore the relation between historical forces and canonical activity; and, if possible, to provide some account of the values implicit in the data. My analysis is by no means exhaustive. I simply followed the data in some of many possible directions.

The study is organized around a table that summarizes the short-story contents of 65 anthologies of Canadian literature published between

1922 and 1992 (see appendix A; appendix B [page 149] provides a full list of anthologies consulted, and appendix C [page 152] a chronological list of those anthologies). I also draw on a much larger database (not published here) that lists the specific stories in each anthology, their frequency of appearance over time, the percentage of space devoted to stories by specific authors in each anthology, and the percentage of space devoted to stories by specific authors in all 65 anthologies studied.[2] The numbers and percentages in the table are based on an analysis of the contents of these 65 works.[3] Revised editions of anthologies are counted as new anthologies. In the discussion that follows, fractional figures are rounded to the nearest whole number.

The frequency of anthology representation shown in the table was calculated by dividing the total number of anthologies in which a given author was represented by the total number of anthologies surveyed. It is important to note that the table indicates the number of anthologies an author appeared in in a given decade, and not the number of stories (which in many cases is a larger figure) included by that author. (Although space does not permit its dissemination here, the data collected for this survey also make it possible to calculate the number of short-story inclusions by author as a percentage in relation to the total number of stories contained in all 65 anthologies.[4] In addition, it is now possible to determine which stories by a particular author are most anthologized,[5] and what trends appear in the selection of stories by a particular author over the years.)

I also provide a breakdown by decade. There were 6 anthologies from the 1920s, 4 from the 1930s, 3 from the 1940s, 5 from the 1950s, 12 from the 1960s, 19 from the 1970s, 13 from the 1980s, and 3 from the 1990s. (The study ends at 1992, so it is impossible to reach any firm conclusions about this decade's trends. The information is provided only to indicate possible directions; all interpretations regarding this decade must therefore be considered speculative and potentially misleading.)

To the best of my knowledge, this database includes all anthologies of Canadian literature that represent themselves as being national (as opposed to regional) in orientation, since the aim was to determine what trends could be observed in anthologies of Canadian literature that included whatever they defined as Canadian fiction in English. The database therefore includes nongeneric anthologies devoted to Canadian literature, and anthologies devoted specifically to Canadian short stories. The database excludes special-interest anthologies (e.g., Canadian mystery stories), anthologies focused on specific periods (e.g., anthologies of short fiction in the 1960s), anthologies devoted to particular regions, and gender-based anthologies. The attempt was to be as inclusive as possible within the historical framework.[6]

The table does not include translated selections by Native or French-Canadian writers; nor does it include anthologies of Canadian essays, even though these sometimes include pieces that could fall into the category of prose fiction (for example, excerpts from MacLennan's *Barometer Rising* are often included as historical essays). Novelists (e.g., Davies, Findley, Richler) are, of course, underrepresented in this study, since novels are seldom excerpted in anthologies (often these novelists are represented by essays that, given the focus on fiction, were not counted in the study). Note also that authors known as both prose writers and poets (e.g., Atwood, Ondaatje) are also underrepresented since their prose tends to be subordinated to their poetry in nongeneric anthologies (possibly because of space considerations and permissions costs).

A fuller consideration of the relationship between permissions costs and anthology selection would put the table in another perspective. However, the table nevertheless represents actual transacted value (it records which stories by which authors various anthologists and their publishers were willing to pay for at particular times). In this sense, it provides a reliable picture of which authors anthologists have continued to invest in, even though the cash value of their inclusion might have risen over the years. Critics too often forget that publishing is a business in which selection and dissemination become functions of cost. These costs may have a profound effect on editorial direction, particularly in the case of anthologies, for which many permissions fees may need to be negotiated.

There are many other ways of measuring canonical activity in anthologies. One could, for example, compare short-story publication trends in periodicals, or chart the relation between the availability of anthologies and their frequency of adoption in high-school and university curricula, or examine the relationship between permissions costs and anthology inclusion. One could also consider the identity of anthologists — their institutional affiliations, where they're from, who they know, who they like or dislike, and so on. Yet the focus on the selection made by these anthologists remains an important element in any canonical assessment. Anthologies tend to ratify canonical values. At the same time, they express the market value of certain writers and certain forms of writing. As Johnson says:

> The anthology may be the means by which the canon reaches the broadest segment of the rising educated class. For professionals of literature, current and apprentice, the anthology is an intersection: it

ratifies whatever consensus exists about the canon; it perpetuates that consensus in the act of presenting it and preserves the consensus through assuring that the works are accessible; and it is a forum for changing the consensus through additions, deletions, or changes in format. The dynamics are indeed those of the market. (113)

Anthologies are almost always authorized by institutional needs and values. Canons are, first and foremost, the expression of those needs and values. Anthologies therefore provide an excellent record of canonical activity. They also provide a record of those writers who have been excluded from such activity. Considered historically, and as a group, anthologies chart the rise and fall of certain reputations and show how those reputations have been valued over time.

Anthologies of Canadian literature are usually compiled by academics (and sometimes by nonacademics) who have academic ends in mind, even though the idea of creating pedagogically based anthologies with public appeal is often the challenge. This means that whatever canonical observations are made here are implicitly curricular observations as well. Anthology-makers are inspired by institutional demands; the satisfaction of those demands serves to reinforce institutional authority.

One thing this study reveals is that the blue-chip reputations of several Canadian short-story writers remain intact even at a time when those very authors are seen as dated or when their work seems out of play. There is consensus among anthologists (and presumably among the anthologists' audience) concerning a few figures whose work has been published over the period covered by the survey (1922–92), and in many cases this consensus has endured for decades. There is also consensus about the importance of certain writers on a decade-by-decade basis. Because many figures do lose their place in anthologies over time, it seems reasonable to conclude that those who maintain their position are still seen as valuable, for whatever reasons.

Findings

There is considerable information to be gleaned from the table in appendix A. In what follows I present several examples of how the data can be applied. These short applications are simply the reflection of some findings that were of interest to me when I consulted the figures. Other people who consult the data will undoubtedly find other applications, as I would in a longer study based on this information.

Most Anthologized

The most anthologized Canadian short-fiction writer in English is Morley Callaghan. He is represented in 41 of the 65 anthologies, an inclusion rate of 63 percent. My impression is that Callaghan's short fiction is relatively conservative; certainly it could not be called experimental, though the directness of its language might have seemed somewhat unusual for Canadian fiction published in the 1920s and 1930s. I would have thought that Callaghan had been devalued in the 1980s, displaced by more experimental writers. Yet the table shows him holding his own. His success peaked in the 1940s, when he was represented in 100 percent of the 3 anthologies published in that decade. In the 1970s he was included in 15 of the 19 anthologies published, an inclusion rate of 79 percent. In the 1980s he appeared in 7 of 13 anthologies, an inclusion rate of 54 percent. The decline of 25 percent between the 1970s and 1980s might at first glance seem substantial, but not when it is compared with the shifting inclusion rates of other short-story writers who would seem to have a much more popular (or contemporary) following. For example, Hugh Hood's inclusion rate in the 1970s is identical to Callaghan's. Mordecai Richler matched Callaghan in the 1970s (79 percent inclusion rate), but fell below him in the 1980s (46 percent inclusion rate), a drop of 33 percent over a decade.

A graph representing Callaghan's inclusion rate by decade in Canadian anthologies appears in figure 1. A comparison of his rate and

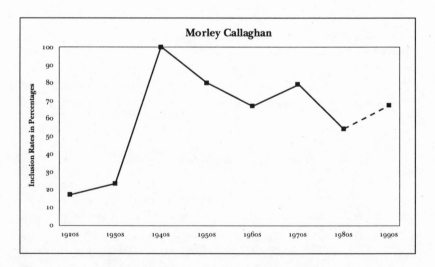

Figure 1

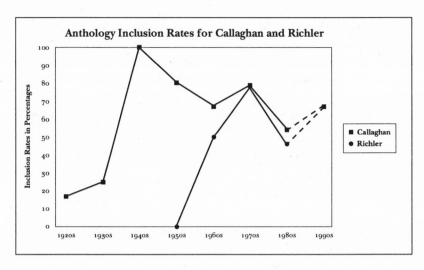

Anthology Inclusion Rates for Callaghan and Richler

Figure 2

Richler's appears in figure 2. The second graph demonstrates that the inclusion rates of these writers has been very close since the 1970s.

The second most anthologized Canadian fiction writer is Stephen Leacock, followed by Sinclair Ross. Leacock had a respectable showing in the 1980s, appearing as he did in 46 percent of the anthologies published that year — down from his 100 percent record in the 1940s, true, but still strong for an author whose work is seldom considered by contemporary literary critics. This suggests that an author can remain curricular without engaging the support of contemporary critics. In fact, Leacock now seems to be increasing in popularity, an interpretation suggested by the fact that his inclusion rate was 46 percent in the 1980s and is 67 percent to this point in the 1990s (see figure 3). Leacock's work did not enter the public domain until 1994, so this is one case in which it cannot be argued that an author has been revived because his work is now available without charge.

The same is true of Charles G.D. Roberts, whose work entered the public domain as recently as 1993. Roberts's strength has been reasonably consistent throughout the period surveyed; he has appeared in 50 percent or more of the anthologies published in every decade but one since the 1920s. In the 1980s his position actually advanced, since his inclusion rate increased by 12 percent over the 1970s figure while authors such as Callaghan, Richler, or Hugh Garner were falling (see figure 4). It is too early to predict how he will fare in the 1990s, although his current inclusion rate is 33 percent.

"Tradition"

There are several ways of explaining the sustained interest in the short fiction of such writers as Callaghan, Leacock, and Roberts. Perhaps they are excellent writers, and their writing is selected decade after decade as examples of literary excellence. Those who do not consider them excellent writers must find another reason to account for their continuing presence in national anthologies of Canadian fiction.

One way of explaining this presence is to see it as a means through which numerous anthologists have asserted the existence of a Canadian literary tradition, which is in turn associated with the valorization of historical development, breadth, lineage, and (implicitly) class-conscious literary pedigree. The argument about tradition is the hegemonic, exclusionary argument that pedigree can be identified, contextualized, transmitted from generation to generation — our jewel box of narrative inheritance.

Anthologists' ability to represent this inheritance through their editorial selections demonstrates the extent to which they have participated in an exercise of tradition-making. To facilitate this exercise, the anthologist needs figures such as Haliburton, Roberts, Leacock, Callaghan, Ross, and other "central" figures from successive decades in order to demonstrate historical development, linkages, influence, continuity. This is especially true in the case of anthologies that claim to represent the historical breadth of Canadian literature. In order to illustrate breadth and development, the anthologist comes to rely on

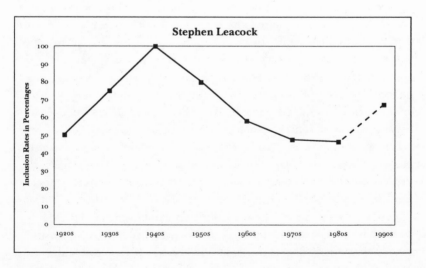

Figure 3

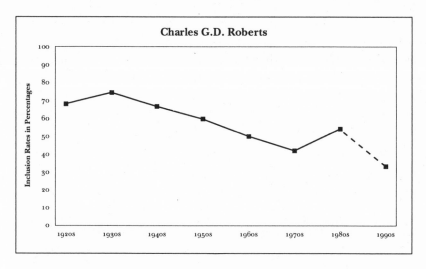

Figure 4

token figures in a manufactured chain. Duncan Campbell Scott (or Roberts) becomes the father of the Canadian short story because of the realistic elements in his fiction — a realism refined by Callaghan, who is usually (mistakenly) seen as the first true practitioner of modernism in the country. And so the story of our patrimony unfolds.

To lend further credibility to the inheritance, other writers come to represent essential generic trajectories within the so-called tradition. The editor is no longer responsible for choosing "the best" or "most representative" short fiction; he or she must present the best or most representative humour, animal stories, modernist fiction, experimental fiction, ethnic writing, writing by women, writing from different regions. The result is, again, that certain figures become the representative figure of certain ways of writing or being, while other practitioners of the genre simply fade away. Roberts is The Animal-Story Writer; Leacock is The Humorist; Moodie is The Nineteenth-Century Woman Writer; Alistair MacLeod is The Atlantic Canadian (even though he hasn't lived in Atlantic Canada since the 1960s). Perhaps Wilson is the Canadian woman writer of the 1950s, Hodgins the magic realist, Bowering the postmodernist, Carr the female artist figure (when such a figure is required), Austin Clarke the token ethnic, and so on. If we ask why a writer such as E.W. Thomson has disappeared from the Canadian anthologists' canon, it may be because, given the demand for broad-based representation and the certification of a tradition, there is simply no longer enough room for two humorists, or animal-story writers, or postmodernists for that matter. The anthologists' canon reduces authors and texts to symbolic functions within a tradition that must display these functions in order to validate the anthologists' pursuit.

These generic choices become more and more restricted as the concept of tradition widens. The more expansive the definition of tradition, the more pointed the representative choices have to be. As a bigger and longer literary history unfolds, and as it becomes increasingly pluralist, the space available for a comprehensive representation of Canadian literature gets smaller, simply because so much more has to be included in every new anthology that claims to do the country justice. When this form of consolidation is applied to the representation of a particular period, the effect is — in anthologies and literary histories — to create the impression that a certain age is demarcated and spoken for by a few so-called key figures, when in fact these writers were sharing the stage with several others in their time. This is one way in which the process of selection distorts history.

More on Genre

If one looks down the list of overall inclusion rates (the extreme right column of the table in appendix A), it is possible to see that Canadian anthologists have not embraced experimental writing, unless one argues that writers such as Callaghan, Leacock, Ross, Munro, or Roberts are experimental. With a few exceptions (Hodgins, Rooke, and Thomas), authors usually considered to be postmodern or experimental actually seem to have fallen out of favour in the 1980s and early 1990s. Dave Godfrey's inclusion rate is down (26 percent inclusion rate in the 1970s, 23 percent in the 1980s, zero in the 1990s); Ray Smith is down (21 percent in the 1970s, 8 percent in the 1980s, zero in the 1990s)[7]; Robert Kroetsch is down (16 percent in the 1970s, 11 percent in the 1980s, zero in the 1990s).

The exclusion of experimental writers from the English-Canadian short-story canon, as reflected in national anthology selections, says something about the value of such writers in a pedagogical setting. Right up to World War II, and especially after it, most Canadian anthologists believed that literature should provide a picture of the nation, and that literature reflected a coherent, understandable, unified world. In part this was a response to modernist and New Critical assumptions about the relation between literature and its cultural milieu. Postwar criticism and pedagogy valued those works that reinforced mimetic assumptions about correspondence, containability, and closure.

These assumptions persist today. The result is what Frank Davey calls "genre subversion" — the suppression or neutralization of particular modes of writing that are not encoded with the appropriate ideology (in this case, the mimetic). Some of the writers who have maintained their status over the years are clearly those whose work can be used, in the classroom, to reinforce New Critical assumptions about unity, coherence, and closure, as well as modernist assumptions about the power of metaphor and symbol (Callaghan, Ross, and Munro come to mind here). Others whose work does not immediately reinforce these values (Leacock, Roberts, or Haliburton) remain important to anthologists because they can function as generic ambassador-representatives, thus enabling the creation of a retrospective canon that provides a sense of temporal continuity — the so-called Canadian tradition. The continuing presence of these writers is the result of a negotiation between anthologists' desire to show the world as a coherent and knowable modern phenomenon, and the desire to claim that it was always knowable (as Canadian) in one form or another.

However, in the negotiated atmosphere that lends Canadian anthologies their particular value, extremes are almost always avoided. Comic writers such as Leacock and Haliburton serve to validate the objects of their derision; after all, comedy about a place and its people says that the place and its people exist and are worth poking fun at. That is one form of negotiation. As Davey suggests in "Genre Subversion in the English-Canadian Short Story," Roberts's writing transmits another strategy of compromise: it mixes modernist, Darwinian assumptions about progress and morality with sentimental plotting and romantic diction. It blends realistic and romantic narrative modes.

Although the demands for historical continuity and generic representativeness do lead to the inclusion of certain key figures in some anthologies, it remains equally true that many of these same figures are excluded by other anthologists precisely because they do not conform to the dominant view of what constitutes valuable fiction. There are many ways in which an author's work can be refused, particularly in terms of genre.

In Canada, as elsewhere, the influence of New Criticism and the advent of literary theory have privileged modernist — and modern — fiction over earlier narrative forms. This may mean that a nineteenth-century writer's work is excluded from the national canon because it is not "modern" enough. The mechanism of exclusion may be quite subtle, as when an anthology presents itself as historical when in fact its historical starting-point privileges more modern works. For example, when modernist anthologists such as Richler, Metcalf, Nowlan, or

Struthers define anthologizable Canadian fiction in terms of the modernist story, they indirectly demote all writers who are not modernists, even though their anthologies may not make overt claims to modernist preferences. Although these anthologists may not comment explicitly on the writings of such authors as Moodie or Haliburton, they are nevertheless pronouncing their work noncanonical and devalued.

Such judgements do more than exclude particular writers or forms of writing: they also serve to redefine the concept of short fiction. Those anthologists who exclude Moodie's sketches from their texts are also saying that these sketches do not constitute short fiction. Those who exclude Norman Duncan's work are suggesting that stories for children are not short fiction, which is to say they are not "serious" enough. Those who shun prose romance are saying that it cannot be considered legitimate short fiction. And so on. The cumulative effect of such exclusionary practices is to create a distorted rendition of the meaning of the short story itself — a rendition that ignores the modern short story's connection to precisely those forms that are most often expunged: folk tales, essays, romances, fairy tales, legends, parables, sketches, and the *fabliau,* to name a few.

Because a number of anthologists who call their collections "modern" insist that this modernity is in fact representative of some kind of Canadian tradition, I have included their work in the survey. Indeed, for many modernist editors, and even for those who might deny the modernist label, there is no contradiction between the assertion of historical coverage and the exclusion of whole chunks of literary history. A good example of this form of exclusion appears in Atwood and Weaver's *The Oxford Book of Canadian Short Stories in English.* In her introduction to the book, Atwood asserts that

> several forms of short prose narrative were written before people got
> around to talking about art, and I like to think the Canadian short story
> owes something to them, as recent poetry certainly does. These were the
> explorers' journals, which were naturally episodic, and the later travel-
> lers' accounts, such as Anna Jamieson's (sic), and descriptions of the
> country, such as Susanna Moodie's and Joseph Howe's, which also
> contain many "character sketches" and short narrative episodes. (xiv)

While Atwood seems to recognize the importance of these writers and the genres they adopted, her anthology excludes them, even though she asserts that "the Jamesian psychological study and the Zolaesque slice of life are only two of the Canadian short story's many forebears" (xiv). In his introduction to the same volume, Weaver does not mention any Canadian short-story writing prior to 1948, even though he says that "*The Oxford Book of Canadian Short Stories in English* has been compiled as a historical anthology — the writing covers more than 100 years" (xix). One hundred years? Here we see an expression of the frequently held belief among Canadian anthologists that Canadian literary history is no more than a century old, or that, if it *is* longer, we don't need to know about it.

Most Anthologized by Decade

The table in appendix A to this chapter demonstrates that despite the consistency shown by such writers as Callaghan, Leacock, Roberts, and Ross, there is a considerable amount of shift in the reputations of writers on a decade-by-decade basis. If we look at the 1980s, for example, it is possible to see that the most anthologized author of that decade was Alice Munro, whose work appeared in 12 out of 13 anthologies, an inclusion rate of 92 percent. Certainly this figure suggests some kind of consensus. But Munro has not been alone in commanding such recognition. In the 1920s Gilbert Parker was perhaps more popular, with an inclusion rate of 100 percent, followed closely by authors such as E.W. Thomson, Norman Duncan, and John Richardson.

The second edition of the *Literary History of Canada* (1976) describes Thomson as "one of the most skilful story-tellers of the Canadian writers of his day" (336), and speaks of how his " 'The Privilege of the Limits' has been a favourite of Canadian anthologists." Yet he warrants only a paragraph in the *Literary History*, perhaps because "he published

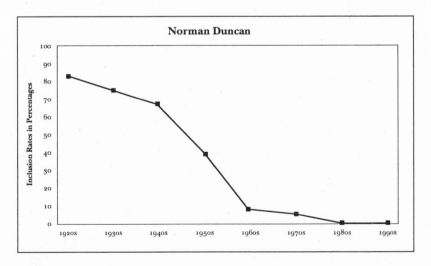

Figure 5

so few stories for adults" (336). This represents another form of genre subversion — the devaluation of literature that is not sufficiently "adult" in its subject matter, literature that is not realistic enough to warrant serious consideration by anthologists and their most important audience — students and teachers in search of mimetic and modernist values. When *The Oxford Companion to Canadian Literature* (1983) speaks glibly about how Thomson's fiction "endures," we know that from the anthologists' perspective the claim is ludicrous, since his rate of inclusion has been falling steadily since the 1950s, and, at this point in the 1990s, it stands at zero. In her commentary in the *Companion*, Lorraine McMullen imagines that what is enduring about Thomson (what constitutes his "best" fiction) are "fine realistic stories of early Canadian life," rather than the "simple boys' stories" or those that are "excessively sentimental" (790). The bias of this judgement is clear: the mimetic is more valuable than the sentimental; what should endure are stories of Canadian life, rather than stories for children.

Duncan's work receives eight lines of commentary in the second edition of the *Literary History of Canada*, even though he appears in 5 of the 6 anthologies published in the 1920s, 3 of the 4 published in the 1930s, and 2 of the 3 published in the 1940s. In fact, Duncan appears in anthologies up to 1973, when he is represented in Edwards's *The Evolution of Canadian Literature in English.* Figure 5 provides a visual illustration of Duncan's popularity (and eventual decline) over the decades.

What accounts for his fall? Like Thomson and Lucy Maud Montgomery, Duncan wrote mainly for children. Did anthologists of the 1980s consider children's literature unworthy of inclusion? Despite their enormous popularity in their time, recent literary histories tend to treat these writers as though they didn't exist, or to express confusion about how to reconcile their earlier popularity with contemporary taste. W.J. Keith's *Canadian Literature in English* (1985) makes no mention of Duncan or Montgomery. W.H. New's *A History of Canadian Literature* (1989) omits Montgomery and devotes nine lines of commentary to Duncan's work. In her survey of the Canadian short story, Michelle Gadpaille dismisses Thomson ("his banal, unfelt language prevents his stories from coming to life"), yet finds that his language is not really so banal or lifeless (he has "an ability to convey human psychology under conditions of great stress" [10]). The conflicting assessments are the product of Gadpaille's inability to reconcile her distaste for Thomson's preferred genre with her recognition that, even within this outmoded genre, Thomson could still convey "human psychology." Presumably this quality is a central ingredient of stories that are worthy because they have "come to life," whatever that means.

Tastes shift. In 1927 Lorne Pierce wrote that Norman Duncan "excelled in short stories for boys" and called his novel, *Doctor Luke of the Labrador* (1904), "his outstanding achievement" (39). Comments such as these make concrete what I had already suspected: contemporary literary histories do little to recreate historical perspectives or to rehistoricize value. Regardless of the genre he adopted, the fact remains that Norman Duncan was the most popular figure in Canadian anthologies of the 1920s, 1930s, and 1940s. There is a reason for this, and even contemporary histories of Canadian literature need to address it. A study could be made of the ways in which certain genres — sentimental romance, writing for children, social and political commentary, adventure stories — were purged from the modernist anthologists' canon to make room for the increasingly predominant genre: teachable, realist fiction that attested to the recordability of time and place.

The 1930s were dominated by Duncan, Leacock, Moodie, Roberts, and Arthur Heming (who wrote popular animal stories); the 1940s by Callaghan and Leacock; the 1950s by Ethel Wilson (who edged out Callaghan in that decade); the 1960s by Callaghan (followed closely by Leacock, Wilson, and Grove); the 1970s by Laurence and Munro; the 1980s were Munro's.

These observations lead me to conclude that there is no direct correlation between the value implicit in anthology recognition and the extent of critical commentary devoted to specific authors recognized by anthologists. Ethel Wilson has an inclusion rate of 100 percent in the 1950s, 58 percent in the 1960s, 63 percent in the 1970s, 46 percent in the 1980s, and 100 percent in the 1990s. These figures suggest that her reputation has been solid for more than forty years. She almost ties Munro in overall percentage of anthology representation, yet her work has generated considerably less critical commentary than Munro's.

Perhaps this comment on Wilson is just an impression that could not be supported by an actual measure of critical output. The table in appendix A makes it clear that such impressions can often be misleading. For example, Alan Young writes that "in the later 1950s and early 1960s [Thomas] Raddall's reputation seems to have evaporated" (223). But this impression is not supported by the table, which shows that Raddall had an inclusion rate of 60 percent in the 1950s and 50 percent in the 1960s. This means that in the 1950s Raddall was included as frequently as Roberts and Moodie, and that in the 1960s he was included as frequently as Duncan Campbell Scott and Brian Moore. Even in the 1970s, the table shows that Raddall was included more frequently than Mavis Gallant or Clark Blaise, and with a frequency equal to that of W.O. Mitchell and Alden Nowlan. It was only in the 1980s that Raddall's reputation declined (rather than "evaporated"), when his inclusion rate dropped from 32 percent in the 1970s to 23 percent, a fall of 9 percent. But even this drop is not the plunge apparent in the case of, say, Mitchell, whose inclusion rate dropped from 32 percent in the 1970s to 8 percent in the 1980s, a fall of 24 percent.

Most Anthologized Stories

The survey of anthologies conducted for this project makes it possible to identify trends in the selection of stories on an author-by-author basis. For example, Callaghan was represented in 41 of the 65 anthologies surveyed, but he was often represented two or even three times within a single anthology. He published a total of 64 stories (or excerpts from novels) in the 65 anthologies covered. His most anthologized story is "Two Fishermen" (from *Now That April's Here*), which appears in 8 of the 64 selections, followed by "A Sick Call," which appears 6 times out of 64.

Margaret Laurence's most anthologized short story is "To Set Our House in Order," which appears 8 times among the 38 stories by Laurence selected for inclusion in anthologies since the 1960s.

In the case of some writers — notably Alice Munro — no clear preference can be discerned among anthologists. In other cases — such as that of Sinclair Ross — there is an overwhelming preference for a single story ("The Lamp at Noon").

What becomes clear in looking at the patterns of short-story selection is that anthologists generally tend to stick with the tried and true. The extent to which they do reveals much about their individual values, and also demonstrates how different anthologists align an author's most representative fiction with a particular period.

In his *Canadian Short Fiction: From Myth to Modern* (1986), W.H. New selected Callaghan's "Ancient Lineage" (first published in 1928) and "A Sick Call" (first published in 1932). "A Sick Call" was originally anthologized in Broadus and Broadus's 1934 collection. The same story was selected by Weaver, Bissell, Klinck and Watters, and Rimanelli and Ruberto in the 1960s, and by Metcalf in the 1970s. Its appearance as recently as 1986 attests to a tradition of selection, but it also raises questions about how anthologists choose to represent one phase of an author's career over another. It would seem that for New, and others, Callaghan remains a late-1920s or an early-1930s author, even though he published short fiction into the 1970s. New says that these two early stories demonstrate "both the moral and the stylistic dimensions of Callaghan's finest short fiction" (154). This statement raises questions. Are Callaghan's earliest short stories his best? Did the quality of his work fall off? Is this what we are meant to understand by the anthologists' selection? Even in 1990, Brown et al. suggest through their selection that Callaghan's best work appeared as early as 1936.

Ethel Wilson was actively writing throughout the 1950s; she published her last short story in 1964. Most anthologists in the 1970s and 1980s choose stories from *Mrs. Golightly* (1961) — the most popular being "The Window." But in some cases the selection is driven by an anthologist's desire to valorize an earlier phase in a writer's career. New selects "We Have to Sit Opposite," a story originally published by Wilson in 1945 (it was also selected by MacNeill and Sorestad in 1973).

Selections such as these attest to more than the worthiness of a writer; they also tend to validate a particular point in a writer's career. At the same time, the selection says something about the anthologizer's individual tastes or longings. One thing remains clear: most anthologists are caught in a time warp. Few are willing to risk betting on a work that has not stood the test of time. For this reason, the introduction of any author's work into the anthologists' canon is often a gamble. As the Canadian canon solidified after World War II, anthologists proved less and less willing to validate the new, preferring instead to select those works that were "safe" because other anthologists had selected them before. A study could be made of the safest Canadian anthologies, and of the riskiest, by determining the extent to which individual anthologists perpetuated, or departed from, their predecessors' canon(s).

Gender

In two recent articles, Carole Gerson has shown that women writers were systematically excluded from the canon — especially between the wars — because the importation of modernist values placed a "critical embargo on 'feminine' concerns" and downgraded writing that focused on social and domestic issues.[8] In addition, Gerson observes that

> simply by virtue of their sex, women have lacked the opportunity to acquire the professional credentials (possessed by professors, clergymen, judges, elected officials, civil administrators, publishers, etc.) that both dignify a nascent national literature and foster the personal connections within the power structure that fortify literary value. ("Canon" 47)

As Gerson notes, this devaluation of the feminine corresponded to the institutionalization of reading choices through which the domain

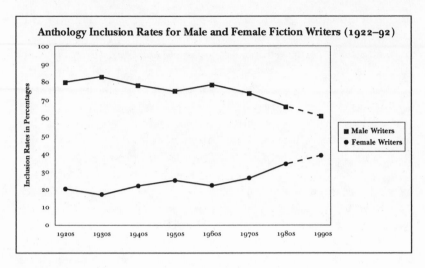

Figure 6

of literary appreciation became the postsecondary classroom — a classroom dominated by "an almost exclusively male professoriate and their influential friends, whose choices inevitably reflected their own class, gender, and racial orientations" (49). Early anthologies of Canadian literature were the products of this professoriate. Many were explicitly designed for use in the classroom, and were organized around mimetic-nationalist themes. Because the fiction women wrote did not always reinforce these themes, and because they were not part of the new institutional power base, they were frequently excluded from these anthologies.

It is tempting to assume that this form of exclusion decreased over the decades; it did. But the table in appendix A demonstrates that no substantial shift occurred until the 1980s, and even the figures for the 1980s show that women were underrepresented in the anthologists' canon in that decade.

The six anthologies published in the 1920s included a total of 92 fiction writers. Of these, 75 (82 percent) were male. In the 1930s, 78 percent of the material in 4 anthologies was by men. In the 1940s, contributions by men accounted for 78 percent of the material. A similar figure (75 percent) applies to the 5 anthologies published during the 1950s. The 12 anthologies released in the 1960s actually demonstrated a return to the 1940s ratio. Even in the 1970s, in 19 anthologies, inclusions by female Canadian fiction writers amounted to only 26 percent, similar to what it had been in the 1950s. By the

1980s things had begun to shift: writing by women accounted for an average of 34 percent of the contributions to 13 anthologies (Weaver was far above the average: 55 percent of the material in the first edition of *Canadian Short Stories* [1952] was by women). In the 3 anthologies published to date in the 1990s, the female inclusion rate has risen further, to an average of 39 percent. Yet it is interesting to note that these 3 anthologies differ considerably in their individual inclusion rates. Brown, Bennett, and Cooke's anthology achieves 46 percent representation by women fiction writers; Ondaatje's anthology maintains an inclusion rate of 37 percent for women, similar to the ratio evident throughout the 1980s. Of the contributors to Struthers's anthology, 38 percent are women. Figure 6 plots the inclusion rates for male and female writers since the 1920s. As the graph indicates, the gap is closing, but it is not yet closed. The figures support Gerson's assertion that "nascent editors of anthologies (and teachers who use them) have been unwittingly conditioned to regard literature as primarily a male preserve" ("Anthologies" 56).

By comparing the male/female inclusion rates in individual anthologies with the average rate for specific decades (or any time segment), it is possible to determine which anthologists were deviating from the trend. For example, there were 19 anthologies containing fiction published during the 1970s; 17 of these were edited by men. Some of the editors exceeded the average inclusion rate (26 percent) for women in this decade. Mary Jane Edwards included 36 percent material by women, Klinck and Watters 33 percent, Pacey 25 percent. Alec Lucas's *Great Canadian Short Stories* (1971) included 16 percent material by women. Lucas looked good next to Kilgallin, who included no stories by women in his *The Canadian Short Story* (1971).

Kilgallin's total exclusion of women is surprising to find in the 1970s, particularly because it had never happened before. Even in the 1960s, no anthology completely excluded women, although one came close. McGechaen and Penner's *Canadian Reflections* (1964) includes 19 authors, only one of whom (Sheila Burnford) is female (inclusion rate of 5 percent). In contrast, Green and Sylvestre's *A Century of Canadian Literature* (1967) contained 33 fiction contributions, 10 of which were by women (inclusion rate of 30 percent). McGechaen and Penner's anomalous position stands out clearly in a graph representing the inclusion rates for women in anthologies published during the 1960s (see figure 7). The anthology also demonstrates that Gerson is correct in her assertion that, for many anthologists, writing by women has no place in the classroom. McGechaen and Penner's anthology is aimed at high-school students; its intent is to give them a greater appreciation of the "entertainment" value of Canadian literature. According to the editors' preface, the primary criterion of selection is teachability: "certain books are eminently teachable and lead to the wealth of discussion so necessary to the life of the subject we call English." This must mean that, for McGechaen and Penner, stories by Canadian women are not entertaining and cannot be taught, even to those students "who relish a genuine involvement with life."

Plunge to Oblivion

By scanning the table in appendix A horizontally, from decade to decade, it is possible to identify those authors who were once popular and frequently anthologized, yet who suddenly fell out of favour with anthologists and never returned again. The most apparent plunge appears in the case of Marjorie Pickthall, whose work appeared in 8 of the 30 anthologies published from the 1920s through the 1960s, a respectable inclusion rate of 27 percent for those five decades. Yet after the 1960s Pickthall falls from grace; in fact, she has made no appearance in anthologies since 1962, when Desmond Pacey included her "The Worker in Sandalwood" in his *A Book of Canadian Stories*. Pacey had included this same story in his 1947 anthology of the same title. Pacey's selection was picked up by Nelson in his *Cavalcade of the North* (1958). In three decades the same story was considered worthy of inclusion in three anthologies, yet it has faded away. What accounts for this decline? The literary histories do little to explain this shift. In his *A History of Canadian Literature*, W.H. New seems to object to Pickthall's

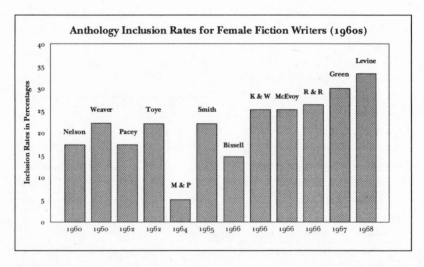

Figure 7

"sentimentalism and religiosity," which I suppose fell out of style, but what about her "feminist commitments" (112)? One would think that these would reawaken interest among anthologists, who have resurrected other early writers with feminist concerns such as Jessie Georgina Sime.

The same question could be asked in relation to authors such as Arthur Heming (who was extremely popular among anthologists in the 1920s and 1930s and was then suddenly excluded from all future anthologies), Will R. Bird (who was popular in the 1950s), or Leslie Gordon Barnard (who was popular in the 1940s and 1950s, but then never heard from again). Let's see what the most recent edition of the *Literary History of Canada* has to say about these figures. In "Nature Writers," Alec Lucas dismisses Heming's two books in three lines because they are "grim and unimaginative" (388). In "Fiction 1920–1940," Desmond Pacey dismisses Bird in one line as an author of "historical romance" (207). Pacey also refers to Barnard as an author of "historical romances" (173). Perhaps this genre fell out of favour with 1980s' anthologists, an indication of the extent to which anthology-makers respond to shifting tastes on the part of readers and critics.

The table allows us to test this assertion by looking at the case of other writers of historical romance. As it turns out, the table confirms the trend: Gilbert Parker is very popular through the 1950s (inclusion rate of 80 percent), then he takes a plunge and disappears by the 1980s; John Richardson is quite popular in the 1920s and 1930s, takes a dip in the 1940s, climbs back to respectable status (16 percent inclusion

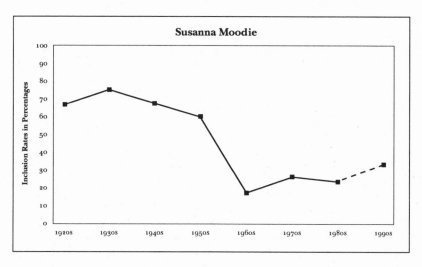

Figure 8

rate) in the 1970s, then he too disappears. These trends might lead one to conclude that the qualities recent critics associate with romance are not those qualities that make a writer worthy of anthologization. So when Desmond Pacey says that Barnard's stories are "sensitive" (173), we realize that this, paradoxically, is not a desirable trait; for Pacey, the "flaw" in Barnard's work is that "the author's detached objectivity [gave] way to sentimentality" (185). Nevertheless, Pacey is able to describe Barnard's early stories as "excellent" (184). Pacey's double-sided stance shows him grappling with the notion that historical romance could still strike him as "excellent," even though the "detached objectivity" that signalled its masculine dimension sometimes gave way to the supposedly feminine impulses that Pacey could not finally endorse.

In contemporary fiction it is David Helwig who has plunged the most in anthologists' esteem. His case is quite startling. He was unknown in the 1960s. In the 1970s anthologists bet heavily on him, including his work in 32 percent of the anthologies published in that decade. But then every anthologist lost interest in him: the following decade, not a single anthology out of thirteen included his work. Other writers who have moved out of anthologists' favour in recent years include Alden Nowlan, Brian Moore, Farley Mowat, W.D. Valgardson (a major drop in inclusion rates), Dave Godfrey, John Glassco, Thomas McCulloch, Ray Smith, Leonard Cohen, and Adele Wiseman.

Meteoric Rise

Just as some authors eventually fall from view, others come into the picture quickly. Their work is hardly known to anthologists when, suddenly, it breaks on the scene. The table in appendix A allows us to track this kind of rapid rise in status. To do this, I look horizontally for patterns of noninclusion followed by sharp, rather than gradual, increases in the inclusion rate.

Mordecai Richler bursts into anthologies in the 1960s, moving from an inclusion rate of zero in the 1950s to 50 percent in the 1960s, when he appeared in 6 of the 12 anthologies published in that decade. Ernest Buckler moves from an inclusion rate of zero in the 1950s to 58 percent the following decade. Clark Blaise also makes a substantial jump, moving from zero in the 1960s to a 26 percent inclusion rate in the 1970s.

Other authors who have experienced a rapid rise in inclusion rates are Margaret Atwood, John Glassco, Dave Godfrey, and David Helwig. Sharp rises such as these can also be tracked in earlier writers. William McConnell was one of the most anthologized authors of the 1940s (67

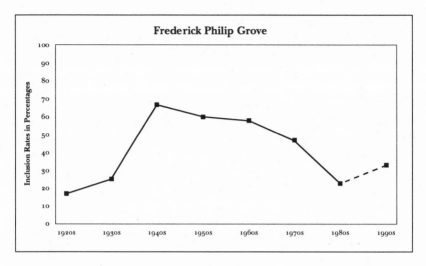

Figure 9

percent inclusion rate — up from zero the previous decade). He occupies 8 percent of the space in Gustafson's *Canadian Accent* (1944), and Pacey allots him 6 percent of the space in his *A Book of Canadian Stories* (1947). Yet if one consults the first edition of Pacey's *Creative Writing in Canada* (1952), there is no mention of McConnell. Leslie Gordon Barnard, best known for the short stories in *One Generation Away* (1931), was ignored by anthologists during the 1930s, but suddenly embraced by them in the 1940s (33 percent inclusion rate) and even more in the 1950s (60 percent inclusion rate). Ethel Wilson hit a 100 percent inclusion rate in the 1950s — up from zero the previous decade (Wilson published her first story — "I Just Love Dogs" — in 1937, so her widespread appearance in the 1950s' anthologies certainly indicates the belated discovery of a star).

In more recent times the most meteoric rise is identified with Jack Hodgins. By calculating the increase or decrease in inclusion rates by decade, it is possible to see that Hodgins's inclusion rate jumped from 5 percent in the 1970s to 69 percent in the 1980s, an increase of 64 percent. Few other authors rival this type of sudden increase. Margaret Laurence does. Her inclusion rate jumped from 25 percent in the 1960s to 89 percent in the 1970s, an increase of 64 percent. Although one might argue that this rapid increase can be explained by the fact that Laurence simply published more in the 1970s than she did in the 1960s, the figures still indicate a meteoric rise and sudden, widespread acceptance of her work. As it happens, however, Laurence was widely published in magazines and journals in the 1960s, with 16 stories to her credit during that decade and four in the 1940s and 1950s; many of these later appeared in *The Tomorrow-Tamer* (1963) and *A Bird in the House* (1970). Laurence published only one short story in the 1970s, and none after that. It seems clear, then, that anthologists in the 1970s suddenly decided that Laurence was worthy of inclusion, even though her stories had appeared in respected journals for more than twenty years. Why? The answer lies in her novels. Often short-story anthologists try to capitalize on authors whose reputations have been made as novelists. If this is true, it suggests that gaining acceptance as a novelist, rather than as a short-story writer, is the preferred means of establishing canonical value.

Other writers who are gaining favour with anthologists in the 1990s include Leon Rooke, Timothy Findley, Wallace Stegner, Sandra Birdsell, and David Adams Richards.

Representing Reception

Scanning the table in appendix A from left to right reveals six types of reception over the period surveyed: rising, falling, rising then falling, falling then rising, flat, and variable. These trends are easiest to see in graphs where the percentage inclusion rates are plotted decade by decade for any given author. For example, Susanna Moodie is clearly falling, then rising (figure 8). Frederick Philip Grove is variable (figure 9), as is David Thompson (figure 10). Norman Duncan is falling or fallen (see figure 5); Marjorie Pickthall is rising, then falling (see figure 11);

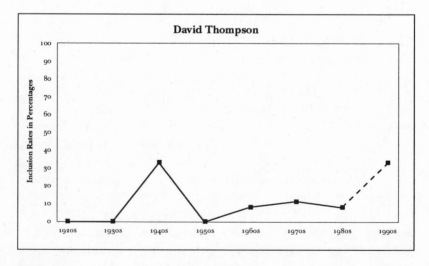

Figure 10

Catharine Parr Traill is variable (see figure 12) and obviously resurgent.

The patterns described above are difficult to explain. One can attribute the return of Catharine Parr Traill to an opening up of the canon and to expanding interest in nineteenth-century women's fiction (the same might be said for Montgomery), but there is clearly some reason why anthologists have not been willing to include Pickthall in this resurgence. Ralph Connor (figure 13) is the last author I would have expected to see back again, but the graph shows that he disappeared during the 1950s, only to return in the 1960s and 1970s, and then to disappear in the 1980s. The pattern of his reception suggests that he is an author whose reputation might be born again. I would bet on his resurrection before I would bet on Norman Duncan's, since Duncan has never recovered from his descent.

By scanning the table and figures it is possible to identify those authors who are experiencing the greatest resurgence of interest in their work. For example, David Thompson is included in 9 percent of the anthologies surveyed. He appears in 33 percent of the anthologies published in the 1940s, is not included for the next decade, then reappears consistently through the 1960s, 1970s, and 1980s, and in 1 of the 3 anthologies published to date in the 1990s — surely a sign of revitalized interest in travel narratives (or perhaps a sign of the modern anthology's ability to neutralize genre by reconfiguring travel literature as short fiction). Other resurgent writers include Anna Jameson and P.K. Page.

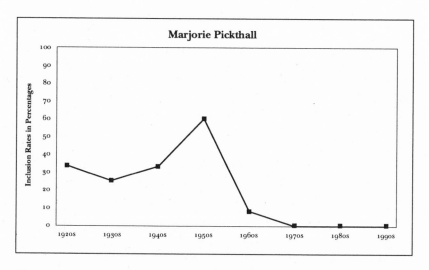

Figure 11

Outside Influences

No one is under the illusion that anthologists make objective choices. All kinds of material, political, and personal considerations come into play during the selection process. The history of anthology-making is as much a history of feuds and disputes as it is of aesthetic correctness. Frequently, an outside event or a perceived cultural imperative will prompt anthologists to make specific choices. These are the most difficult choices to explain — especially in hindsight — because the specific external catalyst is often forgotten or remains unknown.

One of the most ignored catalysts is the value conferred by prize-giving or other forms of certification. Since they were introduced in 1936, the Governor General's Awards have traditionally been regarded as the most prestigious form of literary certification in Canada. The table of anthology inclusions makes it possible to speculate about how anthologists have altered their view of writers who have received one of these awards (or other prizes).

For example, Roderick Haig-Brown (1908–76) published his first book in 1931, and was very active throughout the 1930s and 1940s. In those two decades, none of his work appeared in anthologies. But in 1946 he won the Canadian Library Association Award for best juvenile fiction, and, in 1948, the Governor General's Award for juvenile fiction. By 1955 he had made his way into Klinck and Watters's anthology. By the 1960s he had an inclusion rate of 33 percent. Haig-Brown was still writing in the 1970s, but there were no more prizes. By the 1970s his

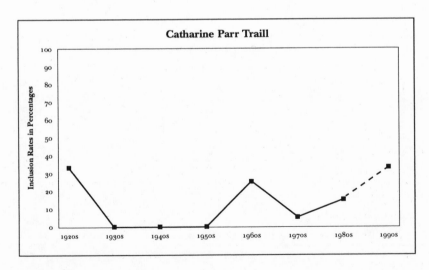

Figure 12

work had disappeared from national anthologies; to date, it has not returned.

Alan Sullivan received the Governor General's Award for Fiction in 1941 for his romance entitled *Three Came to Ville Marie.* Sullivan (1868–1947) had been around for a while. His 1913 *The Passing of Oul-I-But* was written in the nature-story genre. He later tried a novel about Canadian expansion and industry, *The Rapids* (1922), but in 1926 returned to what had become his specialty — stories about the Canadian North — in *Under the Northern Lights.* Although Sullivan's works were popular, he appeared in only one anthology in the 1920s, and in none during the 1930s. Only after he won the Governor General's Award did anthologists begin to take note of him: by the 1950s his inclusion rate had risen to 40 percent. By the 1960s the effect of the award had obviously worn thin: Sullivan never appeared in a Canadian anthology again.

Thomas Raddall is much better known than Sullivan. His works appear in 29 percent of all the anthologies surveyed (he ranks sixteenth among the authors considered in this study). Like Sullivan, Raddall (1903–94) had been writing for years. His first story was published in 1921, and his work appeared regularly in such well-known magazines as *Maclean's* and *Blackwood's* during the 1930s. In 1943 he won the Governor General's Award for *The Pied Piper of Dipper Creek* (1939). Prior to his reception of this award, none of Raddall's work had been anthologized. It would have been too late for Gustafson to include Raddall in *Canadian Accent*, which was already set for publication in

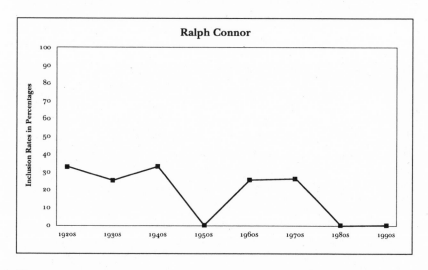

Figure 13

1944. But the next anthology, Robins's *A Pocketful of Canada* (1946), did include two stories from the award-winning book. It is significant that the two works Robins chose for inclusion had been published in 1939 — four years before Raddall won the award — but were apparently neglected until Raddall received the seal of approval. In Raddall's case, this approval ensured his presence in national anthologies of Canadian literature for the next four decades. By the end of the 1940s, Raddall's work was included as frequently as Charles G.D. Roberts's. In the 1950s it was as anthologized as fiction by Duncan Campbell Scott. In the 1960s Raddall was as popular among anthologists as Sinclair Ross. In the 1970s he was as popular as Malcolm Lowry and W.O. Mitchell. Even in the 1980s he was included in anthologies as frequently as Dave Godfrey. These comparisons serve as reminders that Raddall's work has somehow been deemed important and of particular use to students. A thorough study of his work might attempt to account for this longevity and apparent pedagogical value.

Conclusion

There are many more ways in which the data informing this essay might be used. However, this brief study does serve to reinforce some of my previous assumptions about canonicity in Canadian literature, and to undermine others. Although there is clearly no fixed group of works that could be described as canonical, particular works have been favoured by anthologists over the years. These are identifiable. By the same token, while the reputations of certain authors may rise and fall, several Canadian writers continue to have a strong presence in anthologies of Canadian literature. This sustained presence allows us to refer to certain writers from the past as canonical, insofar as "canonical" means they have withstood the test of time and continue to be treated as valuable by virtue of their inclusion in national anthologies. In the historical view, there are authors who dominate the pages of the anthologies considered here. And in every decade, there are specific writers that anthologists value and promote. There is a strong element of consensus in this valuation.

Other potential studies are suggested by this brief statistical excursion. We have some studies of inclusion in Canadian literature; we need other studies — of exclusion — that consider such factors as gender, genre, ethnicity, and race. There is room for detailed analysis of the particular choices made by anthologists in relation to their predecessors (Farrell and Gerson have broken new ground in this area, but much remains to be done). A broad examination of the canonical effects of prize-giving and certification would be worthwhile, as would an examination of the ways in which shifting definitions of such crucial terms as "modernism" or "the short story" have affected anthologists' choices over the years. In a similar vein, there is room for much more discussion about the exclusionary biases inherent in various concepts of Canadian literary tradition, and for more analysis of how tokenism has coloured our perception of literary value.

Most of all, there is a need for new kinds of Canadian literary histories. Many of the histories we have are full of useful information. But, despite the fact that they are histories, they remain preoccupied with an immediate, rather than a historical, sense of value. For this reason, writers considered to be of great importance as recently as 30 years ago are reduced to a few lines of coverage in our most comprehensive literary histories. This means that, for the contemporary reader, real literary history has been more than truncated; it has been destroyed. Of course, it has always been this way, since literary historians, like most people, tend to privilege the contemporary view as the authoritative one.

Notwithstanding this observation, there is considerable room for new literary histories of Canada that would rehistoricize the authors and the works they treat. Such histories would attempt to explain shifts in value and taste, and would comment on the ways in which readers — not just academic readers — responded to the works that were popular and meaningful to them in different times. This type of rehistoricization might be reflected in new anthologies that chose to include works that were once considered valuable (I think here of banished writers such as Norman Duncan or Marjorie Pickthall) in order to allow students to imagine the assumptions of another age. I could imagine another history of Canadian literature that was about negotiating value, and another one about the literary feuds whose legacy we have inherited. Or one about all the writers from our past who are now considered worthless. Or another one about writers, or editors, or critics who made choices, who imagined the country and made it real.

APPENDIX A

Inclusion Rates for Authors in Anthologies of Canadian Literature Containing Fiction, 1922–92

(in descending order by rate of anthologization)

DECADE	20s	30s	40s	50s	60s	70s	80s	90s	Total & %
Anthologies published	6	4	3	5	12	19	13	3	65/65 =100

NAME									
Callaghan, Morley	1	1	3	4	8	15	7	2	41/65 = 63
Leacock, Stephen	3	3	3	4	7	9	6	2	37/65 = 57
Ross, Sinclair	–	–	2	4	6	12	8	3	35/65 = 54
Munro, Alice	–	–	–	–	3	16	12	3	34/65 = 52
Roberts, Charles G.D.	4	3	2	3	6	8	7	1	34/65 = 52
Laurence, Margaret	–	–	–	–	3	17	10	3	33/65 = 51
Wilson, Ethel	–	–	–	5	7	12	6	3	33/65 = 51
Richler, Mordecai	–	–	–	–	6	15	6	2	29/65 = 44
Haliburton, Thomas C.	5	2	2	4	3	7	4	1	28/65 = 43
Hood, Hugh	–	–	–	–	3	15	8	2	28/65 = 43
Grove, Frederick Philip	1	1	2	3	7	9	3	1	27/65 = 41
Moodie, Susanna	4	3	2	3	2	5	3	1	23/65 = 35
Garner, Hugh	–	–	–	2	4	12	4	–	22/65 = 34
Scott, Duncan Campbell	2	–	1	3	5	4	6	–	21/65 = 32
MacLennan, Hugh	–	–	2	2	6	7	1	2	20/65 = 31
Raddall, Thomas H.	–	–	2	3	6	6	3	–	20/65 = 29
Gallant, Mavis	–	–	–	–	2	5	9	3	19/65 = 31
Parker, Gilbert	6	2	1	4	1	2	–	–	16/65 = 25
Lowry, Malcolm	–	–	–	1	5	6	3	–	15/65 = 23
De la Roche, Mazo	2	1	1	4	4	2	1	–	15/65 = 23
Thomson, E.W.	5	2	1	2	2	2	1	–	15/65 = 23
Duncan, Norman	5	3	2	2	1	1	–	–	14/65 = 22
Mitchell, W.O.	–	–	–	2	4	6	1	1	14/65 = 22
Atwood, Margaret	–	–	–	–	–	2	8	3	13/65 = 20
Blaise, Clark	–	–	–	–	–	5	5	3	13/65 = 20
Duncan, Sara Jeannette	–	–	–	1	4	6	1	1	13/65 = 20

Author	1	2	3	4	5	6	7	8	Rate
Hodgins, Jack	–	–	–	–	–	1	9	3	13/65 = 20
Metcalf, John	–	–	–	–	1	7	4	1	13/65 = 20
Richardson, John	5	2	–	1	2	3	–	–	13/65 = 20
Buckler, Ernest	–	–	–	–	7	2	3	1	13/65 = 20
Connor, Ralph	2	1	1	–	3	5	–	–	12/65 = 18
Levine, Norman	–	–	–	–	2	3	6	1	12/65 = 18
Knister, Raymond	–	–	2	2	2	2	2	1	11/65 = 17
Nowlan, Alden	–	–	–	–	2	6	3	–	11/65 = 17
Wiebe, Rudy	–	–	–	–	–	3	5	3	11/65 = 17
Davies, Robertson	–	–	–	–	4	4	1	1	10/65 = 15
MacLeod, Alistair	–	–	–	–	–	2	5	3	10/65 = 15
Moore, Brian	–	–	–	–	5	4	1	–	10/65 = 15
Thomas, Audrey	–	–	–	–	–	1	6	3	10/65 = 15
Brooke, Frances	–	–	–	1	2	4	1	1	9/65 = 14
Marshall, Joyce	–	–	–	1	2	1	4	1	9/65 = 14
Mowat, Farley	–	–	–	–	5	3	1	–	9/65 = 14
Page, P.K.	–	–	2	3	2	–	1	1	9/65 = 14
Traill, Catharine Parr	2	–	–	–	3	1	2	1	9/65 = 14
Valgardson, W.D.	–	–	–	–	–	2	7	–	9/65 = 14
Godfrey, Dave	–	–	–	–	–	5	3	–	8/65 = 12
Pickthall, Marjorie	2	1	1	3	1	–	–	–	8/65 = 12
Rooke, Leon	–	–	–	–	–	1	4	3	8/65 = 12
Carr, Emily	–	–	–	–	1	5	1	–	7/65 = 11
Cohen, Matt	–	–	–	–	–	2	4	1	7/65 = 11
Glassco, John	–	–	–	–	–	5	2	–	7/65 = 11
Hearne, Samuel	–	–	–	–	2	3	1	1	7/65 = 11
Kinsella, W.P.	–	–	–	–	–	–	6	1	7/65 = 11
Kreisel, Henry	–	–	–	–	2	1	3	1	7/65 = 11
Ludwig, Jack	–	–	–	–	3	4	–	–	7/65 = 11
McClung, Nellie	2	1	1	–	1	2	–	–	7/65 = 11
Montgomery, L.M.	3	–	–	–	2	2	–	–	7/65 = 11
Bird, Will R.	–	–	1	3	2	–	–	–	6/65 = 9
Heming, Arthur	3	3	–	–	–	–	–	–	6/65 = 9
Helwig, David	–	–	–	–	–	6	–	–	6/65 = 9
Howe, Joseph	–	–	1	3	2	–	–	–	6/65 = 9
McConnell, William	–	–	2	3	–	1	–	–	6/65 = 9
Thompson, David	–	–	1	–	1	2	1	1	6/65 = 9
Watson, Sheila	–	–	–	–	–	2	2	2	6/65 = 9
De Mille, James	2	–	–	–	–	3	–	–	5/65 = 8
Findley, Timothy	–	–	–	–	–	1	1	3	5/65 = 8

Haig-Brown, Roderick	–	–	–	1	4	–	–	–	5/65 = 8
Harvor, Beth	–	–	–	–	–	1	2	2	5/65 = 8
Jameson, Anna	2	–	–	–	1	1	–	1	5/65 = 8
Klein, A.M.	–	–	–	–	2	1	1	1	5/65 = 8
Mackenzie, Alexander	1	1	1	–	–	2	–	–	5/65 = 8
McCourt, Edward	–	–	–	2	–	3	–	–	5/65 = 8
McCulloch, Thomas	–	–	–	–	1	3	1	–	5/65 = 8
Seton, Ernest Thompson	2	2	–	–	1	–	–	–	5/65 = 8
Smith, Ray	–	–	–	–	–	4	1	–	5/65 = 8
Barnard, Leslie Gordon	–	–	1	3	–	–	–	–	4/65 = 6
Bowering, George	–	–	–	–	1	1	1	1	4/65 = 6
Clarke, Austin	–	–	–	–	–	2	1	1	4/65 = 6
Cohen, Leonard	–	–	–	–	–	3	1	–	4/65 = 6
Hardy, W.G.	–	–	1	3	–	–	–	–	4/65 = 6
Innis, Mary Quayle	–	–	2	2	–	–	–	–	4/65 = 6
Kirby, William	3	1	–	–	–	–	–	–	4/65 = 6
Kroetsch, Robert	–	–	–	–	–	3	1	–	4/65 = 6
Layton, Irving	–	–	–	–	3	1	–	–	4/65 = 6
McDougall, Colin	–	–	–	–	3	1	–	–	4/65 = 6
Nicol, Eric	–	–	–	–	3	1	–	–	4/65 = 6
O'Hagan, Howard	–	–	–	–	1	2	1	–	4/65 = 6
Reaney, James	–	–	–	1	1	1	1	–	4/65 = 6
Schroeder, Andreas	–	–	–	–	–	2	2	–	4/65 = 6
Slater, Patrick	–	–	1	1	2	–	–	–	4/65 = 6
Stegner, Wallace	–	–	–	–	2	–	–	2	4/65 = 6
Sullivan, Alan	1	–	1	2	–	–	–	–	4/65 = 6
Wallace, F.W.	3	1	–	–	–	–	–	–	4/65 = 6
Whalley, George	–	–	–	–	1	3	–	–	4/65 = 6
Wiseman, Adele	–	–	–	–	2	1	1	–	4/65 = 6
Allan, Ted	–	–	–	1	1	1	–	–	3/65 = 5
Allen, Ralph	–	–	–	–	3	–	–	–	3/65 = 5
Bailey, Don	–	–	–	–	–	3	–	–	3/65 = 5
Birdsell, Sandra	–	–	–	–	–	–	1	2	3/65 = 5
Birney, Earle	–	–	1	–	2	–	–	–	3/65 = 5
Blake, W.H.	1	1	1	–	–	–	–	–	3/65 = 5
Dobbs, Kildare	–	–	–	–	1	1	1	–	3/65 = 5
Fraser, Keath	–	–	–	–	–	–	2	1	3/65 = 5
Gotlieb, Phyllis	–	–	–	–	–	2	1	–	3/65 = 5
Gustafson, Ralph	–	–	–	1	2	–	–	–	3/65 = 5
Henry, Alexander	–	–	–	–	2	1	–	–	3/65 = 5

Hiebert, Paul	–	–	–	–	2	1	–	–	3/65 = 5
Johnson, Pauline	1	–	–	–	–	2	–	–	3/65 = 5
Kennedy, Leo	–	–	1	1	1	–	–	–	3/65 = 5
Livesay, Dorothy	–	–	–	–	–	1	1	1	3/65 = 5
MacEwen, Gwendolyn	–	–	–	–	–	2	1	–	3/65 = 5
McArthur, Peter	2	–	1	–	–	–	–	–	3/65 = 5
Ondaatje, Michael	–	–	–	–	–	1	1	1	3/65 = 5
Perrault, E.G	–	–	–	1	–	2	–	–	3/65 = 5
Richards, David Adams	–	–	–	–	–	–	1	2	3/65 = 5
Roberts, Theodore G.	–	–	1	2	–	–	–	–	3/65 = 5
Robins, John D.	–	–	1	–	2	–	–	–	3/65 = 5
Ross, Alexander	1	1	–	–	1	–	–	–	3/65 = 5
Rossignol, James E.	–	2	1	–	–	–	–	–	3/65 = 5
Rule, Jane	–	–	–	–	–	1	1	1	3/65 = 5
Salverson, Laura G.	1	–	1	–	1	–	–	–	3/65 = 5
Thompson, Kent	–	–	–	–	–	2	–	1	3/65 = 5
Waddington, Patrick	–	–	1	2	–	–	–	–	3/65 = 5

The following writers are represented in only 2 of the 65 anthologies:

Anderson, Patrick (40s & 60s)
Bailey, Jacob (50s & 60s)
Berton, Pierre (60s & 70s)
Bodsworth, Fred (60s & 70s)
Brand, Dionne (90s)
Burnford, Sheila (60s)
Campbell, Patrick (60s & 70s)
Clark, Gregory (60s & 90s)
Clutesi, George (70s)
Costain, Thomas (50s & 60s)
Crawford, Isabella Valancy (80s)
Denison, Merrill (20s & 30s)
Dunlop, William (50s & 60s)
Engel, Marian (80s)
Faessler, Shirley (70s)
Fontaine, Robert (60s & 70s)
Gibson, Margaret (70s & 80s)
Guy, Roy (70s & 90s)
Gyles, John (60s & 70s)
Harrison, Susie Frances (80s)
Hickman, Albert (20s)
Horwood, Harold (80s)
Keith, Marian (20s)
King, Basil (20s)
Kogawa, Joy (90s)
Leechman, Douglas (60s)
Leprohon, Rosanna (70s)
Lighthall, W.D. (20s)
Livesay, J.F.B. (20s)
Lizars, Robina and Kathleen (60s & 70s)
Macbeth, Roderick G. (20s & 30s)
MacMechan, Archibald (20s)
Markoosie (70s)
Marlatt, Daphne (60s & 90s)
Mistry, Rohinton (90s)
Mitchell, Ken (70s & 80s)
Mukherjee, Bharati (80s & 90s)
North, Anison (20s)
Pacey, Desmond (50s & 60s)
Ringwood, Gwen (50s)
Ritchie, Charles (80s & 90s)
Saunders, Marshall (20s)
Shields, Carol (90s)
Sime, Jessie Georgina (30s & 80s)
Sinclair, Bertrand (20s & 30s)
Spencer, Elizabeth (80s and 90s)
Spettigue, Douglas (50s & 60s)
Stead, Robert J.C. (20s & 30s)

Vanderhaeghe, Guy (80s & 90s)
Virgo, Sean (80s & 90s)
Walker, David (60s)
Weinzweig, Helen (80s)
Willison, John (20s)
Wood, S.T. (20s)
Woodcock, George (70s & 80s)
Young, Scott (50s and 60s)

The following writers are represented in only 1 of the 65 anthologies:

Adamson, Rigmore (50s)
Aitken, Kate (60s)
Alford, Edna (80s)
Alline, Henry (70s)
Annett, R. Ross (60s)
Annett, William (50s)
Barker, H.J. (60s)
Beames, John (30s)
Bissoondath, Neil (80s)
Black, Martha Louise (40s)
Blackburn, Robert (50s)
Bone, P.T. (60s)
Boyle, Harry (60s)
Braithwaite, Max (80s)
Branden, Vicki (60s)
Brewster, Elizabeth (80s)
Broadus, E.K. (40s)
Brown, Randy (70s)
Bruce, Charles (60s)
Bruce, Harry (70s)
Bruce, Michael (70s)
Butler, William Francis (70s)
Callaghan, Barry (80s)
Campbell, A.P. (80s)
Campbell, Grace (40s)
Carrier, Jean-Guy (70s)
Carroll, John (60s)
Child, Philip (60s)
Christie, Robert (60s)
Clark, Ella (60s)
Clay, Charles (40s)
Copeland, Ann (80s)
Cuevas, Ernesto (50s)
Day, Frank Parker (30s)
Deacon, William Arthur (60s)
De Coccola, Raymond and Paul King (60s)
Denison, Mrs. Muriel (30s)
Dent, W. Redvers (30s)
Douthwaite, L.C. (40s)
Downie, Mary Alice (70s)
Duncan, Frances (70s)
Duncan, W.T. (70s)
Eaton, Flora McCrea (60s)
Edwards, Bob (60s)
Eggleston, Wilfrid (40s)
Elliott, George (90s)
Every, Jane van (60s)
Fraser, William A. (20s)

Freeman, Bill (70s)
French, Alice (90s)
Garber, Lawrence (80s)
Gard, Robert E. (60s)
Gillese, John Patrick (60s)
Goldman, Alvin (50s)
Govier, Katherine (80s)
Graham, Angus (40s)
Grant, George (60s)
Grey Owl (30s)
Hailey, Arthur (60s)
Hall, Basil (60s)
Hargreaves, H.A. (80s)
Harrington, Michael F. (60s)
Hart, Anne (70s)
Hiemstra, Mary (60s)
Hilliard, Marion (60s)
Hoogstraten, Vinia (60s)
Hospital, Janette Turner (90s)
Howarth, Jean (50s)
Hutchinson, Sybil (40s)
Imrie, Walter McLaren (20s)
Ingersoll, Will E. (20s)
Itani, Frances S. (90s)
Janes, Percy (70s)
Jiles, Paulette (90s)
Johnson, Vera (60s)
Johnston, Basil (80s)
Kilbourn, William (60s)
Laing, Hamilton (20s)
Lampman, Archibald (50s)
Landmann, George T. (60s)
Lawrence, R.D. (70s)
LeBourdais, Isabel (60s)
Lewis, Gwen (60s)
Longstreth, Thomas (30s)
Machar, Agnes M. (20s)
MacPhail, Andrew (60s)
Mair, Charles (70s)
Marcuse, Katherine (40s)
Marriott, Anne (80s)
Mather, Barry (60s)
McAree, J.V. (60s)
McFarlane, Leslie (20s)
McLaren, Floris (50s)
McNamara, Eugene (70s)
Meade, Edward (60s)
Miller, Orlo (60s)

Moses, Daniel D. (90s)
Moore, Tom (70s)
Murtha, Thomas (20s)
O'Higgins, Harvey (20s)
Ostenso, Martha (70s)
Peate, Mary (70s)
Phillipps, Alan (50s)
Porter, Helen (80s)
Pugsley, William H. (40s)
Richardson, Evelyn (60s)
Rosenblatt, Joe (90s)
Ross, Dan (70s)
Ross, John (60s)
Ross, Veronica (80s)
Ross, W.W.E. (40s)
Russell, Franklin (70s)
Rutledge, Joseph Lister (50s)
Sandwell, B.K. (70s)
Sawai, Gloria (80s)
Schermbrucker, Bill (80s)
Scott, Frederick G. (20s)
Shapiro, Lionel (50s)

Sharp, Edith (70s)
Simpson, George (60s)
Simpson, Leo (70s)
Sleigh, B.W.A. (60s)
Smart, Elizabeth (90s)
Stein, David Lewis (70s)
Strange, Kathleen (40s)
Symons, R.D. (60s)
Teskey, Adeline (20s)
Thibaudeau, Colleen (50s)
Thompson, George (60s)
Thompson, Samuel (60s)
Townshend, Elizabeth M. (70s)
Vancouver, George (70s)
Wees, Frances Shelley (60s)
Weintraub, William (60s)
Wells, Kenneth McNeill (50s)
Wilkinson, Anne (60s)
Wood, Edward J. (60s)
Wright, J.F.C. (60s)
Wuorio, Era-Lis (60s)

APPENDIX B

Anthologies Consulted

Andrews, Allen, Diane Thompson, and Douglas Cronk, eds. *Canadian Viewpoints: An Anthology of Canadian Writing.* Victoria: B.C. Ministry of Education, 1983.

Atwood, Margaret, and Robert Weaver, eds. *The Oxford Book of Canadian Short Stories in English.* Toronto: Oxford UP, 1986.

Becker, May Lamberton, ed. *Golden Tales of Canada.* Toronto: McClelland, 1938.

Bissell, Claude Thomas, ed. *Great Canadian Writing: A Century of Imagination.* Toronto: Canadian Centennial, 1966.

Boswell, William, Betty Lamont, and John Martyn, eds. *Canadian Stories, Poems and Songs.* 2 vols. Toronto: Van Nostrand Reinhold, 1979.

Broadus, Edmund Kemper, and Eleanor Hammond Broadus, eds. *A Book of Canadian Prose and Verse.* Toronto: Macmillan, 1923.

——, eds. *A Book of Canadian Prose and Verse.* 2nd rev. ed. Toronto: Macmillan, 1934.

Broughton, Katheryn Maclean, ed. *Heartland: An Anthology of Canadian Stories.* Scarborough: Nelson, 1983.

Brown, Russell, and Donna Bennett, eds. *An Anthology of Canadian Literature in English.* 2 vols. Toronto: Oxford UP, 1982–83.

Brown, Russell, Donna Bennett, and Nathalie Cooke, eds. *An Anthology of Canadian Literature in English.* Rev. and abr. ed. Toronto: Oxford UP, 1990.

Daymond, Douglas, and Leslie Monkman, eds. *Literature in Canada.* 2 vols. Toronto: Gage, 1978.

——, eds. *On Middle Ground: Novellas by Clark Blaise, Keath Fraser, Mavis Gallant, Malcolm Lowry, John Metcalf, Audrey Thomas, Ethel Wilson.* Toronto: Methuen, 1987.

Edwards, Mary Jane, Paul Denham, and George Parker, eds. *The Evolution of Canadian Literature in English: Beginnings to 1970.* 4 vols. Toronto: Holt, 1973.

Grady, Wayne, ed. *The Penguin Book of Canadian Short Stories.* Harmondsworth: Penguin, 1980.

——, ed. *The Penguin Book of Modern Canadian Short Stories.* Harmondsworth: Penguin, 1982.

Green, H. Gordon, and Guy Sylvestre, eds. *A Century of Canadian Literature/Un Siècle de littérature canadienne.* Toronto: Ryerson, 1967.

Gustafson, Ralph, ed. *Canadian Accent: A Collection of Stories and Poems by Contemporary Writers from Canada.* Harmondsworth: Penguin, 1944.

Kendrick, William K.F., ed. *Canadian Stories in Verse and Prose*. Toronto: Clarke, 1932.

—— , ed. *Canadian Stories in Verse and Prose*. 2nd ed. Toronto: Clarke, 1936.

Kilgallin, Tony, ed. *The Canadian Short Story*. Toronto: Holt, 1971.

Klinck, Carl F., and Reginald E. Watters, eds. *Canadian Anthology*. Toronto: Gage, 1955.

—— , eds. *Canadian Anthology*. Rev. ed. Toronto: Gage, 1966.

—— , eds. *Canadian Anthology*. 3rd ed. Toronto: Gage, 1974.

Knister, Raymond, ed. *Canadian Short Stories*. Toronto: Macmillan, 1928.

Lecker, Robert, and Jack David, eds. *The New Canadian Anthology: Poetry and Short Fiction in English*. Scarborough: Nelson, 1988.

Levine, Norman, ed. *Canadian Winter's Tales*. Toronto: Macmillan, 1968.

Lucas, Alec, ed. *Great Canadian Short Stories: An Anthology*. New York: Dell, 1971.

MacNeill, James A., and Glen A. Sorestad, eds. *Tigers of the Snow: Eighteen Canadian Stories*. Don Mills: Nelson, 1973.

McEvoy, Bernard L. *Stories from across Canada*. Toronto: McClelland, 1966.

McGechaen, John, and Philip Penner, eds. *Canadian Reflections: An Anthology of Canadian Prose*. Toronto: Macmillan, 1964.

Metcalf, John, ed. *Kaleidoscope: Canadian Stories*. Toronto: Reinhold, 1972.

—— , ed. *The Narrative Voice: Short Stories and Reflections by Canadian Authors*. Toronto: McGraw, 1972.

—— , ed. *Sixteen by Twelve: Short Stories by Canadian Writers*. Toronto: Ryerson, 1970.

Mickleburgh, Brita, ed. *Canadian Literature: Two Centuries in Prose*. Toronto: McClelland, 1973.

Nelson, George E., ed. *Cavalcade of the North: An Entertaining Collection of Distinguished Writing by Canadian Authors*. New York: Doubleday, 1958.

—— , ed. *Northern Lights: A New Collection of Distinguished Writing by Canadian Authors*. Garden City: Doubleday, 1960.

New, W.H., ed. *Canadian Short Fiction: From Myth to Modern*. Scarborough: Prentice, 1986.

Nowlan, Michael. *A Land, a People: Short Stories by Canadian Writers*. St. John's: Breakwater, 1986.

Ondaatje, Michael, ed. *From Ink Lake: Canadian Stories*. Toronto: Lester, 1990.

Owen, Ivon, and Morris Wolfe, eds. *The Best Modern Canadian Short Stories*. Edmonton: Hurtig, 1978.

Pacey, Desmond, ed. *A Book of Canadian Stories*. Toronto: Ryerson, 1947.

—— , ed. *A Book of Canadian Stories*. 2nd ed. Toronto: Ryerson, 1950.

—— , ed. *A Book of Canadian Stories*. 3rd ed. Toronto: Ryerson, 1952.

—— , ed. *A Book of Canadian Stories*. 4th ed. Toronto: Ryerson, 1962.

—— , ed. *Selections from Major Canadian Writers: Poetry and Creative Prose in English*. Toronto: McGraw, 1974.

Peck, Edward, ed. *Transitions II: Short Fiction: A Source Book of Canadian Literature*. Vancouver: Commcept, 1978.

Richler, Mordecai, ed. *Canadian Writing Today*. Writing Today Series. Harmondsworth: Penguin, 1970.

Rimanelli, Giose, and Roberto Ruberto, eds. *Modern Canadian Stories.* Toronto: Ryerson, 1966.

Robins, John D., ed. *A Pocketful of Canada.* Toronto: Collins, 1946.

Selected Stories from Canadian Prose. Toronto: Macmillan, 1929.

Smith, A.J.M., ed. *Early Beginnings to Confederation.* Toronto: Gage, 1965. Vol. 1 of *The Book of Canadian Prose.* 2 vols. 1965–73.

——, ed. *The Canadian Century: English-Canadian Writing since Confederation.* Toronto: Gage, 1973. Vol. 2 of *The Book of Canadian Prose.* 2 vols. 1965–73.

——, ed. *The Canadian Experience: A Brief Survey of English-Canadian Prose.* Toronto: Gage, 1974.

Stephen, A.M., ed. *The Voice of Canada: A Selection of Prose and Verse.* London: Dent, 1926.

Stevens, John, ed. *Best Canadian Short Stories.* Toronto: McClelland, 1981.

——, ed. *Modern Canadian Stories.* Toronto: McClelland, 1975.

Struthers, J.R. (Tim), ed. *The Possibilities of Story.* 2 vols. Toronto: McGraw-Hill Ryerson, 1992.

Toye, William, ed. *A Book of Canada.* London: Collins, 1962.

Watson, Albert Durrant, and Lorne Pierce, eds. *Our Canadian Literature: Representative Prose and Verse.* Toronto: Ryerson, 1922.

——, eds. *Our Canadian Literature: Representative Prose and Verse.* 3rd ed. Toronto: Ryerson, 1923.

Weaver, Robert, ed. *The "Anthology" Anthology: A Selection from 30 Years of CBC Radio's "Anthology."* Toronto: Macmillan, 1984.

——, ed. *Canadian Short Stories.* London: Oxford UP, 1960.

Weaver, Robert, and Helen James, eds. *Canadian Short Stories.* Toronto: Oxford UP, 1952.

Weaver, Robert, and William Toye, eds. *The Oxford Anthology of Canadian Literature.* Toronto: Oxford UP, 1973.

——, eds. *The Oxford Anthology of Canadian Literature.* 2nd ed. Toronto: Oxford UP, 1981.

APPENDIX C

Chronological List of Anthologies Consulted

1922. Watson and Pierce. *Our Canadian Literature: Representative Prose and Verse.*

1923. Broadus and Broadus. *A Book of Canadian Prose and Verse.*

1923. Watson and Pierce. *Our Canadian Literature: Representative Prose and Verse.*

1926. Stephen. *The Voice of Canada: A Selection of Prose and Verse.*

1928. Knister. *Canadian Short Stories.*

1929. *Selected Stories from Canadian Prose.*

1932. Kendrick. *Canadian Stories in Verse and Prose.*

1934. Broadus and Broadus. *A Book of Canadian Prose and Verse.*

1936. Kendrick. *Canadian Stories in Verse and Prose.*

1938. Becker. *Golden Tales of Canada.*

1944. Gustafson. *Canadian Accent: A Collection of Stories and Poems by Contemporary Writers from Canada.*

1946. Robins. *A Pocketful of Canada.*

1947. Pacey. *A Book of Canadian Stories.*

1950. Pacey. *A Book of Canadian Stories.*

1952. Pacey. *A Book of Canadian Stories.*

1952. Weaver and James. *Canadian Short Stories.*

1955. Klinck and Watters. *Canadian Anthology.*

1958. Nelson. *Cavalcade of the North: An Entertaining Collection of Distinguished Writing by Canadian Authors.*

1960. Nelson. *Northern Lights: A New Collection of Distinguished Writing by Canadian Authors.*

1960. Weaver. *Canadian Short Stories.*

1962. Pacey. *A Book of Canadian Stories.*

1962. Toye. *A Book of Canada.*

1964. McGechaen and Penner. *Canadian Reflections: An Anthology of Canadian Prose.*

1965. Smith. *Early Beginnings to Confederation.* Vol. 1 of *The Book of Canadian Prose.*

1966. Bissell. *Great Canadian Writing: A Century of Imagination.*

1966. Klinck and Watters. *Canadian Anthology.*

1966. McEvoy. *Stories from across Canada.*

1966. Rimanelli and Ruberto. *Modern Canadian Stories.*

1967. Green and Sylvestre. *A Century of Canadian Literature/Un Siècle de littérature canadienne.*

1968. Levine. *Canadian Winter's Tales.*

1970. Metcalf. *Sixteen by Twelve: Short Stories by Canadian Writers.*

1970. Richler. *Canadian Writing Today.*

1971. Kilgallin. *The Canadian Short Story.*

1971. Lucas. *Great Canadian Short Stories: An Anthology.*

1972. Metcalf. *Kaleidoscope: Canadian Stories.*

1972. Metcalf. *The Narrative Voice: Short Stories and Reflections by Canadian Authors.*

1973. Edwards, Denham, and Parker. *The Evolution of Canadian Literature in English: Beginnings to 1970.*

1973. MacNeill and Sorestad. *Tigers of the Snow: Eighteen Canadian Stories.*

1973. Mickleburgh. *Canadian Literature: Two Centuries in Prose.*

1973. Smith. *The Canadian Century: English-Canadian Writing since Confederation.* Vol. 2 of *The Book of Canadian Prose.*

1973. Weaver and Toye. *The Oxford Anthology of Canadian Literature.*

1974. Klinck and Watters. *Canadian Anthology.*

1974. Pacey. *Selections from Major Canadian Writers: Poetry and Creative Prose in English.*

1974. Smith. *The Canadian Experience: A Brief Survey of English-Canadian Prose.*

1975. Stevens. *Modern Canadian Stories.*

1978. Daymond and Monkman. *Literature in Canada.*

1978. Owen and Wolfe. *The Best Modern Canadian Short Stories.*

1978. Peck. *Transitions II: Short Fiction: A Source Book of Canadian Literature.*

1979. Boswell, Lamont, and Martyn. *Canadian Stories, Poems and Songs.*

1980. Grady. *The Penguin Book of Canadian Short Stories.*

1981. Stevens. *Best Canadian Short Stories.*

1981. Weaver and Toye. *The Oxford Anthology of Canadian Literature.*

1982. Grady. *The Penguin Book of Modern Canadian Short Stories.*

1982–83. Brown and Bennett. *An Anthology of Canadian Literature in English.*

1983. Andrews, Thompson, and Cronk. *Canadian Viewpoints: An Anthology of Canadian Writing.*

1983. Broughton. *Heartland: An Anthology of Canadian Stories.*

1984. Weaver. *The "Anthology" Anthology: A Selection from 30 Years of CBC Radio's "Anthology."*

1986. Atwood and Weaver. *The Oxford Book of Canadian Short Stories in English.*

1986. New. *Canadian Short Fiction: From Myth to Modern.*

1986. Nowlan. *A Land, a People: Short Stories by Canadian Writers.*

1987. Daymond and Monkman. *On Middle Ground: Novellas by Clark Blaise, Keath Fraser, Mavis Gallant, Malcolm Lowry, John Metcalf, Audrey Thomas, Ethel Wilson.*

1988. Lecker and David. *The New Canadian Anthology: Poetry and Short Fiction in English.*

1990. Brown, Bennett, and Cooke. *An Anthology of Canadian Literature in English.*

1990. Ondaatje. *From Ink Lake: Canadian Stories.*

1992. Struthers. *The Possibilities of Story.*

5

The New Canadian Library:
A Classic Deal

IN ROBERTSON DAVIES'S *Leaven of Malice*, a young academic in English literature is told that he must either publish or perish. His department head urges him to "jump right into Amcan," because "Amcan's the coming thing, and particularly the Canadian end of it. But there isn't much to be done, and the field is being filled up very quickly" (196). Davies's tongue-in-cheek novel was published in 1954, the same year that Malcolm Ross was contemplating the formation of a paperback reprint series that would eventually provide academics with enough material to keep them filling up the field for years. In 1957 McClelland and Stewart launched its New Canadian Library series, under Ross's general editorship. By 1978, the year Ross retired as general editor, 168 titles had appeared in this library of mass-market paperback reprints. It continues today, under the editorship of David Staines.

The New Canadian Library was the product of a decade central to the recognition of Canadian culture. The Massey Commission Report on national development in the arts, letters, and sciences appeared in 1951. Canadian television began in 1952. The National Library was established in 1953. In 1954 George Whalley planned the first conference for Canadian writers, which was held in 1955. Then came the establishment of the Canada Council in 1957, the Canadian Opera Company began in 1958, and the journal *Canadian Literature* was founded in 1959.

Much had changed by the end of the decade. To many, it seemed that Canadian literature had arrived. The climate was right. Yet when it comes to studying Canadian literature, we tend to forget that even in the mid-1950s, the topic was not taught as a discrete subject in

Canadian schools or universities. It was the New Canadian Library that made such teaching possible by providing inexpensive texts and the critical introductions to them that were part of the NCL formula. At the same time, the New Canadian Library encouraged the production of literary criticism devoted to specific authors. In many cases, the introductions commissioned for NCL volumes "marked the first serious literary study of an individual author" (Staines 15). Because it contributed so much to the Canadian literature industry, one can only agree with Margaret Laurence's assessment that the New Canadian Library was "one of the most valuable, significant and far-reaching events in our literary history" (quoted in Staines 15). W.J. Keith reinforces this view when he notes that

> the founding of the series represented a crucial step — I would say *the* crucial step — in demonstrating the existence of a mature Canadian literature and in making possible its extensive study in schools and universities. Indeed, the successful continuance of the New Canadian Library has been in large measure responsible for the confident identification of a Canadian literary tradition. (71)

In many ways, Ross's New Canadian Library selections *formed* this imagined tradition. They influenced a generation of students, and helped to define which texts would become the subject of serious critical inquiry during the 1960s and 1970s. I can't think of any other canonical activity in Canada that would rival this. Given its enormous impact on the teaching and study of Canadian literature, we might well ask why Ross chose the texts he did for inclusion in the New Canadian Library. Think, for example, of the first four titles to appear in the series: Grove's *Over Prairie Trails*, Callaghan's *Such Is My Beloved*, Leacock's *Literary Lapses*, and Ross's *As for Me and My House*. Why were students and teachers given these particular texts? Or why the selections that followed? These questions imply larger ones: What values informed the pedagogical canon at its inception? What was the controlling vision behind the selection process that would determine so much of what would come to be received in Canadian classrooms as the canonical norm? What kind of critical standards accounted for the choice of scholars who were asked to contribute introductions to NCL volumes?

Although these seem like obvious questions to ask about a series of such influence and scope, I have yet to find any research that addresses them. This suggests that the subject of my inquiry — the New Canadian Library — truly has achieved the high point of canonical status: it is a powerful collection of culturally relevant texts that has been accepted, institutionalized, utilized, studied, praised, and never once interrogated.

Actually, I am not being completely honest here. The current general editor of the New Canadian Library, David Staines, has written an introduction to a collection of Ross's critical essays, though it seems somewhat hyperbolic and therefore possibly one-sided in its assessment. For Staines, Ross remains "the selfless servant of his country's literature," a man motivated by a "natural understanding born of passionate dedication to his country and its cultural self-expression." He is "an ardent nationalist," a "committed regionalist," and "a dedicated humanist" who has "served with distinction his country and its cultural traditions" and whose early work "was a very blaze of revelation" in a distinguished career marked by "careful and caring" interpretations that make Ross's "passionate and eloquent voice for Canada" as unique as his "judicious eye," which has projected "a wide and sensitive vision of the country" (7, 8). Whew!

In describing his own involvement in Canadian literature, Ross is much more direct and honest than Staines's adjectival overkill might suggest. When he retired as general editor of the series, Ross described his own interest in Canadian literature "as a hobby, something he has done for fun" (quoted in Slopen 22). This statement raises a disturbing question: Could it be that so much of what we recognize as the pedagogical canon in Canadian literature was the product of one man's fun?

There is no doubt that Ross's selections were enormously influential in defining those texts that would be worthy of commentary and study. Ross wanted good Canadian literature available in paperback. He also wanted to make available earlier works of Canadian literature, French-Canadian works in translation, and books by Jews, immigrants, and other minority writers. He succeeded in doing this, and Canadian literature as we know it would scarcely exist without his efforts. The importance of Ross's achievement is beyond dispute. At the same time, it can be said that Ross's personal interests led him to select some odd titles for inclusion in the series. The New Canadian Library was never really intended to be new. It was designed as a reprint series that would resurrect important texts that had gone out of print. But the very nature of this exercise raises a central question: If these works were so important — if they were truly of classic status, as McClelland and Stewart's promotion would eventually claim — why were they out of print?

In some cases, the answer to this question is that the books had never aroused much interest when they were first published and had quickly faded from public view. In other cases the works in question had simply fallen by the wayside, mainly because the public had not judged them worthy of being kept in view. Consider the first four titles in the series.

Grove's *Over Prairie Trails* had been published in 1922 and was long out of print. Let's face it: Mordecai Richler was right when he said that, at his best, Grove is " 'a good speller' " (quoted in Metcalf, *Kicking* 58). Callaghan's *Such Is My Beloved*, originally published in 1934, was also out of print and had not been available to the Canadian public for more than twenty years. *Literary Lapses* by Leacock was the oldest of the initial group; it was "new" in 1910, but some of the sketches it included had been published in the nineteenth century. *As for Me and My House*, first published in New York in 1941, was out of print and had received mixed to negative reviews when it was first published (it was never released in Canada).

Did Ross have extraordinary foresight in deciding to reprint works — such as *As for Me and My House* — that would go on to become Canadian classics, or was the process of selection more haphazard? How much did Ross's aesthetic preferences influence the selection of titles to be included in the series? To what extent were the selections the result of market forces? How much of what came to be called a collection of Canadian classics was produced by a business decision that determined which texts would be made available to teachers, students, and the public?

My interest in these questions, and in those posed earlier, led me to the McClelland and Stewart papers in the Archives and Research Collections Division at McMaster University and, later, to the Malcolm Ross correspondence held in the Thomas Fisher Rare Book Library at the University of Toronto. The McMaster papers, in particular, contain important correspondence between Malcolm Ross and Jack McClelland concerning the origins and development of the New Canadian Library series, covering the period from 1954 through 1982. For the purposes of this examination, my interest in these letters ends with the 1978 correspondence, for it was in that year that Ross retired as general editor of the series, and it was also in that year that Ross's contribution was honoured at the infamous Calgary Conference on the Canadian Novel.[1] A reading of these letters led me to some unsettling conclusions about the ways in which the pedagogical canon was established in Canada. Moreover, when I asked the archivists at McMaster how many people had consulted this correspondence, I was told, to my astonishment, that I was the first.[2]

* * *

There are two ways of looking at the values informing the pedagogical canon established by the New Canadian Library. The received view is that the selection of titles to be included in the series was made chiefly by Ross, who was motivated by personal conviction and informed aesthetic values. From this perspective, Ross becomes the visionary depicted by Staines — the man whose single-handed choices constructed a national literary tradition and made possible its industrialization. At the centre of Ross's aesthetic was a fervent belief in the cultural value of studying literature. Adele Wiseman recalls that Ross taught his students "to look to literature not simply as a by-product but as a prime value, as the expression of the quality of a society, as witness to the soul of a culture" (quoted in Staines 11). Perhaps it is this emphasis on cultural self-recognition that accounts for Ross's initial interest in titles that were so firmly rooted in mimetic assumptions about the relationship between people and place. Perhaps it also accounts for his reluctance to include titles that challenged cultural norms. What is certain is that the series was eminently conservative in its formation; its version of newness was grounded in books that were old. The New Canadian Library emphasis on works that were not contemporary (which also accounted for the exclusion of works that were experimental) had far-reaching effects that can still be felt today. In the classroom, and in the study of Canadian literature, the main effect was to introduce the idea that contemporary texts had less confirmed cultural relevance than historical texts, that experimentation or culturally transgressive works had no place within the canon that was being established with each new title in the NCL series.

Although I have no doubt that Ross believed in the value of the works chosen for inclusion in the New Canadian Library — conservative as those values might be — his choices were, in many ways, restricted by forces beyond his control. Because the series was devoted to reprints, Ross had to find titles that were available because they were in the public domain, or that could be purchased by his publisher for a reasonable amount of money. Contemporary works — the rights to which were not usually owned by McClelland and Stewart — were simply too expensive to acquire, if they could be acquired at all. This meant that in the early years of the series, before it gained status and prestige, selection on the basis of purely aesthetic criteria was impossible. Ross and McClelland had to confront the reality faced by all anthologizers: the fact that what gets reprinted and collected is a direct function of cost and availability. Canons are often the product of market forces, and they always transmit an ideology that is market-centred. Not all readers know this; consequently, they may be led to assume that the "classics" before them are somehow uncontaminated by the market, when in reality it is precisely this contamination that determines a large part of their value.

From a business perspective, McClelland's decision to reprint inexpensive works made perfect sense; it was a smart thing to do. Publishers must capitalize on market forces if they want to stay afloat. Yet it is also important to recognize that such capitalization does not always promote — or even allow — aesthetic forces to take precedence over economic ones. The New Canadian Library canonized older texts before newer ones because it was cheaper to do so. It canonized certain writers and excluded others in response to the cost of obtaining the rights to their works. What needs to be challenged is the frequently made assumption that any canon — in this case the influential NCL canon — is the product of purely aesthetic concerns.

In Canada, the rhetoric associated with the New Canadian Library was designed to convince readers, and particularly teachers, that a rigorous standard had been applied in the selection of these texts. As this rhetoric evolved, McClelland came to call these books the "classics" of Canadian literature, and many people accepted them as such. Yet in the first ten years of the series, the word *classic* was never mentioned by either McClelland or Ross. No standards of selection were ever articulated.

Although the original choices in the series were Ross's, the series soon came to respond to other forces. Ross recalls that "everything there is not my choice" (Slopen 21). Far from it. For example, "salesmen on the road were receiving requests and others were consulted" (Slopen 21), a statement which suggests that books that came to be described as "classics" in the 1970s might have achieved that status because one salesperson suggested they be included in the series during its expansion in the 1960s. The emphasis was on inclusion rather than exclusion, on monopoly rather than on judgement or taste. As a result, the pedagogical canon as we know it evolved with secondary attention to quality; of primary importance was the book's availability and price. If this is true, then any claim for the classic status of books in the series becomes highly dubious. By extension, the study of a national literature based on these texts must also be considered dubious. In short, the pedagogical canon as we have come to know it may be described as a myth, founded on a grandiose marketing plan.

Much of what we now recognize as the canon of Canadian fiction exists as the result of a marketing scheme. Ross's genuinely noble intentions in conceiving the series were soon overrun by McClelland's businesslike ability to capitalize on the commercial benefits inherent in the idea of promoting a national literature at the mass-market level. Before the New Canadian Library, nationalism had been seen as a value worthy of expression, of course, and many nineteenth- and twentieth-century Canadian critics encouraged writers to represent a national ideal. But the exploitation of nationalism was something different, for now it was linked to the deliberate founding of an institutional canon. In other words, the New Canadian Library defined the pedagogical canon in terms of exploitation rather than expression. This definition shifted the notion of value away from what was produced (the literary work itself might be good) toward the conditions of its production (the literary work was good if it was Canadian and obtainable and cheap).

Of course, there also had to be an audience for the New Canadian Library. McClelland realized from the start that the series would never be profitable if it was marketed solely to the public, which was largely unfamiliar with these "classic" texts; it was essential that school sales be secured. Course adoptions would guarantee profit, and guaranteed profit would ensure the continuing classic status of books included in the series. No sales, no status. Because there were practically no courses devoted strictly to Canadian literature at that time, the success of the series rested on Ross and McClelland's ability to convince institutions and individual teachers to offer courses in the subject, or to include Canadian literature texts in their course readings.[3] Right from the start, professional involvement was crucial to the canonical enterprise.

One of McClelland's first letters about the series, dated 20 April 1954, indicates that its conception was tied to his hope that he and Ross would be "able to convince the majority of University English departments in this country that every student studying English at the University level should be familiar . . . with Canadian literature." To accomplish this, McClelland suggested to Ross that "at some convention or meeting of professors" they must "get complete endorsation of the idea that Canadian literature should be at least a fringe subject in first-year University." McClelland felt that "theoretically this idea should not be too hard to sell," yet he was bothered by the fact that "we still get graduates from the English language and literature course at Toronto who apply for jobs with us and who have never heard of people like Thomas Chandler Haliburton, etc."

To overcome this problem, McClelland hatched an interesting marketing scheme, which he also described in the letter to Ross dated 20 April 1954. Books to be included in the New Canadian Library would first be sent to students in page proofs, "without identifying the author" (perhaps to avoid any negative identification of the author as a Canadian). The students would be required to read the novel and "to submit an original criticism of something that has not yet been published." In this way McClelland hoped to secure his market in advance, and also to determine whether students would like the books he planned to publish in the series. Although this idea was never implemented, it gives some sense of the extent to which McClelland was willing to allow the selection process to be determined by an early form of market-testing and research. It also demonstrates the extent to which the New Canadian Library canon was the product of economic, rather than aesthetic, forces. As McClelland wrote to Ross, "the key to the whole problem, as you realize, is the economic one." McClelland knew that if the students could be involved in the marketing plan — he called it "something of a game" — then "it wouldn't matter a damn whether the book were good, bad or indifferent." So much for Canadian classics.

By 1957 McClelland was ready to propose a name for the series. On 2 April he wrote to Ross suggesting "New Canadian Library" as the title, not only to avoid such "blatant symbols" as beavers and maple leaves, but also because "we hope these books will appeal to immigrants as an opportunity to bone up on Canadian literature." (Here we see in embryo a concept that would later become crucial to the NCL marketing plan — the idea that titles in the series had value because they could be used as nationalist teaching aids that would educate people about Canada.) Ross liked McClelland's suggestion. He replied on 3 May that "the series title seems O.K. — if 'new Canadian' doesn't suggest immigrant literature and/or very *recent* literature."

I don't want to suggest that there was a great deal of discussion about the meaning of "Canadian" in the correspondence devoted to the series. In fact, there is very little attention devoted to this question, a silence that speaks volumes. Instead, most discussions centre on financial questions. Leacock will sell well enough to carry some of the less popular titles for a while. Grove's work can be reprinted cheaply because the rights are held by McClelland and Stewart itself. *Such Is My Beloved* is available for purchase at a decent price. Sinclair Ross won't ask for much money.

What was chosen was what was available at bargain-basement prices. The only proven seller was Leacock. This is why McClelland decided to include one Leacock for every six new NCL titles in the series' developing years; Leacock supported the other books, which gave new meaning to the oxymoron "loss leaders." The minutes of a 20 January 1962 meeting devoted to the New Canadian Library provide some sense of the extent to which economic considerations determined the choice of titles that McClelland and Stewart would later designate classics:

The meeting opened with a brief discussion of sales and costs. It was decided that if a book is long and unlikely to have a college market, we should forget it. Some have to be included as loss leaders, and a few should go in to preserve the purpose of the Series, but generally 256 is a safe limit for an NCL publication. This would accomodate [sic] a normal 320-page book. Above 85,000 words we begin to run into cost trouble.

The minutes suggest one perfectly clear way of recognizing a classic: it is no longer than 85,000 words. If it is longer, then it will just have to be chopped down to NCL classic size. It was this type of chopping that produced the original, severely truncated NCL version of *Roughing It in the Bush*, a Canadian classic that was cut almost in half, then taught to many students, over many years, in its abridged form. Another way of recognizing a classic was to consider what provincial education boards wanted students to read. For example, at the 20 January 1962 meeting,

> Jim Totton reported that the education departments are increasingly interested in books that show kids growing up — such as TOM SAWYER, MAN FROM GLENGARRY, WHO HAS SEEN THE WIND. GRAIN would seem to go well in this category and Dr. Ross was strongly in favour of including the book, which we own.

Ralph Connor's *The Man from Glengarry* soon appeared in the series. So did *Grain*, which had originally been published as far back as 1926. The 20 January meeting also indicated that there was a third way of determining whether a book should be admitted to the series — a consideration of the royalty demanded by an author or his or her estate:

> Jim Totton suggested we might get a university commitment for UNDER THE VOLCANO, in view of the current interest in Malcolm Lowry. It is a long book — 380 normal pages — and still available in Vintage. Our edition would be more expensive, and J. McClelland is against doing books already in another series.

A fourth consideration concerned the contemporary nature of the book. At the 20 January meeting, Colin McDougall's *Execution* and Adele Wiseman's *The Sacrifice* were discussed, but were put on hold because they were "too recent."

Of all the correspondence I saw concerning the development of the series (approximately two hundred letters and internal McClelland and Stewart memos), only five items discuss the actual literary merits of specific titles in any detail. Three of these are devoted to one title —

Leonard Cohen's *Beautiful Losers.* Ross's objections to the inclusion of this title emphasize his conservative leanings, but they also demonstrate that he did not want to be associated with art he could not condone. In a letter to McClelland dated 18 September 1968, he wrote:

> I am sure it "represents" something in the culture of the moment. I am not surprised that Cohen has his following. And the problem raised by this consideration is indeed fascinating. I think that the book — and its vogue — is a visible sign of the cancer which is eating away at the marrow of our life in our time. The artist in our time must leave himself open to the phenomenon which Cohen perceives. But the artist if he *is* the artist must have a certain attitude of his own. He cannot avoid or deny the dirt of our life in a time of disintegration. But it just doesn't do to take a bath in a dirty tub! Cohen wallows in the stinking wreckage of the West. Because there is despair in his eye and in his voice. There is despair in the whole post-civilized posture which this book exemplifies. There is only debasement in this wallowing of Cohen's because Cohen has neither the desire nor the spiritual *muscle* to lift himself up from his dirty tub. Not really.
>
> My objection to the book is at once aesthetic, moral, philosophical *and* theological. It is also visceral. The book turns my stomach. Quite literally, Jack!

Ross concluded that "I simply cannot put my name on that book." Yet, as he confesses in his letter, Ross had not really read Cohen's novel carefully when it was first suggested for inclusion in the series: "I had thumbed through the book months before but without giving it serious attention. . . . This is merely to *explain* how I slid into an indefensible editorial blunder. I *certainly* should not have agreed without more time for a careful reading."

Although Ross's name continued to appear as general editor on each of the NCL titles, McClelland's staff made more and more of the suggestions concerning books to be included in the series. Sometimes, when Ross did recommend titles for inclusion, McClelland would question whether Ross had actually read what he was recommending. In a memo to his assistant dated 9 April 1969 concerning a new title, McClelland writes:

> Malcolm suggested the book. Has he in fact read it? I think this should be clarified. I would like to know the reasons for recommending it for inclusion. The book is unknown to me. Is it likely to be used in Canadian literature courses? Is it a recognized Canadian classic?

The book was Francis William Grey's *The Curé of St. Philippe* (1899). If McClelland had to ask whether it was a classic, how classic could it be? In fact, McClelland required some practical information before he could decide whether to include the title in the series:

> The copyright situation should be investigated very carefully. I think you realize that copyright prevails for 50 years after the death of the author. When did he die? Who was he? What was his background? What is known about him?

Soon this title, which was unknown to McClelland in 1969, had entered the library of Canadian classics.

This 1969 memo represents the first time McClelland uses the term *classic* in his internal correspondence, although the series had been in existence for more than a decade. It's pretty clear that McClelland was not particularly selective in choosing these classics; his goal was to include as many titles as possible, so as to squeeze out the competition. The fact that the correspondence includes no mention of the literary merits of these titles suggests that the fundamental criterion for selection remained commercial rather than critical or aesthetic. But the chief point is this: even if we could determine the principles of selection that prompted Ross to choose certain texts over others, it wouldn't really matter, because the series responded to market forces in a way that Ross never anticipated. In the end, the object of selection was not to exclude poor work, but to include as much material as possible. This is a strange way to determine and promote a nation's classics.

By 1974 the canonical rhetoric was much more assured. On 24 June of that year McClelland wrote to Dorothy Bloore, Jean Parkin, and David Silcox (prominent supporters of Canadian art) about a new plan aimed at promoting the series. (As he says in the letter, he had also thought of approaching "a distillery or a tobacco company or the government or something like that.") He introduces the NCL list by saying that "theoretically the list comprises 150 most important Canadian novels ever published [sic]. These are the Canadian classics. It is not a perfect world however and our claim is not a perfect one. . . . but for practical purposes talk about 150 great Canadian books." In McClelland's view, "these classics are permanent and very few of them are going to disappear. These are the books that will be read 50 years from now and many of them will still be read 150 years from now." McClelland wanted Bloore, Parkin, and Silcox to endorse a scheme that would make it possible for well-known Canadian artists to execute paintings for specific covers in the series. These paintings would then be sold to collectors in order to pay the artist and to cover the colour reproduction costs: "My theory is a sneaky one. My theory is that we would put an artificially high value on these paintings to save the reputation of the artist involved, but we would actually pay them on a commissioned basis considerably less." Hmmm. What if the artist whose reputation would be saved hadn't actually read the book in question? McClelland was ready for that scenario: "We would actually make the goddamn artist read the book." After all, as McClelland pointed out in his letter, "we have the great Canadian authors — MacLennan, Callaghan, Laurence, Richler, Atwood, Roy, Davies, etc. etc. — you name them, we have them — their books, since they are being used by hundreds of thousands of Canadian school children, deserve great art."

McClelland and Stewart's marketing department didn't always share McClelland's optimistic view of the classic status of books in the series. In June 1975, for example, McClelland received a letter from a Montreal reader who complained about the value judgements implicit in the New Canadian Library cover blurbs. She wrote:

> I realize these are meant to entice people to buy and hopefully read the books, but in reality they are an insult to the authors. For example, on the cover of Sinclair Ross' *As for me and my house* there is: ". . . his prose is of a clarity and vividness rare in Canadian literature" and on the cover of Margaret Laurence's *Jest of God*, there appears: ". . . one of Canada's few really gifted writers . . ." Both of these phrases suggest that Canadian literature is mainly drivel, and that these authors have managed to rise a bit above it. There is very little drivel in Canadian literature, and what there is, is most often published through the American market. (Celia Jeffries to McClelland, 5 June 1975)

McClelland responds on 15 August by saying, "I have certainly drawn this to the attention of our marketing people. . . . it is clear from the examples you have given that we do ourselves from time to time slip into a patronizing attitude about Canadian writing as a whole and we will guard against it." The correspondence makes it clear that, even in 1975, McClelland and Stewart's claims for the classic status of books in the New Canadian Library series could be undercut by the rhetoric of precisely those people whose job it was to convey this status. Jeffries's letter also demonstrates that, from the perspective of McClelland and Stewart's cover-copy writers, there were very few books in the series that could be called "rare" and few Canadian writers who could be called "gifted." The attitudes conveyed by the cover copy express more than "a patronizing attitude." They belie an undercurrent of contempt within McClelland and Stewart for Canadian writing in general. As Jeffries notes in her letter, "I am sure that your marketing department is well aware of the fact that people do choose books by their covers, but they do not seem to be aware of the fact that no comments would be better than derogatory ones."

The New Canadian Library had become a new commercial library. What does this say about the idea that the New Canadian Library introduced students and teachers to the best of Canadian literature? It says that terms like *the best* and *classic* are more often than not simply advertising terms that are eventually claimed by critical rhetoric. Canons evolve; they are also constructed. They all respond to market forces, to pedagogical and cultural demands. The Canadian canon that emerged with the New Canadian Library series shared these origins. But it was an unconventional canon because it had emerged so quickly that its values could barely be questioned. This led to the unchallenged establishment of certain canonical values that continue to inform the way Canadian literature is perceived and taught today.

Here, as in every canonical arena, excellence and exclusion went hand in hand. And here, as in every canonical ethos, certain forms of literature were deemed closer to perfection than others. While the New Canadian Library did reprint poetry and short-story collections, the privileged genre within the series was the realist novel, mainly because such novels tended to be adopted in literature courses, while poetry, short fiction, and experimental fiction were not. Ross and McClelland's correspondence from the summer of 1975 provides one example of how the decision to exclude an author from the series could be a function of genre discrimination. They had been discussing the possible inclusion of Norman Levine's short stories (Levine had written to McClelland, proposing that a collection of his stories be included in the series). In a letter dated 15 July, Ross argues that there are two reasons to exclude Levine:

> 1) the quality of his work and 2) the sale possibilities of a volume of his short stories. It may be that the stories he has in mind are first-rate (although this would surprise me). But, as I recall, we have not had good luck with short story volumes — certainly not in terms of course adoption. I doubt if Levine would be strong in trade sales either.

On 15 August, McClelland responded to Ross with these words:

> Because he is considered to be a writer of stature in some quarters, I think the least we can do is to be polite. I passed the buck by telling him

I was sending the inquiry on to you. I shall now tell him that while you have been generally familiar with his writing over a period of years, that you would want to see the stories he would propose for inclusion in assembled form before reaching a decision. Unless he has changed, this will send him into a mood of outraged fury and we will either never hear from him again (which is to be hoped) or he will send an insulting letter.

The correspondence does more than point to the ways in which a particular author could be manipulated; it indicates the extent to which inclusion in the series was related to the sales potential of certain genres and authors, rather than to literary quality. In another example of genre discrimination directed at "experimental" fiction (here depicted as adversarial), McClelland issues a memo to Anna Porter and Malcolm Ross summarizing "the basics of the decisions" reached at a meeting with Ross held on 11 June 1977. Among other things, "we decided to eliminate the literary curiosity type of novel. In short we are going for the big ones and major authors and not necessarily looking for adversity, i.e. we have retained most of Gabrielle Roy rather than including the Graeme Gibsons, the Dave Godfreys, etc." When decisions are made in this way, as they often are in canon-building activities, the meaning and value of "classic" status are inevitably compromised.

As a businessman, McClelland exploited his discovery of the "classic" designation as much as possible, right up to the planning of the Calgary Conference on the Canadian Novel, which was deliberately but secretly conceived as an event that would ratify the canonical status of books included in the series, to the exclusion of books published by other presses. For McClelland, it was a classic deal.

As early as 1976 McClelland realized that it would become more and more difficult to add new titles to the New Canadian Library. Other publishers had started their own reprint series, and many were reluctant to sign away the rights to their books as willingly as they had in the 1960s. On 14 October 1976 McClelland informed Anna Porter that "the days of the New Canadian Library as far as new titles are concerned are numbered. I will have to give serious thought to the retirement of our friend."

How was this to be done? Over the following five months, McClelland developed a way to ease Ross out of the picture. He knew that the quality of the series was in doubt. On 29 March 1977 he told Ross that "for some time now — and we had discussions about this years ago — it has been necessary to compromise. This series is no longer confined to the great Canadian classics." There were other problems too:

The market for Canadian paperbacks is larger than ever and we have achieved a good ongoing technique in the annual three-for-two paperback sale. While the marketplace is increasing, competition is increasing too. New Canadian Library cover treatment is an impediment although inclusion in the series is a useful marketing technique. Royalty rates are higher than they were when we started and there will be increasing pressure on that front.

By way of addressing these problems, McClelland conceived a redefinition of the New Canadian Library. "Our proposal is to close the New Canadian Library off at 100 titles," he wrote. "It's an arbitrary number, it could be 75 — it could be less." McClelland's use of the word *arbitrary* to describe the number of titles that would eventually be called *classic* underlines the arbitrary nature of the New Canadian Library canon. In the end, McClelland decided that 100 was the right round number of books to be designated classic (not 99, or 98). He proposed a revitalized New Canadian Library that would include "in one series the 100 great works of Canadian fiction." This selection, McClelland argued, "should be known as say 'The Canadian Classic Library' a division of the New Canadian Library." It "would act as a guide to high school and even college teachers, who seem vastly uninformed about Canadian literature."

In order to further educate the uninformed, McClelland wanted to promote these 100 great works through "a variety of specialized marketing techniques." It is in one of these "techniques" that we find the germ of the Calgary Conference on the Canadian Novel. McClelland encouraged Ross to "name the 100 great works of Canadian fiction." How was Ross to do this? "You might choose to do this personally," McClelland wrote, or "you might chair a committee; you might do it by polling or surveying a selected group of experts." There is, of course, one problem with such a procedure, and McClelland spelled it out: "of the 100 titles selected by any one of those three groups at least 90 and possibly more would already be in the NCL. . . . What can we do about those for which we don't have rights?" McClelland speculated that "we might have enough leverage to force the availability of those titles," but "the publishers wouldn't like it. We would probably have to sweeten the royalty rates to satisfy the publishers." How would the Canadian Classic Library be launched? McClelland to Ross: "We would plan to launch the whole program as a major event, at an appropriate Canadian university" in 1978, to mark the twentieth anniversary of the series and Ross's retirement.

The correspondence that follows the initial expression of this idea is interesting because it reveals the extent to which McClelland was behind the Calgary Conference, and also the extent to which he attempted to influence the outcome of the ballot that was distributed in connection with that conference — a ballot that was designed to determine in a kind of Canadian hit parade the most important Canadian novels ever published. Ironically, the list of the 100 most important novels was a creation of the very people whom McClelland had recently described as being "vastly uninformed about Canadian literature." How much could one trust their opinions?

It is difficult not to think of this event as a kind of apotheosis of canonical activity in Canada. Yet even this activity, as McClelland's correspondence reveals, was conceived of as a marketing ploy that revolved around questions of costs, permissions, and rights. The list of the so-called 100 most important Canadian novels was actually produced to many cries of outrage, not only because people objected to the idea of critical ranking by ballot but also because they sensed McClelland's behind-the-scenes manipulation of the entire project, a manipulation he steadfastly denied. Yet the correspondence reveals that he had conceived of such a conference in 1977, and that he very much wanted the conference to be played his way.

By June 1977 all plans for the conference had gone underground. McClelland was perturbed to discover that there were some major Canadian novels not included in the New Canadian Library. This came as a surprise. In a memo to Anna Porter and Malcolm Ross dated 14 June 1977, he wrote that "we can't afford to be impractical enough to find that in the opinion of people we ask the selections have all been crazy and that we had to go out and get another 50 titles or something of that sort." As always, "there is the problem of securing rights for those we don't have." Of course, as McClelland observed, "there is a tremendous advantage in the long run for marketing purposes if we have some sort of peer group selection or approval of selection rather than just the single voice."

McClelland's way of seizing this advantage was to test the ballot by showing it to "10, 12 or 15 people (friendly experts)." These "10 friendly critics" would, of course, "all be college people," a decision that points to the increasingly devalued status of high-school teachers as arbiters of literary taste (there would only be two of these "high-school people," but they, like the "college people," would be "friendly"). Regardless of their status as critics in the eyes of McClelland, these "friendly experts" would have something in common: they would not know how their responses would be used; "they would not be told that it was a survey." In fact, McClelland wrote, "no one will know our precise intent." If the results showed that the idea of a larger survey was "too dangerous," then "we would abandon it. If we found, on the other hand, that the results were more or less predictable, then we would determine precisely how we would proceed."

McClelland concluded "I think this is all very neat," and noted that the conference would be held in Calgary the following year, but only after "we have tried to acquire the rights we are lacking," so as to have exclusive control over the books listed on the ballot. McClelland also realized that he would not want to sponsor a ballot that eliminated some of his best-selling titles: "The next issue relates to what we do with the titles that would thereby be eliminated from the New Canadian Library. Some of them sell very well. It is a complex problem." The solution McClelland proposed was to start a list of quality paperbacks that would include many of the works that might be excluded from the ballot and its resulting list of Canadian classics.

By September 1977, plans for the conference had advanced. In a letter to Ross dated 20 September, McClelland observed that "we must proceed with great care and caution. There are crocodiles in the swamp." By this he meant that many academics had begun to object to the idea of the ballot, and particularly to the possibility that it might be inspired by McClelland's desire to use the conference to foreground his company's books. He told Ross that "there should be no reference to the New Canadian Library at all in the ballot" and "no reference at all to publisher." Then he proceeded to lay out the terms of the ballot, emphasizing that it should focus on books that are taught in Canadian literature classes. McClelland was aware that the curricular canon he controlled might differ markedly from the popular canon known by general readers. When Ross protested against McClelland's secret plans, McClelland responded in a letter dated 11 October 1977: "Nothing has changed except that we are not going to reveal our intent or our plans at all at the meeting"; "Our basic intent remains the same, but we don't want that known to anybody other than ourselves."

The rest, as they say, is history. The conference was held in February 1978. Despite all the honours paid to Ross, he expressed indignation at the way the ballot had been manipulated and at the way the information surrounding it had been presented. On 17 March 1978 he wrote to McClelland, calling this incident "the most painful experience of my entire career." Seven months later, on 5 October, he was still protesting: "I was interested in finding out how 'users' of the NCL series felt about it — its weaknesses and gaps as well as its strengths. I never at any time thought that the '100 best' or the '10 greatest' Canadian books could be fixed by a ballot of this kind."

McClelland's response to the outcome of the conference was quite the opposite. "I regret in many ways the list wasn't 'cooked' a little bit," he wrote on 28 February, and on 16 May he expressed disbelief that Ross "could be so intimidated by a handful of academics at the Calgary Conference." Later, on 17 October, in response to Ross's continuing complaints about the fiasco, McClelland concluded that "the whole thing reeks of inane academic snobbery and snobbery of an unrealistic sort. . . . Your problem, Malcolm, is that you are too susceptible to bullshit."

This comment highlights McClelland's contempt for the academic audience that had supported his series and made it a financial success. In the face of such contempt, could one ever expect that the New Canadian Library choices would do anything more than exploit the teachers and students for whom they were originally designed? Or could one really expect that the entire project of creating a pedagogical canon would be more than the product of a consensus achieved through discussions between the publisher and his clients?

* * *

The formation of the New Canadian Library was essential to the development of Canadian literary studies, and it served the crucial function of creating the canon on which the Canadian literature industry could be built. But the fact that it was industrially valuable should not lead us to conclude that it was the product of a sustained aesthetic/critical vision or that it embodied any recognized expressions of excellence. The values established by the New Canadian Library series were as new and unquestioned as the series itself. For the most part, the series responded to economic, rather than aesthetic, pressures. Right from the start, it was conceived of and constructed as a marketing device. As it turned out — as it *always* turns out in canonical affairs — the great arbiter of taste was the market, which pronounced certain titles to be in or out of demand. Usually, books that are out of demand are dropped from the canon. The evolution of the New Canadian Library, however, demonstrates that just the opposite may occur: in this case, books that were out of demand or out of print for many years (books that had become *un*valuable) became the very works considered to be worthy of inclusion in a series that marketed its titles as classics deserving curricular and critical attention — truly an original concept for determining literary value. In the topsy-turvy world of the New Canadian Library, what was not wanted was often wanted most.

We sometimes assume that it is people who create literary histories and the values they embody. Or we believe that literary excellence is out there, waiting to be found. This brief excursion into the origins of the New Canadian Library should do something to unseat these views. Literary history is often written by the marketplace. Canons centre on what can be bought and sold. And they respond to pressures that have to do with promoting certain kinds of books, to certain audiences, at certain times, for certain financial ends. More often than not, in Canada and elsewhere, the art of the deal is the art.

6

The Rhetoric of Back-Cover Copy:
Sinclair Ross's As for Me and My House

THERE IS PROBABLY NO WORK of Canadian fiction that has received more canonical validation than Sinclair Ross's *As for Me and My House.* In the prefatory note to a collection of critical essays he edited on the novel, David Stouck says that "no single work of fiction in the country has so continuously engaged the attention and interest of writers and critics as this novel" (ix). For Stouck, who also provided the introduction to an American reprint that appeared in 1978, the novel is "one of those books, like *Huckleberry Finn* or *The Great Gatsby,* by which a country measures its imaginative life" ("Introduction" xii). John Moss calls it "the quintessential Canadian novel" (*From the Heart* 1). This may be why the back-cover copy of the most recent New Canadian Library edition of the novel describes it as a "landmark work." It may also be why the back-cover copy of the "classic edition" in 1982 contained the endorsement of McClelland and Stewart's short-lived Canadian Classics Committee, which had somehow determined that *As for Me and My House* was a novel that was "indispensable for the appreciation of Canadian literature." Even the back-cover copy of the first New Canadian Library edition (1957) informs us that it has "become a classic."

It was not always this way. The novel was originally published by Reynal and Hitchcock in New York in 1941. "McClelland and Stewart imported some copies for the Canadian market, which were distributed in April of that same year" (Stouck, *Sinclair* 5).[1] In his introduction to the Bison Book edition, Stouck says that "when *As for Me and My House* came out it was not reviewed in mass publications and few people ever heard of it. The book earned its author exactly $270 in advance royalties" (vi). Although there were some positive Canadian reviews of the first edition, "the book sold only a few hundred copies." It soon "dropped from sight" (Stouck, *Sinclair* 6).

The appearance of the novel in the New Canadian Library series certainly affected its profitability and its canonical status. Stouck records that in its first decade as a New Canadian Library title, the novel sold 50,000 copies. He also notes that by 1992, "sales of *As for Me and My House* in the NCL must be close to a quarter of a million copies" ("Sinclair Ross in Letters" 12).

Although *As for Me and My House* is now undoubtedly recognized as a Canadian classic, this very recognition suggests the extent to which canonical status is a curricular function, for the novel is not known outside academic circles. As Stouck says, "Sinclair Ross's readership for more than 30 years has consisted largely of the students and teachers of his work in colleges and universities" ("Sinclair Ross in Letters" 12). John Metcalf argues that this is only one example of how such Canadian classics "do not connect with any ordinary book-buying public; they are not in a relationship with a readership. The reputations of these books were created and fostered by academics to serve dubious academic and nationalist ends" (*What Is* 43).

Metcalf is almost completely right. The value of Canadian classic texts is constructed, usually by professors, whose interest lies in affirming narratives that promote those forms of interpretive power sanctioned by the institution itself. Where such texts do not exist they must be invented, in order to provide stable objects upon which members of the institution can exercise their pedagogical and critical claims to specialization. Only through such invention can the hegemony of specialization be maintained.

When the credibility of this specialization is unfamiliar or in doubt — as it was in the early years of the Canadian literature industry — the need for fetishized texts becomes particularly strong. The interpretation of these texts must testify to more than their excellence; it must show that this excellence validates the new-found curricular subject — Canadian literature, and, by extension, Canada itself. The viability of a national canon testifies to the viability of the nation. It also testifies to the power of its testifiers. As John Guillory observes, canons are "cultural capital"; they determine "how works are preserved, reproduced, and disseminated over successive generations and centuries." Because it is the school as an institution that is responsible for "the *reproduction* of the social order, with all of its various inequities," those who can effect this reproduction — teachers — hold many of the keys to the ways in which a culture is represented (*Cultural Capital* vii, ix).

To construct a canon, teachers must demonstrate that the connection between nation and narration is inviolable and that it transcends regional distinctions. This is why John Moss tells us that even though Sinclair Ross is a regional writer, his work somehow expresses a Canadian essence (and perhaps Moss's northern dream that such an essence can be identified): "Sinclair Ross writes from the heart of the Canadian heartland" (*From the Heart* 2). At the same time, great Canadian novels must always be something more than just regional or heartily Canadian. *As for Me and My House* must be described as a work that has regional and national and universal power. It is about the Canadian prairies in the Depression; and it is a novel of "universal consideration" that is "paradigmatic of the imaginative life" (Stouck, "Introduction" xii–xiii). It represents a lot.

My current interest in this novel has little to do with its story of Philip Bentley and his wife. I want to focus on the ways in which its treatment by publicists and critics shows how canonical texts are packaged and promoted. I also want to suggest that this packaging and promotion often encourages the creation of discursive strategies that subordinate the discourse of the classic text. Ultimately, the discourse of marketing and promotion inevitably becomes the text. There are a number of questions raised by this assertion. What rhetorical strategies are brought to bear on the promotional conception of texts that are deemed to be of classic status? How do these strategies shift in the case of texts that are rapidly enshrined within the canon? What claims are made for the pedagogical utility of such texts? How does the "classic" label transform it? How does it transform us?

Few Canadian critics have grappled with these questions, and I certainly can't deal with all of them here. But I can begin to approach the topic by identifying some of the features associated with the canonical process in Canada as they appear in the eminently representative canonical text, *As for Me and My House.* There are three points I wish to discuss.

First, the process of a text becoming classic is the process of its disappearance. What we call "the text" is actually the critical commentary that replaces it. As classic status evolves, the primary work becomes increasingly secondary in power; in other words, it begins to have critical rather than creative value. By the same token, secondary work attached to the canonical text becomes increasingly primary in its function; it begins to have creative rather than critical power. We pay more attention to the criticism of a classic text than to the text itself because the critical discourse has usurped the original work and become the central object of inquiry. The presence of a classic text always means there is no classic text to be found.

Second, classic texts are by definition paradigmatic and normative; they are vehicles used to convey ideas about continuity, pattern, coherence, homogeneity. Through them, critics show us the forms that affirm a grounded and "representative" view of national or human experience. Realist literature provides the most transparent means of affirming these forms. Critics also use classic texts to demonstrate the value of sequential temporal placement — the presence of a literary tradition. For this reason, the rhetoric of canonicity must always refer to forces beyond itself; it must address microcosmic and macrocosmic values, even though the canonized text itself may work to subvert one or the other of these values.

Third, because they situate us, critically, in relation to recognizable textual and cultural models, classic texts also remind us of the fact that we are being situated. We don't read them; they teach us how to read. In this sense, they refer us to the very process of interpretation through which we arrive at the designation "classic." The interpretive process is never divorced from the interpretive activity that endorses it. This activity is almost always curricular in function. The act of conferring classic status, of reading canonically, is a self-perpetuating act, one that confirms the teacher's ability to teach literature in a way that confirms his or her ability to teach it that way. For this reason, canonical texts must remain institutional (curricular) property. They cannot be owned by the public because such ownership would socialize institutional power and wealth.

* * *

Classic Texts are Absent Texts

One way of approaching this idea is to remember *As for Me and My House* before it was canonized, before it was invented as the construct we've come to know. The novel was first published in New York in 1941. There was no Canadian edition. Ross, a bank clerk, remained virtually unknown. His story about the bleak life of Philip Bentley, a frustrated prairie preacher and failed artist, and his wife, a frustrated artist and the narrator of the novel, attracted little attention. The book's modest jacket copy stressed its regional interest; nothing was said about Canada. The emotional appeal of the novel was emphasized. There were no canonical claims; in fact, the praise offered by the publisher was qualified by the awareness that this was a first novel by a writer who might go on to deliver more, as the jacket copy of the original edition suggested:

As for Me and My House is a first novel of unusual sensitiveness and promise. Its story is told by the woman whose strength, devotion and sacrifice heal the wounds of the man who is her life. Set against a finely drawn background of the prairies in all of their bleakness and desolation, it is a deeply moving book.

The first American reviewers were as modest as the publisher in their praise. One reviewer noted that this was not a complex novel; it was simply "the story of an unhappy marriage" (Fadiman 72). Another reviewer said: "Miss Ross [sic] does a good job" (Field 14). A third explained that it was "the story of Philip Arnold's [sic] struggle to find himself" ("Fiction" 28), while a fourth said that it was about "country life and farm people" (Colquette and Frye 38). Ross himself said the novel "fell flat on its face" (quoted in Ross 170). This was no classy début.

When the novel was resurrected in its New Canadian Library form sixteen years after its first publication (there was no demand for the book), Roy Daniells thought it appropriate to explain why he was writing a critical introduction to the new paperback version of a novel that was "so unfamiliar to the Canadian public" (v). Apparently the people who wrote the cover copy for McClelland and Stewart did not think the book was unfamiliar, for they described it as "a classic in Canadian literature" — a "classic" that was "long out of print but hailed by critics as one of Canada's great novels."

Was this "classic" the *As for Me and My House* that had been published in 1941, or was it another *As for Me and My House*? Why would a great novel of such classic status be "long out of print"? And who were the critics hailing it? Prior to its release in the New Canadian Library format, exactly four articles had been published on Ross. Roy St. George Stubbs described him as a dedicated worker. A one-page article in *Country Guide and Nor'west Farmer* said Ross's fiction should generate "good healthy discussion on literature and the art of living in this western country" (Colquette and Frye 38). Edward McCourt devoted five pages to Ross in *The Canadian West in Fiction*. Desmond Pacey gave him three pages in his *Creative Writing in Canada*. This was far from the hailing McClelland and Stewart copywriters imagined. In fact, Ross was seen mainly as a new writer from western Canada, and what little commentary there was tended to stress his prairie origins and interests.

It was only with the release of the New Canadian Library edition that Ross's work was described as a "classic in Canadian literature," and for this very reason it could no longer be called strictly regional. Like other New Canadian Library titles, it had become part of a series that was "by design, indeed a library, indispensable to an understanding and appreciation of the country itself." Needless to say, the titles in such an educational series would be "authoritative," to use the publisher's authority-conscious term (*English and Communications 1992*). The 1941 novel was disappearing fast.

In the introduction to the first NCL edition, we learn that *As for Me and My House* has a "permanent appeal" because it is "closely concerned with self-scrutiny of a moral kind"; like other Canadian classics, it displays "the middle-class desire for self-knowledge as a key to self-development." Part of this development involves the realization that "analysis of the Canadian scheme of things must be regional, or at least begin by being regional" (Daniells v). Here we see in embryo the canonical assumption that greatness — particularly national literary greatness — ultimately involves the suppression of claims to regional value. Such claims may provide a beginning, but they are certainly not the end. This is why Daniells's introduction to the original New Canadian Library edition of *As for Me and My House* concludes by equating Ross's literary achievement with national purpose — an expression of the canonical belief that the two go hand in hand:

> Too much has perhaps been said about Ross's technical achievement as a writer. But his theme and its implications are writ large and need no explication. Canada is now in search of itself. This search includes an active examination of our historic and cultural past for indications of the national character. Viewed in this context, one which is congenial to most Canadian readers, *As for Me and My House* is also a little *exemplum* of faith severely tried and of hope, after long waiting, triumphant. (x)

Daniells's rhetoric carries with it several planted axioms. Most Canadian readers find the search for "national character" to be "congenial." Those who do not find it congenial to search for the national character are in the minority; perhaps they are not congenial. To engage in the search for national character is to engage in an act of faith and redemption; to reject this search, as it is exemplified in Canadian literature, is to reject the triumph of faith. The process of finding the nation through its fiction is linked to the process of finding the self; reading *As for Me and My House*, as Daniells says, couples "the desire for self-knowledge" with the ethic of "self-development" through the ideology of middle-class faith.

All of a sudden the stakes involved in reading a Canadian novel have taken on a new dimension: the act of reading is now a form of pilgrimage, aligned with the religious and material search for national identity and purpose. Any novel that partakes in this search cannot remain regional for long. In fact, any novel that partakes in this search begins to disappear as a novel; it starts to become a symbolic narrative, an allegory that directs its reader to higher, larger, more transcendent concerns. No wonder Daniells refers to the "Puritan conscience" at work in the novel. By focusing on this consciousness, Daniells can transform *As for Me and My House* into a Canadian *Pilgrim's Progress*, one that illustrates "the slow realization of forgiveness, redemption and reconciliation after torments too long for any but the Puritan to endure" (vii). Could this be the same novel that was about "country life and farm people"? No way.

Eight years after its New Canadian Library appearance, Hugo McPherson, writing in the *Literary History of Canada*, described the novel as "one of the most finished works that Canada has produced" (706). This was indeed a quick and curious rise to fame. To the best of my knowledge, only one critic has attempted to account for this evaluative turnaround. In "The Canonization of *As for Me and My House*," Morton Ross concludes that critics have used the text to validate their interest in current critical trends. My understanding of the novel's shifting reception follows Ross's point to its logical conclusion.

In the beginning, *As for Me and My House* was just a novel. You can make mistakes about plain old novels, the names of their central characters, or the gender of their authors. But it gets harder to make those mistakes about "one of the most finished works" ever written in Canada, and you certainly can't make them about a "classic." In order to accommodate this new status, the discourse had to change. By 1973, we were being told by Wilfred Cude that the novel is

> so finely structured that it invites comparison with fiction in the first rank of English literature. Ross handles personal relationships with all the delicacy of Jane Austen; he handles first-person narration with all the sophistication of Jonathan Swift; and he handles the bluster of a drought-scourged prairie with all the awareness of Emily Bronte." ("Beyond" 48)

By 1982, in its second paperback incarnation, the novel had been pronounced a New Canadian Library Classic, approved by the Canadian Classics Committee as a certified Canadian classic. In her introduction to this new classic (how *new* can a classic be?), Lorraine McMullen calls it a work that voices "the major concerns of our century," one that expresses "eternal truths." Although she is careful to note that "Ross is first of all a prairie writer," McMullen says that his themes place him "in the mainstream of Canadian writing." Note how the rhetoric has changed. The claims to universality have increased dramatically. This is no longer a book about the Bentleys and their problems of devotion and faith. It is now about "major concerns" that span "our century" rather than life in drought-belt Saskatchewan during the Depression. It voices "truths," and these truths are not particular or even time-bound; they are "eternal."

One would think that such a work would inspire a great deal of commentary. Yet after 1982, at the height of the novel's rise to canonical status, criticism of *As for Me and My House* seemed to dry up. A few scattered pieces on the novel appeared, but they represented an insignificant body of criticism in comparison with the volume of commentary that was published while the novel was in the process of being canonized. This paradox is true of many so-called Canadian classic texts: the more the work is deemed "classic," the sooner it disappears. Or to put it another way, the process of becoming classic is a process of textual erasure and replacement. The original body of the text is gradually replaced by critical commentary on that body. This means that when we study a classic Canadian text, we don't really study "it" at all; we study what we've been told about it and what we think it has become. There is no text. *As for Me and My House* is gone. It is truly *finished*. This may be why the traditional introductions to the certified NCL classics have now become "afterwords" that fulfil the role of obituaries: first the body, now the story of its life.

And yet . . . the object of study still exists. I have the various editions of the novel here before me, with their different covers and critical appendages. The book is still taught in Canadian literature courses across the country. It's out in yet another new edition. Anyhow, if it's a classic, it's certainly not dead. How *could* it be dead when it was the subject of renewed commentary at a symposium on Sinclair Ross held at the University of Ottawa in 1990, or when the University of Toronto Press published a book in 1991 that collects five decades of *As for Me and My House* criticism? And how could such a text really be absent, just when Robert Kroetsch's afterword to the new (1989) NCL edition appears? Remember, Kroetsch is himself a classic Canadian figure. Why would he lend his name to an afterword on a book that wasn't equal to his status?

These questions can be answered by considering what it is that we actually *read* when we hold this new edition in our hands. The 1941 text remains virtually the same. So we don't come to the new edition of the novel for the novel. We come for the new cover, or the new cover blurb, or (most probably) for the new afterword. In other words, we come to hear a new story by Robert Kroetsch. This means that if we want to examine the features that make *As for Me and My House* a classic, we have to examine the features that make Kroetsch Kroetsch. His afterword announces nothing but his own rebirth from the ashes of what was once a novel about prairie life.

In this new text, this reborn text, Mrs. Bentley becomes a surrogate Kroetsch, the author who "writes the beginning of contemporary Canadian fiction" (217), as if the novel had never existed and this was its genesis, now. That's what Kroetsch seems to say about Mrs. Bentley and her story. But whose novel is this? Is it really Sinclair Ross's? Or even Mrs. Bentley's? After all, who wants to be a character who "speaks some of the illusive truths not only of our culture and psyche but of contemporary art itself" (217)? Who wants to write the beginning of contemporary Canadian fiction? Who wants to be named "possibly the most compelling and disquieting character in Canadian fiction" (221)? Mrs. Bentley? Or Robert Kroetsch? In the interpretation of classic texts, the lines between character and critic are quick to disappear.

These statements say everything and nothing about the novel. Everything: its status is such that it has become a shapeless vessel with infinite capacity, ready to hold an equally infinite critical load. (How big is big? *Really* big: the novel speaks of "culture," "psyche," and "contemporary art.") Nothing: its status is such that it has become a formless blur that invites us to participate in what Kroetsch calls "the splendid dance of its evasions" (221).

Why is this splendid dance of evasion so exciting to Kroetsch, Mrs. Bentley, and us? The very phrase — "splendid dance of its evasions" — immediately situates the text (us) in relation to contemporary and not-so-contemporary literary ideas. It calls up memories of the good old days, when we could still speak of unreliable narrators, authors, and even texts. But it also allows us to remember (dutifully) that texts are always at war with themselves, always undermining the truth and power they seem to transmit. The experience of the "splendid dance of its evasions" is reassuringly deconstructive: the text is safe precisely because it is unsafe. We trust it *more* than other texts because we trust it *less*. At the same time, we know it really *can't* be trusted because it is merely a fragment in the flow of discourse; it has no unique authority, no beginning or ending, no integrity, no borders, no body, no truth, no life. As I said, it's dead.

What then is Kroetsch writing about in his afterword to what the book's new cover calls "a landmark work" that's "one of Canada's great novels"? He's writing about what I'm writing about: the way I'll make the novel mine, the way I'll make it become me and my language, so I can die and be revived through it. The classics allow us to be resurrected. They also allow us to flex our critical vocabularies. Here are some words that Kroetsch flexes in the very first paragraph of his afterword: "enigmas," "confessions," "concealment," "telling," "not telling," "presence," "absence," "illusion," "truths," "autobiography," "self-portrait." The progression echoes the progression of the afterword itself: it arrives at the notion of autobiography (self) after passing through enigma, confession, absence. Is this a book about "country life and farm people"? Yes. Kroetsch grew up on a farm.

We too can purge ourselves, disappear and reappear, and be reborn through our reading of this recent classic. It is precisely because we have been taught to read it as a narrative that embodies such profound forces as disappearance, rebirth, confession, and self-invention that it functions paradigmatically.

Classic Texts Are Paradigmatic

The whole thrust of this statement appears to contradict what I've already said, for how can a classic text that disrupts convention, that works against closure, that is seen as a progressively deconstructive force, ever be called paradigmatic, with all the stability and grounding the term implies? The contradiction can only be explained in terms of paradox: while our critical rhetoric is directed toward canonizing the text that is ostensibly liberating, unrestrained, and false (remember "the splendid dance of its evasions"), our critical sentiment is directed toward the text that is ostensibly representational, typical, and true. We want to "make it real" by making it eminently unreal. Kroetsch seems to describe this paradox when he says that Mrs. Bentley's narrative "turns into myth, before our eyes," but the myth is subverted, because "irony tumbles into sincerity, sincerity into contrivance, contrivance into truth" (221).

The paradox that allows a classic text to be both mythical and unmythical, receptive and expressive, credible and evasive, accounts for some of the confusing terms used to describe so-called classics. In his afterword to *As for Me and My House*, Kroetsch seems determined to construct the novel and the narrator and her readers as forces that are false (and therefore free). But if we look more closely, we see that the novel Kroetsch has invented embodies the very confusion he encounters in his dealing with a "classic." He wonders whether he should be the shaper or the recipient of the story. Or, as he says of Mrs. Bentley (a version of Robert Kroetsch): "Is she to be the passive recipient, the gifted interpreter of events (of shapes, of narratives) that are beyond her control? Or is she to be the active shaper of what will come to be recognized as the shaper of the announced world?" (219).

Any character (or author, or critic) who is shaping and announcing a world is also interested in controlling a particular vision of that world. In this case, the controlled vision testifies to the presence of a realist aesthetic. This aesthetic, which promotes the representation of spatio-temporal placement and detail (Sinclair Ross and Mrs. Bentley try to shape a recognizable historical milieu), is valued by Canadian critics because it embodies the structuring forces that mobilize canonical thought and allow it to be related to a nationalist literary agenda. As Donna Bennett observes:

> The notion that a canon is *shaped* also arises out of the relation of canon to national identity, which has been a crucial feature of canons through-out the nineteenth- and twentieth-century eras of nation-building. Coherence is particularly important to most national canons, for their existence is often seen as an outgrowth of a shapely national history. Thus continuity, causality, and development are formative concepts within the structure of the national canon. ("Conflicted Vision" 134)

Although the classic status of Ross's novel is frequently explained in terms of the access it provides to a national vision, it must also be understood in precisely the opposite terms — as a novel that rejects nation in favour of region; as a fragmented, discontinuous story that presents Mrs. Bentley as a narrator who is being shaped, rather than as one who is doing the shaping. Because she is a "classic" figure, she will, paradoxically, be both the teller and the person who is being told. As Kroetsch says, it is because of her "telling and not telling, of her presence and absence" that "Mrs. Bentley speaks some of the illusive truths . . . of our culture and psyche" (217). The paradox allows Kroetsch to see the novel as formed, patterned, and paradigmatic, as a narrative that somehow conveys "the larger story of the Canadian imagination," that speaks of "contemporary art itself" (217), that reveals "illusive truths," that is a story "in need of resolution" (218). Here Kroetsch simply confirms his own need for resolution, echoing his earlier view of the novel in "No Name Is My Name." There, he called *As for Me and My House* "the paradigmatic text in Canadian writing" (44). Yet the moment the paradigm is announced, it must be undercut to sustain its paradoxical essence. Kroetsch can describe the novel as the ultimate paradigm because Mrs. Bentley "names her world in great detail" ("No Name" 46), but also because she invites us to remain open, to "risk the feverish," to participate in "the mystery of narratives that tell us into being" (Afterword 221). The paradox is the paradigm. This is obviously no longer a novel about "country life and farm people." What novel was that early reviewer reading, anyhow?

The concept of the classic text as both paradigmatic and paradoxical allows us to understand why so many classics tend to be described in contradictory terms. The original, unsplit text (the one about "country life and farm people") is gradually replaced by an oxymoronic body. Once canonized, it becomes what we are pleased to call universal and particular, or we say it embodies microcosmic and macrocosmic realities, or that it displays heaven in a grain of sand. It does even more: it instructs us to see these features — to appreciate them.

Classic Texts Are Secondary Texts

While classic texts are ultimately viewed as paradigmatic forms of discourse, they can also be seen to embody the discourse that explains the paradigm. This means that the grammar of the classic is fundamentally critical and pedagogical; we read the classic text for what it tells us about something else. (In "Atwood Gothic," Eli Mandel makes this point in relation to Margaret Atwood's *Surfacing*, another canonized text which he reads as a disguised form of criticism.) If it is true that canonical texts function like critical works, then this ability of the classic to function critically signals another canonical paradox: the primary object of inquiry (the novel) directs us away from itself toward another object of inquiry. In other words, the classic text, by virtue of the referential and critical powers vested in it, is finally self-effacing. It becomes a secondary text. It focuses on something else.

This process is evident in the canonization of *As for Me and My House.* We've seen that when the novel was first published, it received little in the way of commentary; it remained to be discovered as a primary object of inquiry. By 1949, with the publication of Edward McCourt's *The Canadian West in Fiction*, it had become such an object. McCourt's critique served to reinforce the primacy of the text. Roy Daniells's introduction to the 1957 New Canadian Library edition began to undermine this primacy. But something else happened in 1957. As Morton Ross demonstrates, the publication of the novel in the New Canadian Library paperback series represented the departure point in the canonical process that followed: now the book would be institutionalized, made classic. Its interest as a primary text would inevitably fade.

By 1969, W.H. New was suggesting that the novel provided an excellent demonstration of how unreliable narrators performed (see "Sinclair Ross's Ambivalent World"). The increasingly canonized text now had pedagogical value; it could teach students something about Wayne Booth's theories concerning point of view. As Donna Bennett says:

The history of reception of *As for Me and My House* indicates not only that critics from outside the West had difficulty accepting the 'artfulness' of this book until the last two decades, but that its acceptance into the Central-Canadian-defined canon came only after the book was interpreted — with a shift in emphasis onto the unreliability of the narrator — in a way that aligned its techniques with those of modernist literary criticism. What had bothered earlier critics — repetition, the claustrophobic perspective, and the relative lack of drama and dramatization — became virtues, and new values were discovered in the text: irony, psychological intensity, and a vision blurred by ambiguity. (148)

In the hands of modernist critics, the novel had become much more than a prime example of how unreliable narration functioned. It had become a crucial work of literary criticism, a secondary source that could be used to study a number of primary subjects, including unreliable narration and the scope and power of the Canadian novel. It could also be used to study other literary works. When *As for Me and My House* was reprinted in 1982 and designated a New Canadian Library Classic, it included an endorsement by the Canadian Classics Committee assuring readers that the text was "indispensable for the appreciation of Canadian literature." I've quoted this statement before, but I hope it now appears in a new context: the Canadian Classics Committee had defined a classic text as one that allowed readers to appreciate something other than the text — in this case, nothing less than "Canadian literature" itself. On the back cover of the 1989 edition, the publisher made even greater claims for the importance of the book. It was described as "essential reading for anyone who seeks to understand the scope and power of the Canadian novel." For the first time, one's mandatory ("essential") reading of the text was equated with literature and power. In other words, the novel could be used to access the institutional hegemony that had granted the novel its power — an excellent example of how classic texts serve to reproduce and validate institutional authority.

Even in the 1989 edition, then, the referential, secondary nature of the classic text remained implicit in the definition provided by the Canadian Classics Committee. In fact, the same definition was applied to all the volumes designated New Canadian Library Classics. In other words, all Canadian classics were implicitly becoming critical guides, secondary sources that could be used to further the appreciation of Canadian literature (and, of course, the country). This raises the following question: If the classic texts were there to help us appreciate the literature, what then comprised the literature itself? The question remained unacknowledged while the canonical process peaked. At its peak, the ability of the classic text to function as criticism would be announced explicitly; indeed, this critical ability would be seen as the prime reason accounting for the greatness of the text.

This criterion of greatness is cited on the back cover of the latest edition of *As for Me and My House*, the one with the afterword by Kroetsch. We know that the novel has reached its canonical high point because now, for the first time, it is described as a "brilliant classic *study* of life in the Depression era" and as "*essential reading* for anyone who seeks to *understand* the scope and power of the Canadian novel" (emphases added). For these reasons, it is "a landmark work."

The rhetoric reveals the extent to which the classic text shifts our gaze toward another text, another narrative to be studied ("life in the Depression era" or "the Canadian novel" at large). These critical benefits (advertised on the back cover) are also promoted inside by Kroetsch, who sees Mrs. Bentley as someone engaged in the process of what he calls "world-recognizing and world-shaping." He explains that she " 'reads' her own presence in and projects herself onto the world." In Kroetsch's view, the novel does not really exist — it is "a *commentary* on, notes towards, a novel" that Mrs. Bentley might write if she could just stop being "only the commentator," only the critic in search of a text (220; emphasis added). She has become merely a guide to something beyond herself, beyond the text, beyond life. In this construction, critics like Mrs. Bentley appear in diminutive terms: they might do some real writing if they would just stop being critics. Yet critics can find out about canons even if they are not novelists, for Sinclair Ross's "teaching" will show us the way to interpret "greatness." As Kroetsch says, "in refusing to 'name' Mrs. Bentley, Sinclair Ross teaches us to read the greatness of his novel" (221). In this final undoing of the classic text, its author becomes a teacher who promotes his own work. Sinclair Ross is at the podium. Mrs. Bentley is taking notes. We are all in the classroom. Only *As for Me and My House* is absent.

* * *

I'm back to my starting point: *As for Me and My House* is finished, dead. It has become a critical guide. Its author has become a teacher. Does anyone feel particularly saddened — or maddened — by this loss? I don't think so. The lack of response — even to the hypothetical suggestion that a great Canadian classic and its author may no longer exist — demonstrates the extent to which our classic texts have become secondary objects of concern.

I've already noted that when I say "secondary" I refer to the ability of Canadian classics to direct us away from themselves toward another, primary focus. I've suggested that this primary focus is something vast and vague, such as "the scope and power of the Canadian novel" alluded to on the back cover of the most recent edition of *As for Me and My House.* But I've left out another name for this primary focus: *us.* In the end, the classic text points to the institution that created it. It points to the members of the superstructure who have been invested with the right to name the classics, or to define "the scope and power of the Canadian novel," or to create Canadian literary history. It points to the narrative we have created in order to keep our institution viable and safe. Teaching the classics becomes an act of self-affirmation. Literary history is a story we invent to safeguard the haven we have built for ourselves. But deep inside ourselves we know there are no classics. We know that literary history is a sham. And we know that literary criticism explains nothing but the person doing the explaining.

If what I say is true — even as this chapter undermines the canonical features that I presume to call "true" — then it's valid to ask: What good is a classic such as *As for Me and My House* if it's dead, or fake, or self-displacing? The answer is my conclusion. Classic texts — Canadian and non-Canadian — are never any good as primary objects of study, simply because the existence of such objects is an illusion, a sleight of hand. The illusion makes us believe that we are studying a text, rather than the constructs, values, and fantasies of its critics. Still, classic texts can be valuable if we accept them as constructs that reveal a set of shifting values — our values — that we know very little about. These are precisely the unexplored values that prompted us to grant certain texts classic status in the first place. If we examined these values, we might begin to understand the story we are trying to write about ourselves — and how we plan to sustain it.

Part Three

Reading Canonical Criticism

7

"A Quest for the Peaceable Kingdom":
The Narrative in Northrop Frye's
Conclusion to the
Literary History of Canada

THE PUBLICATION of the *Literary History of Canada,* in 1965, was a signal event that transformed the making of Canadian literary history and permanently altered the country's critical and creative landscapes. Although several earlier studies had attempted to place Canadian writers within a distinct literary tradition and had grouped them according to various ideological and aesthetic concerns, the *Literary History* was the first "comprehensive reference book on the (English) literary history" of the country (Klinck ix). As "a collection of essays in cultural history" (Frye, Conclusion 822), it opened the field to diverse forms of literary discourse; it brought together the state-supported work of "the Editors and twenty-nine other scholars" who canonized Canadian literature "by offering reasons for singling out those works regarded as the best" (Klinck, ix, xi)[1]; and it "gave a definitive imprimatur of respectability to the academic study of Canadian writing" (MacLulich, "What Was" 19). Most important, its concluding chapter, by Northrop Frye, introduced an influential theory about the evolution of Canadian literature and about the shifting modes of representing this evolution.

The twenty-eight-page conclusion is the product of an eminent critic who explicitly approved — and therefore concretized — the institution called English-Canadian literature. When it appeared in the 1965 edition, the document seemed to be the culminating essay among many that Frye had written about Canadian art and culture. Although these works — collected in *The Bush Garden* (1971) and *Divisions on a Ground* (1982) — remain "largely unread outside his own country" (Balfour 88), they provide insights into some of the questions that Frye approaches in his better-known critical studies. In *The Bush Garden,* he notes that he "was fascinated to see how the echoes and ripples of the great mythopoeic age kept moving through Canada" (viii–ix). His responses to this age constitute the critical documents on Canadian literature that he describes as "episodes in a writing career which has been mainly concerned with world literature and has addressed an international reading public, and yet has always been rooted in Canada and has drawn its essential characteristics from there" (*Bush* i). Of all these "episodes," Frye's conclusion is arguably the central mythopoeic text. The theories it articulates form the primary basis for how most Canadian critics of the past two decades have envisioned and evaluated their literature. Two prominent editors have expressed the widely held view that "no essay in Canadian literary criticism has been more influential than Northrop Frye's 'Conclusion' " (Daymond and Monkman 460). Yet despite its influential status, I can find no critique devoted exclusively to Frye's text.[2]

I do not know how to explain this curious absence of commentary. I do know that I offer here the first extended reading of Frye's conclusion. In doing so, I focus on a central feature of the essay: its narrative depiction of Frye's evolving sense of how critics necessarily become involved in their critical creations and, further, of how the degree of this involvement provides a measure of their own imaginative development.

If one looks at the conclusion from this perspective, it becomes apparent that Frye is doing much more than establishing some basic terms or theories for the analysis of Canadian literature. He is reading the Canadian literary tradition as a romance that implicates him in its structures. This approach provides an early gloss on his concept of romance, which he calls "the structural core of all fictions." His reading of Canadian literary history as a romance, and of himself as the romance's reader-hero, anticipates his view that "the message of all romance is *de te fabula*: the story is about you." In other words, "one becomes the ultimate hero of the great quest of man, not so much by virtue of what one does, as by virtue of what and how one reads" (*Secular* 15, 186, 156–57). Ian Balfour observes that in *The Secular Scripture,* Frye "rewrites the romance scenario by substituting the reader for the hero, or, more precisely, by inscribing the reader as the hero." Implicit in this "allegory of reading" are the assumptions that "the critical quest is itself a romance . . . and that Frye's particular quest is . . . a romance of romance" (61). The same remarks apply to the critic's quest in the conclusion, which appeared more than a decade before Frye's study of the structure of romance. While the projection of the reader as hero in the conclusion anticipates Frye's later work, it also reflects Frye's earlier commentary on Blake, which argues for the interaction of critical and creative energy. As A.C. Hamilton notes, Frye's vision of "literary-cultural history" recognizes "the Blakean struggle of the artist's imagination to shape reality" (59). As interpreter and moulder of reality, the critic participates in this struggle.

The conclusion exemplifies this point. Frye's representation of Canadian literary history is clearly the product of his deliberate shaping. It is characteristically mythopoeic, formal, centralist, Protestant, male-centred, and overwhelmingly English. As a history, it appears to be fundamentally untroubled by the dual linguistic and cultural heritages that both define Canada and threaten its stability as a nation. In the conclusion, Frye discovers a pastoral version of English-Canadian literary history that transcends the divisiveness endangering his country. Assuming the role of narrator as reader and romantic quester, he moves from a distanced and innocent condition to a final harmonious state that merges innocence and experience, the objective and the subjective, the perceiver and the perceived.[3]

Because the conclusion glosses the romantic myth of fall and redemption that inspires much of Frye's work, it also demonstrates how Frye as narrator-critic can seek redemption through a romantic unification with nature that is linked to a discovery of self. Such a discovery, the conclusion makes clear, is not easy to come by. While the goal of self-discovery is an inspiring narrative force, the actual status and validity of selfhood remain in doubt. As a literary historian, Frye knows that the narrative identity he seeks stems from the cultural and historical roots that define his conception of romance and his own experiences as a minister of religion and teacher; there can be no distinct self in the context of this palimpsest. His self-representation is inevitably a misrepresentation; it is paradoxically undercut by the romantic genre. In appealing to the influence of romantic doctrine, Frye must acknowledge that his notion of identity is necessarily plural, that it is determined by plural notions of cultural and national identity. At the same time, he is driven toward writing a conclusion that traces a change in his perspective, in the way he sees his literary world. It is the tension between these collective and individual impulses that gives the critic-narrator his double-sided stance.

The version of Canadian literary tradition one enters by following this twofold representation expresses what Eli Mandel describes as one

of Frye's critical preoccupations: "the romantic fall into modern consciousness, the wilderness or labyrinth of space and time, and the
antithetical quest for a return to an integrated being" ("Northrop
Frye" 285). Thus the conclusion illustrates how Frye's conception of
literary history-making is simultaneously an act of culture-making and
self-making. It provides an excellent example of how literary criticism
is often the outgrowth of the critic's private dreams and desires. And it
lends credence to Balfour's view that, for Frye, "the distinction between
writer and critic is an unstable one" (78). As Hayden White observes,

> although Frye wants to insist on important differences between poetry
> and history, he is sensitive to the extent to which they resemble one
> another. And although he wants to believe that proper history can be
> distinguished from metahistory, on his own analysis of the structures of
> prose fictions, he must be prepared to grant that there is a mythic
> element in proper history by which the structures and processes depicted
> in its narratives are endowed with meanings of a specifically fictive kind.
> (58)

In the conclusion, Frye assumes the telling role of an "Odyssey critic"
whose narrative about ending is also the story of his "quest for the
peaceable kingdom" of Canada that will satisfy the utopian impulse
informing much of Frye's extended poetics.[4] This pastoral realm
evokes more than an image of Canada and the nation's literary tradition. Lying beyond history, beyond space and time, the peaceable
kingdom represents for Frye "the reconciliation of man with man and
of man with nature" in "a haunting vision of serenity that is both
human and natural." This vision is another expression of Frye's preoccupation with "romantic historical myths based on a quest or pilgrimage to a City of God or a classless society" (*Fables* 53–54). In the end,
the pastoral universe Frye discovers through his Canadian quest is
emblematic. It embodies "a serenity that transcends consciousness"
and locates Canada (and Frye's narrative) in relation to "the mood of
Thoreau's Walden retreat, of Emily Dickinson's garden, of Huckleberry
Finn's raft, of the elegies of Whitman" (Conclusion 848).[5] This experience enables Frye to construct Canada as the apotheosis of metaphor,
while reconstructing the criticism attached to Canada (his apocalyptic
conclusion) as a romance, a fiction, a myth.

In the conclusion, as in his non-Canadian criticism, Frye provides "a
fusing link between poet and critic" (Mandel, "Northrop Frye" 291),
one that will allow him to create an allegory with himself at its mythol-
ogized centre. To apprehend this evolution, one has to focus on the

conclusion as a romance that has its own shifting rhetoric, its own shifting images, and its own developing persona who performs in the narrative he is both observing and creating anew. Frye's involvement in this narrative testifies to his engagement with the subject of his criticism. Yet his focus on identity paradoxically undercuts the very notion of concluding. By emphasizing development over resolution, the essay diverts attention from the *Literary History*'s ostensible end. After all, the conclusion affirms that, for Frye, history-making will in some way enact a dream of self-creation in literary time, a dream that replaces closure with conception and history-writing with fables of identity. Frye's working metaphors are all aligned with origins, creation, birth. His conclusion is no conclusion. It is a meditation on poetic genesis.

I

Frye divides his essay into four distinct sections. In the first of these, in the first sentence, Frye's narrative strategy becomes apparent. He says that "it is now several years since the group of editors listed on the title-page met . . . to draw up the first tentative plans" for a history of English Canadian literature (821). Because his emphasis is on imagination and dream, the precise date of the editorial meeting is unimportant. What matters is the drama of creating literary history, of naming a world called Canadian literature, and of giving it credence through the production of a literary history. In the opening pages of the conclusion, Frye suggests that the production of this history is bound to the production of personal and collective identity: "One theme which runs all through this book is the obvious and unquenchable desire of the Canadian cultural public to identify itself through its literature" (823). For Frye, the power and drama of this form of identification seem akin to the power of literature itself. From the outset, his conclusion assumes the transhistorical status of a myth aligned with what he calls "the autonomous world of literature" (822), a world intimately bound up with the iconographic qualities of dream and descent. In recalling the undated, once-upon-a-time event that gave rise to the *Literary History*, Frye pictures the work as an imaginative structure: "What we then dreamed of," he says, "is substantially what we have got," a romantic narrative that confirms his "intuitions on the subject" rather than any historical fact, a prophecy that focuses attention on how "some writers on Canadian literature" articulate a unifying romantic consciousness that links cultural and national identity. "By 'some writers,'" Frye then confesses, "I meant primarily myself" (831).

His observation that Canada is "preoccupied with trying to define its own identity" might well be applied to his own self-defining romantic quest (827).

The opening paragraph of the conclusion sets the stage for what will unfold as a drama of creation, a drama rooted in the story that Frye, among others, has dreamed. The more he discusses this dream, the more he is led to comment on his own purpose, which is not to evaluate Canadian literature, or to study it, but to show how its forms relate to its perceiver and to Frye's belief that the writing of Canadian literary history is similar to all other forms of writing because it shows how "the verbal imagination operates as a ferment in all cultural life." In this sense, Frye finds in his conclusion precisely what he finds in literature at large: evidence that the critical quest takes one toward the notion of identity at "the centre of literary experience itself." Thus he emphasizes that "many Canadian cultural phenomena are not peculiarly Canadian at all, but are typical of their wider North American and Western contexts." So when he states that anyone reading the *Literary History*, "even [someone] not Canadian or much interested in Canadian literature as such, may still learn a good deal about the literary imagination as a force and function of life" (822), he suggests that he will attempt to discover this form of imagination through the critical quest at hand. This quest allows his "verbal imagination" to operate "as a ferment" in his intellectual life. Because Frye consciously pursues this ferment and narrates his conclusion in response to it, one can say that his quest for the *Literary History* enacts his view of literary historiography. This study, he says, "has its own themes of exploration, settlement, and development," and these are related "to a social imagination that explores and settles and develops [according to] its own rhythms of growth as well as its own modes of expression" (822).

As Frye traces the "rhythms of growth" and "modes of expression" that identify "Canadian verbal culture," he displays the corresponding characteristics in his own development within the conclusion (822). In the first section, he devotes considerable attention to detailing how "Canada began as an obstacle . . . to be explored only in the hope of finding a passage through it" (824). He describes entering the country as an "intimidating experience" that "initiates one" into a consciousness that evokes biblical associations: "The traveller from Europe edges into it like a tiny Jonah entering an inconceivably large whale, slipping past the Straits of Belle Isle into the Gulf of St. Lawrence, where five Canadian provinces surround him" (824). In this first section the "one" being initiated is the speaker, the hero-to-be who will enter uncharted territory — whether literary, historical, or geographic — and confront the obstacle of his inquiry, the Canada he must transcend, just as he transcends himself.

I use the word *hero* with some hesitation, and only to emphasize Frye's interest in presenting his narrator as a recognizable, transhistorical persona whose movement toward knowledge is an archetypal, transspatial quest. Yet Frye carefully destabilizes the individual power associated with the notion of hero, just as he tries to deflate the notion of genius by arguing that genius is a myth, "doubtless of romantic origin," that should be redefined as "a matter of social context" as much as of "individual character" (823). In this sense, the narrator-hero observed at the beginning of the conclusion could equally well be called an Everyman who inhabits a "no-man's land" stretching "from sea to sea" (826). For the narrator, this imagined territory is a devouring land: "to enter Canada is a matter of being silently swallowed by an alien continent." Such an entry, though "unforgettable and intimidating," ensures the narrator's quest: "the experience initiates one into that gigantic east-to-west thrust" that has "attracted to itself nearly everything that is heroic and romantic in the Canadian tradition" (824). Frye's attempt to understand this tradition goes hand in hand with his attempt to solve the conclusion's well-known riddle: "Where is here?" (826). To answer this question, Frye must become involved in charting his own narrative quest.

As he discusses the charting of the frontier, he is drawn to speculate on the ways the frontier affects not only "national consciousness" but also personal consciousness: "One wonders if any other national consciousness has had so large an amount of the unknown, the unrealized, the humanly undigested, so built into it." Frye's narrator is struck by how "the frontier was all around one," how it is "a part and a condition of one's whole imaginative being" (826). For the explorer, it was "the immediate datum of the imagination" that "had to be dealt with first" (827).

As the explorer in the conclusion, Frye also confronts this datum. But because his notion of the frontier is becoming much more personal and creative than cultural or geographic, he meets the challenge by evoking the myth of Canada as the "next year country" that will one day be revealed by a myth, "the myth of the hero brought up in the forest retreat, awaiting the moment when his giant strength will be fully grown and he can emerge into the world" (827). This myth obviously relates to Frye's self-understanding as a critic, for by his own account it "informs a good deal of Canadian criticism down to our own time." He is the critic, but he inhabits the autonomous world of literature he writes about.

Frye's conception of this world often seems to resemble a male dream of potency. If he is the hero of his narrative, then he is also a version of the archetypal hero attached to the romance mode, the one who awaits the moment "when his giant strength will be fully grown." Through his identification with the "unforgettable" experience of entering Canada as a process of gaining both potency and the means to self-expression, Frye can be seen as the romantic hero and, metaphorically, as the erotic quester whose journey into the country is an impregnating act. The critic-explorer enters "into that gigantic east-to-west thrust" that initiates "the growth of Canada" (824).

It is not surprising to find that some of Frye's metaphors are erotically charged. After all, "the romance, for Frye, is 'almost by definition' a love story," while "the trajectory of romance is toward erotic consummation" (Balfour 58). But the imagery he associates with this entering thrust suggests more than a purely sexual encounter and more than a dream of male potency inscribed on a waiting landscape. If the country can be figured as a whale that swallows the explorer, it can also be imaged as an engulfing womb that deprives him of power and agency, presumably the very resources necessary for exploration. For this reason, perhaps, the search for the peaceable kingdom frequently finds Frye pursuing a double narrative stance: while he organizes the conclusion around tropes connected with sexuality, conception, and birth, he responds to another set of tropes that threaten to stifle his quest and to turn the birth image toward suffocation, impotence, and death. His confrontation with the dual implications of his metaphors is reflected in a problem he encounters in creating the entire document as a text that must somehow *end.* The conclusion stretches before him; it is the apocalyptic ending he must reach, a Blakean ending that promises a new reality, a remythologized beginning. Yet to find this ending is to work against the quest, for once the end is reached, the quest ceases to have value. Frye is caught in a bind: his job is to write a conclusion that must not conclude. How does he meet this challenge?

II

In the second section of his essay Frye pulls back from this paradoxical problem after he realizes that "it is not the handicaps of Canadian writers but the distinctive features that appear in spite of them which are the main concern of this book, and so of its conclusion." He would like to believe that possibility lies before him, that he can see the Canadian landscape, through its art, as a metaphorical realm of potential, that he can adopt a sensibility "inherited from the *voyageurs,*" the sensibility that finds one "probing into the distance" or "fixing the eyes on the skyline" (828). This preoccupation with unfathomable distance expresses his desire to find the peaceable kingdom that transcends the here and now. Frye identifies with the "faraway look" of the voyageur relentlessly scanning the horizon (828). But the Canadian voyageur cannot always contemplate this horizon, which signifies potential and release, for all around him there is immediate nature, whose conquest "has its own perils for the imagination." For Frye the critic, and for Frye the self-imagined voyageur, something must be asserted against these perils, because "the human mind has nothing but human and moral values to cling to if it is to preserve its integrity or even its sanity" (830).

The mind asserts these values against "the vast unconsciousness of nature" by developing what Frye calls "a garrison mentality." Critics have conventionally seen this mentality as a negative force and, in the past, have used Frye's concept to justify the view that Canadian literature is characterized by a "tone of deep terror in regard to nature," the product of a "beleaguered society" obsessed with isolation and survival (830). Although such an application of Frye's ideas is now generally discredited, critics continue to ignore his emphasis on the positive aspects of the garrison mentality that develop when "the individual feels himself becoming an individual, pulling away from the group." When this separation occurs, the individual is confronted with "a more creative side of the garrison mentality, one that has had positive effects on our intellectual life" (831).

Frye realizes these effects by asserting intellect over landscape, creativity over culture. His task is to find a poetic means of crossing the various frontiers that he identifies throughout the conclusion. A figurative voyageur, he perceives these frontiers as both psychological and aesthetic. He notes that while quarrels within a society merely produce rhetoric, "the quarrel with ourselves" produces poetry (831). His position at this point is interesting because he finds himself pulled two ways. One way tempts him to explain Canadian literature by "using language as one would use an axe, formulating arguments with sharp cutting edges that will help to clarify one's view of the landscape." He does this. But he knows that using language in this way "remains a rhetorical and not a poetic achievement" (832). So he is pulled in another direction away from language as axe, toward poetic language as a vehicle of connection, toward an ultimate conclusion that envisions the world as myth rather than as event, through synecdoche rather than occurrence ("every statement made in a book like this about 'Canadian literature' employs the figure of speech known as synecdoche, putting a part for the whole" [823–24]). In Frye's expanding narrative the part known as Canada becomes the whole world; similarly, the part called the conclusion becomes a metaphor of apocalyptic consciousness. In this world — "an autonomous world of literature" — all human forms may one day be identified (822).

The more Frye writes, the more he pursues this type of identification, and the more he focuses on the literary forms that have begun to construct his world. By the end of the second section, he is no longer speaking about garrison mentalities; instead, he is involved in discussing texts that reflect his developing concern with "the fundamental issue of the role of the creative mind" (833). As he discusses this role, Frye comes to inhabit it. Now he can assert what his readers have suspected from the start: his enemy is not the wilderness, or nature, or society, or rhetoric; it is "the anti-creative elements in life as he [the writer] sees life. To approach these elements in a less rhetorical way," by which Frye means a more poetic way, is to "introduce the theme of self-conflict, a more perilous but ultimately more rewarding theme." This theme anticipates the third section of the essay, in which Frye describes the conflict he has entered through his pilgrimage toward the conclusion of a world made into art: "The conflict involved is between the poetic impulse to construct and the rhetorical impulse to assert, and the victory of the former is the sign of the maturing of the writer" (834).

If readers continue to see this conflict as something external to the conclusion, they become victims of "the rhetorical impulse to assert," for it is this impulse that directs them away from what Frye sees as the poetic centre of truly creative and critical pursuits. But if they see the conflict as a struggle that informs the conclusion and energizes its critic-protagonist, then the essay opens up a double-sided story: Frye writes about the process of entering an allegorical literary consciousness that he is in the process of creating. He is writing transformation literature and transformation criticism; his metamorphosis could be, and should be, his readers' as well. But their entry into this allegorical creative and critical realm is blocked, as it is for Frye's narrator, by the overwhelming presence of history. The Canadian literary mind, Frye asserts, "was established on a basis, not of myth, but of history" (835). His distinction between myth and history is crucial. Myth releases the individual from time and space; it bridges the gap between subject and object. In contrast, "the Canadian attitude to time as well as space" — its "preoccupation with its own history" — restricts the individual to a social perspective bound up in the "need for continuity" (829) and the valorization of linear thought. To find the peaceable kingdom, one must transcend history and embrace myth.

III

The means of transcending this "historical bias" is the subject of Frye's third section, which deals with the problems inherent in the "conceptual emphasis" that is "a consequence" of the Canadian preoccupation with history and determinism (835). This bias detracts from the essence of literature, Frye argues, because "literature is conscious mythology," which one must enter in order to experience literature. If this mythology does not exist, the authentic writer is driven to create it. Frye's insistence on the need to create "an autonomous world that gives us an imaginative perspective on the actual one" emerges in the conclusion through the narrator's increasing devotion to "a recreated view of life." Such a view is illuminated by the "metaphor-crystallizing impetus" that transcends the "habitual social responses" aligned with various forms of mimetic thought that endorse "the separation of subject and object." Only by overcoming this separation can the writer discover "the real headwaters of inspiration" (836–38).

As Frye moves toward these headwaters, he contextualizes himself in relation to the "heroic explorers" who know that identity can be located only within the story itself, not through commentary. The critical act of commenting distances him as writer from self-consciousness and the social mythology he is trying to absorb. From this removed perspective, Frye as external spectator remains "dominated by the conception of writing up experiences or observations" and thus thwarted in his attempt to find the peaceable kingdom. In contrast, the critic who "enters into a structure" and who embraces "metaphorical thought" becomes not merely an observer but also "a place where a verbal structure is taking its own shape" (836). Locating this place involves an act of devolution: one must undo literature that is "rhetorical, an illustration or allegory of certain social attitudes," and return to those genuine forms of experience that "exist within literature itself, and cannot be derived from any experience outside literature" (834, 835). Such a movement allows the writer to withdraw from "a country without a mythology into the country of mythology" that Frye seeks (840).

In these comments Frye reveals the extent to which his own goals have changed through his narration of the conclusion: now he implies that his task is to become a creator rather than a curator of Canadian literary life. He will free himself from literary history. He will leave behind the academic school that encouraged his undertaking in the first place. He will move away from the concept of closure, away from his own conclusion, away from his narrative death. Finally, he will act out his assertion that "the imaginative writer, though he often begins as a member of a school or group, normally pulls away from it as he develops" because such a writer "is finding his identity within the world of literature itself" (839–40). As Frye comes closer to this autonomous world, he gradually becomes a different kind of reader and writer of literary history. In this double role, he can identify with the members of his audience, each of whom has witnessed his transformation and each of whom is eligible to share in this transformation by joining Frye's quest for the peaceable kingdom and all it has come to symbolize. Frye invites his readers to partake in the particular difference that characterizes his own journey: "The difference is in the position of the reader's mind at the end, and in whether he is being encouraged to remain within his habitual social responses or whether he is being prodded into making the steep and lonely climb into the imaginative world" (838).

IV

By the time Frye reaches the fourth and final section of his conclusion, he has become deeply involved in making this climb. His discussion of Canadian literature has set the stage for a critical epiphany to be realized in the heights associated with "the imaginative world." The bald declaration that begins this section contrasts sharply with the speculative observations that mark the opening of the conclusion. Now Frye can say that there is a myth, a "pastoral myth . . . at the heart of all social mythology" (840). On one level, this myth can be a "senti-mental or nostalgic" one that promises the dream of "a world of peace and protection" whose inhabitants have "a spontaneous response to the nature around it" and "a leisure and composure not to be found today" (840). But on a more complex level, the "genuine" pastoral myth identifies nature as "the visible representative of an order that man has violated, a spiritual unity that the intellect murders to dissect" (845). It is "the sense of kinship with the animal and vegetable world" that affirms a profound "identifying of subject and object, the primary imaginative act of literary creation" (842).

As Frye comes closer to this form of identification, his narrator explores "the mythopoeic aspect of Canadian literature" that provides access to the peaceable kingdom Frye equates with pastoral conscious-ness. Because one who reaches this kingdom finds harmony with nature, not so much physically as imaginatively, the search "for a North American pastoral myth in its genuinely imaginative form" becomes a means by which one "tries to grasp the form" of a "buried society" that the imagination can resurrect. By this reasoning, "the conception

'Canada' can also become a pastoral myth in certain circumstances"
(841, 842).

To promote these circumstances, Frye openly embraces the identification of subject and object by relating his own developing perceptions
to the developing perceptions of the nation and by allowing the story
he comments on to become his story. This narrative traces a three-part
movement from prelapsarian to postlapsarian to prelapsarian awareness: (1) The conclusion begins in a once-upon-a-time realm of genesis
and dream where Frye's consciousness remains free by virtue of its
distance from history and the historically oriented task at hand. (2) But
then there is a fall — embodied in the garrison mentality, the speaker's
increasing self-consciousness, and the act of writing a literary history
— that excludes its creator, Frye. (3) Finally, the narrator retreats to
the pastoral ideal of the peaceable kingdom that appears as the conclusion approaches its ending. By embracing this resolution, the speaker
finds his way out of the creative and critical paradox I have described:
the need to produce a conclusion that does not conclude.

Only by evoking a pastoral myth can Frye approach the true object
of his quest — an ending that finds human beings not exiled from the
garden and at odds with their world, but pursuing the peaceable
kingdom that Frye has been seeking. The peace he finds in realizing
this quest is conveyed by his closing affirmation that "an imaginative
continuum" inspires him and all writers. By participating in this continuum, Frye can transcend both the conclusion he has apparently
reached and the title of his essay as well, for his conclusion actually
brings him back full circle to his dreamed-of beginning, back to a
consciousness that elevates the imaginatively conceived over the historically determined. From this perspective, Frye is able to see his conclusion as only the first step in a narrative process that links him with the
"writers of Canada" who "have identified the habits and attitudes of
the country" and "left an imaginative legacy of dignity and of high
courage" (849). In his expanding story, these writers have become
heroes, the voyageur-heroes who are sharing his steep climb to a new
"imaginative world."

If one ignores the direction of Frye's own imaginative involvement in
his conclusion, one is forced to endorse a diminished response to the
work's literary value — the kind of response that characterizes most of
the well-known Canadian criticism the essay ostensibly influenced. By
focusing deliberately on the practical application of his observations to
a theory of culture, such criticism becomes preoccupied with all the
by-products of the pastoral vision denied: garrison mentalities, or
themes of isolation, survival, and national identity. But the conclusion

appears in a new light when it is examined from the vantage-point of Frye's own transforming voyage through it. It depicts the creation, through a romance narrative, of the idea of Canada, a metaphoric conception that is transhistorical, autonomous, and distinctly literary before it is cultural. Frye's narrative leads his readers away from history toward self-creation, away from isolation toward integration. At the end of this movement — this quest — lies the peaceable kingdom of Frye's original dream. His vision of this once-upon-a-time kingdom antici-pates its resurrection, through his telling, at the very moment the kingdom seems most displaced. As Frye says: "The moment that the peaceable kingdom has been completely obliterated by its rival is the moment when it comes to the foreground again as the eternal frontier, the first thing that the writer's imagination must deal with" (848).

In concluding his essay, then, Frye points the way to a new beginning. Now beyond history, he leaves his readers contemplating his distance from time, space, and any version of mimesis. He is not in the *Literary History*. He is not in literary history. He is out there, in the autonomous world he has always sought. "Again," he reminds his audience, "noth-ing can give a writer's experience and sensitivity any form except the study of literature itself" (849). The conclusion that closes with these words is nowhere near its end.

8

Nobody Gets Hurt Bullfighting Canadian-Style: Rereading Frank Davey's "Surviving the Paraphrase"

My message to you is that one never does escape oneself, that when one is writing a poem about shipwrecks one is still writing a poem about oneself. Every experience that one has, every activity that one undertakes is subjective, reflects upon oneself. And that is the secret of form; form always testifies whether it's to what you think it's testifying or to something else. And this is why I object to criticism that does not pay attention to form.

— Davey, Interview with Komisar (53)

I think of my books as simply records of a journey.

— Davey, "Starting at Our Skins" (130)

1974. FRANK DAVEY is presenting his paper entitled "Surviving the Paraphrase" at the founding meeting of the Association for Canadian and Quebec Literatures in Toronto. The presentation creates a stir. Two years later, the essay appears in *Canadian Literature*.[1] In 1983, a decade after he wrote it, Davey is still thinking about this early work: he publishes a book-length collection of essays entitled *Surviving the Paraphrase*.

Around this time, people begin to refer to the 1974 essay as a departure point for the development of antithematic criticism in Canada. Writing in 1983, Stephen Scobie calls it "a seminal attack" (173). In 1984 W.J. Keith observes that "it has itself become a critical classic." He goes further: "Were I dictator," he says, "I would require all

Canadian teachers of literature to display a knowledge of its arguments before they were permitted to step into any classroom" (Review 459). By 1986 Barbara Godard could claim that "Surviving the Paraphrase" was "the rallying point in the critical debate" about the aims and methods of Canadian criticism ("Structuralism/Post-Structuralism" 28). This assessment is endorsed by Barry Cameron in the 1990 *Literary History of Canada.* Cameron says that Davey's attack was responsible for the "widespread reaction" to criticism that was "grounded in cultural criteria" (116). One year later, Lynette Hunter confirms the widespread opinion that Davey's essay was "the scourge of thematic criticism." In her view, it has become "a landmark" (145).

Clearly "Surviving the Paraphrase" has been canonized, appropriated by Canadian theorists as a crucial resistance narrative. Davey has participated actively in this canonizing process. In a letter to the *Globe and Mail* published in 1985, he referred to the essay he wrote more than ten years earlier as "my rather notorious essay on thematic criticism." He further magnified its status in his 1988 collection of essays entitled *Reading Canadian Reading,* in which he looks back to the Future Indicative Conference on Literary Theory and Canadian Literature (held in Ottawa in 1986) and endorses the view (voiced by other Canadian theorists at the conference) that "there was a narrow field of recurrent reference" in the papers presented at the conference — "of Canadian theoretical texts, mostly my 'Surviving the Paraphrase,' of non-Canadian ones, mostly work by Kristeva, Derrida, Barthes, Lacan and (especially) Bakhtin" (2).

Davey's words point to his need to associate his criticism with the work of big-name, non-Canadian critics. He wants to mythologize himself. The vehicle for this mythologizing remains "Surviving the Paraphrase." Even in 1988, fourteen years after it was first delivered and dozens of essays later, he still focuses his act of self-definition on *that* essay, as if it remains for him a central point of departure and return, the focal point in his career as a critic, a central narrative he must tell and retell. For other Canadian critics it also remains a canonical narrative — a story that has affected their values and the language they use.

Why is this story so important to Davey? Why has it seemed so important to his readers? If Hunter is correct in her assertion that " 'Surviving the Paraphrase' is not a particularly sophisticated piece of criticism" (145), why do we keep referring to it year after year? We call the document a "seminal attack" or a "landmark," and forget about its technique and form. In short, we treat the document in the very way Davey objected to treating literature in "Surviving the Paraphrase" itself.

For some reason (perhaps because it is too sacred?), critics have been "reluctant to focus" on "Surviving the Paraphrase" as *writing* — "to deal with matters of form, language, style, structure, and consciousness as they arise from the work as a unique construct" ("Surviving" 5). They have not tried to "illuminate the work on its own terms without recourse to any cultural rationalizations." They have not considered its "formal complexities" (5) or its "structure, language, or imagery" (6). They have not paid attention to its "unique or idiosyncratic qualities" (7). They have said nothing about its "technical features" (6). They have behaved like the thematic critic Davey so pointedly rejected — the critic who "extracts for his deliberations the paraphrasable content and throws away the form" (6). They have "rejected or ignored" its internal "conflicts," and have shown a "disregard for literary history" by treating the document as if it were somehow divorced from its author, the very author who argues that "*every* experience that one has, every activity that one undertakes is subjective, reflects upon oneself" (Davey, Interview 53). In short, critics have never illuminated "Surviving the Paraphrase" as a literary document that is related to its author's career, his consciousness, his life.

I

His life. I know practically nothing about it. Whatever commentary I provide concerning Davey's aims or motives is emphatically interpretive, based solely on what Davey has written or said in interviews. I want to emphasize that, for me, Davey remains a figure I have encountered primarily through his writing — a fiction, a biographical fallacy, a construction. He encourages this type of encounter and invites us to read his criticism as a personal narrative; in his words, "The best criticism is creative and I'm personally impressed by criticism that dares to venture into areas considered the province of fiction" (quoted in Ryval 12). Although he claims that "I'm not a literary writer, I'm not writing about literary topics," he also says that "I'm writing about my life and my experience with it" ("Starting" 179), as if writing about one's life and experiences is somehow antiliterary.

It is precisely because he denies the literariness of his writing life that it becomes such an interesting fiction. E.D. Blodgett observes that, for Davey, "the crafts of poetry and criticism are coterminous" ("Frank Davey" 130). Because his poetry and his poetics are related, Davey's sense of self-definition is always self-reflexive and metaphoric. As David Clark explains, Davey's criticism provides an opportunity for self-display "because in many ways specularity (or self-display) is the master trope at work" in much of Davey's criticism (76). My access to this trope is through other fictions about it — things that Davey has said and written, things other people have said about him and his work — a palimpsest that makes no claim to truth or objectivity. Davey remains masked. Therefore, I can interpret — and wonder: How does the fiction of Davey's life encode his own stance as the author of "Surviving the Paraphrase"? What kind of story does this "landmark" essay tell? How does Davey position himself as a persona in this story? What gives the essay its canonical clout?

Many readers encountering this "landmark" document for the first time may not know what kind of historical forces contributed to its production.

Above all, "Surviving the Paraphrase" is the product of a man who grew up in British Columbia, aligned himself with a West Coast universe from youth, wanted to create a history of West Coast culture, wrote poems about West Coast love and loss, edited two magazines oriented toward West Coast thinking, saw his role models as West Coast models, got his undergraduate and graduate degrees on the West Coast, was married and divorced on the West Coast, and made the West Coast — and specifically Vancouver — the centre of his human universe.

Davey saw himself as a poet developing within this milieu. Although he was involved in founding two literary journals — *TISH* (1961) and *Open Letter* (1965) — in which he published letters, editorials, and the occasional polemical essay, Davey did not define himself first as a literary critic, even after he graduated with a PhD from the University of Southern California in 1968. By that year he had published four books of poetry and had two more in the works; there were no books of criticism. Davey thought of himself primarily as a somewhat radical West Coast poet and editor, experimenting with language and working with new forms inspired by the poetics of such writers as Creeley, Duncan, Olson, and Pound.

Although Davey defined himself first as a poet, the lure of academia clouded this identity. When Davey returned to Vancouver after completing his degree in California, he was regarded with suspicion by fellow poets. In 1967 he accepted a post as assistant professor at Royal Roads Military College in Victoria. George Bowering recalls that at this time,

> One of the things that people felt about you [Davey] is that you were moving into academia, not only in the work you were doing, but in your poetry. That you were tending toward getting academic or something; and they felt as if you were betraying all the things that we'd always thought about poetry then. ("Starting" 134)

Davey recognized that "there was also a feeling that I was exploiting my connection with the Vancouver scene for personal gain" ("Starting" 134). While he was encountering this hostility, he was also dealing with the breakdown of his first marriage, which had figured prominently in most of the poetry he had written since his wedding in 1962. I imagine he was confused, angry, and anxious to prove that he had not sold out to academia, that the poet in him was still central and strong.

These feelings would not have been alleviated by Davey's move to Montreal in 1969. All of a sudden, he found himself a teacher in the Creative Writing program at Sir George Williams University — away from the sea, away from his past, away from the West and everything he associated with it: childhood, family, passion, poetry, learning, love, anger, divorce. Now he had taken a big step toward aligning himself with some of the bureaucratic structures he had spent so much time working against. Now he was *within* the structure — and in the East. He was twenty-nine years old and very few people in Montreal knew he was a poet. Davey's situation was unimaginable. How could *he* (who was in his heart a West Coast poet) have ended up teaching *here*, in Montreal?

Davey confronted this tension by writing new poems about loss (almost all of his poems up to this point are about shipwrecks, division, drowning, frustrated relationships, wasted seed). But there was also the lure of criticism and its promise of power. Soon after Davey arrived in Montreal, Gary Geddes offered him the opportunity to write a book on Earle Birney for a series published by Copp Clark. The study, released in 1971, was Davey's first book-length foray into Canadian criticism.

Davey recognizes that this first extended exercise in criticism (excluding his doctoral dissertation) reveals much about his own preoccupations at the time of its writing. Issues of power and marginalization were central. Davey realized that in order to advance in the profession, he now had to attend the appropriate cocktail parties, because "a British Columbian . . . or a Maritimer, an Albertan, was unlikely to be given an opportunity to write about Canadian literature unless she or he happened into the appropriate Toronto cocktail party" (*Reading* 20). With these words Davey casts himself in the role of perpetual outsider, the marginalized poet forced to participate in the central-Canadian cocktail party in order to gain acceptance from his newly apparent and imperialist peers. The activity must have accentuated his sense of being far from home, in alien territory, and his determination to maintain a purchase on his western identity and his past.

The book on Birney provided an ideal means of bridging the gap between the two worlds Davey had come to inhabit — the two worlds that were pulling him apart. As an act of criticism, as the book of a professor, as the product of a central-Canadian publishing house, it represented Davey's entry into powerful foreign territory. At the same time, it was focused on a writer — Birney — who had faced many of the same challenges experienced by Davey himself over the years:

> When I came to write the book on him it was a process of discovery for me. Here was a writer who had been an only child, who had grown up in a rural isolated area, far more isolated than I was but certainly isolated from the main stream of culture in a way that I was; who was brought up by a working class family of minimal education very similar to mine; who had gone as a student, as an undergraduate to the same university that I had; who had grown up on the west coast, in the ranges — him in the deep Rockies, me in the Coast Ranges . . . he'd also been very tall and skinny as I have been; he'd also been tempted by an academic career in the way that I was; he had red hair, yes; he had been attracted to journalism as I had been — I had thought of working for the *Ubyssey*; he actually became Editor-in-Chief of the *Ubyssey*; he had been involved in student publication in a way that I had wanted to be, and finally was in a peripheral way with *Tish*; and he'd been attracted so much to an academic career that he eventually got a PH D and had embarked upon the same curious process that I was embarked on, being an academic and a poet simultaneously, and being a PH D academic and a poet simultaneously, which was something nobody else in the *Tish* group has tried to do. ("Starting" 146)

It seems clear that Davey had found his *doppelgänger* in the first book of criticism he came to write. In many ways the process of writing about Birney was a process of writing about himself.

Although Davey admired Birney's two-sidedness — his ability to be both poet and professor — he felt uncomfortable with the professorial role, both as it emerged in Birney — who also felt uncomfortable in this role — and, presumably, as it was emerging in himself. This discomfort was partly a response to the fact that Davey's aim was to treat Birney's discourse as fraudulent:

> I wanted to expose the fraudulence of "objective" discourse, of what I came in the book to call Birney's "professorial stance." . . . I wanted also to endorse idiosyncratic, "local," discourses, to argue that all human discourses are specific, idiosyncratic, limited, that they emerge . . . from one's "own cultural, geographic, historical context." (*Reading* 21–22)

In arguing against Birney in this way, Davey was also arguing against himself. He was exposing his own sense of fraudulence as a professor who had abandoned his " 'own cultural, geographic, historical context' " and who, by adopting the professorial stance implicit in the book he was writing for a central-Canadian publisher, had symbolically sold out to the very interests he wanted to write against. Through this book he was indeed exploring "the problematics of combining writing with university teaching" (*Reading* 21).

The conflict between professorial and poetic allegiance is the central problem in Davey's career. The book on Birney in no way resolved this problem; on the contrary, it seemed to increase Davey's confusion and anxiety about the type of writing he should produce and, further, about the kinds of writing he should endorse as a teacher and critic.

By the time *Earle Birney* appeared, Davey had moved to Toronto to accept an assistant professorship at York University. Now he was a professor at a central-Canadian institution. And now he was publishing his poetry in Toronto, too: his *Weeds* was released by Coach House Press in 1970, and *Arcana* (also published by Coach House) in 1973, the same year Davey was writing "Surviving the Paraphrase." Yet Davey remained aloof, troubled, alienated. He was being encouraged by Geddes to write a book about Birney that would "speak almost as much about myself as about Birney" (*Reading* 23). If Davey's description of Birney is self-reflexive, then we can find in him what he found in Birney at that time: a "dogged individual" who faced "overwhelming odds"; "the strong, perceptive outsider, marginalized by others' lack of understanding"; "the precocious child who struggled against solitude, poverty, and ignorance"; the "trusting graduate student who was sacrificed to faculty politics"; "the only academic who would act on his social conscience"; "the only 'real' poet in the Department of English"; an academic who was "marginalized, excluded, punished for each of these singularities"; a person whose writing emphasized "solitary, abandoned, ineffectual, yet semi-heroic figures" who "made themselves vulnerable to betrayal or rejection by having sought entry into the value and language system of others" (*Reading* 23–24).

In moving east, in entering into the value systems of others, Davey discovered that Birney's story was his. If we turn away from Davey's retrospective view to the analysis in *Earle Birney* itself, we find the same preoccupations. For example, Davey writes:

> Divided loyalties continue to bedevil Birney's career. The anomalies at the beginning of this chapter are symptomatic of them. Country versus

city, western Canada versus eastern Canada, worker versus bourgeois, revolution versus establishment, and eventually, poet versus academician. (16)

By now it should be apparent that the conflict between poet and academician — writer and professor — is by no means strictly professional. For Davey, it is a profoundly existential conflict, for it concerns who he is and what he will choose to become. It is important to realize that at this point in his career — 1971 — Davey did not consider himself to be a literary critic; he still defined himself as a poet. As he himself says, "Frank Davey would have been unlikely to have attempted to write any critical book at this time had not Gary Geddes, or Copp Clark, offered the possibility" (*Reading* 22). Even in 1974, the same year he presented "Surviving the Paraphrase" and published *From There to Here*, Davey did not think of himself as a critic. In an interview with George Bowering he said: "I think of myself as a poet who teaches rather than a teacher who writes poetry, and if someone asks me, what are you? I dont say, a professor. I say, a writer. Or writer and editor." He also notes that "it was very clear when I was hired at York that I was being hired as a writer and editor whom they wanted to have on their faculty. And that's just fine with me" ("Starting" 101). When he wrote "Surviving the Paraphrase," then, he saw criticism as a distinctly secondary form of writing: "I'm angered by it. I'm led to introspection and reconsiderations but I'm seldom persuaded by it" ("Starting" 117).

When we consider Davey's opinions about criticism at this time, and his own sense of divided allegiance between West and East, writing and professorhood, we can see that the prevailing myth surrounding the origins of "Surviving the Paraphrase" needs to be repositioned. The man who walked up to the podium at the first meeting of the Association for Canadian and Quebec Literatures at the University of Toronto was not a self-confident critic thoroughly immersed in the theoretical issues of his time. He was a West Coast poet in the process of becoming a centralist, Ontario-based, Canadian literary critic. This realization may have delighted him, for it promised a new route to power. But the same realization must have terrified him, for it promised to close the door on poetry itself, especially since he had spent so much time distinguishing authentic writing (poetry) from inauthentic writing (criticism).

Because the act of presenting "Surviving the Paraphrase" to a group of academics crystallized this dilemma in the form of an oral, and later a written, document, the essay can be seen as the expression of an individual divided by the opposing loyalties and tensions I have been enumerating (with Davey's help). It also attempts to resolve the conflicts that were plaguing Davey at this time, for it records Davey's own attempt to negotiate a route between the worlds of poetry and criticism, both of which he hoped to renew and synthesize through something called "writing."

At first the route seems clear cut: if you looked at Davey in 1974 you would call the document an anomaly; you would think of him primarily as a poet and editor working in an academic milieu. But the problem with this picture is that Davey was not really gaining recognition as a poet. Although he had been publishing poetry for more than a decade, he had not received serious critical attention. By the time he presented "Surviving the Paraphrase," Davey had published twelve books of poetry. At this time, the most serious treatment of his work was by Warren Tallman, a former teacher and mentor who published a small article on Davey in 1965. The only other considerations of Davey's poetry had been in short reviews. However, he had learned early on that polemical writing inspired controversy, that it could focus people's attention on him and his work. He wanted to change critical values so that his writing would be intelligently (and positively) received. In an interview recorded in 1973, shortly before he presented "Surviving the Paraphrase," Davey observed that

> if I had an ideal world I would not have to be a critic and I would not have to be an editor. I would be able to be just a writer. But I'm aware that the literary environment is unsatisfactory for my own work, and I'm aware that it's unsatisfactory for other writers, and I know that I am capable of changing this environment. And I see myself as, yes, changing the way in which writing is criticized. Changing the way, providing alternate ways of criticism, which would be more useful to the writers and would do a better job of dealing with their work. ("Starting" 100)

In order to begin effecting this change, Davey took the most expedient route. He stood up in front of a group of academics and delivered a polemical address that fulfilled three functions.

First, it provided a means of naming and so exorcizing the East-West tensions that had haunted him since his move to Montreal in 1969. From this perspective, "Surviving the Paraphrase" can be read as a confession and redemption narrative. It traces Davey's personal sense of loss in moving east as a loss of self and voice, and expresses his desire to redeem himself (reclaim his voice) in this fallen world by positing a noncentralist vision of recovery *through* form (which he equates with the authenticity of "writing as writing").

Second, it provided a means of justifying his new persona as critic to his fellow writers by defending "writing as writing" over criticism. In this sense, it can be read as a defence of poetry in the guise of criticism, and therefore as a statement of loyalty to his West Coast origins. Through this defence, Davey seeks to justify his position as a poet who has been excluded from the centralist canon. But this allegory of exclusion and justification is conflicted, because Davey must use criticism (a potentially tainted form of discourse) to recuperate poetry (his sacred language). The very act of privileging criticism to achieve this end robs poetry of its pre-eminent status. Ironically, Davey must use criticism to promote poetry that is disempowered by the means through which it is promoted.

Third, its strategies were designed to appeal to critics who, like Davey, were eager to position themselves in the rapidly expanding institution called Canadian literature. In this universe, in 1974, there were still very few signs indicating which way to go, how to speak, or how the collective should operate. Davey not only recognized this community by addressing it, but the story he told also promised to deliver this collective from the wilderness. To those who felt marginalized by their involvement with Canadian literature in this early phase of its institutionalization, Davey's essay held out the hope of social coherence through new critical and collective effort, even though its rhetoric of idiosyncrasy and individualism seemed to be anticorporate. By surviving the paraphrase, Canadian literature and its literary critics would find their promised land.

II

Here is the opening paragraph of Davey's essay:

> It is a testimony to the limitations of Canadian literary criticism that thematic criticism should have become the dominant approach to English-Canadian literature. In its brief lifetime, Canadian criticism has acquired a history of being reluctant to focus on the literary work — to deal with matters of form, language, style, structure, and consciousness as these arise from the work as a unique construct. It has seldom had enough confidence in the work of Canadian writers to do what the criticism of other national literatures has done: explain and illuminate the work on its own terms, without recourse to any cultural rationalizations or apologies. Even the New Criticism's espousal of autotelic analysis did not move Canadian critics in this direction. Instead, in every period they have provided referential criticism: the evaluative criticism of Brown

and Smith looks away from Canadian writing toward other national achievements; the anti-evaluative thematic criticism of Frye, Jones, Atwood, and Moss looks away toward alleged cultural influences and determiners.

In the first sentence of this paragraph, Davey does something very new: he gives thematic criticism its name. But by christening it in this way, Davey introduces an immediate paradox. Through the act of naming, he identifies and therefore empowers the very ideology he wishes to undercut. Within a few words he has replicated the tension evident in all his work up to 1974: a critique of authority that desires authority; a condemnation of referentiality that relies on referential language; a preoccupation with individualism voiced in terms of group dynamics and group control.

These tensions account for the contradictory images so present in the opening paragraph — images that simultaneously invoke weakness and strength, blindness and insight. They also account for the dense-ness of Davey's language as it moves forward in theoretical assertion, doubles back on itself in terminological doubt, jams together a lexicon of freedom and transcendence with a vocabulary of domination and loss.

The document presents us with a narrator who is obsessed with evasion and weakness: he tells us that Canadian criticism is "reluctant to focus"; it "looks away"; it has "seldom had enough confidence" (5). But all of this denial is described in terms that are clearly aligned with power, legality, proof. Although "Surviving the Paraphrase" is ostensibly anti-authoritarian in theory, in practice it is very prescriptive and authority-centred. We are presented with a speaker who uses traditional rhetoric and traditional images of control and domination to object to a rhetoric of control and domination that he finds too traditional.

The first noun in the essay is the word *testimony* — a statement made under oath, a form of confession, the biblical announcement of com-mandments, rules. (*Testimony* finds its etymological origin in the male act of bearing witness to virility by swearing an oath on one's testes — an act that can appear in many guises in its contemporary and discursive forms, as Davey's essay will show.) This word is followed by others that share in the discourse of power, location, and subordination: "limi-tations," "direction," "confidence," "apologies," "rationalizations," "recourse," "espousal," "determiners," "alleged cultural influences" (5). The language is both penitential and prescriptive. It verges on the legal. We seem to be participating in a trial narrative. Who or what is being tried?

At first glance the criminal appears to be thematic criticism itself, as if it were a body, a being who "looks away" from concrete evidence toward "alleged cultural influences." The criminal is young, not yet hardened. The narrator reminds us that this offender has only had a "brief lifetime" (5). Let the court provide mercy. But mercy cannot be provided to a school of criticism, even if it *were* a school. Something, someone else, must be on trial. Perhaps it is the person *giving* testimony, the narrator himself, who presents all of Canadian criticism in a grain of sand called thematic criticism, as if Canadian critical discourse begins and ends here.

What is his crime? Crime number one: to have come into the land of E.K. Brown, A.J.M. Smith, Northrop Frye, D.G. Jones, Margaret Atwood, and John Moss. To have come east. (By Davey's own account he was "a British Columbian who was excluded from a Canada defined as Ontario" [*Reading* 4].) To have left the garden. To have ventured into an undifferentiated wilderness where everything looks the same — where there are no signs. To have deserted, jumped ship, left home, mutinied, aligned yourself with the territory of another crew. (Davey's poetry up to 1974 is full of mutineers and shipwrecks.)

The second crime: to have left home. To feel as if you had evaded your responsibilities. To see in those around you in this new wilderness what you see in yourself: a hardening; a preoccupation with "cultural influences and determiners"; a reluctance to focus; a referential gaze that looks away (5). Away from what? Cast out, adrift, alone, the narrator looks away from himself. The evasion he sees in thematic criticism is his self-evasion. The domination he fears in thematic criticism is his fear of domination by others whom he cannot control. What is on trial is nothing less than the narrator's very being, his survival in a place where the theme of survival is deemed absurd.

How to survive: *make yourself known.* Adopt a subversive stance so that people will pay attention to you. (Just before he delivered "Surviving the Paraphrase" in 1974, Davey talked about "exploiting controversy as a way of reaching a public" and about how "you just have to get in a controversy in order to get anybody to pay attention to the criticism" ["Starting" 144].) Demand that people treat "writing as writing" so that all writing has the same status, regardless of genre. This perspective undoes the distinction between creative and critical writing. It means that you can be a critic *and* a writer who is respected *as* writer. Or you can be a writer who is a critic. You can bridge the gap. In other words, you can be what Frank Davey wanted to be in 1974: writer as critic. (Many of Davey's pre-1974 poems are preoccupied with bridges. For Davey, "The bridge is . . . anything which reaches across, whether it be the sexual, the male penis, or right through to the bridge" ["Starting" 120]. Bridge-building is male. Being writer as critic is male. Writing "Surviving the Paraphrase" is male. It is the act of being a man. Of giving testimony.)

The critics whom Davey approves of are called "writers who appear to have the greatest understanding of the technical concerns and accomplishments of their fellows" (5). All of the writer-critics Davey mentions in this context are from the West (Doug Barbour, Stephen Scobie, George Bowering, Dorothy Livesay), with the exception of William Gairdner, Eli Mandel, and Miriam Waddington (all Davey's colleagues when he was at York University), and also Gary Geddes (who was, as we know, responsible for Davey's first book-length critical venture). In other words, the valorization of certain forms of critical activity is aligned not only with region, but also with political and institutional allegiance. And the best examples of this criticism are practised by writer-critics, who are privileged because of their hybrid status.

Once we see that the critic is a writer, a narrator, it becomes easier to see how attending to "writing as writing" also serves the interest of any writer's self-expression. For Davey (I'm deliberately blurring the distinction between the author of "Surviving the Paraphrase" and its narrator), one alternative to thematic criticism is criticism that deals with "form, language, style, structure, and consciousness as these arise from the work as a unique construct" (5).

The emphasis here involves more than distinguishing one writer from another on the basis of technique as opposed to content; it is about consciousness, uniqueness, and illuminating the work "on its own terms." In other words, the examination of writing as writing reveals difference, and difference is essential to an author — particularly a critic — who remains an immigrant to part of a country that is central to the country he calls home. The first page of "Surviving the Paraphrase" consistently equates writing and writers with individual illumination, so much so that they appear like mantras. The words *writing* or *writers* appear nine times on the first page — more than any other word.

A central problem, according to Davey, is that thematic criticism silences writing. In contrast, formalism allows writing to speak. By recognizing particularity and idiosyncrasy, it allows the writer to define himself as unemasculated by thematics. Being particular means being male. In a review he published just prior to writing "Surviving the Paraphrase," Davey criticizes several mythopoeic poets for having "retreated from the reality of themselves and their country into an emasculated international world of myth and archetype"

("Reflections" 64). Never retreat. Have courage. Avoid emasculation. Be particular. Be pointed. Be male. Sometimes this is hard.

Although the narrator's strategy is to bridge the gap between authentic voice (writing) and false voice (criticism), he must continually assert the binary distinction he establishes between writing and criticism in order to maintain his structural model. For this reason, "Surviving the Paraphrase" develops as a narrative that operates against itself. It wants us to pay attention to "form, language, style, structure," but it doesn't *do* much to illustrate this sort of attention. Instead, it aligns attention to form with *courage*, with the ability to *face*, rather than evade, writing. The masculinist narrative here is about having the courage to read — to plunge into the fold between poetry and criticism, to claim the space in which writing can act. Any narrative about courage is also a narrative about power. But any narrative about power also testifies to the impotence it denies. In this case, to look away from writing is to be thematic, to be impotent, finally to be less of a man. To look *into* the writing is to be courageous, focused on the work, illuminating it as from the vantage point of God. *That* is to be a man.

Because he does not illuminate the work in this way, the narrator in "Surviving the Paraphrase" runs the risk of becoming what he became the moment he started speaking: a critic, an undifferentiated Everyman, just another archetypal wanderer dreaming about gardens, apocalypse, orgasm, closure, grand myths of truth. Even in 1988 Davey was still describing the landscape of his journey in archetypal terms as "the wilderness of thematic criticism" (*Reading* 2).

By the time the narrator comes to the end of the opening page of "Surviving the Paraphrase" we realize that the wilderness he must traverse is the wilderness that is his. The crime of silencing the work through criticism is both without and within; the crime of going east finds narrative expression as a struggle between voice and silence; the crime of abandoning local history is addressed through a confession that extols the particular over the universal and individual utterance over culture.

III

I can only imagine how people responded when Frank Davey read the first two paragraphs of "Surviving the Paraphrase." I want to pretend I was there. They hear the words. They say, "This is an attack." Like most attacks, this one contains a counternarrative. In this case, the counternarrative serves to reassure the audience that witnesses the attack. The counternarrative says: this attack on thematic criticism is not too dangerous because thematic criticism is not yet sacred. (How could it have become sacred in the four years since Jones published *Butterfly on Rock*? How much thematic criticism was actually being written during this time? Can we get any distance on this question?)

The counternarrative says: you may not have thought that thematic criticism was sacred, but now, through this attack, it will become sacred. Now it will be worthy of analysis and sustained attack. It says: don't worry, this won't be a rough ride because you will be able to fall back on all the terms that comfort humanists, even though this is also an attack on humanist assumptions. You will be able to believe in "testimony," the work as a "unique construct," "consciousness," illumination, "movements," and even "an odyssey in novelistic technique." There will always be something to hold on to. A bridge. A force.

We are about to enter "the wilderness of thematic criticism." In this wilderness, the narrator will guide the way. One of his methods of leading is to allow his audience, his followers, to escape the wilderness, to realize that he always means the opposite of everything he says. He will always be ironic. This is why he supports "a principle formulated by Frye: 'the literary structure is always ironic because "what it says" is always different from "what it means" ' " (6).

What "Surviving the Paraphrase" *says* is that support for thematic criticism is synonymous with support for the corporate body, which Davey associates with "Arnoldian humanism," "responsibility to culture," "the group," and the collective "expression of ideas and visions"; this expression is variously called "our imaginative life" (Jones), "national being" (Moss), or "cultural history" (Frye). What it *means* is that corporate bodies — call them what you will — are fundamentally technocratic and religious. They represent "messianic attempts" to create "formulae" that will define collective identity (6).

In rejecting this humanist vision, the narrator asserts more than his alignment with a poetics focused on structure, language, and imagery. He asserts the value of individualism, the achievement of identity through writing and voice. But this search for identity is itself ironic, not only because "identity" is a concept traditionally aligned with the humanism that "Surviving the Paraphrase" ostensibly rejects, but also because the question of identity here is presented as a discussion about who will represent whom. Davey's quarrel with humanism is a quarrel about representational power. In this case, the question is a political one addressed to an academic group. Framed in this way, "Surviving the Paraphrase" becomes a document about anticorporate individualism that is empowered by an individual's political appeal to a new corporate body — the Association for Canadian and Quebec

Literatures — which was founded on the belief that national literatures are distinct, identifiable, and worthy of study.

Both in its assertion of individual over corporate power, and in its questioning of corporate values, "Surviving the Paraphrase" announces itself as a narrative that paradoxically subverts the audience it would convert. The issue of theme versus technique, of culture versus writing, is displaced by the essay's controlling metaphors, which align strength with individualism, rebellion, and writing, and cowardice with culture, consensus, and criticism. To witness the presentation of this document, then, is to be caught in a double bind. If I want to make statements about Canadian culture, I am cowardly and writing in bad faith. If I want to write about writing, I am joining the narrator in his subversive activities.

Far from presenting its listeners or readers with a clear choice, "Surviving the Paraphrase" presents them with two ambivalent options, neither of which is entirely acceptable under the terms of institutionalized academic behaviour. While such behaviour must lay claim to some form of solidarity, it must also reject solidarity in favour of increasingly powerful theories of language and text. In brief, the power of "Surviving the Paraphrase" is that it is the first critical document in English-Canadian criticism to make its audience nervous. Now we are in the plot and it scares us. This controversy makes us feel uncomfortable.

The creation of this controversy is, in one respect, a by-product of Davey's argument. But in another way, the formulation of a double bind becomes a powerful tool in the hands of its conceiver, for he is the one who can deliver the audience from its nervousness. He is the one who can show the way. *What* way does not yet matter. All that matters is that there is someone here who seems to understand the problem he has constructed, someone who knows what to do. By publicly formulating a problem he can solve, Davey empowers himself both as a storyteller who speaks and as a critic who can get us out of the mess we didn't know we were in until he started to describe it. In two pages, then, he has built one of the bridges that will serve as metaphoric reference points throughout his career: the bridge between the radical, experimental, marginalized writer from the West and the established, institutionalized, centralized critic from the East. This activity is deliberately syncretic: it unites the old and the new in a single breath.

Because this bridge-building is so active, the audience is distracted from a number of other subnarratives that position Davey as he speaks. For example, one of the most arresting essays in thematic criticism was published long before the books by Atwood, Jones, and Moss which Davey attacks. This was Warren Tallman's "Wolf in the Snow" (1960).

Tallman supported Davey when he was a student at the University of British Columbia, and in fact it was Tallman who wrote the introduction to Davey's first book of poetry, as well as the first article on Davey's work. Not a word is said about Tallman's criticism, which had much longer to influence critical trends than did the work of the more recent thematic critics Davey repudiates.

Tallman's work may not be discussed in "Surviving the Paraphrase," but Tallman is there. He appears when Davey quotes approvingly from Robert Creeley, who remarks that "it cannot be simply what a man proposes to talk about in a poem that is interesting. . . . We continue to define what is said/happening in how it is said" (6–7). Creeley's words are reproduced from a tape-recorded lecture given at the home of Warren Tallman in Vancouver in 1962. In other words, Tallman, Creeley, the West Coast, and 1962 (the year Davey's first book of poetry was published) are still very much present in this 1974 document, but they are ironically present, displaced as they are to the list of footnotes that gives "Surviving the Paraphrase" the academic *cachet* it wants, and doesn't want, to have.

IV

The narrator in the second section of "Surviving the Paraphrase" is deeply divided. He speaks with critical authority about the need to defy critical authority. He wants freedom, so he is preoccupied with rules. Although this is apparently an attack on the main thematic critics — Frye, Moss, Atwood, Jones — it really turns out to be an attack on Jones. Davey dismisses Frye because his "genuinely thematic criticism of Canadian literature constitutes a small body of work" (7), as if *size* really *is* important. He thus dismisses the conclusion to the first edition of the *Literary History of Canada* (1965), the very document that inspired the thematic critics Davey attacks. Moss is dismissed because his work is "largely derivative of Frye and Jones" (7). Atwood had been dealt with elsewhere.

So Jones becomes the synecdoche, the Christ figure who must pay for the sins of those who preceded and followed him. It is Jones who embodies the "messianic attempts" (6) of the thematic critics to define a corporate, humanist society. This may be true, but in *Butterfly on Rock* Jones committed a greater crime. He cast the search for national identity in terms that would have been particularly distasteful to Davey, for Jones saw the achievement of national identity as the product of successful "westward expansion" that was now complete, a phrase that revealed precisely the imperialist assumptions behind the centralist values Davey abhorred. Jones was the colonizer from the East — and a humanist to boot. His criticism had taken the West, written it into a University of Toronto Press book, and converted it into property held by powerful interests from the East.

Davey saw in Jones's work an embodiment of the five features he objected to in thematic criticism: its "humanist bias"; its "disregard for literary history" (7); its "tendency toward sociology"; its "attempt at 'culture-fixing' "; and "the fallacy of literary determinism" (8). While Davey's brief discussion of these objections focuses our attention away from Davey, the terms of his discussion serve to make the objections self-reflexive.

Davey objects to humanism because it pretends to be all-inclusive in its perpetuation of mass value. What Davey wants is a recognition of "unique," "idiosyncratic," "unusual," "original," and "eccentric" qualities that identify individual works. The problem here is that all these qualities fit quite comfortably within the humanist and nationalist ethos, in which the concern for shared value is a distinct product of the recognition of difference. As David Clark observes, "Davey's post-modernist escape from 'metaphysics' may be a displaced figure for the oldest metaphysical gesture of them all," a belief in "originality" and in the "foundationalist opposition of self-same and 'other' upon which nationalisms of all kinds are based" (86).

Davey's sustained quarrel with humanism, which he consistently effects through humanist discourse, is not so much with humanist ideology as it is with the fact of *his* difference, *his* exclusion from the perceived mainstream discussed in the works of Frye, Jones, Atwood, and Moss — none of whom mention what seems most important to Davey at this point in his career: his poetry.

In this context, the final words of his objection to Jones's humanism are revealing: he complains that "whatever conflicts" with "mass-values" is "rejected or ignored" (7). In a strange leap, humanism becomes "mass-value," and mass value becomes canonical. What begins as an attack on humanism becomes an attack on the forces of literary exclusion. As the agent of this attack, Davey becomes the self-appointed outsider, the wanderer in the wilderness, the questing antihero whose difference marks him as both outcast and prophet. Paradoxically, Davey's defence of difference serves to position him as a self-styled victim, as a subject who constructs himself in precisely those terms of thematic criticism that his essay sets out to reject. As Lynette Hunter says, "Davey's postmodernism is at this time thoroughly tied into a form of Canadian nationalism that validates Canada in the name of the counter-culture, the (implicitly heroic) anti-hero. . . . [T]he contradiction of the denial of essentialism running hand in hand with implicitly essentialist statements about form and politics underwrites a form of individualistic pluralism" (49).

This paradoxical construction explains much about Davey's view of literary history. What literary history proves to him is that victimization is not unique to Canadian literature; it is ubiquitous in contemporary world literature: "the traditional subject of the novel has been the person who is 'isolated' by his not being able to fit comfortably into society" (7). In other words, the problem of being different — apparently Davey's problem — is a universal problem of archetypal status. But if victimization is so ubiquitous, so traditional, then it is not different; it is normal. And if victimization is ubiquitous, then no victim can have special status; the role of antihero becomes the status quo. Davey's arguments threaten to become self-neutralizing. He concludes his discussion of literary history in words that are as revealing as those that closed his earlier discussion of humanism. He recognizes that he has become involved in "a dilemma from which there appears to be no scholarly escape" (8).

One does not think about escape unless one is imprisoned. But in this case, scholarship offers no route to liberation. Scholarship (by now aligned with the "academic critics" whom Davey calls thematic) is a dead end. The scholarship that we are reading about our scholarly problem gets embroiled in a scholarly dilemma about how to solve the scholarly problem. It begins to turn in on itself, to become preoccupied with the question of how it will transcend its own identity as an exercise in academic criticism that might go nowhere.

This preoccupation with escape leads Davey to focus obsessively on the metaphor of isolation, perhaps his own. If this metaphor appeared only a few times, its presence would be easy to explain: Davey is simply drawing on the works of the thematic critics to illustrate his points. But in this eight-page essay about surviving, the metaphor is associated with a cluster of words that appear far too often for us to attribute them to scholarly evidence or exegesis. And the frequency of these word clusters increases as the essay unfolds. By the time he is dealing with thematic criticism's "tendency toward sociology," we notice that he returns to the problem (expressed by Jones) of how the Canadian "will feel at home in his world," of how this same Canadian will experience "the end of exile" (8). By now we understand what is most frightening to Davey about Jones's stance: it is his own. Is he not the wanderer in search of home? Is he not the ubiquitous victim in contemporary literature, the isolato divorced from his community and his own history? Is he not Adam cast out?

Because he identifies so strongly with the problems faced by Adam, the narrative begins to sound like a commentary on the biblical story, rather than a comment on D.G. Jones. Although Davey describes what he calls the "culture-fixing" supported by thematic critics, or the "fallacy of literary determinism" through which the artist is presumed to speak for a people, his descriptions and discussions return again and again to patterns of isolation and oppression. Here Davey focuses repeatedly on the presence in his own work of the patterns he denies: the "transition from an Old Testament condition of exile and alienation toward a New Testament one of affirmation, discovery, and community"; "restricting and potentially paralyzing" formulae; definitions that "intimidate"; criticism that "fails to make clear that the writer is in some small way free," rather than "passively formed" by forces beyond his or her control (8). This repeated appeal to freedom in the face of restriction and paralysis marks the speaker as profoundly unfree.

V

What are the alternatives to this enslavement — to pattern, to criticism, to nation? This is the question addressed by Davey in the last section of his essay. My interest here is not in the various approaches that Davey proposes as alternatives to thematic criticism. I am more concerned with showing how the concluding section resolves the narrator's own sense of isolation, and how its closing images pacify an audience that has been following a narrative that seems subversive, and possibly threatening, in its intent.

Davey uses an effective technique to increase the solidarity between speaker and audience. By this point in the paper, the audience has been told, repeatedly, that thematic criticism is inadequate. Readers have been victimized by thematic criticism, which promotes restriction, potential paralysis, passivity, and subordination; it makes people feel reduced, isolated, ignored, fixed, imprisoned, rejected, and intimidated. Now, through a subtle manipulation, Davey tells his audience that thematic criticism exploits its readers, deceives them, makes them the victims of a conspiracy that is bent on distorting the truth about Canada and its literature. In this new formulation, there are "motivations" behind thematic criticism, "motivations" that soon become the "undeclared motive" behind the "ruse of sociological research" (9). The reader of thematic criticism has obviously been duped. The perceptive reader will acknowledge this deceit. All of a sudden, the rejection of thematic criticism is equated with the ability to expose a sham.

There are some interesting forces at work here. Those who heard the first few pages of Davey's essay might not have been aware that thematic criticism was a school, much less a conspiracy with hidden motives. By the end of the essay, the school has been named, invented, and identified with power structures that need to be destroyed. In short, Davey's narrative takes its readers from creation to destruction. It identifies them as believers in false gods, and it proposes to deliver them from these gods. In this scenario, the audience is given no means of asserting its commonalty, particularly because the symbol around which this commonalty organizes itself — cultural nationalism — is being undercut. No one wants to be entirely alone. And in an industry devoted to the teaching of Canadian literature, no one wants to believe, ultimately, that there is no such thing as national identity.

In order to deliver his listeners from their potential isolation, and in order to deliver himself, Davey must find a way to question national identity while affirming it. He must subvert the paranoia his own narrative constructs. He must find a way of providing his readers with access to community at the very moment that he questions its value. Ultimately, he must show that "writing as writing" is not strictly eccentric and subjective, not strictly divorced from culture. If he is to be a critic-leader, he must unite the group at the very moment it confronts the insecurity he has aroused.

Davey employs several tactics to achieve this end. Right after he tells us that the thematic critics have deceived us, he provides reassurance. He addresses "Canadian critics" as a group, saying that "it is extremely important that Canadian critics not forget that there are indeed alternatives to thematic criticism" (9). (When he reprinted "Surviving the Paraphrase" in his 1983 book by that title, the only substantive change he made was to replace the words "extremely important" with the word "essential" [7].) Moreover, "these alternatives, like thematic criticism, do allow the writing of overviews of all or parts of Canadian literature" (9). It begins to sound as though the alternatives are really not too dangerous, not too risky, because they are like the devil we already know.

Although it might have seemed as though national identity were being questioned, this turns out not to have been the case. The alternatives Davey recommends would assume "a national identity's existence and a national literature's significance" (9). A study of prosody, for example, would yield an important "by-product": "an implicit statement about Canadians, Canada, and its evolution" (10). Wouldn't such a by-product offer precisely the totalizing formulation that Davey's essay rejects?

Davey's conciliatory position at the end of "Surviving the Paraphrase" serves to reaffirm the value of the group he is addressing, as well as his position as a speaker for that group. By the end of the essay, he has become the persona he was so hesitant to become — an academic Canadian critic, living in Toronto, speaking about Canadian criticism, at the Learned Societies meetings, at the University of Toronto, in the East. But the regional voice is still there. Close to the end of the essay Davey asserts that "the bulk of Canadian literature is regional before it is national, despite whatever claims Ontario or Toronto writers may make to represent a national vision." He wants us to know that "the regional consciousness may be characterized by specific attitudes to language and form" (11). This assertion of difference remains the expression of Davey the poet. But Davey the Canadian critic must undermine this claim to poetic specificity if he is to gain acceptance in the East. His defensiveness at this point ("it is not unfair to say" [11]) is understandable. So is his concluding message: that to surrender to the totalizing, boring conformity of thematic criticism is to live in ignorance. Yet one suspects that Davey's fear, his concern about the "dangers" of thematic criticism, is a fear of criticism itself, associated as it is for Davey with control, power, and exclusion.

VI

It is in the face of this alienating force of criticism that Davey writes "Surviving the Paraphrase," a document that rejects power structures as its prescriptive argument seeks them, a document that would disempower communal values while it mourns the community's extinction. Finally — most importantly — it is the expression of a narrator who wants a home. Although the emphasis on "writing as writing" is designed to focus our attention on difference, Davey's ultimate purpose is to find a means of integrating the eccentric into a social universe. As it turns out, criticism that focuses on "the writing itself" produces a milieu in which "no writer can be excluded because of his attitudes or subject matter" (12).

In this egalitarian milieu, all writing is open to critical discussion. By emphasizing this openness, Davey suggests in his concluding words how the hard distinctions between criticism and creative writing might be bridged. Such a bridging (such a force) would resolve the central conflict behind "Surviving the Paraphrase" — Davey's apparent desire to be both writer and critic, to speak from within a community of poets and to establish his authority within a new community that is academic in orientation. This desire for community, for belonging and connection, is far from subversive. In fact, it has much in common with Frye's need to imagine the peaceable kingdom, an alternative he proposed to the isolation of the garrison mentality in his conclusion to the first *Literary History of Canada*. Davey never deals with this document, perhaps because it is too close to his own.

If "Surviving the Paraphrase" narrates a conversion experience, as did Frye's conclusion, it is because it represents the first expression of Davey's realization that criticism can be a creative act, and that consciousness can be articulated as much through exegesis as through poetry. The final sentence of the document brings this connection home. Davey asserts that the type of criticism he is advocating "would turn the critic's attention back to where the writer's must always be" — to "writing as writing" (12). This closing gesture both privileges writing over criticism and simultaneously equates it with the critical act. But the most important value Davey upholds, right to the end, is "loyalty" to language, an allegiance that positions him firmly among those he may well be leaving behind. His future as a critic may promise "power, complexity, and ingenuity" — writerly qualities all — but it promises to locate those qualities in a new community of scholars that, even in 1974, Frank Davey was still coming to know.

In retrospect, it does not seem as though "Surviving the Paraphrase" is the radical document it is often presented to be. Its appeal lies both in the contradictions it embodies between loyalty and liberation and in the way these contradictions are presented as issues that are relevant to a professional community faced with questions about its own identity and future. To this community, "Surviving the Paraphrase" is a subversive document that appeals for a new social order while remaining loyal to a previous one — a dream of Canada — that cannot, ultimately, be eliminated or repressed. And in the midst of this document is Frank Davey, tossed on his sea, talking about criticism, and writing, and loss.

Making It Real (Again)

"IT'S THE PROFESSOR. How are you today, Mr. Professor?"

I am being greeted, as I am every month, by the nurse who will soon be giving me my allergy injection, protection against the fatal sting of wasps.

"Fine. Fine."

I sit down and flip through a copy of *People* magazine, waiting nervously for the moment when she calls me into the scary little room where the injecting is done.

"Okay, Robert. Come in."

I roll up my sleeve and get ready for the small talk she always makes to distract me.

"So. . . . What is it you said you teach?"

"Literature."

"What kind of literature?"

"Canadian."

"Oh. I guess that must mean there is some."

"Right."

I distract myself by looking at the wall calendar.

"All done, Mr. Professor. See you next month."

* * *

The study of Canadian literature — and Canadian literature itself — remains foreign to most members of the public. Of course there are the big-name Canadian writers who command public attention and sell thousands of books, but there is practically no public sense of Canada as a country with a literary history, no sense that there are literary connections out there, no deeply ingrained civic feeling that it is worthwhile to have a national literature or to find out how it evolved. Those who do read Canadian literature on a regular basis may feel they are ensconced in a community. They are. But it is a tiny community, supported mainly by federal and provincial arts agencies. Without such support, the remaining signs of literary life in Canada would probably vanish. There would be no more readings, no more authors on tour, hardly any advertising, few new books. Most publishing companies would fold. Academics would find it impossible to publish their studies. Popular journalism on Canadian writing would dry up, simply because the audience would be too small to justify the writer's salary. While this scenario may seem extreme, anyone who is involved in writing about or publishing Canadian literature knows (or needs to know) that the end of government support is the end of the game.

This alarms me, mainly because I still believe that there is a relationship between literature and culture, and that a government that is interested in culture ought to support this relationship. Yet, in the face of inevitable future budget cuts and attempts to reduce federal and provincial deficits, it will be increasingly difficult to argue that a knowledge of Canadian literature contributes to Canadian cultural literacy, especially if the public seems apathetic about the issue. In what I hope is not an indication of things to come, the Conservative MP for North Vancouver argued, in 1991, that not enough Canadians read books to justify subsidizing the Canadian book-publishing industry to the extent the federal government does. When asked if there should be less subsidization, the MP — Chuck Cook — said, "Yeah, I'm afraid so" ("So Who Reads Books?" C1). I'm afraid that Cook was serious. Can we really rest secure that the Liberals will not adopt Cook's stance?

Even if government continues to buy the idea that *cultural* literacy is essential, it does not necessarily follow that the support of Canadian *literature* will be seen as one means of achieving such literacy. After close to forty years of federal and provincial efforts designed to create a Canadian literature industry and to foster public support for Canadian writers and artists, the public seems more alienated than ever. In a recent issue of the *OAC Notepad*, a publication of the Ontario Arts Council, Yolande Grisé speaks as a director of the council's board of directors when she says that "artists don't have a lot of public support. . . . We have to educate Canadians about the arts and culture, and help politicians and decision-makers understand what we are achieving with the arts in different communities in Ontario" ("We Do Not Retreat" 4).

One might wonder why nearly forty years of government funding has failed to educate Canadians in this way. Have things really changed much from the time the Massey Report was released in 1951? In that report, the authors argued that it was "necessary to find some way of helping our Canadian writers to become an integral part of their environment and, at the same time, to give them a sense of their importance in this environment" (227). The authors of the report believed that "if we in Canada want a more generous and better cultural fare we must pay for it" (381).

Canadians have been paying for this cultural fare since the founding of the Canada Council in 1957. Although federal and provincial arts agencies are the most prominent bodies responsible for investing in "cultural fare," there are many other funding programs designed to support the idea of a national culture and its literature.

What kind of success has this investment produced? When it comes to the appreciation of Canadian literature, it seems clear that government intervention has simply not created a substantial readership outside the schools, while the readership in schools is largely a manufactured one comprised of students who seldom buy Canadian literature after they leave their classes. It's worth remembering that a strong sale for a Canadian novel is 5000 copies. A respectable sale for a poetry book is 500 copies. Books of Canadian literary criticism that sell 1000 copies are considered to have done quite well, even though 50 percent or more of these sales are usually to libraries with a mandate to purchase Canadian criticism. If the other half of those critical books are bought by interested readers, this means that one in every 50,000 Canadians will invest in a reasonably successful work of literary criticism, or about .000017 percent of the total population. In fact, most of the critical works not bought by libraries are bought by academics, so that the actual number of nonacademic readers of Canadian literary criticism is even smaller than the figure above. I would imagine that, with a few notable exceptions, the voluntary readership for a reasonably well-received book of Canadian criticism would be fewer than 100 people (not counting students who are assigned such reading in their courses).

Anyone who is surprised by this assertion should remember just how few literate readers Canada actually has. Despite the frequently made assertion that "Canadians are voracious book readers" and that we have a "robust literary culture" (*Reading in Canada 1991* 20, 35), a recent Decima survey indicates that "only 10% of Canadians buy books from bookstores" (Scott Anderson). Perhaps this is because we are not a nation of readers. In the first survey to provide real statistics about the state of literacy in Canada, the Southam Literacy Report, entitled *Broken Words* (1987), revealed that "five million Canadians cannot read, write or use numbers well enough to meet the literacy demands of today's society," and that 50 percent of Canadian adults have serious trouble using bus schedules and can't find a store listing in the Yellow Pages (7, 14). Eight percent of Canadian university graduates are functionally illiterate. In Toronto, 27 percent of the population is functionally illiterate; the rate is 23 percent in Montreal.

A recent survey by Statistics Canada confirms the findings of the Southam report: in Canada, 38 percent of the population cannot read or "tend to avoid situations requiring reading" (*Adult Literacy in Canada* 18). For this reason, "illiteracy represents a major challenge facing Canadian society in the 1990s" (77). In a commentary entitled "Canada Must Improve Literacy Performance," Neville Nankivell observes that although Canada spends more per capita on education than most countries in the world, it ranks 24th "in terms of the educational system meeting the needs of a competitive economy." This is because "Canada's adult illiteracy rate as a percentage of population is high," and, as a result, Canada is not competitive — it stands "only 16th overall on the 1994 world competition ladder" (17). All the government funding directed toward the identification and promotion of Canadian culture through the reading and study of Canadian literature might have been better invested in creating a nation that, first, could read. As Jon Bradley says: "It's not as life-threatening as AIDS, nor as terrible as mass murder, nor as current as acid rain. . . . But in the long run it could be a far more damaging threat to Canadian society" (*Broken Words* 8).

In an article entitled "An End to Audience," Margaret Atwood points to one reason why this threat is so profound:

A country or a community which does not take serious literature seriously will lose it. *So what?* say the Members of Parliament. *All we want is a good read. A murder mystery, a spy thriller, something that keeps you turning the pages. I don't have the time to read anyway.*

Well, try this. It could well be argued that the advent of the printed word coincided with the advent of democracy as we know it; that the book is the only form that allows the reader not only to participate but to review, to re-view what's being presented. With a book you can turn back the pages. You can't do that with a television set. Can democracy function at all without a literate public, one with a moral sense and well-developed critical faculties? Can democracy run on entertainment packages alone? (357)

No. But entertainment packages may be all that are left to a country that has forgotten its literature, or that never got to know it. Obviously the noncurricular audience for Canadian literature is extremely small; the audience for critical works is minuscule. It may not feel that way at the annual learned society meetings attended by hundreds of academics from different disciplines, but the reality is that the actual reading community inhabits a tiny island in a sea of illiteracy. There is no way that, under current circumstances, the study of Canadian literature will have any effect on the public at large. It may be possible to affect a small number of literate readers outside the schools, and it is certainly possible to affect students — at the high school, college, and university levels. However, as I argue in "Privacy, Publicity, and the Discourse of Canadian Criticism," academic professionals have shown little interest in reaching a broader public, even those members of the public who do read Canadian literature enthusiastically and on a regular basis. The nature of the study has become much too specialized for public consumption. Besides, tenured academics really have no compelling incentive to address the public, since they are not publicly accountable. I know of one prominent scholar in Canadian literature who insists that academics (especially literary theorists) have every right to speak in terms as esoteric as those employed by nuclear physicists. Implicit in this position is the idea that academics really only need to speak to each other, or, if they deign to address the nonspecialist, it will be through an inferior, degraded form of discourse.

All this is fine so long as your job is secure, the university provides the students, and the government makes it possible for physicist-critics to publish their books. But the system will not be able to function this way for much longer. There is too great a discrepancy between the stated aims of the funding agencies and the aims of academics. The agencies want to advance Canadian cultural literacy at a time when Canadian academics seem bored by the whole idea. What was the last book written by an academic that focused on teaching cultural literacy in Canada, or on the centrality of literature to an apprehension of Canadian culture, regardless of how fragmented and polycultural it has become? I haven't encountered one in many years. Instead, academics write for each other, in order to obtain promotion, power, and prestige. There is no public end within the current system, and nobody seems upset about this fact. Instead, we have political infighting, power grabs, territorial disputes.

Most of these disputes are played out in the university milieu, another indication of the extent to which the study of Canadian culture — such as it is — has been hijacked by PhDeified specialists who have no patience with public discourse and no time for dialogue with teachers who do not work at the university level. When the study of Canadian literature was being industrialized in the 1960s and 1970s, high-school and college teachers were considered to be part of the ball game. There were books designed for use in Canadian high schools, and bibliographies designed for teachers at all levels. For example, the Writers' Development Trust published a series of books for the English intermediate curriculum in Ontario high schools. Margery Fee and Ruth Cawker published *Canadian Fiction: An Annotated Bibliography*, which, the authors said, was intended for use by secondary-school teachers ("although we hope it will also prove useful for librarians, students and those who simply read Canadian literature for pleasure" [ix]). I do not believe it would be possible to find the same appeal to such a varied audience in a contemporary reference work. I cannot remember the last time I saw a book of Canadian criticism directed toward a high-school audience. Perhaps this is because the days of governments investing heavily in library acquisitions and programs devoted to Canadian literature are over. Without this support, there has been little interest in producing critical books for the high-school market. The same observation can be made about anthologies of Canadian literature. At one time, publishers designed anthologies that were meant for use in secondary-school classrooms; today, fewer anthologies are produced, and they are directed primarily at the university market.

If similar support is withdrawn at the university level, how long would academics continue to do research in the field of Canadian literature? Not very long. The established, tenured professor can survive such a shift in funding priorities, which I predict will come about by the end of the decade. He or she does not need to publish in order to keep a job. But the untenured faculty member does need to perform. If public activity is discounted at the expense of publishing activity, as it currently is in the eyes of most promotion and tenure committees, then the withdrawal of government support for Canadian cultural projects (synonymous with cultural protection) will create a crisis for young academics as they discover that there is no outlet for their work, particularly if it happens to be devoted to Canadian literature, which will inevitably be seen as an area of secondary concern in the face of the growing problem, not of cultural literacy, but of literacy itself, since illiteracy is a major economic problem that government will be forced to address and redress. This will be costly.

Given these assertions, it seems logical to ask whether a book such as this one — which is written by a university professor who specializes in Canadian literature — can make any contribution to a discussion about the contemporary relation between Canada and its literature. At least it proposes that such a discussion is crucial. There are some very hard questions that need to be asked about the study and teaching of this country's literature. Why do it? How has it been done? Why invest in it? Why claim it is worthy of government support? So long as Canadian literature is singled out as a field that is distinct — as an industry that has journals, courses, books, and teachers devoted to it — then those who work in the industry should be capable of explaining, and even defending, its distinct status and value.

Many of the chapters in this book argue that this status and value is a function of displaced literary nationalism. When this displacement becomes a silencing of nationalist discourse, as it has in recent Canadian criticism, then the power of that discourse needs to be identified, precisely because something so forcefully avoided obviously retains force. Although every comment on a body of work called Canadian literature implies the construction of a nation called Canada, there is virtually no recent commentary on how contemporary literary critics and teachers have participated in this construction, or tried to alter it. Those who teach and study Canadian literature generally ignore what Heather Murray calls "the relation between education and the state" and "the relationship of literary training to national formation" ("Institutions of Reading" 5). Or they treat the idea of speaking about their relation with this force as quaint, romantic, reactionary, a relation that is out of style. Or they speak of it in terms that can only be understood by professional colleagues, rather than the educated reader outside the university.

This book shares some of the problems I describe above and it has not solved them. In many ways, its stance is contradictory, since many of the issues it raises are academically centred, a sign of my own involvement in the institution that has taught me how to think and speak about literature. Writing now, in retrospect, in conclusion, I see that each chapter in this book is part of a process of rewriting myself, and of discovering how difficult this process is. *Making It Real* encourages me to be suspicious about my critical language, to question my voice, to ask how the issues I raise can be made relevant to people beyond the institution's walls.

Such inquiries are not at all comforting, because they confirm what I suspected: I have not felt free to develop a more public discourse; I have not felt encouraged to write criticism for high-school readers; I have been thoroughly immersed in an institutional setting that reinforces my separation from the public. In some instances, the members of this "public" are my own former students, who are already forgetting how to speak about literature in the language of their school. How can they be addressed? What can professors do to ensure that some of the relevance we see in the study of literature is transmitted to people who are no longer in the classroom?

If "The Canonization of Canadian Literature" marks an attempt to question institutional values, it also demonstrates how hard it is to engage in such questioning when it is the very institution itself that provides the inquirer with his or her grammar. In order to move out of the received institutional discourse, it is necessary to make a conscious break — to engage in forms of research and talk that are strange or uncomfortable, to enter different critical and pedagogical milieux that are not one's own.

The irony of wanting to think outside the institution is this: I want to be outside and inside; I want to inhabit both spaces at once. This double desire is predictably consistent with the attitudes toward canonicity that I see in many contemporary discussions of Canadian literature, including those in *Making It Real.* On one hand, academic critics will insist that there really is no canon of Canadian literature, that what we call a canon is actually a fluid grouping of texts that have more or less authority at certain historical moments. Because conceptions of the canon tend to be conceptions of the nation when the study of national literatures is involved, I think it's fair to say that contemporary doubts about the solidity of a Canadian canon are also doubts about the canonicity of Canada. This observation is quite conservative; it suggests that there is a fairly direct correspondence between the conception of authority in the study of a nation's literature and the perception of authority in the nation itself. In other words, it promotes the idea that textual and national value are related.

Although this is the assumption that has always encouraged people to study Canadian literature, there are no recent studies of how a historic conception of the nation figures in the conception of literary value, mainly because it is no longer acceptable to generalize about the construct called Canada or to promote theories of unity and coherence. While this process of dismantling canon and country takes place, teachers and critics continue to define themselves as specialists in something called Canadian literature, as if one could specialize in a nation's literature and never mention the nation. The country just is. Or isn't. Who cares? After all, its literature is there.

But how long will it be there? As I argue in "A Country without a Canon?" it is not possible to proceed in the study of a national literature without recognizing some version of authority. Failing such recognition, a national literature is not national, or different. It is literature. And if it is literature — minus the Canadian — then there is no reason to promote courses in Canadian literature, or to support journals or books devoted to its study. In fact, there is no reason to write about *Canadian* literature at all. This is why is it finally impossible to argue that Canadian literary criticism can ever really be "minus Canadian," as Barry Cameron and Michael Dixon imagined it could be when they wrote their "Mandatory Subversive Manifesto" in 1974, or as Frank Davey wanted it to be when he presented "Surviving the Paraphrase" in the same year. If Canada has no special status when it comes to the study of literature, then there is no reason for governments to fund its study, or for critics to comment on Canada's literature as if it did have special status by virtue of its being Canadian. You can't have it both ways. The peculiarity of recent Canadian criticism is that it insists on having it both ways: it seems to want to be called Canadian, but never to explain this want.

This conflicted understanding of the function of Canadian criticism is a product of the institution of Canadian literature that developed during the late 1960s and 1970s. Prior to this institutionalization, critics tried to explain the discrete status of the country and its literature. Sometimes, they idealized the connection, or saw it as a means of exploring their own motivations as writers. Frye does this in his conclusion to the *Literary History of Canada;* so does Davey in "Surviving the Paraphrase" and Kroetsch in his afterword to *As for Me and My House.* So do most of the anthologists whose works are surveyed in chapter 4. As I say in "Privacy, Publicity, and the Discourse of Canadian Criticism," the belief that there is a link between the Canadian critic and the nation has never really died. The problem is that, in recent years, the connection has been denied. If denial becomes acceptance, then the idea of Canadian literature will vanish. Something more will have been lost. In order to reverse this trend, those involved in the study and teaching of Canadian literature need to reassert the Canadian aspect of what they do. This does not mean returning to the nationalistic cheerleading that blinkered so much early Canadian criticism. It does not mean finding Canadian themes in, say, *The English Patient* or *Such a Long Journey.* It does mean that we consider these books different because they are written by Canadians, and that one aspect of studying them involves an investigation of this difference. In order to do this, Canada itself needs to be reimagined. This process of reimagining should be an explicit part of Canadian literary study. It is a necessary form of critical positioning. Those who teach Canadian literature carry a conception of the country. This conception needs to be foregrounded.

I have already argued that there will be increasing demands on academics to alter their sense of audience as the pressure to serve more people for less money increases with budget cutbacks. How much longer will it be possible to offer graduate courses for a handful of students who face dim employment prospects, or to subsidize the publication of books that will be read by a few dozen people, or to fund the editing and production of learned journals that have a few hundred subscribers? Will the university presses continue to invest in publishing Canadian criticism? Have people noticed that the University of British Columbia Press, which once published Canadian literary criticism, has quietly withdrawn from the field? Or that the Canada Council is rethinking its policy of funding critical works that are not substantially trade oriented?

There are other signs of increasing demands for public accountability, even if the demands are not framed in those terms. For example, scholarly journals that do not have a broad enough domestic and foreign subscription base will no longer receive support from the Social Sciences and Humanities Research Council's learned journal program. Professors who cannot demonstrate that their work will be disseminated widely — beyond the university — may not receive the funding they once did. In short, it is already becoming more and more necessary to think in specialist *and* nonspecialist terms, to work in new areas that remain foreign to many (I include myself) who have spent their professional lives within a strictly academic milieu. This will pose an enormous challenge, and will entail an entire rethinking of the profession.

As this process of rethinking gains momentum, academics involved in the study of Canadian literature will have to reconceive their mandate. Because many of the funding sources for the publication of specialized scholarly works will dry up, academics will be forced to seek publication in a market-driven system. At present, publishers of Canadian literary criticism do not have to make the market their primary consideration, simply because their losses are offset by grants from government programs that anticipate such losses. This luxury cannot last long. When the funding plug is pulled and the safety blanket is gone, academics in the field of Canadian literature will be under pressure to write books with more popular appeal in order to generate greater sales. Books on obscure Canadian poets — good as they may be — will be difficult to get published, unless they are written in a way that captures public interest, and unless the public has a reason to *be* interested.

If a scholarly book that is currently supported by government funding must sell, say, 1000 copies in order for the publisher to break even after the receipt of various forms of government support, it will have to sell five times that amount, at least, in order for it to break even without government support. It doesn't take long to realize that, given the cutbacks we can anticipate in all kinds of federal and provincial programs, it will no longer be possible for publishers to invest in esoteric studies of Canadian literature. The market is just not there, as it is, say, in the United States, where the academic population is ten times the size of what it is in Canada. A book about American literature that is sold exclusively to 5000 American academics can break even without subsidy; an equally good book about Canadian literature that is sold to 500 Canadian academics cannot. There is no reason to believe that funding for scholarly journals and books will continue indefinitely in Canada; the tendency is in the direction of cutbacks, increased selectivity, and demands for broader dissemination of material that is supported by grants.

If even minor shifts in government funding can have a serious impact on the publication of Canadian literary criticism, then major shifts in funding policies will transform the critical landscape. Although it is entirely possible that we may see such shifts over the next five years, there seems to be little concern with the consequences. Many academics who publish in the field of Canadian literature are so used to dealing with subsidized publishing houses that the idea of living without subsidy is inconceivable, even though most academics are also unaware of the extent to which subsidy makes the publication of their work possible. (At the University of Toronto Press, for example, one-third of all scholarly publications are supported by a grant.) It is time to end this innocence and to prepare for a future in which subsidy is eliminated or dramatically reduced.

What does such preparation involve? In many ways, it involves an entire rethinking of what academics have been trained to do and how they have learned to speak. It does not mean that academics have to stop writing academic books, or that they will not be able to pursue theoretical interests and to employ theoretical discourse, however specialized it may be. What it does mean is that the public side of Canadian criticism, which has diminished over the past few decades, needs to be reaffirmed and practised by academics in a very deliberate way. Only if the public is involved and understands the importance of the topic will it tolerate the funding of specialization and esoteric discovery. And because basic illiteracy is such a pressing issue in Canada, those who work in the profession will also have to convey the importance of reading itself. I think the attitude of most professionals involved in higher education is that this is a problem that is out of their domain. A high-school problem, perhaps. In any case, a problem that is out there, not in here. This attitude is reinforced by a promotional system within the universities that does not truly reward professors for getting "out there," for doing community work or contributing to literacy programs, even though many university promotion committees pay brief lip service to the idea of community service. It is ironic that one could get tenure by writing a book that a few dozen people might read, while teaching a few people to read for the first time would not be considered a central element in a tenure application. It is ironic that universities expect students to enrol in courses in Canadian literature (this enrolment is frequently mandatory) while we say nothing in public about why such enrolment is necessary. Courses on Canadian literature are simply assumed to be valuable, an assumption that leads to pedagogical and ideological complacency.

So who is it who *will* explain to students why they should study Canadian literature? This explanation is frequently left to high-school teachers and librarians, the first line of educators encountered by students who are being introduced to their country and its literature, if they are introduced at all. These are the very educators who are by-passed by the Canadian literary institution as it now stands. These people ought to be welcomed and their experiences valued. If there is more widespread discussion about what the study of Canadian literature involves and why such discussion is valuable beyond the university classroom, then it might be possible for specialization and public interest to coexist in a balance that benefited schools, students, and the granting agencies that are, however remotely, answerable to the public.

Are there specific measures that can be undertaken to facilitate a more public awareness of, and involvement in, the study of Canadian literature? There are. Most important, academics need to articulate their understanding of the value of studying Canadian literature, and must act upon their recognition of this value. They need to talk about why it is a subject worth teaching. If the answer is because such professional pursuits are culturally significant, then this significance needs to be described. I am not suggesting that academics adopt the hackneyed view that it's good because it's Canadian, but that they reconsider the fundamental nature of the rubric under which they teach and write. They should make this reconsideration an active and ongoing process that leads to interrogation and debate, rather than to tacit endorsement of the idea that the country's literature is worthy of study because it just is, and that's enough said about that.

As I argue in "Privacy, Publicity, and the Discourse of Canadian Criticism," it is equally important for students to learn to be critical of their milieu in the most constructive sense. While there is no absolute wall that separates the professor and the public (some professors do contribute to nonacademic discussions and assessments of Canadian writing), there are some concrete steps that can be undertaken to encourage the development of a more communal approach to the study of Canadian literature — one that might republicize it. It's worth repeating Shirley Neuman's recommendations in this regard. She suggested that in order to reach a wider public and to increase public awareness of what professors do, academics should get involved in community-service work on theatre and library boards, coordinate public reading groups, review in local newspapers, give lectures in local libraries, become more involved with alumni, engage more directly with popular culture, help people learn to read and write, and speak understandably and unpretentiously. These measures would certainly affect the public visibility and activity of professors.

There are other measures that would more directly involve the public in academic pursuits and in determining the nature of those pursuits. The chief link between academics and the public is students. After all, students originate in and ultimately constitute the public. Academics need to develop practical, accessible, and meaningful ways of interesting students in literature as a force that has social relevance. When it comes to the teaching of Canadian literature, it means educating students about the country that gives the literature its name. It involves saying that this literature comes from this place. It involves affirming that part of being educated means being educated about where one lives. Obviously there is no single methodology that can ensure this type of knowledge, but it is important for educators to agree that such knowledge is crucial. Any method that allows students to be critical of their milieu, and to see that criticism can address them, will go a long way toward encouraging a more public understanding of what specialists in Canadian literature can do. It might also encourage those specialists to re-imagine Canada. Again. And again. And again.

NOTES

Making It Real

[1] Some of these questions were raised in the volume entitled *Problems of Literary Reception/Problèmes de réception littéraire*, edited by Blodgett and Purdy. Their publication was the first of several to be released in a series entitled Towards a History of the Literary Institution in Canada/Vers une histoire de l'institution littéraire au Canada. It announces that a future volume (which has not yet appeared) will consider the question of "La canonisation" (5).

[2] As Kroetsch writes, "The fiction makes us real" (*Creation* 63).

[3] There are some important exceptions to this statement. Useful attempts to rehistoricize or re-evaluate Canadian literary history and criticism include Bennett, "English Canada's Postcolonial Complexities"; Blodgett, "Is a History of the Literatures of Canada Possible?"; Fee, "Canadian Literature and English Studies in the Canadian University" and "English-Canadian Literary Criticism, 1890–1950"; Gerson, "Anthologies and the Canon of Early Canadian Women Writers," "The Canon between the Wars," and *A Purer Taste*; Godard, "Canadian? Literary? Theory?" and "Structuralism/Post-Structuralism: Language, Reality and Canadian Literature"; Lawson, "Values and Evaluation"; MacLulich, "Thematic Criticism, Literary Nationalism, and the Critic's New Clothes"; McCarthy, "Early Canadian Literary Histories and the Function of a Canon"; Moyes, " 'Canadian Literature Criticism': Between the Poles of the Universal-Particular Antinomy"; Murray, "Resistance and Reception: Backgrounds to Theory in English-Canada"; and Weir, "The Discourse of 'Civility': Strategies of Containment in Literary Histories of English Canadian Literature."

[4] The Aux Canadas conference held at the Université de Montréal in April 1993 is an obvious recent exception to this statement.

[5] See Bennett, "English Canada's Postcolonial Complexities"; and Hutcheon, "Circling the Downspout of Empire" and "Eruptions of Postmodernity: The Postcolonial and the Ecological."

1 The Canonization of Canadian Literature

[1] Although there is no study that examines the evolution and meaning of value in the English-Canadian canon from a historical perspective, a few studies do address the question of value in recent Canadian criticism or in relation to specific, canonized texts. The most rewarding of these are Godard, "Structuralism/Post-Structuralism"; Murray, "Reading for Contradiction in the Literature of Colonial Space"; Ware, "Notes on the Literary Histories of Canada"; and Weir, "The Discourse of 'Civility.' " The collection I edited — *Canadian Canons: Essays in Literary Value* — appeared in 1991.

[2] The full list of titles selected through the ballot appears in Steele, *Taking Stock* (151–53). In fact, Margaret Laurence's *The Stone Angel* came first on the actual ballot, but was inadvertently dropped from the top of the list published in *Taking Stock*.

[3] In a perceptive review of Keith's book, Alan Lawson observes that "The domination of language is one with the language of domination. And one can't help but notice how frequently Keith uses 'dominate' in a laudatory way. It is part of his anxious quest for order, and part of a vocabulary that includes 'command,' 'discipline,' 'control,' 'mastery,' and 'unity' " (112). Lawson points out that "the military language is part of the urge to order" (112).

3 Privacy, Publicity, and the Discourse of Canadian Criticism

[1] I would like to thank the following people who provided helpful commentary on an early draft of this chapter: Neil Besner, Gary Boire, Russell Brown, Nathalie Cooke, Michael Darling, Jack David, Margery Fee, W.J. Keith, Angela Marinos, John Metcalf, Donna Pennee, Denis Salter, Lorraine York, and Mary Williams. I am also grateful to Shirley Neuman, who was kind enough to send me the notes for her presentation at the ACCUTE session on "Explaining Ourselves to the Public" at the 1993 conference in Ottawa.

[2] See Neuman for a rough survey of what was actually being offered in Canadian universities in 1992.

[3] See Bennett, Brown, Cameron, Godard, Murray, and Weir.

[4] See Fee, Jasen, Lecker, MacLulich, and Murray.

[5] Heather Murray writes that "concern over the 'professionalization' of literary study through increasing specialization, either of teaching or inquiry, has worried English-Canadian academicians for some decades now" ("Resistance" 56–57). I can find no sustained historical expressions of such worries when it comes to the study of English-Canadian literature. Recent discussions of the topic are almost as scarce. See Murray's own work, and that of John Fraser and Lorraine Weir.

[6] Since it was in 1957 that the New Canadian Library reprint series became available to high-school and university students, this marks the point at which Canadian literature — specifically Canadian *novels* — became available for pedagogical use within a post-Massey Commission institutional framework that encouraged widespread curricular dissemination. This form of industrialization was concretized and affirmed through the publication of the *Literary History of Canada* in 1965. Of course, Canadian literature was taught sporadically prior to 1958 (see Fee), and, in one way or another, it was always institutionalized. But the pedagogical dimension of the shift that occurred after 1958 remains distinct and unprecedented. MacLulich provides a good account of industrialization in each of his works cited.

[7] See Robbins for an insightful summary of the issues involved in the debate about professionalism. Susan Horton provides an equally perceptive summary of recent commentary on the politics of criticism.

[8] Jim Merod's *The Political Responsibility of the Critic* is an informative discussion about the politics of professionalism and the relationship between theory and culture. From a different perspective, Cornel West also addresses the contemporary aspects of the debate. West identifies "three major models" of professional politics: "the *oppositional professional intellectual* model that claims that we must do political work where we are in the academy. . . . the *professional political intellectual* model that encourages academicians to intervene into the public conversation of the nation. . . . the *oppositional intellectual groupings within the academy* which seek to create, sustain, and expand intellectual subcultures inside the university networks" (31).

[9] See Bennett, "Conflicted Vision," for an excellent discussion of the relationship between genre and literary value.

[10] As of this writing, the most recent conference I attended was the Aux Canadas conference, held at the Université de Montréal in April 1993. I thought many of the papers were excellent, and the conference was certainly well organized. But I reflected that this conference, which sported such a public title and which was perhaps designed to bridge the stereotypical two solitudes of English Canada and Quebec and to acknowledge the multi-ethnic composition of the country, was attended only by professors and students or their friends. The papers were highly specialized and esoteric, and many relied on theoretical concepts unfamiliar to most well-read people and even to some conferees. I witnessed no passionate debates. By contrast, any well-read person who attended the Queen's conference would have understood the discourse and could have participated in the debate.

[11] Recent editions in the New Canadian Library reflect general editor David Staines's decision to downplay the academic image associated with the series. Now writers are providing afterwords to each volume, rather than professors providing forewords. This shift away from the professional frame

may be market driven, or it may simply reflect Staines's desire to foreground the text and to downplay its theoretical treatment. (What other reason would there be for choosing writers over critics?) The effect of this new strategy is, ironically, to force the writer to behave as a critic, a fact that accounts for some of the anxiety-ridden, self-conscious discourse evident in the new afterwords. In this case, the strategy of subordinating criticism serves only to demonstrate that, given the current market for these titles, criticism cannot ultimately be subordinated but must simply assume new forms of address.

[12] Lee obviously abandoned his concern with publicity in *Savage Fields: An Essay in Literature and Cosmology* (1977). As Nell Waldman says, this is a "turgid tractate" that provides a phenomenological reading of the oppositions between "world" and "earth" as they appear in Michael Ondaatje's *The Collected Works of Billy the Kid* and Leonard Cohen's *Beautiful Losers* (374). I read *Savage Fields* as a displaced struggle between privacy and publicity, cast in terms of a nature/culture dichotomy. The details of this reading are the subject of a work in progress.

[13] See "Kim Campbell and the Endless Summer."

[14] For a discussion of the different historical and pedagogical forces behind the teaching of national literature in Canada, England, and the United States see MacLulich, "Thematic Criticism, Literary Nationalism, and the Critic's New Clothes."

[15] A rare example of this type of debate can be found in *Volleys*, edited by J.R. (Tim) Struthers.

4 Anthologizing English-Canadian Fiction

[1] In applying this criterion I understood that some anthologists claim to have created anthologies that are national in scope when, in fact, these anthologies appear to be more partial in their selection than others. Because every anthology considered in this study is an expression of partiality, I decided to include any anthology that did not openly claim to represent particular groups of writers, or special interests, or distinct historical periods. In this way, I hoped to create a level playing field on which all the players would be equally biased in their claim to representing Canada and its fiction.

[2] For a similar analysis of short fiction published in anthologies devoted exclusively to short fiction, see Farrell.

[3] Many of the statistics I am examining were compiled by Cynthia Sugars. I am indebted to her rigorous and detailed library work, and to her mathematical calculations, without which this study would not exist.

[4] For example, a total of 1663 stories appear in the sixty-five anthologies. Of these stories, 4 percent (64/1663) are by Morley Callaghan, 1 percent (13/1663) by Gilbert Parker, 2 percent (38/1663) by Alice Munro, and so on.

[5] For example, stories by Ethel Wilson appear in 33 out of the 65 anthologies. Wilson's most anthologized short story is "The Window," which appears in 6 out of her 40 inclusions in 33 anthologies, or 15 percent. Stories by Alice Munro also appear in 33 out of the 65 anthologies. Munro's most anthologized short stories are "Walker Brothers Cowboy" and "Dance of the Happy Shades," each of which appears in 3 out of her 38 inclusions in 33 anthologies, or 8 percent. In contrast, Jack Hodgins's short stories appear in 12 out of the 65 anthologies. His most anthologized short story is "By the River," which appears in 3 out of his 12 inclusions, or 25 percent.

[6] Some problems in arriving at these calculations must be noted. In anthologies containing fiction and prose, it was sometimes difficult to determine whether a given prose piece should be classed as fiction. Many early anthologies include explorers' narratives, public speeches, and so on. In the end, the distinction was inevitably subjective, but it was based on an assessment of whether the piece in question had narrative interest as a story, and whether it focused on personal experience rather than on a political question or, descriptively, on a historical event; I also considered the author's conception of the work in question.

Another factor that must be considered in reading the table is what I will call the birthday factor. If a popular author was born in 1888, for example (here I am using the case of Ethel Wilson), she stands a greater chance of being included in a greater number of anthologies, simply because she has been around longer than, say, Alice Munro. This means that while the table demonstrates that a writer such as Callaghan (born 1903) is historically more anthologized than Munro, a correction for the difference in their birth years (or, alternatively, the year in which they first published fiction) might suggest a different historical perspective and a different indication of their value (in the 1970s and 1980s, Munro was more anthologized than Callaghan and Wilson). For this reason, the figures provided for individual authors should not only be seen in the global historic picture offered by the table, but should also be viewed in relation to trends evident on a decade-by-decade basis (as in the table).

[7] In Smith's case, the figures can be explained by the fact that John Metcalf edited 3 anthologies in the 1970s, 2 of which included Smith.

[8] See Gerson's "Anthologies and the Canon of Early Canadian Women Writers" and "The Canon between the Wars: Field-Notes of a Feminist Literary Archaeologist."

5 The New Canadian Library

[1] The proceedings of the conference, as well as the ballot and its outcome, can be found in Steele. Since my focus here is on the years leading up to the Calgary Conference, I do not consider developments in the New Canadian

Library after 1978, particularly the establishment by McClelland of the short-lived Canadian Classics Committee. A good summary of post-1978 developments is provided by Keith in "The Quest for the (Instant) Canadian Classic."

² I wish to thank the Social Sciences and Humanities Research Council of Canada for a grant in support of the research connected with this work. I am grateful to Sarah McClelland and Jack McClelland, who gave me permission to consult the New Canadian Library files at McMaster University Archives, and for their permission to quote from this material in my commentary on the development of the New Canadian Library series. I am equally grateful to Malcolm Ross, for granting me permission to quote from his letters. I also wish to thank Carl Spadoni and Charlotte A. Stewart-Murphy for permitting me to access the New Canadian Library material held by The William Ready Division of Archives and Research Collections at the McMaster University Library.

³ For an examination of Canadian literature in the university curriculum, see Fee.

6 The Rhetoric of Back-Cover Copy

¹ In his dissertation entitled "A History of a Canadian Publishing House: A Study of the Relation between Publishing and the Profession of Writing, 1890–1940" (U of Toronto, 1969), George L. Parker records a 1941 McClelland and Stewart issue (348), as does the *Canadian Catalogue of Books: Published in Canada, about Canada, as Well as Those Written by Canadians, with Imprint 1921 through 1949*, 2 vols. (Toronto: Toronto Public Libraries, 1959). However, in their *A Bibliography of McClelland and Stewart Imprints, 1909–1985: A Publisher's Legacy* (Toronto: ECW, 1994), Spadoni and Donnelly indicate that no copies of such an issue have been located.

7 "A Quest for the Peaceable Kingdom"

¹ The general editor, Carl F. Klinck, says in his introduction that the *Literary History* treats "not only works generically classified as 'literature,' but also, chiefly in separate chapters, other works which have influenced literature" (xi). Frye notes in his conclusion that the editors of the *Literary History* went out of their way to broaden the concept of literature by including "chapters on political, historical, religious, scholarly, philosophical, scientific, and other non-literary writing" (822). (Unless otherwise indicated, all citations of Klinck's introduction and Frye's conclusion refer to the first edition of the *Literary History* [1965].)

Klinck points out that "the support provided by the Humanities Research Council of Canada and the Canada Council can never be suitably acknowledged. During every year of preparation the Humanities Research Council provided funds." In addition, "the Canadian Council made twenty-two short term grants in aid of research to individuals who were working for the *Literary History*; not one application was refused" (xiv).

² While reviews of the *Literary History* comment on Frye's conclusion, the 1965 text of the chapter has never been considered a discrete document. Similarly, a revised version published in Frye's *Bush Garden* was treated only in the context of that collection. While Robert Denham lists twenty-six reviews of *The Bush Garden* in his bibliography on Frye, he cites no studies devoted to the conclusion, in either its original or its revised form. Eli Mandel's perceptive essay identifies Frye's "romantic reading of a Canadian literary tradition" and emphasizes "critical problems arising from questions having to do with a definition of a national literature" ("Northrop Frye" 285); but while Mandel provides important commentary on much of Frye's Canadian criticism, he merely mentions Frye's "extraordinary" conclusion without discussing it.

Most Canadian criticism published in the two decades following the appearance of Frye's conclusion bears his imprint. Thematic in orientation, such criticism promotes the notion that literary texts can be approached as expressions of national identity. The best-known of these critical works include those by D.G. Jones, Margaret Atwood, Laurence Ricou, and John Moss. Although the influence of Canadian thematic criticism is still apparent today, several important essays and books have challenged the notion of a poetics based on cultural criteria and have implicitly questioned the authority of Frye's culturally grounded vision of a stable, unfragmented nation. Among the most frequently cited antithematic texts are those by E.D. Blodgett, Barry Cameron and Michael Dixon, Frank Davey, and Paul Stuewe.

³ When the second edition of the *Literary History* appeared in 1976, Frye wrote a new conclusion that hardly resembled the first version. Expressing concern over the deepening linguistic tensions that were dividing Canada, he noted that "the trends [he] studied in the previous conclusion have reached something of a crisis since then" (318). In the context of such a crisis, it was difficult for Frye to sustain the pastoral vision that characterized the earlier document. In 1965 the notion of a Canadian literature and Canadian literary history was but "a gleam in a paternal critic's eye"; the emphasis was on the future, on infinite potential. But now that Canadian literature had achieved a certain identity, the focus had turned back on a present that made the original vision harder to find. As Frye observes, "to achieve, to bring a future into the present, is also to become finite, and the sense of that is always a little disconcerting, even though becoming finite means becoming genuinely human" (319).

⁴ In *A Natural Perspective*, which was published the same year as the *Literary History*, Frye differentiates, "in the manner of Coleridge," between "Iliad critics [and] Odyssey critics" (1). The *Odyssey* critic, like the critic in Frye's conclusion, is aligned with the romance quest.

The phrase "peaceable kingdom" derives from Edward Hicks's painting of that title — a work completed, Frye says, "around 1830" (Conclusion 847–48).

5 In his attempt to find appropriate metaphors of pastoral experience, Frye curiously neglects to mention several Canadian models that were clearly important to him. Of these, the most influential is perhaps Lawren Harris, one of the Group of Seven painters. In an essay on Harris published in 1969, Frye observes that Harris interests him in part because the painter also wrote poetry and "a great deal of critical prose" (*Bush* 207). Another reason is that Harris shared in his group's "direct imaginative confrontation with the North American landscape which, for them, began in literature with Thoreau and Whitman" (*Bush* 206). This confrontation encouraged a romantic view that had again become fashionable during the 1960s, when Frye's conclusion appeared. His reflections on these artists, and on their milieu, is therefore germane to any attempt to establish the conclusion as a romance that traces a search for redemption through faith. Frye writes that the Group of Seven painters, as a result of their reading of Thoreau and Whitman, "developed an interest for which the word theosophical would not be too misleading if understood, not in any sectarian sense, but as meaning a commitment to painting as a way of life, or, perhaps better, as a sacramental activity expressing a faith, and so analogous to the practising of a religion. This is a Romantic view, following the tradition that begins in English poetry with Wordsworth. While the Group of Seven were most active, Romanticism was going out of fashion elsewhere. But the nineteen-sixties is once again a Romantic period, in fact almost oppressively so" (*Bush* 208).

8 Nobody Gets Hurt Bullfighting Canadian-Style

1 Unless otherwise noted, all references are to the 1976 publication in *Canadian Literature*.

WORKS CITED

Adam, Ian, and Helen Tiffin, eds. *Past the Last Post: Theorizing Post-Colonialism and Post-Modernism.* Calgary: U of Calgary P, 1990.

Adams, Hazard. "Canons: Literary Criteria/Power Criteria." *Critical Inquiry* 14 (1988): 748–64.

Adult Literacy in Canada: Results of a National Study. Ottawa: Statistics Canada, 1991.

Allen, Carolyn, and Katherine Anderson. "Course Objectives." Lauter, *Reconstructing* 3–5.

Altieri, Charles. *Canons and Consequences: Reflections on the Ethical Force of Imaginative Ideals.* Evanston: Northwestern UP, 1990.

——. "Canons and Differences." Nemoianu and Royal 1–38.

——. "An Idea and an Ideal of a Literary Canon." *Critical Inquiry* 10 (1983): 37–60.

Anderson, Benedict. *Imagined Communities: Reflections on the Origin and Spread of Nationalism.* 1983. Rev. ed. London: Verso, 1991.

Anderson, Scott. "Price Matters." *Quill and Quire* July 1994: 5.

Arac, Jonathan, and Barbara Johnson, eds. *Consequences of Theory.* Selected Papers from the English Institute, 1987–88. New Series 14. Baltimore: Johns Hopkins UP, 1991.

Ashcroft, Bill, Gareth Griffiths, and Helen Tiffin. *The Empire Writes Back: Theory and Practice in Post-Colonial Literatures.* London: Routledge, 1989.

Atwood, Margaret. "An End to Audience?" *Second Words: Selected Critical Prose.* Toronto: Anansi, 1982. 334–57.

——. *Survival: A Thematic Guide to Canadian Literature.* Toronto: Anansi, 1972.

Atwood, Margaret, and Robert Weaver, eds. *The Oxford Book of Canadian Short Stories in English.* Toronto: Oxford UP, 1986.

Balfour, Ian. *Northrop Frye.* Twayne's World Authors Series 806. Boston: Twayne, 1988.

Ballstadt, Carl, ed. *The Search for English-Canadian Literature: An Anthology of Critical Articles from the Nineteenth and Early Twentieth Centuries.* Toronto: U of Toronto P, 1975.

Bennett, Donna. "Conflicted Vision: A Consideration of Canon and Genre in English-Canadian Literature." Lecker, *Canadian Canons* 131–49.

— . "Criticism in English." Toye 149–66.

— . "English Canada's Postcolonial Complexities." *Essays on Canadian Writing* 51–52 (1993–94): 164–210.

Bhabha, Homi K., ed. *Nation and Narration.* London: Routledge, 1990.

— . "Representation and the Colonial Text: A Critical Exploration of Some Forms of Mimeticism." *The Theory of Reading.* Ed. Frank Gloversmith. Brighton: Harvester, 1984. 93–122.

Blodgett, E.D. *Configuration: Essays in the Canadian Literatures.* Downsview, ON: ECW, 1982.

— . "Frank Davey: Critic as Autobiographer." *West Coast Line* 25.1 (1991): 130–43.

— . "Is a History of the Literatures of Canada Possible?" *Essays on Canadian Writing* 50 (1993): 1–18.

Blodgett, E.D., and A.G. Purdy, eds. *Problems of Literary Reception/Problèmes de réception littéraire.* Proc. of a Conference on Problems of Literary Reception at the Research Institute for Comparative Literature, University of Alberta. 16–18 Oct. 1986. Towards a History of the Literary Institution in Canada 1. Edmonton: U of Alberta P, 1988.

Bloom, Harold. "Criticism, Canon-Formation, and Prophecy: The Sorrows of Facticity." *Raritan* 3.3 (1984): 1–20.

Boire, Gary. "Canadian (Tw)ink: Surviving the Whiteouts." *Essays on Canadian Writing* 35 (1987): 1–16.

— . "Transparencies: Of Sexual Abuse, Ambivalence, and Resistance." *Essays on Canadian Writing* 51–52 (1993–94): 211–32.

Bové, Paul A. "Discourse." Lentricchia and McLaughlin 50–65.

Bowering, George, and Robert Kroetsch. "Writer Writing, Ongoing Verb." Moss, *Future Indicative* 5–24.

Braendlin, Bonnie, ed. *Cultural Power/Cultural Literacy: Selected Papers from the 14th Florida State University Conference on Literature and Film.* Tallahassee: Florida State UP, 1991.

Braendlin, Bonnie. "Introduction: Cultural Power/Cultural Literacy." Braendlin, *Cultural Power/Cultural Literacy* 1–11.

Brand, Dionne. "Who Can Speak for Whom?" *Brick* 46 (1993): 13–20.

Brennan, Timothy. "The National Longing for Form." Bhabha, *Nation and Narration* 44–70.

Broken Words: Why Five Million Canadians Are Illiterate. Toronto: Southam Newspaper Group, 1987.

Brown, Russell M. "Critic, Culture, Text: Beyond Thematics." *Essays on Canadian Writing* 11 (1978): 151–83.

Butler, Judith. *Gender Trouble: Feminism and the Subversion of Identity.* New York: Routledge, 1990.

Cameron, Barry. "Lacan: Implications of Psychoanalysis and Canadian Discourse." Moss, *Future Indicative* 137–51.

——. "Response." Steele 21–33.

——. "Theory and Criticism: Trends in Canadian Literature." *Literary History of Canada: Canadian Literature in English.* Ed. W.H. New. 2nd ed. Vol. 4. Toronto: U of Toronto P, 1990. 108–32. 4 vols. 1976–90.

Cameron, Barry, and Michael Dixon. "Mandatory Subversive Manifesto: Canadian Criticism vs. Literary Criticism." *Studies in Canadian Literature* 2.2 (1977): 137–45.

The Canadian Catalogue of Books: Published in Canada, about Canada, as well as Those Written by Canadians, with Imprint 1921 through 1949. 2 vols. Toronto: Toronto Public Libraries, 1959.

Chambers, Ross. "Irony and the Canon." *Profession 90.* New York: MLA, 1990. 18–24.

Clark, David L. "Disfiguring the Post-Modern." Rev. of *Reading Canadian Reading,* by Frank Davey. *Canadian Poetry: Studies, Documents, Reviews* 26 (1990): 75–86.

Colquette, R.D., and H.S. Frye. "A Canadian Writer." *Country Guide and Nor'west Farmer* Apr. 1942: 38.

Cude, Wilfred. "Beyond Mrs. Bentley: A Study of *As for Me and My House.*" *Journal of Canadian Studies* 8.1 (1973): 3–18. Rpt. Cude, *A Due Sense of Differences* 31–49.

——. *A Due Sense of Differences: An Evaluative Approach to Canadian Literature.* Lanham, MD: University P of America, 1980.

Dafoe, Chris. "Adventures in the Book Trade." *Globe and Mail* 29 June 1993: D2.

Daniells, Roy. Introduction. *As for Me and My House.* By Sinclair Ross. New Canadian Library 4. Toronto: McClelland, 1957. v–x.

Darling, Michael. "A Hard Twayne's Gonna Fall." Rev. of *John Metcalf,* by Barry Cameron. *Essays on Canadian Writing* 37 (1989): 172–83.

Davey, Frank. "Critical Response I: Canadian Canons." *Critical Inquiry* 16 (1990): 672–81.

——. *Earle Birney.* Studies in Canadian Literature. Toronto: Copp Clark, 1971.

——. *From There to Here: A Guide to English-Canadian Literature since 1960.* Our Nature — Our Voices 2. Erin, ON: Porcepic, 1974.

——. Interview. With Elizabeth Komisar. *White Pelican* 5.2 (1975): 49–58.

——. Introduction. *The Open Letter* 1 (1965): 3.

——. "Kim Campbell and the Endless Summer." *Globe and Mail* 16 Sept. 1993: A19.

—— . Letter. *Globe and Mail* 20 Apr. 1985: D7.

—— . *Post-National Arguments: The Politics of the Anglophone-Canadian Novel since 1967.* Toronto: U of Toronto P, 1993.

—— . *Reading Canadian Reading.* Winnipeg: Turnstone, 1988.

—— . *Reading "Kim" Right.* Vancouver: Talonbooks, 1993.

—— . "Reflections while Reading Canadian." Rev. of *Read Canadian,* ed. Robert Fulford, David Godfrey, and Abraham Rotstein. *Open Letter* 2.3 (1972): 62–65.

—— . "Starting at Our Skins: An Interview with Frank Davey." With George Bowering. *Open Letter* 4.3 (1979): 89–181. [The interview was conducted in 1973.]

—— . "Surviving the Paraphrase." *Canadian Literature* 70 (1976): 5–13. Rpt. *Surviving the Paraphrase: Eleven Essays on Canadian Literature.* Winnipeg: Turnstone, 1983. 1–12.

Davies, Robertson. *Leaven of Malice.* Toronto: Clarke, 1954.

Davis, Lennard J., and M. Bella Mirabella, eds. *Left Politics and the Literary Profession.* The Social Foundations of Aesthetic Forms. New York: Columbia UP, 1990.

Daymond, Douglas, and Leslie Monkman, eds. *Towards a Canadian Literature: Essays, Editorials and Manifestos.* Vol. 2. Ottawa: Tecumseh, 1985. 2 vols.

Denham, Robert. *Northrop Frye: An Annotated Bibliography of Primary and Secondary Sources.* Toronto: U of Toronto P, 1987.

Dewart, Edward Hartley. *Selections from Canadian Poets with Occasional Critical and Biographical Notes and an Introductory Essay on Canadian Poetry.* 1864. Literature of Canada: Poetry and Prose in Reprint. Toronto: U of Toronto P, 1973.

Dooley, D.J. *Moral Vision in the Canadian Novel.* Toronto: Clarke, 1979.

Eagleton, Terry. *The Function of Criticism: From "The Spectator" to Post-Structuralism.* London: Verso, 1984.

English and Communications 1992. Catalogue. Toronto: McClelland, 1992.

Fadiman, Clifton. Rev. of *As for Me and My House,* by Sinclair Ross. *New Yorker* 22 Feb. 1941: 72.

Farrell, Dominic. "Reading Canadian Short Story Anthologies: Theoretical Contexts, a History, and a Case Study." MA thesis. U of Guelph, 1993.

Fee, Margery, and Ruth Cawker. *Canadian Fiction: An Annotated Bibliography.* Toronto: Peter Martin, 1976.

Fee, Margery. "Canadian Literature and English Studies in the Canadian University." *Essays on Canadian Writing* 48 (1992–93): 20–40.

—— . "English-Canadian Literary Criticism, 1890–1950: Defining and Establishing a National Literature." Diss. U of Toronto, 1981.

"Fiction." Rev. of *As for Me and My House,* by Sinclair Ross. *Toronto Daily Star* 22 Mar. 1941: 28.

Field, Rose. Rev. of *As for Me and My House,* by Sinclair Ross. *New York Herald Tribune Book Review* 23 Feb. 1941: 14.

Findlay, L.M. "Writing the Canadian Flag." *Alphabet City* [Toronto] 2 (1992): 46–47.

Fogel, Stanley. *A Tale of Two Countries: Contemporary Fiction in Canada and the United States.* Toronto: ECW, 1984.

Fox-Genovese, Elizabeth. "The Claims of a Common Culture: Gender, Race, Class and the Canon." *Salmagundi* 72 (1986): 131–43.

Fraser, John. "The Production of Canadian Literature." *In Our Own House: Social Perspectives on Canadian Literature.* Ed. Paul Cappon. Toronto: McClelland, 1978. 148–73.

Fraser, Nancy. "Rethinking the Public Sphere: A Contribution to the Critique of Actually Existing Democracy." *Habermas and the Public Sphere.* Ed. Craig Calhoun. Cambridge: MIT, 1992. 109–42.

Frye, Northrop. *The Bush Garden: Essays on the Canadian Imagination.* Toronto: Anansi, 1971.

——. Conclusion. Klinck, 1965 ed. 821–49.

——. Conclusion. Klinck, 1976 ed. 3: 318–32.

——. *Divisions on a Ground: Essays on Canadian Culture.* Ed. James Polk. Toronto: Anansi, 1982.

——. *Fables of Identity: Studies in Poetic Mythology.* New York: Harcourt, 1963.

——. *A Natural Perspective: The Development of Shakespearean Comedy and Romance.* New York: Columbia UP, 1965.

——. *The Secular Scripture: A Study of the Structure of Romance.* Cambridge: Harvard UP, 1978.

Gadpaille, Michelle. *The Canadian Short Story.* Perspectives on Canadian Literature. Toronto: Oxford UP, 1988.

Gellner, Ernest. *Thought and Change.* London: Weidenfeld, 1964.

Gerson, Carole. "Anthologies and the Canon of Early Canadian Women Writers." *Re(Dis)covering Our Foremothers: Nineteenth-Century Canadian Women Writers.* Ed. Lorraine McMullen. Proc. of a Conference at the University of Ottawa. 29 Apr.–1 May 1988. Reappraisals: Canadian Writers 15. Ottawa: U of Ottawa P, 1990. 55–76.

——. "The Canon between the Wars: Field-Notes of a Feminist Literary Archaeologist." Lecker, *Canadian Canons* 46–56.

——. *A Purer Taste: The Writing and Reading of Fiction in English in Nineteenth-Century Canada.* Toronto: U of Toronto P, 1989.

Glassco, John, ed. *English Poetry in Quebec.* Proc. of the Foster Poetry Conference. 12–14 Oct. 1963. Montreal: McGill UP, 1965.

——. Preface. Glassco, *English Poetry* 5–8.

Godard, Barbara. "Structuralism/Post-Structuralism: Language, Reality and Canadian Literature." Moss, *Future Indicative* 25–51.

Goldberg, Jonathan. "The Politics of Renaissance Literature: A Review Essay." *ELH* 49 (1982): 514–42.

Grady, Wayne, ed. *The Penguin Book of Canadian Short Stories*. Harmondsworth: Penguin, 1980.

Greenblatt, Stephen. "Introduction." *Genre* 15 (1982): 3–6.

——. *Renaissance Self-Fashioning: From More to Shakespeare*. Chicago: U of Chicago P, 1980.

Greenblatt, Stephen, and Giles Gunn, eds. *Redrawing the Boundaries: The Transformation of English and American Literary Studies*. New York: MLA, 1992.

Guillory, John. "Canon." Lentricchia and McLaughlin 233–49.

——. "Canonical and Non-Canonical: A Critique of the Current Debate." *ELH* 54 (1987): 483–527.

——. *Cultural Capital: The Problem of Literary Canon Formation*. Chicago: U of Chicago P, 1993.

——. "The Ideology of Canon-Formation: T.S. Eliot and Cleanth Brooks." *Critical Inquiry* 10 (1983): 173–98.

Habermas, Jürgen. *The Structural Transformation of the Public Sphere: An Inquiry into a Category of Bourgeois Society*. Trans. Thomas Burger. Cambridge: MIT, 1991.

Hamilton, A.C. *Northrop Frye: Anatomy of His Criticism*. Toronto: U of Toronto P, 1990.

Harrison, Bernard. "Back to Liberalism." Rev. of *Canons and Consequences: Reflections on the Ethical Force of Imaginative Ideals*, by Charles Altieri. *Times Literary Supplement* 1 Nov. 1991: 25.

Hinchcliffe, Peter, ed. *Family Fictions in Canadian Literature: Six Essays, Six Stories, Three Poems*. Proc. of a Conference on the Theme of the Family in Canadian Writing at the University of Waterloo. May 1987. Waterloo: U of Waterloo P, 1988.

Hjartarson, Paul. "The Literary Canon and Its Discontents: Reflections on the Cultural Reproduction of Value." Poff 67–80.

Hobsbawn, Eric, and Terence Ranger, eds. *The Invention of Tradition*. Cambridge: Cambridge UP, 1983.

Horton, Susan R. "The Institution of Literature and the Cultural Community." *Literary Theory's Future(s)*. Ed. Joseph Natol. Urbana, IL: U of Illinois P, 1989. 267–320.

Howard, Jean E. "The New Historicism in Renaissance Studies." *English Literary Renaissance* 16 (1986): 13–43.

Hunter, Lynette. "War Poetry: Fears of Referentiality." *West Coast Line* 25.1 (1991): 144–60.

Hutcheon, Linda. "Circling the Downspout of Empire." Adam and Tiffin 167–89.

——. "Eruptions of Postmodernity: The Postcolonial and the Ecological." *Essays on Canadian Writing* 51–52 (1993–94): 146–63.

——. *A Poetics of Postmodernism: History, Theory, Fiction.* London: Routledge, 1988.

Jasen, Pat. "The English-Canadian Liberal Arts Curriculum: An Intellectual History, 1800–1950." Diss. U of Manitoba, 1987.

Johnson, Glen M. "The Teaching Anthology and the Canon of American Literature: Some Notes on Theory in Practice." Nemoianu and Royal 111–35.

Jones, D.G. *Butterfly on Rock: A Study of Themes and Images in Canadian Literature.* Toronto: U of Toronto P, 1970.

Kaplan, E. Ann. "Popular Culture, Politics, and the Canon: Cultural Literacy in the Postmodern Age." Braendlin, *Cultural Power/Cultural Literacy* 12–31.

Keith, W.J. *Canadian Literature in English.* London: Longmans, 1985.

——. "Canadian Tradition and the (New) New Canadian Library." *American Review of Canadian Studies* 21 (1991): 71–80.

——. "The Function of Canadian Criticism at the Present Time." *Essays on Canadian Writing* 30 (1984–85): 1–16.

——. "The Quest for the (Instant) Canadian Classic." Metcalf, *Bumper Book* 155–65.

——. Rev. of *Surviving the Paraphrase: Eleven Essays on Canadian Literature,* by Frank Davey. *University of Toronto Quarterly* 53 (1984): 459–62.

——. "The Thematic Approach to Canadian Fiction." Steele 71–91.

——. " 'To Hell with the Family!': An Open Letter to *The New Quarterly.*" *New Quarterly* 7 (1987): 320–24.

Klinck, Carl F., gen. ed. *Literary History of Canada: Canadian Literature in English.* Toronto: U of Toronto P, 1965.

——, gen. ed. *Literary History of Canada: Canadian Literature in English.* 2nd ed. Toronto: U of Toronto P, 1976. 3 vols.

Kolodny, Annette. "The Integrity of Memory: Creating a New Literary History of the United States." *American Literature* 57 (1985): 291–307.

Kroetsch, Robert. Afterword. *As for Me and My House.* By Sinclair Ross. New Canadian Library. Toronto: McClelland, 1989. 217–21.

——. "Contemporary Standards in the Canadian Novel." Steele 9–20.

——. "No Name Is My Name." *The Lovely Treachery of Words: Essays Selected and New.* Toronto: Oxford UP, 1989. 41–52.

Kroetsch, Robert, James Bacque, and Pierre Gravel, eds. *Creation.* Toronto: New, 1970.

Kroetsch, Robert, and George Bowering. "Writer Writing, Ongoing Verb." Moss, *Future Indicative* 5–24.

LaCapra, Dominick. *History and Criticism.* Ithaca: Cornell UP, 1985.

Lauter, Paul. "Canon Theory and Emergent Practice." Davis and Mirabella 127–46.

——, ed. *Reconstructing American Literature: Courses, Syllabi, Issues.* Old Westbury, NY: Feminist, 1983.

Lawson, Alan. "Values and Evaluation." Rev. of *Canadian Literature in English*, by W.J. Keith. *Canadian Literature* 110 (1986): 111–13.

Lecker, Robert, ed. *Canadian Canons: Essays in Literary Value*. Toronto: U of Toronto P, 1991.

Lecker, Robert. "The Canonization of Canadian Literature: An Inquiry into Value." *Critical Inquiry* 16 (1990): 656–71.

——. "A Country without a Canon? Canadian Literature and the Esthetics of Idealism." *Mosaic* 26.3 (1993): 1–19.

——. "Critical Response II: Response to Frank Davey." *Critical Inquiry* 16 (1990): 682–89.

——. "Making It Real: Representations of Value in English-Canadian Criticism." *Canada Ierie Oggi 3*. Atti dell '8° convegno internazionale di studi Canadesi. 25–28 aprile 1990. 3: sezione anglofona. Ed. Giovanni Bonanno. Biblioteca della ricerca. Cultura straniera 44. Fasano: Stazione, 1992. 9–21.

——. "Nobody Gets Hurt Bullfighting Canadian-Style: Rereading Frank Davey's 'Surviving the Paraphrase.'" *Studies in Canadian Literature* 18.2 (1993): 1–26.

——. "Privacy, Publicity, and the Discourse of Canadian Criticism." *Essays on Canadian Writing* 51–52 (1993–94): 32–82.

——. "'A Quest for the Peaceable Kingdom': The Narrative in Northrop Frye's Conclusion to the *Literary History of Canada*." *PMLA* 108 (1993): 283–93.

Lecker, Robert, and Jack David, eds. *The Annotated Bibliography of Canada's Major Authors*. 8 vols. to date. Toronto: ECW, 1979– .

Lecker, Robert, Jack David, and Ellen Quigley, eds. *Canadian Writers and Their Works: Essays on Form, Context, and Development*. 20 vols. to date. Toronto: ECW, 1983– .

Lee, Dennis. "Cadence, Country, Silence: Writing in Colonial Space." *Open Letter* 2.6 (1973): 34–53.

——. *Savage Fields: An Essay in Literature and Cosmology*. Toronto: Anansi, 1977.

Lentricchia, Frank, and Thomas McLaughlin, eds. *Critical Terms for Literary Study*. Chicago: U of Chicago P, 1990.

"Letter to the Panelists." Steele 156–57.

Lorde, Audre. "The Master's Tools Will Never Dismantle the Master's House." *Sister Outsider: Essays and Speeches*. Trumansburg, NY: Crossing, 1984. 110–13.

Lucas, Alec. "Nature Writers and the Animal Story." Klinck 1: 380–404.

MacLaren, I.S. "Defusing the Canon: Against the Classicization of Canadian Literature." Poff 49–55.

MacLaren, I.S., and C. Potvin, eds. *Questions of Funding, Publishing and Distribution/Questions d'édition et de diffusion*. Proc. of a Conference on Funding, Publishing and Distribution at the Research Institute for Comparative

Literature, University of Alberta. 9–11 Apr. 1987. Towards a History of the Literary Institution in Canada 2/Vers une histoire de l'institution littéraire au Canada 2. Edmonton: U of Alberta P, 1989.

MacLulich, T.D. *Between Europe and America: The Canadian Tradition in Fiction*. Toronto: ECW, 1988.

——. "Thematic Criticism, Literary Nationalism, and the Critic's New Clothes." *Essays on Canadian Writing* 35 (1987): 17–36.

——. "What Was Canadian Literature? Taking Stock of the Canlit Industry." *Essays on Canadian Writing* 30 (1984–85): 17–34.

Malcolm Ross Papers, Thomas Fisher Rare Book Library, University of Toronto.

Mandel, Eli. "Atwood Gothic." *Malahat Review* 41 (1977): 165–74.

——, ed. *Contexts of Canadian Criticism: A Collection of Critical Essays*. Chicago: U of Chicago P, 1971.

——. "Northrop Frye and the Canadian Literary Tradition." *Centre and Labyrinth: Essays in Honour of Northrop Frye*. Ed. Eleanor Cook, Chaviva Hosek, Jay Macpherson, Patricia Parker, and Julian Patrick. Toronto: U of Toronto P, 1983. 284–97.

——. "The Regional Novel: Borderline Art." Steele 103–21.

Marchand, Philip. "A Novel State of the Nation." Rev. of *Post-National Arguments: The Politics of the Anglophone-Canadian Novel since 1967*, by Frank Davey. *Toronto Star* 21 July 1993: D3.

Mathews, Lawrence. "Hacking at the Parsnips: The Mountain and the Valley and the Critics." Metcalf, *Bumper Book* 188–201.

Mathews, Robin. *Canadian Literature: Surrender or Revolution*. Ed. Gail Dexter. Toronto: Steel Rail, 1978.

McCarthy, Dermot. "Early Canadian Literary Histories and the Function of a Canon." Lecker, *Canadian Canons* 30–45.

McCourt, Edward. *The Canadian West in Fiction*. Toronto: Ryerson, 1949.

McGechaen, John, and Philip Penner, eds. *Canadian Reflections: An Anthology of Canadian Prose*. Toronto: Macmillan, 1964.

McClelland and Stewart Papers. William Ready Division, Archives and Research Collections. McMaster University Library, Hamilton, Ontario.

McMullen, Lorraine. Introduction. *As for Me and My House*. By Sinclair Ross. New Canadian Library 4. Toronto: McClelland, 1982. N. pag.

——. "Thomson, Edward William (1849–1924)." Toye 789–90.

McPherson, Hugo. "Fiction, 1940–1960." Klinck, 1965 ed. 694–722.

Merod, Jim. *The Political Responsibility of the Critic*. Ithaca: Cornell UP, 1987.

Metcalf, John, ed. *The Bumper Book*. Toronto: ECW, 1986.

——. "The Curate's Egg." *Essays on Canadian Writing* 30 (1984–85): 35–59.

——. *Kicking against the Pricks*. Downsview, ON: ECW, 1982.

——. *What Is a Canadian Literature?* Guelph: Red Kite, 1988.

Montrose, Louis. "New Historicisms." Greenblatt and Gunn 392–418.

——. "Renaissance Literary Studies and the Subject of History." *English Literary Renaissance* 16 (1986): 5–12.

Moss, John. "Bushed in the Sacred Wood." *The Human Elements*. Ed. David Helwig. 2nd ser. Ottawa: Oberon, 1981. 161–78.

——, ed. *From the Heart of the Heartland: The Fiction of Sinclair Ross*. Proc. of a Symposium on Sinclair Ross at the University of Ottawa, 1990. Reappraisals: Canadian Writers 17. Ottawa: U of Ottawa P, 1992.

——, ed. *Future Indicative: Literary Theory and Canadian Literature*. Proc. of a Symposium on Literary Theory and Canadian Literature at the University of Ottawa. 25–27 Apr. 1986. Reappraisals: Canadian Writers 13. Ottawa: U of Ottawa P, 1987.

——. *Patterns of Isolation in English Canadian Fiction*. Toronto: McClelland, 1974.

——. *A Reader's Guide to the Canadian Novel*. 2nd ed. Toronto: McClelland, 1987.

——. *Sex and Violence in the Canadian Novel: The Ancestral Present*. Toronto: McClelland, 1977.

Moyes, Lianne. " 'Canadian Literature Criticism': Beyond the Poles of the Universal-Particular Antinomy." *Open Letter* 8.3 (1992): 18–46.

Mukherjee, Arun. *Towards an Aesthetic of Opposition: Essays on Literature, Criticism, and Cultural Imperialism*. Toronto: Williams-Wallace, 1988.

Murray, Heather. "Delivering the Curriculum." *ACCUTE Newsletter* (June 1992): 14–18.

——. "Institutions of Reading: New Directions in English-Canadian Literary History." *Textual Studies in Canada* 3 (1993): 2–7.

——. "Reading for Contradiction in the Literature of Colonial Space." Moss, *Future Indicative* 71–84.

——. "Resistance and Reception: Backgrounds to Theory in English-Canada." *Signature* 4 (1990): 49–67.

Nankivell, Neville. "Canada Must Improve Literacy Performance." *Financial Post* 13 Sept. 1994: 17.

Nemoianu, Virgil. "Literary Canons and Social Value Options." Nemoianu and Royal 215–47.

Nemoianu, Virgil, and Robert Royal, eds. *The Hospitable Canon: Essays on Literary Play, Scholarly Choice, and Popular Pressures*. Philadelphia: Benjamins, 1991.

Neuman, Shirley. "Of the 'Threat' to the Canon and English Departments' Course Guides." *ACCUTE Newsletter* (June 1992): 1–9.

New, W.H. *Canadian Short Fiction: From Myth to Modern*. Scarborough: Prentice-Hall, 1986.

——. *A History of Canadian Literature*. New York: New Amsterdam, 1989.

——. "Sinclair Ross's Ambivalent World." *Canadian Literature* 40 (1969): 26–32.

Ohmann, Richard. "The Function of English at the Present Time." Davis and Mirabella 36–52.

Pacey, Desmond. *Creative Writing in Canada*. Toronto: Ryerson, 1952.

———. "Fiction 1920–1940." Klinck 2: 168–204.

Parker, George L. "A History of a Canadian Publishing House: A Study of the Relation between Publishing and the Profession of Writing, 1890–1940." Diss. U of Toronto, 1969.

Pierce, Lorne. *An Outline of Canadian Literature (French and English)*. Toronto: Ryerson, 1927.

Poff, Deborah C., ed. *Literatures in Canada/Littératures au Canada*. Proc. of a Conference on Literatures in Canada held in Hamilton, ON. 31 May–2 June 1987. *Canadian Issues* [Assoc. for Canadian Studies] 10.5 (1988).

Powe, B.W. *A Climate Charged*. Oakville, ON: Mosaic, 1984.

Rashley, R.E. *Poetry in Canada: The First Three Steps*. Toronto: Ryerson, 1958.

Reading in Canada 1991. Toronto: Ekos Research, 1991.

Renza, Louis A. "Exploding Canons." Rev. of *Canons*, ed. Robert von Hallberg. *Contemporary Literature* 28 (1987): 257–70.

Ricou, Laurence. *Vertical Man/Horizontal World: Man and Landscape in Canadian Prairie Fiction*. Vancouver: U of British Columbia P, 1973.

Ricou, Laurie. "Dialogue: From a Continuing Correspondence between Lorraine Weir and Laurie Ricou." *Canadian Literature* 110 (1986): 2–6.

———. Panel comment. Steele 96–99.

Robbins, Bruce. "Oppositional Professionals: Theory and the Narratives of Professionalization." Arac and Johnson 1–21.

Roper, Gordon, S. Ross Beharriell, and Rupert Schieder. "Writers of Fiction 1880–1920." Klinck 1: 327–53.

Ross, Morton L. "The Canonization of *As for Me and My House*: A Case Study." *Figures in a Ground: Canadian Essays on Modern Literature Collected in Honor of Sheila Watson*. Saskatoon: Western Producer, 1978. 189–205. Rpt. Metcalf, *The Bumper Book* 170–85.

Royal Commission on National Development in the Arts, Letters and Sciences. *Report*. Ottawa: King's Printer, 1951.

Ryval, Michael. "Cornering a Clamour of Critics." *Quill and Quire* May 1978: 4, 12.

Said, Edward. "Opponents, Audiences, Constituencies, and Community." *Critical Inquiry* 9 (1982): 1–26.

———. *The World, the Text, the Critic*. Cambridge: Harvard UP, 1983.

Scholes, Robert. "Canonicity and Textuality." *Introduction to Scholarship in Modern Languages and Literatures*. Ed. Joseph Gibaldi. New York: MLA, 1992. 138–58.

Scobie, Stephen. "Davey, Frank." Toye 172–73.

Scott, F.R. Introduction. Whalley, *Writing* 1–10.

Slemon, Stephen. "Modernism's Last Post." Adam and Tiffin 1–11.

Slopen, Beverly. "Malcolm Ross: Caretaker of CanLit." *Quill & Quire* May 1978: 21–22.

Smith, Barbara Herrnstein. "Contingencies of Value." *Critical Inquiry* 10 (1983): 1–35.

"So Who Reads Books? MP Asks." *Globe and Mail* 30 Oct. 1991: C1.

Spadoni, Carl, and Judith Donnelly. *A Bibliography of McClelland and Stewart Imprints, 1909–1985: A Publisher's Legacy.* Toronto: ECW, 1994.

Staines, David. Introduction. *The Impossible Sum of Our Traditions: Reflections on Canadian Literature.* By Malcolm Ross. Toronto: McClelland, 1986. 7–19.

Steele, Charles, ed. *Taking Stock: The Calgary Conference on the Canadian Novel.* Proc. of a Conference on the Canadian Novel. 15–18 Feb. 1978. Downsview, ON: ECW, 1982.

Stouck, David. "Introduction to the Bison Book Edition." *As for Me and My House.* By Sinclair Ross. Lincoln, NE: U of Nebraska P, 1978. v–xiii.

——. *Major Canadian Authors: A Critical Introduction.* Lincoln: U of Nebraska P, 1984.

——. "Sinclair Ross in Letters and Conversation." Moss, *From the Heart of the Heartland* 5–14.

——, ed. *Sinclair Ross's* As for Me and My House: *Five Decades of Criticism.* Toronto: U of Toronto P, 1991.

Struthers, J.R. (Tim), ed. *Volleys.* Erin, ON: Porcupine's Quill, 1990.

Stubbs, Roy St. George. "Presenting Sinclair Ross." *Saturday Night* Aug. 1941: 17.

Stuewe, Paul. *Clearing the Ground: English-Canadian Literature after Survival.* Toronto: Proper Tales, 1984.

Surette, Leon. "Creating the Canadian Canon." Lecker, *Canadian Canons* 17–29.

——. "Here Is Us: The Topocentrism of Canadian Literary Criticism." *Canadian Poetry: Studies, Documents, Reviews* 10 (1982): 44–57.

Tallman, Warren. "Wolf in the Snow. Part One: Four Windows onto Landscapes." *Canadian Literature* 5 (1960): 7–20.

——. "Wolf in the Snow. Part Two: The House Repossessed." *Canadian Literature* 6 (1960): 41–48.

Tompkins, Jane. *Sensational Designs: The Cultural Work of American Fiction, 1790–1860.* New York: Oxford UP, 1985.

Toye, William, ed. *The Oxford Companion to Canadian Literature.* Toronto: Oxford UP, 1983.

Waldman, Nell. "Michael Ondaatje." *Canadian Writers and Their Works: Essays on Form, Context, and Development.* Ed. Robert Lecker, Jack David, and Ellen Quigley. Poetry Series vol. 8. Toronto: ECW, 1992. 362–412. 20 vols. to date. 1983– .

Ware, Tracy. "A Little Self-Consciousness Is a Dangerous Thing: A Response to Robert Lecker." *English Studies in Canada* 17 (1991): 481–93.

——. "Notes on the Literary Histories of Canada." Rev. of *Canadian Literature in English*, by W.J. Keith. *Dalhousie Review* 65 (1985–86): 566–76.

"We Do Not Retreat." *OAC Notepad* March 1994: 4–7.

Weinsheimer, Joel. *Philosophical Hermeneutics*. New Haven: Yale UP, 1991.

Weir, Lorraine. "Dialogue: From a Continuing Correspondence between Lorraine Weir and Laurie Ricou." *Canadian Literature* 110 (1986): 2–6.

——. "The Discourse of 'Civility': Strategies of Containment in Literary Histories of English Canadian Literature." Blodgett and Purdy 24–39.

——. " 'Maps and Tales': The Progress of *Canadian Literature*, 1959–87." MacLaren and Potvin 141–59.

——. "Normalizing the Subject: Linda Hutcheon and the English-Canadian Postmodern." Lecker, *Canadian Canons* 180–95.

West, Cornel. "Theory, Pragmatisms, and Politics." Arac and Johnson 22–38.

Whalley, George. Preface. Whalley, *Writing* vii–xii.

——, ed. *Writing in Canada: Proceedings of the Canadian Writers' Conference, Queen's University, 28–31 July 1955*. Introd. F.R. Scott. Toronto: Macmillan, 1956.

White, Hayden. *Tropics of Discourse: Essays in Cultural Criticism*. Baltimore: Johns Hopkins UP, 1978.

Williams, Raymond. *Marxism and Literature*. Oxford: Oxford UP, 1977.

Wilson, Milton. "The Reviewer of Poetry." Glassco, *English Poetry* 51–57.

Woodcock, George. Editorial. *Canadian Literature* 1 (1959): 3–4.

——. "Possessing the Land: Notes on Canadian Fiction." *The Canadian Imagination: Dimensions of a Literary Culture*. Ed. David Staines. Cambridge: Harvard UP, 1977. 69–96.

Young, Alan R. "Thomas H. Raddall (1903–)." *Canadian Writers and Their Works: Essays on Form, Context, and Development*. Eds. Robert Lecker, Jack David, and Ellen Quigley. Fiction Series. Vol. 5. Toronto: ECW, 1990. 215–57. 20 vols. to date. 1983– .

INDEX